THE
HIDDEN KEY

Ernie,
I hope you enjoy
The Hidden Key!

David E. G

THE
HIDDEN KEY

A Steve Stilwell Thriller

DAVID E. GROGAN

CAMEL
PRESS

Seattle, WA

Epicenter Press
6524 NE 181st St.
Suite 2
Kenmore, WA 98028

www.epicenterpress.com
www.camelpress.com
www.coffeetownpress.com

For more information go to: www.davidegrogan.com

Cover design by Dawn Anderson

The Hidden Key
Copyright © 2019 by David E. Grogan

ISBN: 9781603815802 (Trade Paper)
ISBN: 9781603815864 (eBook)

Produced in the United States of America

To military members deploying to the far-flung reaches of the globe and the families who wait for their return.

Also by the author

Sapphire Pavilion

The Siegel Dispositions

ACKNOWLEDGMENTS

As with the first two Steve Stilwell thrillers, I am indebted to a host of people for helping me with *The Hidden Key*. First among them is my wife, Sharon, who not only lets me seclude myself in my basement office to write, but who also is my primary pre-Camel Press editor and critic. If something isn't right or doesn't work, Sharon tells me the truth. I couldn't ask for a better partner.

I subjected five other friends and family members to the first draft of *The Hidden Key* before sending it to Camel Press. On the family side, my father Mike Grogan, my sister Jenny Scharner, and my sister-in-law Carolyn Grogan, plowed through the manuscript and helped me smooth out the rough spots. Retired ambassador Marisa Lino, a brilliant and cherished friend from my Navy days and the U.S. Ambassador to Albania from 1996-1999, also reviewed the manuscript and used her keen diplomatic eye to tighten the story. My daughter, Erin Grogan, did a final review and made sure all was in order.

To make sure I accurately described the events taking place in India, I visited Chennai in July 2018. Two highlights of my visit were speaking to Padmaja Anant and Malavika Harish. Both women graciously sacrificed time out of their busy days to meet and speak with me about life and customs in Chennai. I could not have written about Chennai without their help and I am so thankful for having had the opportunity to meet them. To the extent I have not accurately captured South-Indian customs, it is due to my shortcomings as an author and not due to their gracious advice.

One other subject matter expert I relied upon was Mitchell Nixon.

Mitchell, who currently lives in Saipan and is a merchant mariner, helped me with some important international insights I could not otherwise get on my own. I am indebted for his assistance.

Finally, *The Hidden Key* would not have been possible without the gentle sculpting of Jennifer McCord and Phil Garrett at Camel Press and the advice and guidance of my agent, Steve Hutson, and my publicist, Wiley Saichek. Jennifer and Phil took the rough rock that was *The Hidden Key* manuscript and helped hew it into the finished product you are about to read, while Steve and Wiley helped guide it to where it needed to go. I cannot imagine a better team of professionals to work with and thank them from the bottom of my heart for helping to breathe life into *The Hidden Key*.

—*David E. Grogan*

1

———— ∾ ————

10:32 p.m. on Wednesday, September 22, 2004
Independence, Missouri

THE DOORBELL TO THE BROWN-SHINGLE BUNGALOW rang just as Kevin Jones settled deep into his leather sofa to watch the *Late Show*. Alfalfa, his six-year-old yellow lab, didn't alert to the visitors before the doorbell rang. Now he sprang from his blanket on the far side of the living room and charged the front door, barking as he crossed the room and positioning himself to welcome whoever was there.

"Who in the world can that be at this time of night?" Jones asked Alfalfa as he got up to answer the door. He didn't care that he was wearing only an undershirt and jeans. When someone came by this late on a Wednesday night, they took him as he was. He set the can of beer he had just popped open on the coffee table's glass top, turned down the TV's volume, and headed for the door. "This better be important." More out of habit than necessity, he turned on the living room ceiling light with the switch by the front door.

Jones reached down and grabbed Alfalfa by the collar and forced him to sit. Alfalfa whimpered but begrudgingly complied. "Now you be good," he cautioned Alfalfa. The lab looked at him with his big brown eyes, eager to please and even more eager to see who was there. He let loose a staccato bark, still sitting with Jones restraining him by his collar.

When Jones opened the door, two men he didn't recognize stood before him, their faces illuminated by the front porch light protruding from the siding just above their heads. Both men, one black and one white, looked to be in their mid-thirties. They both wore jeans while the African-American man added a lightweight navy blue jacket, wet from drizzle. His partner had closely cropped sandy blond hair and sideburns. Jones surmised they were Marines he'd met in Iraq, although he couldn't place either man's face or fathom how they might have found his house.

Neither looked like he was coming to visit a fellow veteran. They appeared instead as if they had something they needed to get done, and that something involved Jones. He suddenly felt vulnerable, like when he was exposed to Iraqi mortar fire randomly pocketing patches of desert. He never knew if the patch he occupied would take the next hit. Alfalfa began an uncharacteristic growl, showing his teeth.

Jones' instinct told him to slam the door. He felt his right arm trying to throw the door shut until his rational self took control and held the door open just in case these were kindred military spirits. That left him with only one defense—show no sign of weakness or fear. If they were there to roll him, he had to make them believe it wouldn't be easy. He and Alfalfa would make them feel pain, and his chiseled upper body, accentuated by an undershirt one size too small, reinforced the message.

"It's pretty late to be ringing doorbells," Jones began, stooping just enough to restrain Alfalfa by the collar.

"You Kevin Jones?" the man in the jacket asked, ignoring Jones' remonstrance.

"Yeah, that's me. Who's askin'?"

"You advertised a clay brick on the Internet and we want to see it." The man in the jacket did all the talking, while his buddy stood behind him, staring at Alfalfa. Alfalfa's growl grew meaner. Jones didn't do anything to discourage his dog's warning, especially after what he'd just heard. He hadn't posted his name or address in the ad, so he figured these guys had to be undercover cops. There was no way he was going to own up to posting the ad, especially since it had to do with a clay tablet he'd smuggled into the United States from Iraq when he and his Seabee unit returned from the war.

"Not me. I got nothin' posted online."

"Look, man," the guy continued. "We know you got a brick to sell, so cut the shit and let's talk business."

"Like I said, you got the wrong person." Jones reached out and tried to shove the door closed, but the guy in the jacket stuck out his work boot and stopped the door short of closing. Jones wished he'd followed his initial instinct and slammed the door in their faces. Now it was too late.

The man reached forward and shoved the door open, leveraging his way partially inside. Alfalfa barked and then lunged at the intruder. Jones, still holding onto Alfalfa's collar, yanked him back. Alfalfa's growl grew deeper and more vicious. The intruder took a half step back, leaving his other foot in place so Jones couldn't close the door. His accomplice moved up close behind him. The two men looked like they were ready to exploit the open door and force their way inside.

"Here's how we're doing this," the intruder commanded. "We're coming in and you're get'n us that brick. Then I give you one hundred bucks and we leave." He forced a grin. "Now ain't that easy?"

Jones flashed a defiant smile. "How about you guys piss off or I call the cops. That's easy too, ain't it?"

The intruder shed his grin and stepped forward, pushing Jones away from the door and bumping into Jones' shoulder in a display of machismo as he strutted to the center of the room. His accomplice moved to block the door, coming in just far enough to close it behind him. The intruder spoke as he pivoted to face Jones.

"Look man, we both know you ain't calling no cops. What you gonna do, tell 'em somebody's trying to steal the brick you stole from Iraq?" He laughed at the irony. "Come on, man, you're smarter than that. Just get me the brick."

Jones knew if something went down, it would turn out badly since he had no way to escape. He would just have to play along until they made a mistake he or Alfalfa could take advantage of. Alfalfa was ready, too. For the first time in his life, the usually friendly lab seemed primed to tear into someone. It was all Jones could do to hold him back.

"So how do I know you ain't cops?"

"You don't," the accomplice countered for the first time. "But it don't matter, 'cause one way or another, we're taking us a brick, ain't we Charles?" He smiled and laughed a foul laugh, like one that presaged evil. Alfalfa lunged forward when he heard it, catching Jones off guard. Alfalfa's collar slipped through his fingers and he leapt toward the accomplice, snarling like a trained attack dog. His jaws clamped onto the man's outstretched left arm and he started to shake it violently, like he did with stuffed toys in the back yard. The man screamed, popped open a switch blade Jones hadn't seen before and jammed it deep into the dog's neck. Alfalfa yelped and let loose his grip, crying as he dropped off the man. The man stabbed the dog again as he fell to the floor and wrenched the knife upward, mortally wounding Alfalfa.

"Nooooo!" Jones screamed. He charged the man bending over the stricken dog, kicking him in the face with as much force as he could muster. His target flew backward and landed on his back with blood streaming from his nose, still holding the knife he'd used to fend off Alfalfa. Jones jumped on him and pinned the knife-wielding hand to the floor, while his free hand pummeled the man's face. Rage fueled every blow, making him impervious to fear and pain. "You killed my dog! You killed my dog! I'm gonna kill you, you bastard!" With two successive blows, he could feel the man's nose break and his cheekbones cave in.

Jones didn't see Charles run to the melee. Charles' work boot struck him in the ribs with an uppercut, cracking something and throwing him off his bloodied opponent, who lay there groaning. Jones felt a crushing pain in his left chest. He tried to suck in oxygen, but his lungs refused, so he lay on the floor immobilized trying to breathe. He twisted his head toward Charles, who stood a safe distance away pointing a pistol at him. Alfalfa's killer moaned and rolled over on his side so Jones got a glimpse of what used to be the man's face. His left eye was already swollen shut and his mouth and tooth-torn lips oozed blood and saliva. His nose was no longer a recognizable shape. Seeing how he'd at least partially avenged Alfalfa had a morphine-like effect and Jones' lungs responded by allowing him to gasp in just enough air so he could struggle to his feet. He couldn't let himself be in a defenseless position should the wounded accomplice revive enough to seek his own revenge.

"You happy now?" Charles shouted. "Your dog's dead and you and my man are messed up." He pointed his gun at Jones, shaking it to the rhythm of his words to drive home he was deadly serious. "But you're still gonna get me that brick. You got that?"

Jones glared at him, his eyes filled with rage. Alfalfa's dying shrieks reverberated in his ears and his adrenaline commanded him to take Charles down. But his Navy Seabee training yelled louder and told him to get control of his anger or he was dead. He had to find a way to counteract the gun. He tried to breathe deeply but couldn't, so he took a quick, shallow breath just to get some air inside. He didn't know if they intended to kill him, although he figured his actions thus far had increased the chances of that outcome. At least until Alfalfa's killer revived, it was one-on-one.

There was one obvious option. He could give them the clay tablet. At this point, he really didn't care about losing it, but figured he was safest when only he knew where it was. Once they had it, he was a witness they might be inclined to snuff out. On the other hand, murder was a long way from theft, so they might be content to lick their wounds and leave if he gave them what they came for. He could also tell them to piss off again, but that hadn't worked so far. Plus, separating Charles from his wounded ally opened up one additional possibility.

"Man, you deaf?" Charles shouted angrily. "I said get me the damn brick." He brought the pistol to the ready position, sighting it at Jones' head. Jones could see the man's fist tightening its grip on the pistol. He was a hair's breadth away from pulling the trigger.

"It's not here," Jones asserted. "No way was I keeping it at the house. I got it in storage."

"You're one lying piece of shit," Charles quipped. He jerked the gun and pulled the trigger. A bullet ploughed through Jones' muscular thigh, exiting out the back of his leg. Jones screamed in pain and fell to his knees, covering the entrance wound with his hands to stop the bleeding.

"Look man, I'm done playing games. One way or another, I'm leaving here with a brick. Whether you're dead or alive don't make no difference to me. Now are you gonna get it for me so we can leave, or are you gonna make me shoot you again so you can bleed to death while we're looking for it?"

Jones grimaced, still on his knees and pressing hard on his thigh with both hands. Blood ran between his fingers and streamed down the back of his leg from the exit wound. "Alright," Jones assented. "It's in my bedroom at the back of the house. You'll find it on the floor underneath the corner bookcase." Jones doubled over in pain, groaning as he did. He tried to straighten up but couldn't. His leg hurt too badly.

"That's where you're wrong." Charles' subtle smile returned. "That's where you're gonna find it. You're gonna limp your ass back to that room and get it for me. I ain't letting you out of my sight."

Still scrunched over, Jones looked up to beg Charles to get the clay tablet and just leave. "Look, I can't—

"This ain't no negotiation. Get me the brick." Charles pointed the gun at Jones' stomach. Failure to comply meant a painful death.

Jones forced himself to his feet, letting out a gasp. He turned and started moving toward the hall to the back bedroom, taking small steps with his good leg and dragging the wounded leg behind. His lungs weren't cooperating either, so he moved slowly, each step zapping pain through every nerve in his body. When he reached the hall, he steadied himself using his bloody hand, sliding it along the wall to keep himself upright. When he reached the bedroom door on the left, he let go of the wall and slipped forward, falling on the foot of the bed just a few feet inside the door. Charles was right behind him, switching on the light to the room and revealing a trail of blood on the floor.

Jones pointed to the bookcase in the room's corner across from the foot of the bed. "I swear to God," Jones promised, "it's on the floor under that bookcase. All you got to do is slide the bookcase forward and you'll have what you came here for. Please, just take it and leave."

"You don't listen too good, do you?" Charles chuckled. "You move the bookcase and get the brick. If it ain't there, you're a dead man." He coaxed Jones on with his gun. "Come on now, get going."

Jones slid along the foot of the bed until he got to the other side. Still putting pressure on the entrance wound with his left hand, he put his right hand behind him on the dark brown bedspread and pushed himself upward to his feet. He fell toward the bookcase and grabbed onto the third shelf from the bottom to steady himself, but lost his balance and fell backward, pulling the bookcase with him. Books and framed pictures of his Seabee shipmates spilled from the shelves, cascading to the floor. He would have been crushed by the heavy oak cabinet, except he fell to the floor on the side of the bed while the bed stopped the bookcase mid-fall. Jones' head hit the shag carpet with a thud.

"Ahhhh," he shrieked in agony. He wriggled himself backward toward a nightstand with a glass lamp at the head of the bed. Charles moved further into the room toward where the bookcase lay across the corner of the bed.

"Get up on that bed where I can see you," he demanded. He kept the gun pointed at Jones and used his peripheral vision to see whether there was anything on the floor where the bookcase had been. A big smile covered his face.

Jones tried to pull himself onto the bed then fell back to the floor, hitting the nightstand on the way down. The lamp wobbled as Jones braced himself on the floor with both hands. Now it was Jones who wanted to sit up on the bed as close to the nightstand as possible. Unwittingly, Charles had facilitated his final option. It was a nuclear option, but at least it was an option. "Ahhhh," he screeched as he jolted himself onto the bed. He doubled over in pain, still only able to take short, shallow breaths.

With his gun trained on Jones, Charles reached down behind the base of the bookcase and grabbed the sand-colored clay tablet he had been looking for. He held it up to admire it, or at least to show off to Jones that it was now in his possession. Still pointing the gun at Jones, he brought the tablet closer to his eyes like a nearsighted old man trying to read the instructions on his latest prescription. He looked at the side with compass-like carvings first, then twisted it in his fingers until he could see the other side covered with the intricate characters of an ancient alphabet. Satisfaction flooded his face, as if he had read the writing and understood what it said. He laughed and stuck the tablet into his jacket pocket.

Jones had to decide quickly whether to use his nuclear option. Charles had what he wanted, so if he intended to finish Jones off, now would be the time. The moment of indecision answered the question for him when Charles lowered his weapon.

"See?" Charles asked, vindicated by leaving Jones in the room alive. "All I wanted was the brick. It didn't have to be this hard. All I wanted was the damn brick." Charles eased backward to the doorway, when a hand came from behind and slap-grasped the doorframe. Jones flinched and Charles jumped forward, startled by whoever was behind him. He aimed the gun toward the silhouette leaning against the door.

"Charles, it's me!" shouted his accomplice, the right side of his face all black and blue and his eyeball invisible behind ballooning flesh. "Don't shoot, it's me!"

"You idiot!" Charles chided. "You ever sneak up on me like that again and I'll kill you. You ain't got no sense, man. You just ain't got no sense."

The accomplice bent over and breathed deeply before he stood up semi-straight and continued talking. "You got the brick? You got the brick yet?" His words sounded eager, like someone trying to please.

"Yeah, I got it. Now let's get out of here."

"You just leaving him here, Charles?" the wounded man protested. "He'll call the cops! You can't just leave him here. I ain't going back to jail for no brick. You got to shoot him."

"I ain't shooting no one," Charles countered. "We ain't getting paid to kill somebody. We got the brick, now let's get out of here before the cops come." He pushed past his partner and started down the hall.

The remnants of the accomplice's face looked crestfallen. Still propped against the doorframe, he looked over his shoulder with his good eye as Charles retreated toward the living room. "Man, look what he did to my face. He ain't getting away with it, Charles. It don't work that way." A knife reappeared in his hand. Jones could see the blade, still streaked with Alfalfa's blood.

Charles stopped and pivoted toward his partner. "Look. I'm pulling out of the driveway in one minute, with or without you. If you got some business to do, you get it done. But I got no part of it. You got that?"

That was all the leash the accomplice needed. He pushed himself from the doorframe holding the knife in front of him at a slash-ready angle. He maneuvered around the bed and neared the bookcase, his eyes locked on Jones.

Jones had no choice—it was time for the nuclear option. He leaned over to the nightstand and threw open the drawer. As he reached inside, the accomplice waved his knife and said something, but Jones couldn't recognize what it was. He flung some papers out of the way, grabbed a steel object, and pulled it from the drawer. The accomplice leapt onto the bed and Jones pulled the trigger, blowing the man backward with blood spurting from his neck. Jones started to drop to the floor behind the bed for cover when Charles rushed back to the door. Two more gunshots burst through the room, followed by the moans of dying men.

2

6:56 p.m. on Thursday, September 30, 2004
London, England

STEVE STILWELL STOPPED IN FRONT OF the Madras Star's two retractable
royal blue awnings. The restaurant glowed through its white lattice
windows, transforming the cool night air on the brick-paved street just
outside with its soft yellow light. From where he stood, he could see inside
the restaurant's two dining rooms flanking the entrance. The chamber on the
right was the livelier of the two, with tables near a small bar at the back of the
room full of Londoners conversing mid-meal. The dining room to the left
looked empty by comparison, with only a young couple sitting at a table for
two at the front by the window, and a middle-aged man wearing a dark khaki
suit at a table for four in the rear-most corner of the room.

Reaching for the door, Steve thought the Madras Star an odd venue for a
first meeting with a wealthy client. The restaurant seemed more the place for
expatriate Indians to enjoy a taste of home or for young professionals to grab
a beer and a quick meal after grinding away in London's massive financial
district. It would not have been Steve's first choice for discussing complex
estate planning with a potential new client, but since he wasn't familiar with
the city, he acquiesced.

Steve knew even less about Arul Ashirvadam than he did the City of
London. His associate counsel, Casey Pantel, researched the man to give
Steve background and context prior to his departure for the meeting. Casey
discovered Ashirvadam was a 54-year-old international real estate tycoon

from India, with significant hotel property holdings in Northern Virginia. Steve assumed the Virginia properties were the reason he was being retained, although there were plenty of qualified trust and estates attorneys practicing closer to Ashirvadam's properties.

Ashirvadam himself contacted Steve's office and asked Steve to meet him on Thursday, September 30th, at the Madras Star. Neither Steve's hourly rate nor his travel per diem deterred the invitation. Within minutes after arranging the meeting, Ashirvadam wired sufficient funds for Steve to fly first class from his Williamsburg, Virginia, law office to London. Steve accepted the invitation, reasoning the size and international aspects of Ashirvadam's estate would challenge him professionally. He also knew if a client like Ashirvadam dropped his name in the right circles, it could significantly expand his practice and reputation. Beyond those business reasons, meeting with the Indian entrepreneur in London injected excitement into his daily routine. His Williamsburg trusts and estates practice was a far cry from his prior life as a Navy attorney advising warfighters in the Judge Advocate General's Corps.

As soon as Steve opened the Madras Star's door, the aroma of exotic spices engulfed him, pulling him inside. Suddenly the thought of a few interruptions by a waiter as he discussed his potential client's estate didn't seem so burdensome as long as a spicy lentil stew followed the session. Two steps inside, a dark-skinned maître d' wearing black slacks and an open collared deep purple shirt approached him.

"Mr. Stilwell?" The maître d' spoke the King's English without even the hint of an Indian accent.

"Why yes," Steve responded, surprised the maître d' knew who he was.

"Please, follow me." The maître d' led him into the dining room on the left, past the couple by the window and toward the rear. The room itself was narrow, with a row of tables covered with saffron table cloths pushed against the wall on the left and a row of stand-alone tables similarly adorned on the right. As they wove down the aisle between the settings, it became obvious the maître d' was escorting Steve to the man in the khaki suit sitting in the far corner of the room. The back-wall tables were the only two that had black vinyl bench seats protruding from the wall, and the man sat on one of them with his back braced against the corner on the left side of the room. He didn't stand to greet Steve.

"Mr. Ashirvadam," the maître d' began once he reached the table, "Mr. Stilwell has arrived."

Ashirvadam nodded, which was all the maître d' needed because he pulled out the chair across from him and motioned for Steve to sit down. Steve did, and the maître d' departed. Ashirvadam broke his silence, but his face remained stern. Unlike the maître d', he spoke with an Indian accent.

"Thank you for coming on such short notice, Mr. Stilwell. I assure you it was more than necessary." He eased over on the bench so he was closer to being directly across from Steve, still preserving his access to the corner. His eyes looked painfully bloodshot and his three-inch long jet-black hair furrowed from front to back. As Steve slid closer to the table, Ashirvadam ran his fingers through his toniced hair, brushing it back from his forehead and revealing the source of the furrows. His hand came to rest on the table, although he withdrew it slightly to clench the table's edge, as his other hand already did.

"Well," Steve began, hoping to calm Ashirvadam's agitation with a matter-of-fact approach to a subject he assumed Ashirvadam found difficult to discuss. "I appreciate you considering me for your estate planning needs. But before we get to that, I take it you are Arul Ashirvadam?"

"Yes, I'm so sorry. I've been rude, haven't I?" Ashirvadam reached across the table to shake Steve's hand. "I am Arul Ashirvadam, and I am pleased to make your acquaintance, Mr. Stilwell. Your reputation precedes you."

"Thank you, and it's my pleasure," responded Steve, shaking Ashirvadam's sweat-drenched hand. "How long have you been in London?" He smiled at Ashirvadam, nonchalantly withdrawing his hand and reaching under the table to adjust his posture, wiping his hand dry on his pants as he did. He noticed sweat beading around Ashirvadam's thick, dark sideburns and above his black mustache, even though the restaurant felt cool.

"Please accept my apologies in advance, Mr. Stilwell, but can we dispense with the pleasantries? I wouldn't have called this meeting if I wasn't familiar with your reputation for taking on tough international cases. I was particularly impressed by the newspaper reports about how you grappled with the Vietnamese and U.S. governments for one of your clients a few years ago. That's what I'm looking for, Mr. Stilwell—tenacity in protecting my estate and providing for my family. Now, I'm keen to get down to business. I haven't much time."

Ashirvadam's exchange took Steve by surprise. He hadn't agreed to accept the engagement yet—he wasn't even sure what it was. While he fully expected to be retained, the usual protocol involved a discussion where the terms of representation would be worked out and agreed upon. An essential by-product of that discussion was understanding his client and his client's needs. Reaching that understanding was part of the dance that needed to happen before the legal work commenced.

"That's fine," Steve acquiesced. Then he laid down a marker to avoid misunderstandings down the road. "But I've got to understand what your estate planning needs and objectives are. Whether we call that pleasantries or something else, we'll have to have the discussion if I'm going to represent you effectively."

Ashirvadam glanced behind Steve toward the window and the entrance to the dining room as he began to speak, apparently concerned about something other than Steve's desire for simpatico. "Of course, Mr. Stilwell. In the interest of time, let me be blunt. I need you to be the executor of my estate in the U.S. I've already forwarded my American will to your office via international courier appointing you as executor. I trust you will find everything in order."

"That sounds very good, Mr. Ashirvadam. I still will want to do an engagement letter and review the will to make sure there is nothing in it that creates confusion. And, I'll also need to—"

"You don't understand, there is no time for that!" Ashirvadam's outburst caused the young woman sitting by the window to raise her eyebrows and cock her head in Ashirvadam's direction, pretending not to listen. A bearded Sikh waiter wearing a blue turban approached Steve's table, but Ashirvadam brushed him away. He leaned forward and got right in Steve's face. "I have already wired five hundred thousand dollars to your office as an initial payment to secure your services. You will receive it on Monday." Ashirvadam sat back on the bench seat, reigning in his impatience. As the vein in his temple receded, he added in a subdued voice Steve had trouble hearing, "Of course, any additional charges will be paid by my estate."

Although Ashirvadam's outburst shocked Steve, it was the five hundred thousand dollar payment that grabbed his attention. Six-figure retainers weren't part of his vocabulary despite his success over the last few years. He tried to maintain a poker face so as not to convey his surprise. He needed to portray confidence and competence so his new client—and he had no doubt now this was his client—would continue to believe he was the right lawyer to manage a complex international estate. He also realized he had to ask succinct and pointed questions to get the background information he needed. Ashirvadam had a low tolerance for prattle.

"Well, thank you so much for retaining my services," Steve said with a degree of genuineness extending beyond mere business courtesy. "I will, of course, be honored to serve as your executor. However, you must tell me, why is there so little time? Do you have a terminal illness?"

Ashirvadam slid further along the bench toward the center aisle of the restaurant as if he were preparing to depart. "In a manner of speaking yes, but that's not important now. I just need to make sure you will take care of my family."

"Of course, I'll do whatever your will says. If your will doesn't adequately take care of your family, then I'll suggest how we can revise it so it does. Why don't you tell me a little bit about your family?"

"I must go." Ashirvadam started to get up, looking toward the exit and the window at the front of the dining room. His eyes got huge and he exhaled loudly. "My God, it is time!" He dropped back onto the bench and retreated into the corner, bracing himself like an animal waiting for the hunter to arrive.

Steve had little time to react. He looked over his shoulder to see what was disturbing Ashirvadam, but only saw two men hurrying toward the door to the restaurant from the outside. By the time he turned back around, Ashirvadam was shrinking into the corner. Steve scooted his chair directly in front of Ashirvadam, leaning toward him with both elbows on the table.

"What's wrong?" he asked. "Are you ill? You've got to tell me what's going on."

Tears gushed from Ashirvadam's eyes. "I've sold my soul, Mr. Stilwell," he shrieked. "I've sold my soul. Now I must pay." The turbaned waiter approached the table from the kitchen door at the rear of the dining room. Steve looked at the waiter, wondering whether his client was psychotic and might need an ambulance. As the waiter bent down to speak to Steve, Ashirvadam reached inside his suit coat and pulled out a pistol. The first man Steve saw outside threw open the front door, shattering its glass against the wall. He burst into the dining room with his partner close behind.

Steve's first instinct was to grab Ashirvadam's gun, but he didn't know who the bad guys were, so he didn't want to prevent Ashirvadam from defending himself. He dove for the floor, hitting his head on the chair next to him. As his face slammed onto the tile, he heard his nose crack. He could no longer see what was going on and felt the table being pushed toward him as the center pole pressed against his waist. He heard tables and chairs crashing to the floor from the direction of the two men, who yelled something he couldn't decipher. The woman at the table by the window screamed. Afraid he might be caught in the crossfire, Steve covered the back of his head with his hands and flattened himself on the floor.

"God forgive me!" he heard Ashirvadam yell. A gunshot exploded in the room and the woman's scream crescendoed beyond fear to panic. Chaotic shouting came from the direction of the two men as tables and chairs flew in the wake of something Steve knew was getting closer but couldn't see. He twisted his head just in time to see Ashirvadam's legs lurch forward, and a hard object banged on the table near the wall. Streams of blood raced down the wall behind Ashirvadam's legs, losing momentum as they neared the floor. Steve contorted himself to look towards the men and saw two legs almost upon him. He closed his eyes and tried to negotiate with God but ran out of time before he could close the deal.

3

1:17 a.m. on Friday, October 1, 2004
London, England

STEVE TOOK A SIP OF THE stagnant coffee someone gave him after he arrived at New Scotland Yard from the hospital. The facility wasn't the creepy Elizabethan building he imagined after watching movies as a kid. Instead, he found himself in a steel and glass high-rise in central London with the two men from the restaurant, who turned out to be detectives. The older of the two, his salt and pepper hair made him look about fifty, sat behind a modular desk that transitioned into a faux-wood credenza with bookshelves and cabinets once it reached the wall. The younger detective, black and of slighter build, looked to be in his early thirties. He sat next to Steve in front of the desk with a pad of paper in his lap, prepared to take down anything Steve said. The older detective, Cavendish, began the conversation, nonchalantly sliding his elbows across his desk toward Steve and resting his chin on his clasped hands.

"That was an ugly one, wasn't it, Mr. Stilwell?" He didn't give Steve time to respond. "It's not every day you see someone blow their brains out at dinnertime, now is it?"

Tired, shaken, and surprised by Detective Cavendish's callous characterization of his client's death just a few hours before, Steve answered without the restraint he might otherwise have shown. "What the hell was that all about?"

"That's what we were hoping you would tell us, Mr. Stilwell. You were the one talking to the man when he killed himself, now weren't you?" Cavendish slid back to his original position, keeping his eyes pegged on Steve.

"I guess I was," Steve admitted. He put his hands on his thighs, straightened his arms, and flexed his back to relieve the tension compressing his chest. He felt like he had to tell himself to breathe. "I'm afraid I can't tell you very much. Arul Ashirvadam hired me to do some legal work and we had just finished our discussion when you came into the restaurant. You saw the rest."

"Well, that's a start, Mr. Stilwell. That's certainly a start. But we'll need more information than that, now won't we?" Cavendish leaned forward and decreased his volume, but not his intensity. "The man's dead, Mr. Stilwell. He's dead, and the Crown Prosecutors will want to know why. You can understand that, can't you, Mr. Stilwell? You being an American attorney and all?"

Steve knew Cavendish had to investigate Ashirvadam's death. He also knew prosecutors would need to review the investigation file as a matter of course. But hearing Cavendish articulate it during what was seeming more and more like an interrogation and less and less like an interview caused reality to set in. Obviously, Cavendish had something on Ashirvadam or he wouldn't have cornered him at the restaurant. Steve didn't want to be guilty by association, so he intended to cooperate, although there were limits on what he could say. Cavendish had to know that.

"There's not much more I can tell you, Detective," he began, his reset nose throbbing as the painkillers wore off. "Ashirvadam contacted my office and arranged for us to meet in London at the Madras Star. I flew in this morning from the United States and we met at seven for the first time. He was in a hurry, so we went over the terms of representation and then he had to go. That's when you came in. There's not much more to it than that."

"Well, it seems a reasonable question might be why he retained your services? You can answer that, Mr. Stilwell, can't you? After all, your client is dead."

Cavendish's question opened Steve's eyes. Cavendish wasn't some bumpkin detective stumbling through the interview. He was a savvy interrogator asking seemingly unobtrusive questions that hid his deeper understanding. Cavendish knew Steve was bound by the attorney-client privilege not to disclose the confidences of his client, so he was trying to get Steve to lower his guard by implying the privilege no longer applied because Ashirvadam was dead. Steve needed to let Cavendish know it wouldn't work.

"The fact that my client is dead really doesn't matter, Detective Cavendish. In America, the attorney-client privilege continues even after a client dies. I'm sure that must be the same in England." Asserting his client's privilege gave Steve a certain amount of satisfaction, even though he actually wanted to cooperate.

"Yes, of course," Cavendish replied, sounding more sophisticated. "I suppose you're right." He slid a single piece of paper in front of him that had been obstructed from Steve's view by a wooden in-box filled full of documents. He consulted the paper briefly before speaking. "Unless your client talked to you about his will, which might make sense since you are a trusts and estates attorney, now aren't you, Mr. Stilwell? If that were the case, then you'd be probating his will and it would become a public record, wouldn't it?" Cavendish grinned, communicating his own level of satisfaction. "It's amazing what you can learn on the Internet nowadays, isn't it?"

Now Steve was unsure of whether he was speaking with Detective Cavendish or the reincarnation of Sherlock Holmes. If he didn't watch what he was saying, Cavendish might start to think he was hiding something, or in cahoots with whatever his client was involved in. This wasn't a game.

"I'm sorry," Steve admitted. "You're correct. My client retained me to be the executor of his estate. I don't have the will—he mailed it directly to my office—so I don't know what it says. Once we get it, I expect we'll probate the estate in the appropriate court in Virginia."

"Very good," Cavendish responded, clearly satisfied with the progress he was making. "Very good indeed. Will you be able provide us with a copy of the will?"

"I'd prefer not to do that," Steve answered. "I don't want to take any actions that could be construed as contrary to my client's interests, especially since I've not even seen the will yet. But I can certainly let you know when and where we file the will so you can contact the Clerk of Court directly."

"Brilliant," Cavendish declared. "Now what else can you tell me? Did Ashirvadam tell you why he needed you to be his executor? Did he tell you what he was involved in?"

"You know I can't disclose that. Besides, my guess is you know the answer or you wouldn't have been after him. Why don't you tell me what he was involved in?"

"Fair enough, Mr. Stilwell. But like you, there are limits on what I can discuss. Still, I suppose it wouldn't hurt to give you some details, especially if it helps you keep us informed about your progress with Ashirvadam's estate." Cavendish brought his right hand close to his neck, and motioning from left to right, signaled to his partner to stop taking notes. "You will, I trust, be circumspect with what I am about to tell you."

"Of course," Steve replied, wondering what his fifteen-minute meeting with Ashirvadam had gotten him involved in.

"We've been watching Ashirvadam closely for quite some time. He's a collector, you see." Cavendish reached forward and retrieved an unsharpened pencil sitting on the large calendar ink blotter covering the top of the desk. He tapped the eraser end lightly on the calendar page, which still showed the month of July.

"Collector of what?" Steve asked.

"Antiquities."

"So, I presume you are involved because not all of his purchases were above board?"

"Precisely. In fact, he's rather crafty in that regard."

"What do you mean?"

"His flat and office in London look like bloody museums. He's a wealthy man, Mr. Stilwell, and he doesn't mind showing it off. As far as we can tell, all those artifacts are legitimate acquisitions. It's the ones he doesn't display we are interested in."

"If he doesn't display them, how do you know he's got them? And, if what you say is true, why didn't you just arrest him?"

"Both very good questions, I can assure you." Cavendish opened his desk's middle drawer and stowed the pencil in a tray. He leaned well back into his chair and turned his head slightly, but looked back at Steve out of the corner of his eye as if he were passing an insight he knew Steve would find intriguing.

"Let me just say this. We've had an active black market in antiquities in London since the Iraq War started. I'm sure you've read in the headlines how the Iraqi National Museum and other historical sites were looted after the bombing started. Well, it seems Al Qaida has funneled some of those antiquities through its contacts in London, where they're sold to raise money. We believe Ashirvadam may have purchased some of those items."

Steve's eyes grew large. A few hours ago, he was thrilled to have a new client who'd paid him a six-figure retainer. Now the client was dead, his possible links to international terrorism exposed, and Steve was being questioned by Scotland Yard. This was not the scenario he envisioned when he boarded the plane for London. Realizing his window for asking questions might close at any moment, he pressed Cavendish for more information.

"I don't know what to say," Steve admitted. "I had no way of knowing. But your answer begs the question. If you knew what he was doing, why didn't you arrest him?" Steve thought for a second and then something even more perplexing came to mind. "And why did you burst on the scene in the restaurant? You're not telling me everything, Detective Cavendish. There's got to be more to the story." Realizing he'd tapped into something big, he sat back and crossed his legs. "I need answers too, Detective Cavendish."

"As I said before, good questions. Unfortunately, they are questions I am not prepared to answer. I'm afraid you will just have to accept that."

"That's not good enough," Steve asserted, pressing his newfound advantage. "You drove my client to suicide and could have easily gotten me killed, too. I deserve answers."

"Maybe so," Cavendish replied in a half-volume voice, "but I'm afraid you won't be getting them today." Looking at Steve as if to challenge him, he added, "I think we are quite finished here. Detective Drinkard, do get a copy of Mr. Stilwell's passport and contact information. Then he is free to go."

"Certainly," the younger detective replied as he stood up from his chair. "Mr. Stilwell, please follow me and I will get you taken care of."

Steve didn't stand. He couldn't leave without a better resolution to his questions. "You've got to tell me what was going on here, Detective Cavendish. My client is dead."

"I've already told you more than you needed to know. If I were you, I'd accept the gift I'd been given and move on before things get worse. Good day, Mr. Stilwell, and I do wish you a speedy recovery." Cavendish nodded to his partner, communicating he should act with dispatch.

Steve knew it was futile to attempt to get additional information from Cavendish, at least for the time being. Perhaps after doing a little digging of his own, he would be in a better position to make another run on Cavendish at a time and place of his own choosing. For now, discretion was the better part of valor. He stood up and started to walk out, turning back to Cavendish when he reached the door.

"I'll be in touch," Steve pledged, "and I trust you'll let me know when you are in a position to give me answers."

Cavendish ignored him. He was already pretending to refocus his attention on a handful of papers he pulled from his inbox. Steve wasn't fooled. Despite Cavendish's calm exterior, he knew he'd struck a nerve. He just had to figure out how to exploit it.

4

7:55 a.m. on Monday, October 4, 2004
Williamsburg, Virginia

STEVE HUSTLED PAST THE WROUGHT IRON fence leading to the courtyard of his law offices on the corner of Prince George and North Henry Streets in Williamsburg, Virginia. The wind hitting his face made the unseasonably cold Monday morning seem even colder, amplifying his failure to grab his overcoat on the way out of his house. Those were the things his wife, Sarah, used to help him with. When he reached the end of the brick sidewalk, he hopped up the stone slab steps and pushed through the double doors standing between him and warmth. After a quick turn down the hallway to the right, he entered the offices of Stilwell & Pantel, Attorneys at Law, marked by a new bronze plaque he hadn't seen before bearing his and his law partner's names.

"Mr. Stilwell!" Marjorie Weldman exclaimed as she jumped from her chair and rushed around her desk to greet him. "I'm so glad you're safe." Marjorie stopped a few steps beyond her desk and stared at Steve's face. "Wait a minute. Your eyes are all black and blue. You didn't tell me you were hurt. Are you okay?" Marjorie put her hands on her hips to register her disapproval.

"I'm fine," Steve replied, hoping to deter the chiding he knew would soon follow. "I just bumped my nose when I hit the floor in the restaurant and it gave me a black eye. It's not serious. In fact, after they x-rayed it, they barely had to reset anything. The bone just cracked a little."

"It's more like black eyes," Marjorie retorted, drawing out the plural with her thick Tidewater Virginia accent. "You look like somebody punched you out. Does it hurt?"

"Nothing a little ibuprofen can't handle." Steve knew Marjorie wouldn't let the issue drop until she felt like she'd made her point. She was right, of course. He should have told her about his nose when they spoke on the phone last Friday; he just had too many other things to tell her. Forty-seven and recently remarried, Marjorie had no kids of her own, but she liked to tell Steve her office manager job made her feel like his mom. Although she always said it with a feigned frown, Steve knew she enjoyed looking out for him, even more so since his separation from Sarah. He couldn't fathom practicing law without Marjorie keeping him and the administrative side of his law practice on the right track.

"Welcome back, Steve," Casey Pantel said emerging from her office on the other side of the reception area. "Wow, Marjorie's right. Your eyes look terrible. Are you sure you're okay?"

"I'm sure," Steve replied. "I've got to admit, though, that wasn't the most pleasant trip to London I've ever had. But we've got a new estate to manage, and it's going to take all three of us to pull this one off. How about we get together and talk about it later this morning."

"I can't wait that long, Mr. Stilwell. There's something I've got to tell you." Marjorie looked like a schoolgirl eager to divulge a secret.

"If it's bad news, let's head into my office first.

"It's not, it's not at all," Marjorie said excitedly, relishing in the growing suspense.

"Then let's have it, Marjorie. What is it?" Steve asked.

A grin spread across her face. "We're rich, Mr. Stilwell! We're rich!"

"Whhaaat?" Casey asked.

"It's true. We received a five hundred thousand dollar wire transfer this morning. It's a retainer from Mr. Ashirvadam. He must have sent it right before he died."

"That's exactly what happened," Steve confirmed. "He told me at the restaurant he did it, but I wasn't sure I believed him." Steve shifted his briefcase to his other hand and started to ease toward his office. "This gives us one more thing to talk about. I'm going to grab a cup of coffee and catch up on my emails and any appointments I need to prep for. Then maybe we can get together and come up with a plan for tackling this estate. How does that sound?"

"That works for me," responded Marjorie.

"Thanks Marjorie," Steve answered as he headed toward his office. "I don't know what I'd do without you."

"You just keep thinking that, Mr. Stilwell," Marjorie said in a loud voice. She smiled as she walked back around to her chair.

"You mind if I follow you into your office?" Casey asked.

"Not at all," Steve replied as he walked in and flipped on the light switch. "Come on in." He set his briefcase under the credenza behind his desk and plunked down in his leather desk chair, resting his arms on his blotter. Casey stood in front of him like a junior Army officer getting ready to make a report to the old man. "You're being awfully formal this morning, Casey. Grab a chair and tell me what's on your mind."

"Thanks Steve." Casey sat in one of the two caramel leather tub chairs in front of Steve's desk and scooted forward until she was balancing on the front edge. She'd been working with Steve for over four years and he'd recently let her buy into the practice. Although only in her mid-thirties, she'd proven herself a formidable litigator. Of course, it didn't hurt that she'd clerked for a Federal District Judge and was a favorite of the Williamsburg bar. But what Steve valued most was her honesty and professional courage. If she thought he was wrong, she said so and explained why. But, like any good lieutenant, she also understood when to salute and follow orders, even if she disagreed. Steve assumed after she'd barely survived an Army helicopter crash, nothing in the legal world could shake her. So, when she said she had something to tell him, he figured it had to be significant.

"I just want to make sure you're doing alright." Casey crossed her hands on her lap and leaned forward, conveying her concern.

Steve chuckled at Casey's question. "Aside from my broken nose and two black eyes, I couldn't be better."

"That's not what I meant," Casey retorted, not letting him escape her question. "I know what it's like to survive trauma, Steve. You may think you're too tough to be affected, but don't fool yourself. You just experienced a terrible event. It's okay to talk about it."

"I appreciate your concern, Casey, but there's nothing to talk about. I'll admit my nose throbs when the medicine wears off, but other than that, I'm perfectly fine—really." Steve heard the buzzer in the lobby ring, signaling someone entering the office. He seized the sound as an opportunity to change the subject. "Do you have any appointments this morning?"

"Nice try," Casey countered. "I'm free this morning, so you're stuck with me. And now that you've made me your partner, I've got a vested interest in making sure nothing happens to you." She leaned even further forward in the chair. "Just promise me you'll talk to someone if it starts to get to you. You don't have to deal with it yourself."

"Don't worry, Casey. I promise."

"Can I interrupt, Mr. Stilwell? I've got something here I know y'all will want to see."

Steve looked over at the door and saw Marjorie holding up a cardboard international shipping envelope. "Of course, come on in. What do you have?"

Marjorie walked over to Steve's desk, pulled the contents from the envelope, and handed them to him. "It's Mr. Ashirvadam's will. It just arrived a minute ago."

Steve glanced at Marjorie before he started to peruse the papers. "Now that we've got this, there's no sense waiting until later in the morning to come up with a plan. If you can take notes, I say we go through this and get a sense of what needs to be done for our new client's estate."

"Aye aye, captain," Marjorie responded, alluding to Steve's previous life as a captain in the Navy Judge Advocate General's Corps, or JAG Corps. Marjorie never tired of using worn-out Navy phrases. Although Steve's Navy career was now six years in his rearview mirror, he had to admit he never tired of hearing Marjorie's allusions.

Marjorie scurried to her desk and grabbed a notebook and pen. When she returned, she sat down in the open chair across from Steve's desk, crossed her legs, and positioned the notepad on her lap.

"Fire away, Mr. Stilwell," Marjorie announced.

"Alright, then, let's see what we've got." Steve held the small stack of papers like he was reading the morning newspaper at the breakfast table. "Here's what the cover letter says:

Mr. Stilwell,

Thank you for agreeing to be the executor of my U.S. estate. I've enclosed my U.S. will, including a schedule of my U.S. assets, and notarized copies of my U.K. and Indian wills. I trust you will find the documents in order.

By now you should have received a $500,000 (U.S.) wire transfer to pay for your services. Should this be insufficient, you may withdraw any additional fees allowed by Virginia law to compensate you for your services. If the $500,000 exceeds what is required, you may retain the excess as compensation for executing the following two requests, which I trust you will honor.

First, I want my body buried at St. Thomas Syro-Malabar Catholic Church in Palayur, India. I have previously told my wife this, but I am not convinced she will do so. You must ensure this takes place, even if it means moving my body from another burial site against the will of my wife.

Second, I have enclosed a key to safe deposit box #20316 at the Security International Bank in Vienna, Virginia. Provide the euros you find there to the Cathedral of San Giovanni Battisti in Turin, Italy. Destroy the remainder of the contents of the safe deposit box.

My wife, Rani, and two sons, Nihal and Jivan, are very precious to me. Do not think that my requests detract from my devotion to them. However, my requests represent my penance to God and must be kept.

Sincerely,

//Arul Ashirvadam//

"Hmmhh." Steve set the papers on his desk and thought for a moment. "I sure didn't expect that."

"What do you mean?" Casey asked.

"Well, when I agreed to be Ashirvadam's executor, he directed me to take care of his family, which I said I would do as long as the will permitted it. This sets a different tone."

"If we're getting strange things on the table," continued Casey, "it's pretty presumptuous of Ashirvadam to thank you for agreeing to be his executor when he hadn't even spoken to you yet. He obviously wrote that before he met with you in London."

"He must have figured half a million dollars would be pretty convincing, right Mr. Stilwell?" Marjorie's eyes got big and her lips puckered and twisted to the side of her mouth, as if she surprised herself by what she said. Like Casey, she had a knack for telling it like it is.

"I guess it was a pretty safe bet," Steve admitted. "But I agree with Casey that it's strange."

Marjorie wasn't finished. "And what about telling you to destroy the contents of his safe deposit box? In all the years I've worked here, I've never heard anything like that before."

"Me either," agreed Steve. "It's particularly disconcerting given his troubles with Scotland Yard. We're going to have to tread very carefully here. We're not destroying anything until we're one-hundred percent positive it's not associated with any criminal wrongdoing. I don't want to create any ethical problems."

"Can we go back to his family for a second?" Casey asked. "Does the will actually take care of them?"

"That's a good question, especially in light of what we just read." Steve skimmed through the will until he found its operative provisions and marked the spot with his finger. "It's actually quite simple. The will transfers all of Ashirvadam's U.S. property and ownership interests into a trust for the benefit of his wife and two children, who live in Chennai, India. That should take care of his family, but there's little for us to do other than identify his U.S. assets, pay off his liabilities, and transfer what remains into the trust. It's up to the trustee to take care of his family."

"Maybe Ashirvadam just wanted you to get it done quickly so the trust would be funded and available to his family right away," reasoned Casey.

"Maybe so," equivocated Steve. "I guess that has to be it. Ashirvadam was a sophisticated businessman. He had to know what he was doing. It's just odd that he told me to take care of his family and didn't mention anything about a trust or a trustee. I guess he was so distraught, knowing he was about to die, that he couldn't focus on the details of his will."

"Who's the trustee?" Casey asked.

Steve consulted the will again. "It just keeps getting weirder," he continued. "You'd think it would be someone in the U.S., or London, or even Chennai where his family is. But it's Bertrolli & Associates, in Milan, Italy. I assume that's either a law firm or some sort of investment company, but I wonder why it's in Milan? We've got a lot of work to do, starting with getting the will filed and checking out that safe deposit box."

"Speaking of which," Marjorie interjected, "where's the key he said he sent? Without that, how are you going to open the box?"

"Another great question, Marjorie." Steve picked up the cardboard envelope. He held it open end down and flared the edge so any remaining contents would fall onto his desk, but nothing did. He turned the envelope around and looked inside. "Ahhh, there it is." He reached in and ripped a tape-covered object from the side of the envelope. He pulled away the tape and shreds of cardboard and tossed them into his wastebasket, then held the key up so Casey and Marjorie could admire his discovery.

"It looks like we're in business, Mr. Stilwell," Marjorie noted. "So, what do you need us to do?" Marjorie prepared to jot down what he said, waiting for his pronouncement.

"Alright, here's the game plan. Marjorie, I need you to run down a certified copy of Ashirvadam's death certificate. We'll need that to get the probate process started. Do whatever it takes to get it here ASAP."

"Got it," Marjorie responded.

"Casey, can you research probating an international estate, especially a scenario where there are wills in other countries? I want to make sure we don't get going on this and then find out we're stuck on a technicality. And, see if you can find out anything about the churches in India and Italy."

"I'm on it," Casey said enthusiastically, starting to push herself out of her chair.

"I'll go through the will, too, and determine where in Virginia we need to file the will so I can get qualified as executor. Once that happens, we can see what's in that safe deposit box."

"Sounds like a plan, Mr. Stilwell," Marjorie added, flipping her notebook closed after taking her last note.

"Oh, and Marjorie," Steve said in an afterthought. "When you're getting the death certificate, see if you can find out what the current burial plans are. I'm hoping the body's already on its way to that church in India. If not, I may be in for an unpleasant phone call with Ashirvadam's widow."

"I'll see what I can find out," Marjorie answered. "And don't forget about your appointments this afternoon."

"Thanks Marjorie. I think we're in for an interesting ride."

5

8:16 a.m. on Monday, October 4, 2004
Independence, Missouri

Two late model Fords drove slowly along Berry Road past the brown-shingled bungalow they were looking for and turned around just down from the driveway. Although the house was set back from the road and behind some trees, the lead car had a clear view of the driveway and the front porch, the access points for the search. Everything looked good. A radio call announced the agents in the second car were ready to go.

"Let's do this," Special Agent Sheinelle Fields replied over the tactical circuit. Although she didn't anticipate a violent response or even any resistance from the subject, fourteen years in the FBI had taught her to expect the unexpected. That was why the two agents in the second car would exit their vehicle and wait just outside the back door in case the subject tried to flee. Explaining to the Special Agent in Charge how she'd let the subject escape was a conversation she did not want to have.

Field's partner, Special Agent Neil Crosby, pulled the car into the driveway, nosing it up as close to the one-car garage door as he could to eliminate an escape route. Both agents got out of their vehicle and climbed the porch steps to the front door. Fields, wearing an olive jacket and pants that allowed her to quickly un-holster her mostly concealed weapon, stood in front of the subject's door with her badge in hand so she'd be immediately seen by whoever opened the door. Crosby, wearing a gray suit, stood invisible off to the side, ready to appear in case the situation required a two-agent show of force. So far though, their experience as part of the FBI's newly formed rapid deployment Art Crime Team was that suspects were cooperative, intent more on hiding what they had illegally obtained rather than trying to forcefully fend off the FBI.

"You got the warrant?" Fields asked Crosby as she readied herself to ring the doorbell. She knew, of course, Crosby had it. She'd confirmed that before they left the FBI field office in Kansas City.

"Here you go," Crosby replied, retrieving the tri-folded document from his suit coat pocket and handing it to Fields.

Fields took the search warrant and opened it so she'd be ready to read it when the subject came to the door. "Radio the backup and let 'em know we're ready to go in." Crosby did as instructed and the backup confirmed they were in position behind the house.

"Okay then," Fields announced. "Let's get this done." She reached out and rang the doorbell. She could hear the muffled double chime from just inside the door. She fidgeted with the corner of the warrant waiting for someone to answer, shifting her weight to her back foot to dissipate the stress.

"Maybe he's at work," Crosby conjectured. "It is Monday morning."

"He could be sleeping in. I know that's what I'd be doing if I didn't have to be here. Let's give it one more ring." Fields pushed the doorbell until it droned on for an annoyingly long time. Still no answer.

"He's either passed out or gone," Crosby concluded. "That would have woken anybody up."

"Tell the backup there's no answer and we're going in," Fields directed.

"Wilco," Crosby replied before shifting to the radio and passing Fields' instructions. "You want me to get the bar from the car so we can open the door?"

"Hang on for a second." Fields reached out and grasped the doorknob. "Maybe this will be—it's our lucky day. The door's unlocked." Fields smiled at Crosby and then pushed the door open to walk inside. A wall of stench struck her in the face and she gagged. "Oh my God!"

"Something must be dead in there," Crosby declared, recoiling from the foul cloud now engulfing him, too.

Fields stuffed the search warrant into her back pocket and drew her service pistol. She reached inside the front door to turn on the light but realized it was already on. Just inside in the living room and off to the left, she saw a blood-spattered carpet and a large, bloody yellow lab lying dead on the floor. She could see several deep cuts in the dog's neck and torso. She pulled herself back outside to update Crosby.

"There's a butchered dog in the living room and I think I hear a TV on. You better call the locals and have them get out here right away. Make sure they bring an animal disposal unit with them."

"Wilco," Crosby repeated. He relayed what they had found over the radio and requested support from the Independence Police. He positioned the radio so both he and Fields could hear the response. A moment later, the radio confirmed the locals were on their way.

"I'm not so sure this is our lucky day anymore," Fields quipped. "Let's get in there and secure the scene. We can hold off the search until they get the dog out. And let's leave the front door open to see if we can get this place aired out."

"You want me to go in first?" Crosby asked. "I've done this a few more times than you have, you know." Crosby grinned; this was not braggadocio but concern for his partner's safety.

"That's because you're old. Just keep me straight and I'll be fine." Fields looked back at her partner and smiled. Crosby was ten years her senior and he treated her like his little sister, not in a condescending way, but always wanting to help her succeed. He knew what she was up against, being a black woman in a force dominated by white males. Fields knew that because they drank a lot of coffee together, and they talked. Crosby was a good man, having transferred to the startup Art Crime Team from the International Crimes Division, where he'd come into contact with a bunch of bad actors. Fields felt safe knowing he had her back, but she also had no hesitation going in first. She'd never cut corners when it came to paying her dues. She didn't want to give less forward-thinking agents any reason to question her ability; it was all about proving herself every day, every time. She had no margin for weakness because someone would see it and use it to take her down.

"You got your weapon ready?" she continued.

"I'm good," he responded.

"Here we go then." Fields stepped into the living room, her weapon at the ready, trying to avoid being overcome by the stench. A pool of dried blood radiated from the deep cuts in the dog's body, turning the section of the carpet around the dog a deep, dark color. In its death throes, the dog defecated, contributing to the putrid smell.

"Watch out for those bloody footprints," Fields cautioned Crosby as they walked passed the dog and made their way to the center of the room. "Lookout here, too," she said, pointing to another bloody splotch on the carpet. Fields couldn't tell if it was from the dog or something else, although she had her suspicions. She paused by the glass-topped coffee table and looked around after stepping over the second bloody patch. "You see what I see?" she asked, her face knotted in an effort to combat the smell.

"What's that?"

"It looks like whatever went down happened while he was watching TV." She pointed to the coffee table with her pistol. "See that? There's an open beer and the TV's on." She scanned around the room and the dining area to the rear, covering her nose and mouth with her free hand as if that would help keep the smell of death from intruding on their investigation. "Nothing's knocked over, everything looks in place."

"So, why's there a dead dog in the living room?" Crosby asked, building on Fields' observations. He, too, had his free hand over his nose, and he talked louder, like he was speaking on a cell phone with a bad connection.

"I'm thinking something interrupted him when he was watching TV, and that something killed his dog."

Crosby nodded. "Let's hope that's all the something did."

Fields gestured with her head toward the hall at the back of the room. "Let's check out the rest of the house. Go ahead and tell Allen and McPherson to come in if the door's open. We've got to get some fresh air in this place."

Crosby nodded again. He radioed what they'd found so far to the two agents waiting at the back door and directed them to enter the house. He added if it looked like it wouldn't disturb anything, to prop open the back door. He then returned to the front door and opened it all the way, wedging his wallet between the bottom edge of the door and the carpeting to keep it open. The air in the room started to flow; the agents at the back door had made it inside.

Fields waited for Crosby to return. "Hey Neil, you doing okay?" Fields whispered as she paused before entering the hallway.

"Yeah, but I certainly didn't expect this," Crosby responded, his voice not as hushed as Fields'. "I'm thinking somebody else beat us to the punch. I wonder if they found it?"

"It's not what's missing that worries me." Fields' voice was no longer hushed. "It's what I'm afraid we might find. I got a bad feeling about this." Fields turned to proceed through the hall, following the bloody footprints. She could see two open doors and a third barely ajar on the left side, the two open doors allowing swaths of light to penetrate the hallway. The sunlight revealed a long, crimson handprint wiped along the full length of the interior wall. The finger and palm stain started at the entrance three or four feet from the floor, fading to just fingers the farther down the hall it went. An arched entryway interrupted the streak about half way down, only to continue again on the other side. It disappeared opposite the mostly closed door at the end of the hall.

"Neil, how about you go check out the dining room and I'll start down the hall."

"Why don't you wait here until I can go with you? It'll just take a minute."

"The way that dead dog smells tells me whoever was here is long gone," Fields said confidently. "Besides, I think the archway on the right is coming from the dining room, so we should meet back up anyway."

Crosby nodded and gave a thumbs up. He veered off to the dining room, while Fields took her first tentative steps down the hall, avoiding the bloodstains on the carpet. She moved slowly, processing the details like a sensor analyzing conditions unknown. What concerned her most was that the handprints and footprints led in only one direction—to the door at the end of the hall. That meant whoever went back there cleaned up and came out of the room un-bloodied, or they were still there. She kept her weapon drawn.

As she inched closer to the door at the end of the hall, the smell became more and more wretched. Either the stench from the dog had permeated the walls and furnishings throughout the house, or there was something else dead behind that final door. She prayed it was another dog. When she made it to the first open door, she cleared the room and continued down the hall. The next room on the left was a small bathroom, and it, too, was empty. Now at the last door, she paused to peer through the sliver of an opening between the door and its frame.

"The dining room's clear and I met up with Allen and McPherson in the kitchen," Crosby reported from just behind her.

Fields gasped and jumped back from the door. "You startled me," she whispered angrily. "I was just getting ready to look inside."

"Sorry," Crosby announced a little louder than Fields would have liked, but she didn't say anything. Crosby returned to reciting his report. "It's all clear in the kitchen. They're opening up windows and they know to be careful for fingerprints. You find anything yet?"

"No, but whatever we're gonna find is in this room." Fields pointed to a bloody handprint on the doorframe and whispered her assessment of what it meant. "Somebody was trying to steady themself before they went in. I'm afraid this isn't the dog's blood."

Crosby nodded.

Fields leaned forward and tilted her head so her left eye could see through the crack in the door. All she could see was the right edge of a bed with a dark brown bedspread, and a nightstand with an unlit lamp against the wall at the head of the bed. Everything looked in order, but she knew that couldn't be. She looked back at Crosby. "Let's get this over with." Her heart pounding with a high-octane mix of adrenaline, determination, and fear, she readied her weapon, held her breath, and pushed the door open.

"Oh my God," she said as if she needed the spoken words to help her deal with the reality of what she was seeing. On the floor just in front her, a man lay dead on his back. His nose bent in unnatural angles and one eye was open. The other eye, and the rest of his face for that matter, looked like it had been pulverized with a blunt object. The real damage, though, was the bullet wound in his neck.

Having quickly processed the dead body, Fields started to notice the rest of the room. The midsection of a tipped-over bookcase rested on the end of the bed, with the bookcase's contents strewn onto the floor and the bed itself. Some of the items partially covered a bloodstain on the bedspread, which looked made on the right side, but was a mess on the left. The nightstand at the head of the left side of the bed had its drawer open, and its lamp sat upside down and crooked on its shade on the floor. The room wreaked of death.

Fields took a couple of steps inside, which was all she could do without stepping on the corpse. She stood as tall as her five-foot, five-inch frame allowed and looked over on the floor on the far side of the bed just to make sure there was nothing there. Although she couldn't see the floor immediately to the left of the bed, she saw enough to satisfy herself that the room was clear. She holstered her weapon and looked back at Crosby, who was surveying the room with his hand covering his nose. As he put his weapon away, police sirens started to play in the background, their increasing volume announcing their impending arrival

"Looks like someone got our man," Fields asserted. "Let's have Allen notify the coroner's office and get the evidence techs out here. While they're doing that, we can get some fresh air and notify the boss. I've had about all I can take of this stench." She turned to head out of the room.

"I don't think this is him, Sheinelle," Crosby countered.

Fields stopped in her tracks. "What makes you think that? He's a white male, about the right age with a military-style haircut. This is him alright. They must have beaten him until he gave them the tablet and then they left him for dead. He must have grabbed onto the bookshelf when he fell."

"That would work except it doesn't fit the scene."

"What do you mean?" Fields didn't mind Crosby questioning her theory. She'd worked white-collar crime for fourteen years; he'd spent his career chasing bad guys. If he said the scene didn't fit, there had to be something to it.

"Somebody with a wound fell on the bed. Look at how it's all messed up on the left side with blood on the bedspread. In fact, the bedspread's bunched together on the edge near the middle, like someone grabbed it as they went over the side. What if our guy was on the bed and reached into the nightstand to get a gun, then shot his assailant either before or after he went over the side?"

"That would work," Fields concurred, "but where is he then? Do you see him over there?"

Crosby worked his way past Fields and got as close to the bookshelf as he could without disturbing anything. He leaned over to inspect the floor on the far side of the bed. "No body, but there's a lot of blood on the floor. Someone was definitely over there."

"Wait a minute," Fields announced. She knelt down on a clean patch of the floor and pulled up a corner of the bedspread. The smell coming from under the bed told her she didn't have to look, but she did anyway. "Man, you are good," she said as she stood up. "There's another dead white male under the bed. You are good," she repeated.

"I've seen too much of this kind of thing," Crosby responded. "I transferred to Art Crime to get away from it."

"Looks like you brought it with you," Fields chided, hoping the conversation would lighten the burden of having to deal with the scene. "Did you tell headquarters to get the coroner and the evidence techs here?"

"They're on their way," Crosby confirmed.

"Okay then," Fields concluded. "Let's get out of here and let the boss know what's going on."

6

3:38 p.m. on Tuesday, October 5, 2004
Rome, Italy

THE CAFÉ COULD HAVE BEEN ANYPLACE in Italy. This one happened to be on a busy street in Rome. Inside, a handcrafted wood cabinet filled the back wall of the small establishment, while a marble counter provided food preparation space for the two bartenders in white shirts and blue ties working behind the bar. To prepare for the Tuesday afternoon rush, one bartender wiped the back counter with a wet rag while the other stacked tiny espresso cups and saucers on the counter just below the bar.

A man in a gray suit with his back to the eatery's streetside entrance stood at the bar sipping a cup of coffee. He looked straight ahead into a bottled drink refrigerator with "Pago" emblazoned across the top in red Latin letters, seemingly oblivious to his surroundings. A page-sized envelope lay clasp side up on the counter next to his saucer, and his left hand fidgeted with a spoon in between sips of coffee. His heart raced when he saw in the glass door of the Pago refrigerator the reflection of someone entering from the street. Although he suspected this could be the one, he didn't move or convey interest.

The reflection grew larger until it turned into a woman in a cinnamon-brown business suit. She walked up to the counter on his left. Although he couldn't discern her features from her reflection in the glass, the bartender stacking the saucers could and stopped what he was doing to serve her.

"Ciao," he said with sudden animation and interest. "What can I get for you today?"

"Caffè, grazie," she replied, pulling her wallet from her unzipped bag and placing a two euro coin on the counter. She returned her wallet to the bag and set it on the floor between her feet and the bar. She brushed her golden-brown hair off her shoulders and waited a few more moments before the bartender set her coffee in front of her.

"May I help you with anything else?" he asked, obviously enjoying the sight of his latest customer.

"No, grazie," she replied. She looked away from him toward her coffee, picking it up and taking a disinterested sip. The bartender got the message and retrieved the two euro coin. He started to make change, but she waved him off without saying anything. When he returned to stacking cups and saucers away from where she stood, she began speaking just loud enough for the man in the gray suit to hear.

"Let's sit at one of the tables away from the counter to talk business."

"I'm sorry?" the man said, pretending not to know what she was talking about. He had to make sure she was the right person. He looked at her for the first time. Attractive but stern, she didn't look like she had time for chatter. She responded by picking up her bag and coffee and moving to a table in the corner farthest away from the counter. He took his coffee and the envelope and followed her to the table, sitting across from her.

"Don't play games," she warned. "I've come here for the information and you either have it or you don't. If you don't, you will have bigger problems to deal with."

He felt his palms liquefy with sweat. He had never done anything like this before. It started with a phone call from someone who sounded friendly. All she wanted was a few blueprints and she was willing to pay handsomely for them. She assured him no one would ever know or suspect anything because it was in everyone's interest to conduct the transaction quietly. She promised the only reason she wanted the blueprints was to help her company submit a proposal that would be good for everyone. She also struck a chord by reminding him the Superintendency of Monuments didn't pay him what he was worth. When he hadn't taken any action to deliver the blueprints by her second call, she pushed harder. When he told her during her third call that he had changed his mind and wanted to forget the whole thing, she played a tape recording of him agreeing to provide the blueprints in return for money. She had him and he knew it. Now he just wanted to give her what she wanted, get his money, and get it over with.

"It's all there," he assured her. "The plans, the blueprints, and the security system information. But I want you to give me my money first."

The woman's face twisted and her cheeks reddened, creating an angry look beyond her years. "That's not possible. The agreement was we would first verify the authenticity of the information, then we would pay you."

The man shook his head in an emphatic no. "Do you think I am going to give you the information and then wait patiently for you to pay me? I don't even know who you are. If I give you the blueprints now, I may never hear from you again. We are going to have to change the agreement—you and me, here." Although his hands were still sweating, the discomfort on the woman's face emboldened him. She looked no more than thirty. He was nearly twice her age. She couldn't tell him what to do. Besides, he had the information and there was no way she was going to take it from him.

The woman thought for a moment, then leaned toward him, her anger displaced by a look of optimism. "I have a solution. Let's go to my bank and I'll give you five thousand euros and you give me half the documents. I'll fax my team what you give me and if they tell me it's authentic, I'll pay you the rest of the money in return for the remaining documents. I think that will work, don't you?" The woman smiled, making him want to please her.

Unable to think of a better option, he nodded and said, "I agree." As he started to push his chair back to stand up, she reached across the table and grabbed his arm.

"Just one more thing before we go. You need to show me what's in the envelope so I know you have all the documents with you. I don't want to be played for a fool."

It was his turn to smile. "Of course." He unfastened the brass clasp and pulled the small stack of blueprints and other documents from the envelope. He'd copied everything in the file without regard to what was relevant and what wasn't. At the time, his main interest was making the copies without raising suspicions or being detected. He celebrated that approach now because having given her everything, she wouldn't keep bothering him for more information. He set the documents on the table and let her flip through the stack.

The woman perused each document, taking in each one as if she were confirming its authenticity on the spot. When she finished, she gathered them up and returned them to the man.

"Everything looks in order," the woman concluded. "Do we have a deal?"

"Of course," he replied, stuffing the documents back into the envelope and folding down the clasp to keep the flap closed.

The woman stood up and he followed suit. Before she turned to head for the door, she reached out to shake his hand. "I like to seal my deals with a handshake to show our good faith." Her smile showed her satisfaction with their resolution of what could have been an intractable problem. He shook her hand, smiling to demonstrate his satisfaction, as well.

"So where is your bank?" he asked, tucking the envelope under his left arm and pushing his chair against the table. The woman left her chair where it was when she stood up.

"Let's go outside and flag a taxi," she replied without disclosing more. She led the way out of the café and onto the sidewalk until he caught up with her. They had to weave their way across the Roman sidewalk, now packed with afternoon commuters on their way to the bus stop off to the right. She stopped just back from the curb so they could see any cabs heading their way. After checking out the prospects, she cupped her free hand to amplify her voice over the din of the traffic and the crowd. He bent down slightly so he could hear what she was saying.

"There are a couple of buses and then it looks like there might be a cab. Would you flag it down?" she asked. He nodded and looked toward the oncoming traffic, confirming her observations. He pulled the envelope from under his arm and held it tightly so it wouldn't be lost when they climbed into the cab. After the first bus passed in front of them, he raised his hand so the cab behind the second bus would see them. As he did, the woman imperceptibly slid her right foot in front of his left foot, and then with her right hand on his lower back, shoved him forward. Tripping over her outstretched foot, he flew headfirst into the path of the oncoming bus. The driver slammed on the brakes, but it was too late. The man hit off the front of the bus and fell on his back, only to be crushed by the skidding front tire.

The woman's scream sliced through the afternoon rush hour. "Call an ambulance, call an ambulance," she yelled. She knelt down next to what could be seen of the man and reached under the bus, but quickly withdrew, screaming hysterically and crying. Others pushed past her, including a woman yelling, "Make way. I am a doctor. Make way."

The doctor bent down to assist the man, but he was pinned beneath the wheel, so she could not reach him, nor could he be pulled free. "Back up the bus," the doctor yelled to the driver. "Hurry, you must back up the bus." Several men joined her entreaty by motioning for the bus to back up. "Go slowly," the doctor implored, bracing the man's legs to hold him in place as the bus retreated. It didn't work because the low clearance between bus and street meant once the tire pulled away from the man's abdomen, the reversing bus dragged his body along the concrete road. "Stop, stop," she yelled as she stood up to make sure the bus driver saw her. The men helping out mimicked her impromptu hand signals.

The doctor crouched down again and with the help of two Good Samaritans, wrenched the man from under the bus and pulled him to the curb. Blood ran from his mouth and oozed from his nose, and the belly of his white shirt looked like a blood-soaked rag. The doctor checked the man's breathing and pulse, but found no signs of life. With the sound of an ambulance's siren growing louder, she prepared to turn over the man to the arriving paramedics.

"Where is the woman he was with?" someone shouted.

"I don't see her," another person said. Bystanders near the man looked around, waiting for the woman to step forward to mourn the man's death, but she never did. She'd slipped away through the crowd and commotion, taking the envelope containing the blueprints with her.

7

———

2:17 p.m. on Thursday, October 7, 2004
Fairfax County, Virginia

FRESH FROM QUALIFYING AS ARUL ASHIRVADAM'S executor before the
Clerk of Court for the Fairfax County Circuit Court and admitting the
original will into probate, Steve drove to the Security International Bank in
Vienna to find out what was in Ashirvadam's safe deposit box. Under normal
circumstances, it would have been impossible to get the certified copy of
Ashirvadam's death certificate required by the Circuit Court in just two days,
but Steve used Detective Cavendish's eagerness to get his hands on a copy of
Ashirvadam's will to his advantage. Cavendish jumped at the offer to send the
death certificate overnight in return for the details of when and where Steve
would probate Ashirvadam's estate. Steve still couldn't give Cavendish a copy
of the will directly, but Cavendish was satisfied with requesting it from the
Clerk of Court as soon as it became a public record.

Despite that quid pro quo, Steve didn't show Cavendish his full hand—he
kept the existence of Ashirvadam's cover letter secret. Mentioning the letter to
Cavendish would be too risky without first knowing what was in his client's
safe deposit box. Cavendish would find out eventually, especially if Steve
needed it to move Ashirvadam's body to India for burial. But for now, he
didn't want anything to complicate his access to the box.

After a short wait in the lobby, a young man from the bank escorted Steve
through a security gate and into a giant steel vault filled with safe deposit
boxes.

"It's box 20316, is that correct?" the man asked.

"That's the one."

"Okay then." The young man retrieved the bank's key to the box, stuck it in the lock, and turned it to the right. "Your turn," he said.

Steve inserted his key and turned it to the right. As he did, the man tugged on his key and the door swung open, revealing the box in its slot in the wall. "You can set it on the counter over there and go through it," the young man instructed, pointing to the area behind him. "Call me whenever you're ready to lock it up again."

"Thanks," Steve answered. He pulled the heavy drawer from near the bottom of the wall and cradled it over to the counter before setting it down. By the time he lifted open the lid, the man was already outside the vault.

"Holy cow," Steve said under his breath once he realized what he was seeing. Bundles of colorful hundred-euro notes, each one neatly bound with a paper wrapper and labeled as ten thousand euros, filled the front of the compartment. He counted the bundles as he took them out and set them on the counter. "One hundred thousand euros," he announced to himself once the last bundle hit the pile. Steve opened his leather planner and jotted down the total.

There were only three other items in the box: a rental agreement for postal box 321 at the Vienna, Virginia, Post Office; a key which Steve presumed would open the postal box; and a folded paper page that looked like it had been hastily ripped from an address book. The page had two hand-printed telephone numbers on it, one ten-digit U.S. number and another that appeared to be for someone in Italy. Having deployed to the Mediterranean Sea on the USS Saratoga and gone on liberty in Naples and Rome, he recognized 039 at the start of the telephone number as Italy's country code. Neither telephone number had a name associated with it.

It would have been easy to take the rental agreement and the page from the address book with him. After all, Ashirvadam's cover letter instructed him to destroy everything in the box except the euros. He knew, though, that the items might be important to Cavendish's investigation, and he didn't want to do anything that would make him appear complicit in a cover-up. The Virginia State Bar might also open an ethics investigation if it thought he destroyed evidence of a crime, even though he currently had nothing but Cavendish's unsupported accusations that Ashirvadam had done anything illegal. He jotted down the post office box and two telephone numbers and returned the rental agreement, folded paper, and the cash to the box.

Not so for the key. As Ashirvadam's executor, he had a fiduciary duty to collect and inventory all of Ashirvadam's U.S. assets and liabilities so they could be resolved pursuant to the will. For all Steve knew, the post office box might contain bills that needed to be paid or investment checks that needed to be deposited on behalf of the estate. Ashirvadam's cover letter may have directed him to destroy the key, but it didn't say when that had to occur. The ambiguity allowed him to take the key, use it to check the contents of the post office box, and deal with Ashirvadam's instructions, and possibly Cavendish's investigation, later. Content he'd threaded his duty to his client through the ethical needle, he summoned the young man waiting by the front of the vault to help him secure the box.

Twenty minutes later, Steve was unlocking box 321 in the Vienna, Virginia, Post Office. The only item inside was a U.S. Postal Service notice informing Ashirvadam he had a package waiting for pickup. The receipt was dated October 7th, so whatever the package was, it had just arrived that morning. Steve got in line and waited until it was his turn at the counter.

"Next customer please," the middle-aged postal clerk announced. She sounded tired and didn't smile. Steve noticed she was trying unsuccessfully to avoid looking at his black eyes.

"Hi," Steve said, sounding chipper. He set the package delivery notice on the counter and slid it toward the clerk. "I broke my nose, but it looks a lot worse than it is."

"It looks pretty painful to me," she said, her expression reflecting her concern. She picked up the form and glanced at it like a human bar scanner, capturing everything she needed. "I'll need to see an ID, please."

"Sure," Steve replied. "I'm actually an attorney representing the box holder's estate. He died just last week." The clerk perked up, apparently thrilled to deal with something out of the ordinary. Steve opened his planner and started to pull out some papers when the clerk rattled off her requirements.

"That changes things," she said. "I'll not only need your ID, but I'll also need a copy of your qualification letter from a court of law. I'm afraid without that, I won't be able to give you the package."

"I got that from the court this morning, so we're in good shape," Steve responded, smiling as he removed a copy of his qualification letter from a manila folder in his planner. He passed it to the clerk together with his driver's license. "Is there anything else you need?" He knew the answer was no.

The clerk ran the long edge of Steve's driver's license along the qualification letter until the names on the license and the letter lined up. Apparently satisfied he was who he said he was, she handed him back his driver's license. "No, Mr. Stilwell," she replied, a repressed smile forcing its way to her lips. "It's nice to see someone who knows what to bring. You'd be surprised at how many people come without the right documents. Then they get mad when I can't just turn the mail over to them. What do they expect?"

"I know what you mean," he replied, nodding sympathetically. He didn't want to do or say anything that might squelch the cooperation coming his way.

"I'll get the package," the clerk said. When she returned, she handed him a shoebox-sized package. "Be careful," she cautioned. "It's marked extremely fragile."

"I will," he assured her. "Thanks so much for your help." With package in hand, he walked past the long line that had formed behind him and headed out to his car. Although he still had a three-and-a-half-hour drive back to Williamsburg ahead of him, he couldn't help but count the day a success. He was now officially Ashirvadam's executor, he'd inventoried the safe deposit box, and he'd discovered Ashirvadam's post office box. He hoped managing the rest of Ashirvadam's estate would go this smoothly.

8

2:34 p.m. on Thursday, October 7, 2004
Kansas City, Missouri

SPECIAL AGENTS FIELDS AND CROSBY STUDIED the witness sitting at the
rectangular table in the interrogation room. He looked nervous, clutching
with both hands a large paper cup of what had to be lukewarm coffee and
scouring every inch of the stark white walls. The room had no windows, just
a large mirror all but the most ignorant interviewees understood, but quickly
forgot, allowed people outside the room to scrutinize their every move.

The session, scheduled to begin at two thirty, was not an interrogation.
DaRell Peters had done nothing wrong. His only crime was that he knew
Navy Chief Petty Officer Kevin Jones, one of the dead men found three days
before in the back bedroom of the home in Independence, Missouri. In fact,
they had been in the same Navy Reserve unit, Navy Mobile Construction
Battalion Fifteen, Air Detachment, based out of Kansas City, and they'd
deployed together to Iraq in 2003. Fields was certain the story behind the
killings began in Iraq, so that was where she intended to focus her initial
efforts. She would start by interviewing every person who deployed to Iraq
with Chief Jones, reasoning someone in his unit had to know how he got
himself involved in smuggling antiquities. Jones' officer-in-charge told her
the best person to start with was Peters, since he worked directly for Jones and
they spent a lot of time together during their Iraq deployment. Fields hoped
the officer-in-charge's instincts were correct.

"We better get in there," Fields told Crosby. "We don't want to freak him
out *too* much." She grinned. Everything she and Crosby did was scripted to

get the witness to open up and tell them what he knew. By building just the right amount of pressure and then relieving it by relating to the witness on a personal level, they hoped to make him trust them enough to talk. It was a science requiring an artist's touch. Fields opened the door and went into the room. Peters stood up as soon as he saw her.

"We're sorry to keep you waiting DaRell," Fields began as she walked over to shake his hand. "I'm Special Agent Sheinelle Fields and this is Special Agent Neil Crosby."

"Pleased to meet you ma'am, sir," Peters responded.

"You can sure tell you are Navy," Fields continued. "But I'm not that old, so you don't have to call me ma'am. And please, sit down. You don't have to stand for us." As Peters took his seat at the table, Fields sat across from him. She placed a thin, unmarked manila folder in front of her, which drew Peters' eyes. Crosby took a chair back from the table. The seating arrangement let Peters know Fields was in charge.

"Just so we can get the formalities out of the way, both Special Agent Crosby and I are FBI agents with the Art Crime Team, so we need to show you our credentials." She paused while both she and Crosby retrieved their badges and showed them to Peters. His eyes got larger looking at the badges and he clasped his hands on the table. Fields noticed sweat forming on the side of his face just below his regulation length sideburns. She had one more formality to get out of the way before she could try to calm him down.

"DaRell, just so you know what's going on, Special Agent Crosby's going to take notes while we talk, and our interview's also being recorded so we don't forget anything you tell us. Do you understand?

"Yes, ma'am," Peters replied, either ignoring or forgetting Fields' earlier admonition about calling her ma'am. Fields assumed it was the latter given his military background. His every act showed respect for her authority.

"DaRell, I can tell you're nervous. Everyone is when they talk to the FBI. But you've got nothing to worry about. We don't think you did anything wrong and you aren't under investigation. We just want to talk to you about a member of your unit, Kevin Jones. Do you know him?"

"Yes, ma'am. We was assigned together in NMCB-15 and we deployed together to Iraq."

"NMCB-15, is that Navy Mobile Construction Battalion 15, Air Detachment, headquartered right here in Kansas City?"

"That's it, ma'am. Chief Jones was my chief. I worked directly for him."

Fields' voice softened. "You know he's dead, DaRell, don't you? We found his body on Monday."

Peters nodded, his eyes downcast. "Yes, ma'am. The officer-in-charge put an email out Monday afternoon. He said he'd let us know when the funeral is."

"You know how he died?" Fields asked.

"Some dude shot him in his house," Peters responded. "I heard it on the news. They found the killer dead, too." He added an afterthought. "I'm glad Chief killed him. At least he took somebody out with him."

"No doubt about that," Fields responded. "But now we need to understand why it happened. We think you can help."

"I swear," Peters answered, slowly shaking his head from side to side. "I don't know nothin' about what happened. The last time I seen Chief was at drill weekend last month."

Fields used his answer as a launch pad for the questions she really needed answered. "When you mention drill weekend, you're referring to your Navy Reserve duty?"

"Yes ma'am. We go one weekend a month and do training and stuff like that at the Reserve Center. That's the last time I seen Chief Jones."

"I believe you DaRell," Fields assured him, "but where I think you might be able to help us comes from when you deployed to Iraq last year. We understand you worked pretty closely with Chief Jones building the defenses around a Marine Corps base in the desert. Is that true?"

"That's true."

"Can you tell us about that?"

"Yes ma'am." Peters leaned forward, clasping his hands on the table. "Chief and I was assigned to build a defensive perimeter around Camp Babylon. I'm a heavy equipment operator, so Chief and I went out every day and I'd drive the bulldozer, pushing up dirt and stuff into a mound around sections of the camp."

Fields could tell Peters started to relax when he talked about the work he did in Iraq. The fact that he'd gotten closer to her by leaning forward indicated he felt comfortable talking about something he knew. She wanted to make him even more comfortable before she got to the heart of the matter. She gambled that his mother and father had taken him to church as a kid.

"Is that the same Babylon that's in the Bible?"

"Yeah. There was ruins and stuff all around. We could even see the statue of the Lion of Babylon there until the general put it off limits."

"What's the Lion of Babylon?" Fields asked, hoping to draw Peters further in.

"It's some famous statue that's even on Iraq's flag. It's like thousands of years old."

"That had to be pretty cool, DaRell, being around all of those ancient ruins. In fact, that's where I think you really can help us."

"I don't know nothin' about them, ma'am. I just seen them when we was working over there and thought they was cool."

"Well, here's how we hope you can help us." Fields slid forward on the table and clasped her hands just like Peters had. She looked into his eyes. "Right before Chief Jones was killed, he ran an ad online. The ad was for a clay tablet with a diagram and some ancient writing on the back of it. That tablet had to come from Camp Babylon, DaRell. Do you know how he got it?"

Peters withdrew into his chair, again shaking his head from side to side. "I don't know nothin' about no tablet, ma'am. If he got it there, he didn't tell me." Peters looked down at the floor before reestablishing eye contact with Fields.

"Look DaRell, we're not trying to get you in trouble. I know you may not want to talk about it because you're not supposed to bring stuff like that back with you, but we really need to know where he got that tablet."

Peters looked down and just kept slowly shaking his head from side to side. "Like I said, I don't know about that."

"I understand, DaRell, I got it. If you don't know anything, then that's the way it is. But let me make sure you know a few of the details before you go." She moved the manila folder from the desk to her lap, out of Peters' view. Her eyes fixed on the folder and ignoring Peters, she opened it as she continued speaking. "About a week or two ago, somebody came over to Chief Jones' house while he was watching TV and butchered his dog with a knife." She pulled a color picture of the blood-soaked dog lying dead on the floor in Chief Jones' living room and slid it over to Peters. He twisted his head away after a quick glance.

"Then they shot Chief Jones and he crawled under his bed and bled to death." She retrieved a second picture, this one showing Jones in a pool of blood on the floor, with the bed he hid under propped on its end against the wall. Someone's legs were also visible at the top of the picture, but no more of the other body could be seen. Still reeling from the picture of the dog, Peters didn't look back at the photo of Jones.

"You need to look at this, DaRell. You need to see what somebody did to Chief Jones." Fields pushed the pictures closer to Peters so he couldn't avoid them. The Navy man looked at the photo of Chief Jones as directed and then pushed it away. He scowled at Fields.

"I got it ma'am. I got it." His voice grew more intense with each repetition. "I don't need no more pictures. I got it."

Fields face softened, but she continued to press the point home. "I'm sorry I had to do that, DaRell, but now you understand why we're trying to find the person who did this. We know you had nothing to do with it, but if we're going to get the person, we've got to know where the tablet came from." Fields reached forward and gathered the two pictures together with the one of Jones on top. She started to pick them up by the top right corner, elevating the upper portion from the table an inch or so and then pausing so there was no way Peters could avoid looking down one last time at the image of Chief Jones lying lifeless on the floor. This time, he didn't look away, he just glared down at the photo of his dead shipmate.

"I just want to make sure you really don't know anything about that tablet before we go." Fields pulled the photos away and tucked them into the manila folder.

Peters picked his head up, his shoulders slumping forward, and looked at Fields. "You being straight with me?"

"That's the way it went down, DaRell. They killed your friend."

"I thought Chief Jones killed the dude. If that's true, why do you need to know about some tablet?"

"You're right, Chief Jones got one of the men who attacked him, but there was at least one more. You know how we know that?"

Peters shook his head.

"Because Chief Jones died of a gunshot wound, and the man he killed didn't have a gun, only a knife—the knife that killed the dog. We know the man who killed Chief Jones is still out there somewhere, and the info about the tablet will help us find him."

Peters slouched down low, lifting his head up just enough to barely make eye contact with Fields. "Yeah, he got the tablet in Iraq."

Fields felt her heart beating faster as she closed in on the information she had been hoping for. "How do you know?"

"'Cause I was with him when he found it."

"Explain it to me, DaRell. Where were you and what were you doing when he found it?"

"Like I said, we was making a defensive perimeter for the Marines around Camp Babylon. I took a water break because it was hotter than hell in that armored dozer I was driving, so I climbed down to get a drink and talk to Chief."

"Was there anyone else there with you?"

"Nope, just me and him."

"What happened?"

"As he was walking over to me, he tripped and fell, but he caught himself before he did a face-plant. I was laughing and he was cussing and pissed because he'd need to put on a clean uniform when he got back to his tent. Then he bent over and started brushing the dirt from his knees, when all of a sudden, he stopped. He bent over some more and said 'well looky what I just found.'

"I said 'what's that Chief?' He said it looked like the bricks we seen all around the site, but it had some kind of writing carved on it. He said the bulldozer must've uncovered it.

"I told him to just leave it alone because the general ordered us not to mess with stuff and it would be a pain in the ass to report the brick. But he said it's cool and would look great on his mantle, or maybe even be worth big money once he got it back home. He said the place was loaded with stuff like this and ain't nobody gonna miss one damn brick. He said no one even knew it was there anyway. So, he picked it up, wiped it off with his sleeve, and stuffed it in the pouch on his pants. He said don't tell no one, so I didn't."

"That's really helpful, DaRell. That's what we figured, but we couldn't prove it. Now at least we know where the tablet came from. Let me ask you another question. Did he tell you how he got it back to Kansas City?"

"He never said nothing else about that tablet after he found it, not even when we got back to KC. I forgot he even took it. You bringing it up is the first time I heard anything about it since Iraq."

"Agent Crosby, do you have any more questions for DaRell?"

"No, I think you covered it."

"All right then, DaRell. That's all we need for now. I can't tell you how much we appreciate your help. If we have any more questions, we'll let you know. And, if you think of anything that will help us catch Chief Jones' killer, you give me or Agent Crosby a call."

"Yes, ma'am." Peters started to get up to leave, but then paused. "Am I gonna get in trouble for this? You know, for not telling nobody about Chief taking that brick?"

"I can't say no for sure, but we'll be sure to tell your officer-in-charge how helpful you were. I'll bet he'll be happy with that."

"Yes, ma'am."

Fields stayed seated while Crosby rose and opened the door for Peters, who quietly slipped out of the room and went on his way, escorted by an agent waiting outside. Crosby closed the door and returned to the table, plopping into what had been the hot seat just moments before.

"Where do we go from here?" Crosby asked. "You know, this really doesn't put us any closer to identifying a suspect. I think it's a dead end."

"Maybe so, maybe not," Fields conjectured. "What it tells me is Jones wasn't a professional. He didn't go over there looking for this stuff and he wasn't acting for anybody else. He just found a souvenir and brought it home because it looked cool."

"Why'd he advertise it online then?"

"I don't know. Maybe he got tired of it, or like Peters said, maybe he thought he could make some easy money. I guess it doesn't matter anymore, does it?"

"No," Crosby agreed, "but what does matter is that he's dead and somebody got the tablet. How are we going to find them?"

Fields got up and took a few steps before turning around and facing Crosby. "Let me ask you this first. Why do you think someone wants the tablet?"

Crosby crossed his legs. "I figure they must be a collector. They must have been watching the Internet for things like this to pop up and when it did, they jumped on it."

Fields rubbed her chin and started talking at the same time, but drew out her words so they wouldn't get ahead of her brain processing the logic of what she was about to propose. "A collector, yes, but maybe more than that. This collector sent a couple of thugs to score that tablet and they weren't taking no for an answer."

"I don't get it. Where are you going with this?"

"So," Fields continued, "I'm wondering if there might be something special about this tablet besides being from Babylon and thousands of years old. Maybe they weren't looking for just any tablet. Maybe they were looking for this tablet. We need to find out what it says. Let's get the photos from the website and see if there's anything special about it."

"Alright," Crosby assented. "But it could take some time."

Fields walked back to her chair and grabbed the back with both hands. "Then expedite it," she directed. "Two men are dead and the tablet's gone. The longer it takes, the tougher it's going to be to follow this up. Let's get an expert on it right away."

"Will do," Crosby replied, jotting down the instructions in his notes.

"And I'll follow-up too with the lab to see if they found anything that might help us identify the shooter. I don't want this case turning cold on us." Fields knew it was more than that. This was her first case combining art theft and murder and she could not fail. She had something to prove.

9

7:55 a.m. on Friday, October 8, 2004
Williamsburg, Virginia

WITH THE PACKAGE HE'D PICKED UP at the post office the day before tucked under his arm, Steve set his briefcase down on the hallway floor to free up a hand to open the door to his office. The door was unlocked, of course. Marjorie always arrived around 7:30 a.m. to make sure the office was ready for the day. That meant fresh coffee brewing in the kitchen and his schedule printed out and waiting on his desk. He twisted the knob and leaned into the door with his shoulder to keep it open, then picked up his briefcase and pushed through to the law office lobby where Marjorie waited behind her desk.

"Good morning, Mr. Stilwell," Marjorie announced with a smile that made Steve feel like his Friday was already off to a great start. "How was your trip to Vienna?"

Steve stopped in front of Marjorie's desk to give his mandatory after-action report.

"It went like clockwork," he replied. "I qualified as executor without a hitch and then the International Investment Bank gave me access to Ashirvadam's safe deposit box."

"What was in it?" Marjorie continued. As she spoke, Casey emerged from her office carrying a mug of thick, black, steaming coffee that easily could have been mistaken for used motor oil.

"Good morning, Steve. It sounds like your trip went well." Casey took station a couple of feet from Steve and, holding her mug with both hands, sipped tentatively without taking her eyes off him.

"It did," he replied. Realizing he wasn't going to make it to his office without divulging everything that happened on his trip, he set his briefcase down to make a full report. "I was just filling in Marjorie on the details. Basically, we're good to go with administering the estate, so we need to press forward right away. I also found some very interesting things in the safe deposit box."

"Like what?" Casey asked, picking up where Marjorie left off.

"Well, to begin with, one hundred thousand euros in cash."

"Oh, my. I wish ya'll had sent me to clean out that box," Marjorie quipped. "I'd have taken good care of that money." Marjorie widened her eyes and tilted her head as if she were chastising Steve, but her Virginia drawl and the turned-up corners of her lips wouldn't let her sound serious.

"And that's precisely why you didn't go." Steve grinned.

"That's the money our client wants us to give to the church in Italy," Casey noted, bringing the conversation back to business. "Do you see any way we can do it?"

"Not off the top of my head," answered Steve. "Since the gift to the church wasn't in the will itself, I think the church is out of luck. I'm not ruling anything out, though, until we research whether the international character of the will might make a difference. But that's the way I see it now."

"That's what I thought, too," Casey said, reinforcing Steve's preliminary conclusion. "The church I think we can deal with is the one in India. That's the one where Ashirvadam wants to be buried."

"What's it called?" Steve asked. "I can't remember its name."

"The only reason I can is because I researched it yesterday," Casey noted. "It's the St. Thomas Syro-Malabar Church. It was founded in 52 A.D. by St. Thomas after he settled in India."

"Is that Doubting Thomas the Apostle?" Marjorie asked.

"That's the one," Casey answered.

"I didn't know he went to India," Marjorie continued.

"Neither did I," Steve added. "I wonder why Ashirvadam picked those two churches?"

"Maybe we can find out when we talk to his wife about her husband's burial instructions," suggested Casey.

"Don't ya'll think it's unusual for a rich guy like Ashirvadam to keep that much cash in a safe deposit box?" Marjorie asked, returning to the euro discovery.

"That's what I'm thinking," Casey added. "It makes me wonder where the money came from, especially given your conversation with the police in London. Did you bring the money back with you?"

"No, I left it in the safe deposit box. I don't want the police to think we're trying to hide anything."

"Was there anything else?" Marjorie asked, taking notes for the Ashirvadam estate file.

"There was," Steve replied. "A piece of paper with a couple of handwritten telephone numbers on it. One looked like it was from Italy, while the other looked like a U.S. number. The only other things were a contract and key for a mailbox in the Vienna Post Office. In fact, that's where I picked up this package." Steve pulled the shoebox-size package from under his arm and held it up even though it had been fully visible before. He set it down in the center of Marjorie's desk. "Marjorie, can you record in the file where the package came from and the date it was received, which was yesterday. While you're doing that, I'll grab a cup of coffee and then you can bring it into my office and we'll see what's inside."

"Will do, Mr. Stilwell."

"Casey, how about joining us and you can update me on anything else you've been able to find out."

"Works for me," Casey replied.

Steve was already seated at his round cherry conference table by the time Marjorie and Casey filed into his office. They took their usual seats, then Marjorie slid the package toward Steve, together with a pair of scissors resting on top.

"We think you should open it since you brought it back," Marjorie declared.

"I can't argue with that," agreed Steve. He used the scissor's blades like a knife to slice through the packing tape along the center and edges of the box, then manipulated the now-liberated box flaps until he could see inside.

"What is it, Mr. Stilwell?" Marjorie asked impatiently, bracing her arms on the edge of the table and half-standing to get a better look at the contents.

"Hang on there, Marjorie," chastened Steve, pulling tightly packed newspaper from the top half of the box and setting it on the table. "I was afraid of this," he announced. He left the item in the box and slid it toward Casey and Marjorie so they could look inside. Both women stood at their seats to study the object nested in the crumpled newspaper lining the bottom of the box.

"So now what do we do?" Casey asked.

"Wait a minute," Marjorie demanded. "What the hell is it?"

Steve chuckled. "That's a good question. Assuming what the London police said was true, my guess is it's some sort of ancient tablet Ashirvadam acquired for his collection."

"And that means it's likely stolen," Casey added.

"It could be," Steve replied, "but he could have acquired it legitimately. I don't want to jump to any conclusions, at least not yet."

Casey spun the box around and flipped the top closed so she could see the postal mark and the addressee. She pressed her point. "Let me play devil's advocate for a moment. I think we need to assume it's stolen, Steve. Look," she said, pointing to the top of the box. "There's no return address and the package isn't insured. There's no way a legitimate dealer would have sent this without insurance, let alone without a return address. I recommend treating this like stolen property."

"Fair enough," Steve conceded. "I haven't had to deal with an issue like this since I was a defense counsel in the Navy, and that was a long time ago. As I recall, we have an ethical obligation as attorneys to turn stolen evidence over to the prosecution, but we get to investigate it first. Maybe if we do some digging, we might be able to establish where it came from and whether it was stolen."

"I'll bet I can tell you at least where it was packaged," Casey claimed, reaching for a piece of the balled-up newspaper littering the table. She unfolded one of the pages just enough to read the upper left corner. "It's the Kansas City Star from September twenty-seventh." She set the paper down and checked the postage on the top of the box. "The post mark is also Kansas City and it has the same date. Looks like that's where the trail starts."

"Can we take it out and look at it?" Marjorie asked.

"I'd recommend we not touch it," Casey replied politely. "Even though we could probably get some gloves and take it out of the box, it might be best for the police to see it just like we found it. I suppose there could be fingerprints on it, too, although I'm not sure how well fingerprints would stick to something like this."

"Casey's right," agreed Steve. "But we can certainly take a good look at it." He peered into the box as he continued to speak. "I've got to admit, it's pretty fascinating. I mean, it seems to be in perfect condition. The markings are as clear as can be." He leaned over even further to get a better look. The rectangular clay-brown tablet had rounded edges, chicken-scratch writing etched into the clay at the top, and a sun-shaped object taking up the bottom three quarters of the surface. A small hole marked the center of the sun.

"I wonder what the drawing is?" Steve queried, stepping back to give the others a chance to look at the tablet more closely.

"If you ask me, it looks like some kid drew the sun in a brick and now ya'll are getting all worked up about it," commented Marjorie. "How do you know it's even real, let alone stolen? It could be a fake, you know."

"Hhmm—I hadn't thought about that," Casey remarked. "It does seem to be in perfect condition. I suppose it could be a replica." She crossed her arms and thought for a moment. "There's got to be someone at the College of

William & Mary who can help us with that. They may even be able to tell us if it's stolen. I'll see if can get an appointment to have someone take a look at it."

"That's a great idea," Steve noted. "Why don't you get our 35mm camera and take some pictures first. Then Marjorie can take the film to the photo shop and get it developed right away. That way you'll have something to give them in case they need to research it further."

"Too bad we can't take pictures of the back, too," Casey complained. "If there's something there that's important, we'll never know."

"I've let you two lawyers go at it long enough," Marjorie remarked. "How do ya'll know there isn't something else in the box, like maybe a receipt or something saying where the brick is from? A receipt would solve all your problems, and when you take the thing out to check, you can photograph its backside."

"That's brilliant," Steve exclaimed. The solution was so obvious, he was embarrassed he hadn't thought of it, but with his and Casey's professional ethics at stake, he'd approached the issue conservatively. It took Marjorie's recognition of the obvious to solve the conundrum. Still, he wasn't ready to throw all caution to the wind. "I tell you what, Marjorie. Why don't you get the gloves from the kitchen and we'll take it out of the box and see if there's anything else in there."

"I'll get the camera," Casey added, registering her agreement. "That way we can get the pictures at the same time."

"Sounds like a plan," confirmed Steve. Marjorie was already scurrying out of the office to get the gloves; Casey departed at a more deliberate pace. While they were gone, Steve retrieved two pieces of clean white paper from his printer and aligned them on the conference table with their long sides overlapping slightly. They formed a bright white rectangular background that would accentuate the clay tablet and its markings for the pictures. When Marjorie and Casey returned, Marjorie handed the gloves to Steve.

"I'll let you grab the brick," Marjorie said. "I'm afraid I'll drop it and then you'll have to fire me."

"I don't think you need to worry about that," Steve quipped. "You're the one coming up with all the solutions."

As Steve stretched the first glove onto his hand, Casey fiddled with the camera until she was ready to go. "We've got ten pictures left on this roll," she announced, "so I'm going to start by taking a couple shots of the tablet in the box. That way the police will be able to see just how we found it." Casey pulled the box toward her and with the camera looking straight down on its target, snapped two photographs in quick succession.

"Over to you, Steve." Casey set the camera down as Steve pulled on the second glove, releasing the sleeve end with a snap.

"Ready," he declared. He reached inside the box and cradled the tablet with both hands. As he removed it, he slowly flipped it over and set it face down on the paper he'd laid out. "Mission accomplished."

"That's interesting. The entire back is covered with writing," Casey observed. "I wonder what it says?" She bent down and scrutinized the writing as if she were trying to read the date on a century-old penny. "Maybe I can find out when I talk to the expert at William & Mary."

"Why don't you go ahead and take a few pictures of both sides while we've got it on the table," Steve suggested. "Then Marjorie can get the film over to the photo shop and we should have the pictures back in an hour. If the professor needs some pictures to work with, you can leave them there."

"Roger that," Casey replied, reverting to her Army lingo. "There are still eight pictures left—I might as well use them up." She took four pictures of the back of the tablet, rotating the camera to get both portrait and landscape prints. "That should do it for the back," she announced. Steve gingerly turned the tablet over and Casey started focusing the camera on the side with the sun.

"Since ya'll are almost out of film," Marjorie commented, "shouldn't you check the box just to make sure there's nothing else in there to take a picture of?"

"Thanks, Marjorie. I'm getting ahead of myself, again, aren't I?" Casey set the camera down after taking one close-up of the front and started pulling wads of crumpled newspaper from the bottom of the box. "I can't believe it, Marjorie, but there does appear to be something down there."

"Of course there is," gloated Marjorie. "After packing all your mail, I should know. People always put who it comes from inside the box. That's just the way it's done."

After tossing the last newspaper ball onto the table, Casey pulled out a single sheet of white paper, unevenly folded in half. "Just a telephone number," she said after unfolding the paper. "No name or anything, just the number." She read it out loud.

"Wait a minute," Steve said. "Read me that number again." After Casey did, his eyes lit up like Marjorie's had when she came up with the idea to inspect the bottom of the box. "I'll bet it's the same number."

"What number?" Marjorie asked.

Steve hustled to his briefcase propped up against the credenza behind his desk. He got his leather planner out and opened it as he walked back to the table. "Give me that number one more time."

Casey read the number aloud, this time enunciating each digit like an announcer at a bingo parlor. Steve picked up the analogy and carried it one step further.

"Bingo," he declared. "That's exactly the same number I found in Ashirvadam's safe deposit box yesterday. Now there's no question Ashirvadam knew who sent this to him."

"What are you going to do with it?" Marjorie asked. "Turn it over to the police?"

"Not until I call this number and see who answers," Steve replied.

Casey grabbed the back of the chair closest to her and frowned. "Is that really a good idea, Steve? I mean, you'll be letting someone who probably stole the tablet know you've got their number, and they might figure out you've got the tablet, too."

"They probably know that already," Steve countered, "but I do see your point. Maybe I'll keep the number in reserve, just in case it comes in handy down the road."

"I like that approach better," Casey concluded. "Now we've got the advantage, at least until we have to turn it over to the police."

"Let's see if we can confirm whether it's stolen before we involve the police," suggested Steve. "I'll be interested to hear what the expert at William & Mary has to say."

"Me too," added Marjorie. "I've got a good feeling about this tablet. I think it's gonna bring us good luck from here on out."

"I hope you're right, Marjorie," Steve added, "although I'm not so sure we're off to such a good start. So far, our client's dead and we've got a potentially stolen clay tablet to deal with. I don't know if we can handle any more good luck like that."

Still, Steve was optimistic. He had the tablet in hand and he'd connected the dots enough to know his client had communicated with whoever sent the package. Now he needed to figure out what made the tablet so valuable that Ashirvadam might want to steal for it.

10

───∿───

4:15 p.m. on Friday, October 8, 2004
Williamsburg, Virginia

THE FEW TIMES CASEY'D VISITED PROFESSORS during her undergraduate years at Penn State or during law school at the College of William & Mary, she'd always found them sitting behind desks with the doors to their offices open. Seeing Professor Ivan Lindor's door closed made her hesitate, but the black and white plastic nameplate on the wall next to the door confirmed she had the right office. She knocked, hoping he hadn't forgotten about their appointment. She couldn't imagine that happening, since she'd made it only a couple of hours before. When she heard a muffled "Please come in, it's unlocked," her anxiety disappeared.

With her game face on, Casey twisted the knob and pushed the door open, only to be shocked by what she saw inside the dimly lit office. Giant stacks of paper, boxes, and books filled every inch of the professor's desk, the credenza behind him, the tall bookcases along the wall, and all but a narrow walkway on the floor. She could barely see the professor, a plump man in his fifties with gray hair and a five-o'clock shadow, sitting at his desk with his fingers still moving slowly on a computer keyboard. The clutter so took her by surprise that she almost forgot to say hello or introduce herself. She stepped inside to a clearing just beyond the door and convinced herself to ignore her surroundings and be polite.

"Hello, Dr. Lindor? I'm Casey Pantel. I spoke to you a little earlier this afternoon."

"Yes, of course, Ms. Pantel. Please, do come in." The professor got up from his chair and walked around his desk to shake Casey's hand. "I'm so pleased to meet you."

"I'm pleased to meet you, too. Thanks for seeing me on such short notice late on a Friday afternoon. I hope I've not inconvenienced you."

"Of course not. Please sit down."

Casey glanced toward the two guest chairs in front of the professor's desk. Both had open copier paper boxes filled with folders on them, leaving Casey nowhere to sit. She looked back toward the professor, too embarrassed to say anything. When she didn't take a seat, he looked and saw the problem.

"Oh, look at that," he said as if it wasn't routine or obvious. "I forgot to clear a chair for you. I'm so sorry." He maneuvered in front of the first chair, picked up the box, and stacked it on top of the box in the other chair. "There you go. Now please, sit down."

As soon as the professor backed away enough for Casey to get by, she slipped her way to the chair and took a seat. She wanted to set the tablet under her chair until the time came to show it to the professor, but the space already had yet another copier paper box filled with folders occupying it, so she set the tablet immediately at her feet. She pulled her briefcase onto her lap and retrieved a legal pad and a pen for notes.

"So," the professor began, leaning back with his elbows on the armrests and clasping his hands just below his chin. "I understand you've got a clay tablet you'd like me to take a look at."

"That's right," Casey responded, sitting upright in her chair with the best posture she could muster. Even though she'd been out of law school now for over six years, she felt like a student coming in to see a professor to discuss a writing assignment. It made her feel at once young and old—young because her reaction seemed real and old because she knew her law school days had long since passed.

"I didn't have the chance to give you the full story over the phone," she continued. "A man we're representing recently passed away and it looks like he acquired some sort of ancient clay tablet with drawings and writing on it. We have no idea what it is, so we were hoping you might be able to tell us, or at least get us pointed in the right direction."

"Mmmm, I see. Yes, of course." The professor unclasped his hands, reforming them so they came together at the fingertips. He rested his chin on the tips of his middle fingers and took a deep breath as if he were considering whether to assist or not. "I couldn't help but notice you carried a box when you came in. I take it you have the tablet with you?"

"I do." Shoving her briefcase to her side, Casey reached down and picked up the box with both hands, resting it on her lap where her briefcase had been. She put her hand on top of the box while she made her next point. "I've got to admit, we don't know how our client acquired the tablet, so we're being very careful about taking it from the box. I've got pictures of both the front and back if that will help."

"You should be careful, Ms. Pantel," agreed Professor Lindor. "Depending upon what you have, it could be quite valuable and very fragile. Why don't you let me take a look?"

Casey shifted her briefcase and legal pad to prevent them from tumbling to the floor, then she stood up and handed the box to Dr. Lindor. Without clearing away any of the papers laid out over what appeared to be a calendar blotter several layers below, he set the box down and folded back the flaps so he could see inside. After peering in, he grabbed a pair of reading glasses from somewhere among the clutter. With his spectacles now in place, he took a closer look.

"The light's not very good in here, is it?" he observed.

Before Casey realized what was happening, he reached inside the box and pulled out the tablet. Now she wished she'd been less subtle about handling the artifact. Professor Lindor assuaged her fears when he carefully placed it on his desk with the drawing side up. He bent the metal neck of a reading lamp she hadn't noticed before into position and turned on the light, adjusting the lamp's height until it was just right.

"This is extraordinary, Ms. Pantel. Absolutely extraordinary. It's in mint condition."

"That's what we thought, too. It's so good, in fact, we wondered if it might be a reproduction."

"I suppose that's possible, but I doubt it. Before we get to that, though, let's start at the beginning. Do you know what this is?"

"I tried to research it on the Internet, but I didn't get far. I'm guessing it's some kind of ancient cuneiform writing on a clay tablet, but that's only a guess."

"It's an excellent guess, Ms. Pantel, and it's correct. What made you think it's cuneiform?"

The professor had her and she knew it. She couldn't lie or play dumb—he'd see through it right away. Since he was being kind enough to help her, she decided to be straight with him. Besides, he probably had figured it out already.

"Well, to be honest, professor, I have some concerns that the tablet may have found its way out of Iraq after the U.S. invasion last year. If that's the case, the tablet would most likely be cuneiform."

Without taking his eyes off the tablet, Professor Lindor pulled open a desk drawer to his right. "There are a lot of cuneiform tablets out there, you know. Thousands were taken out of Syria during the late 19th century and this could very easily be one of those. It might have been lost in someone's attic until it worked its way into a garage sale somewhere."

The professor stuck his hand in the drawer and probed around until he pulled out a large black-handled magnifying glass. "My guess, though, is you're right and this is a recent find. There's really no way to tell unless someone admits to bringing it here, or someone else reports it missing." The professor hovered the magnifying glass a couple of inches over the tablet, then let it roam around the tablet's surface in no apparent pattern.

"Do you know what it says?" Casey asked.

"Oh no, of course not. There aren't many people around who can read a tablet like this. In fact, most tablets have never been translated. There are far too many of them and far too few people able to read them. Most sit in storage in museums, but at least they're safe from being worn down by the elements or destroyed by human development. I can assure you, though, this one's different."

Casey perked up. "Why's that?"

"Why, the map, of course."

"Map?" Casey scribbled down "MAP" on her notepad and readied her pen to write more. "How do you know it's a map?"

"I cheated." The professor chuckled. "This actually looks very similar to a famous Babylonian tablet depicting a map of the world. But as I recall, that tablet had to be pieced together and is missing entire sections. This one is intact with all of the markings clear and legible. Historians, museums and collectors will be very interested in this, especially if it fills in the missing details from the existing tablet."

Professor Lindor turned the tablet over and began to examine its backside. Casey winced, but there was little she could do. If fingerprints became an issue, the police would just have to exclude his. She hoped he wasn't destroying others. He didn't use the magnifying glass this time, she presumed because it was nothing but incomprehensible cuneiform script. She waited for him to look up before saying anything further.

He didn't, instead turning the tablet again so the map was on top. He gave it one last examination with the magnifying glass and then returned it to the box.

"What is it you need from me?" he asked, turning off the desk lamp and pushing it to the side. With the room's light restored to its original dullness, he grasped his chair's armrests, his elbows protruding from his sides, and rocked back. The chair squeaked with each change in seat angle.

"Is there anything else you can tell me about it?"

"Not a lot more than we've already discussed. It's definitely cuneiform, so I'd estimate it's between three and four thousand years old. If it is the map, as I suspect it is, it will be very valuable. Historians will want to have it translated, especially if it provides information about the map itself. I'd say you're very lucky, Ms. Pantel."

"Thanks professor, but it's not mine. It belongs to our client's estate, and I'm still concerned about the tablet's origin. Is there a way to determine if someone's reported it missing?"

"The FBI has an art theft unit, as do most major Western countries. They'll have a registry they can check, and they share information with each other. If it's been reported stolen, they'll be able to tell you."

"What if we're not ready to go there yet?"

"I'd be happy to make some inquiries through academic channels. You mentioned you have a photograph of the tablet. If you leave it with me, I'll see what I can find out. I wouldn't expect much, though. Academics tend to be a slow lot. It could take some time."

"That would be really helpful, Dr. Lindor," Casey said as she opened her briefcase and pulled out a manila envelope, which she handed to the professor. "There are two five-by-seven photos inside—one of the front and one of the back. I've also put a copy of my business card in the envelope so you can call or email me if you find out anything." As she let go of the envelope, she wondered if it would become forever lost in one of the professor's endless stacks of paper, much like the tablet had been lost to mankind for over three thousand years.

"This is exciting, Ms. Pantel." Professor Lindor folded the box closed and walked around his desk to hand it to her. "Who knows," he said. "You may have found the key to unlock the secrets of the ancient map of Babylon."

"That is exciting," Casey agreed. "And I really appreciate you delaying the start of your weekend to meet with me. It's been a real pleasure." Casey took the box and tucked it under her arm so she could shake his hand.

"Keep that in a safe place, Ms. Pantel."

"I will, professor, and thank you again." Casey bent down and grabbed the handle of her briefcase, smiled one last time, and left the professor's office. As she made her way out of Washington Hall and looked on the college's Sunken Garden, she paused to check her watch. It was already past five o'clock and she had a rare dinner date at six. She wouldn't have time to go back to the office and get ready for dinner, so she decided to go straight home. She couldn't help but think of the irony. She'd gone from flying helicopters over war-ravaged Iraq to holding the key to the ancient map of Babylon. The thought made her skin tingle.

11

2:13 a.m. on Saturday, October 9, 2004
Williamsburg, Virginia

Although Phan Quốc Cường worked hard to please all of his customers, nothing short of perfection sufficed for the law offices of Stilwell & Pantel. Every night, he made sure the office floors shined, the kitchen sparkled, and the trash cans and recycling bins started each new day fresh and empty. He even scheduled the law offices to be cleaned last so he wouldn't have to rush his work. Marjorie arrived around seven-thirty a.m., but he was always finished well before then. Still, he wanted the time available just in case.

Phan revered Steve because Steve kept a promise and brought him and his family to America. It didn't matter that he'd saved Steve's life once and that Steve felt just as indebted to him. Had Steve not sponsored his family's immigration from Vietnam four years before, he'd still be dirt poor in Ho Chi Minh City trying to hawk motorcycle rides to westerners just so his wife and daughter would have enough to eat. Now they not only had enough to eat—they had hope.

Helping his family come to America would have been enough, but Steve didn't stop there. Once he got Phan's family set up in an apartment, he helped Phan start an office cleaning business. Steve and Casey's law practice was Phan's first customer. Now he cleaned all of the offices in the building, as well as some of the stores on Duke of Gloucester Street. But even beyond the success of his new business, his beautiful five-year-old daughter actually attended school with American children in Williamsburg. He could not believe his good fortune.

Phan unlocked the office's front door early on Saturday morning and rolled his cleaning cart into the lobby, taking care to avoid the Oriental rugs dotting the hardwood floor. A creature of habit, he pulled his equipment to the kitchen so he could dump the trash and wash any dishes Marjorie might have left for him. He found it spotless except for a few small clumps of dirt here and there on the floor. He swept those up, wiped down the already pristine counters, and ran a mop over the tile floor to catch anything he might have missed.

Backing out of the kitchen with the last few swabs, Phan stowed the mop in the bucket on his cart and retreated down the hall to Steve and Casey's offices. He always did Casey's first, so he parked his cart just outside her door and gathered a dust rag and some spray wax for his initial pass. Again, he noticed some small clumps of dirt on the floor by the door, so he put the dusting paraphernalia back and grabbed a broom and dustpan to sweep up the clumps before he stepped on them and made the problem worse. He figured Casey must have had something on her shoes and tracked it around the office either before or after she poured her morning coffee.

Phan swept up the dirt and dusted around Casey's glass-topped desk and end tables, all the time thinking about the dirt on the floor. He hadn't noticed it when he came in, but his focus at the time was on getting started with the kitchen, not looking for tiny clumps of dirt along the way. He retrieved a bottle of glass cleaner from his cart and, after carefully shifting the few papers Casey had on her desk to one side, spritzed the cleaner across the desk. As he was wiping the glass dry, he heard a squeak that sounded like it came from a door, but he knew that couldn't be the case. He was sure he'd locked the front door behind him and he was alone in the office, so he attributed the squeak to the paper towel on the desktop and dismissed what he'd heard. After returning Casey's papers to their original locations, he headed for Steve's office, which was off the lobby and to the left.

Now more attuned to the dirt on the floor, Phan noticed a couple of very small pieces just outside of Steve's door. When he looked at these clumps, he saw the faint outline of a footprint heading into Steve's office. The footprint was waffled like that of a running shoe or work boot, not smooth like Casey's dress shoes would be. Now that he thought about it, it hadn't rained in the last twenty-four hours, so it was unusual that there would be footprints or clumps of dirt anywhere in the office. All he could think of was Marjorie must have hired someone to do some work and they had dirty shoes. He reached inside Steve's office and flipped on the light. With dustpan and broom in hand, he bent down to sweep the floor.

The *whooooshhh* came so fast he didn't have time to react. The door to Steve's office swung toward him, striking the broom handle and jamming it into his face. The blow knocked him off balance and he landed on his rear. He planted his hands on the floor so he could spring up to defend himself, but before he could propel himself upward, an African-American man rushed around from behind the door. He thrust a pistol up from his side and jerked it toward Phan's head.

"You move and you dead. You move and you dead," the man repeated. The look in his eyes screamed to Phan he meant what he said.

Phan froze with his hands glued to the floor. His martial arts training in the Vietnamese Army couldn't help him now; his position was too disadvantaged. His adrenaline pumped and his chest heaved as he sucked in oxygen waiting for the man to say more.

The man held the pistol with both hands and outstretched arms, training it at the middle of Phan's face. "You got some bad luck, my man. You came in at just the wrong time." The man angled his head, his eyes still pegged on Phan. "Now what am I gonna do with you? Huh?"

Still breathing heavily and bracing himself upright with his hands behind him on the floor, Phan said nothing. He wasn't afraid. He was too angry for that. Besides, all he wanted was to survive so he could see his wife and daughter again. Leaving them would be death's real tragedy. He stared into the man's eyes and waited.

"Okay, okay," the man said as if he were confirming in his head the way the scene would play out before he carried it out in real life. "Gimme your wallet."

Phan didn't answer, he just looked up at the man and pretended not to understand.

"Wallet," the man repeated, speaking slowly. He released one hand from the weapon and reached around to his back pocket. He pulled out his own wallet and held it up for display. "Your wallet—you it give to me," he said, motioning with his wallet back toward him.

Not knowing what the man would do if he made him angry, Phan leaned forward and started to pull his wallet from the rear pocket of his green workpants.

"That's it," the man said, smiling with approval. "Just slide it over to me, now. You got that? Just slide it on the floor, over to me."

Phan set his wallet on the floor and did as instructed, but it didn't make it much past where his feet were planted on the floor. It made the man angry. He stuck his own wallet back into his pocket and grabbed the pistol, shaking it right at Phan's face.

"What, you think I'm stupid? You better scoot your ass back away from that wallet or you're a dead man, you got that?"

Phan nodded and crab-walked backwards a few steps until he was clear from the wallet.

"That's it," the man said, calming down. With the weapon still trained on Phan, he squatted down and picked up Phan's wallet. When he opened it, a big smile came across his face. "This your wife and daughter?" He turned the wallet around so Phan could see the picture of his daughter sitting in his wife's lap. Phan flushed with anger and he started rocking forward to get up.

"Now hold on there," the man said, his smile replaced by a smirk. "You sit your ass back down so I don't have to pull this trigger. You got that?" When Phan complied, he took a couple of steps away from Phan and tucked the pistol under his belt. "Now you relax and this is gonna turn out just fine." He pulled the picture and Phan's driver's license from the wallet and tossed it back to Phan, then pointed his gun at him.

"Now I need you to listen to me real good, because now I got a picture of your wife and daughter and I know where you live. You mess with me, and they're dead. You got that?"

Phan barked back, "You leave them alone. They not do anything to you."

The man smiled again. "I figured you were playing me with that don't speak English routine. Now you better understand real good." The man tucked the picture of Phan's family and driver's license into the pocket of his navy blue jacket. "Here's the deal. Somebody in this office got something of mine and you're gonna get it for me."

"I not work here," Phan interrupted. "I not know what they have. I only clean."

"Look man, you ain't got many options. These folks got a brick that belongs to me. It's a flat stone with carvings on both sides. You got until tomorrow night to get it for me or I'm coming for your family. You know what that means?"

"You hurt them and I kill you," Phan shouted defiantly.

"You ain't in no position to kill no one. Besides, nobody's got to get hurt at all. You just get me that brick by tomorrow night. Oh, yeah, and don't be calling the police or trying to hide them away. I got your address, so I'll be watching. I see anything weird going on, and they're dead. You got that?"

Phan nodded.

The man's face tightened, and his look became intense. "I said you got that? I wanna hear you say it. You got that?"

"Yeah, I got that," Phan declared, matching the man's intensity.

"Good. I knew we could do business." The man eased over toward Marjorie's desk and found a small decorative container with the firm's business cards in it. He took one and returned to his original position. "Here's how this goes. I'll call here tomorrow night at about this time." He checked his watch. "I'll call here at two-thirty. You answer and I'll give you instructions on how you deliver the brick." The man smiled. "I'll even give you back the picture and your driver's license when you do. See how easy it is?"

"That no work," Phan responded. "It Saturday now. No one work again until Monday. If brick not here now, no way it be here before Monday."

The man nodded. "Okay, I'll buy that," he said, starting to back down the hall toward the kitchen. "Monday night. You got 'til Monday night at two-thirty. Just pick up the phone and I'll tell you what you need to do. You understand?"

"How you know they bring brick to office? What if it not here on Monday?"

"That ain't my problem, now is it? That's why I got you." The man smiled again. "Now I'm going out the way I came in. You stay still for at least five minutes. I'll be watching from outside the building." He reached into his jacket pocket and pulled out the picture of Phan's wife and daughter. "Man, you got a beautiful family. I'd sure hate for something to happen to them. You know what I mean?" The man smiled again before disappearing into the kitchen.

Phan couldn't move. It wasn't that his muscles wouldn't react, it was more like his brain wouldn't send them signals. He heard the kitchen window open and close. A million thoughts fought for his attention, but one dominated. He would never let anything happen to his family. He would die first. He ran through his options. He could tell the police, but that would put his wife and daughter at risk. Plus, growing up in Vietnam, he had a natural distrust for the police that carried over to America. Besides, his friends in the Vietnamese community had warned him never to involve the police in anything—they wouldn't listen because he was Vietnamese. They said it would ruin his family's chances of becoming American citizens. He could tell Steve—Steve would know what to do. Then again, he might not. What if Steve said they had to call the police? His wife and daughter might be killed. He couldn't let that happen. That left only stealing the brick from his friend and giving it to the man, or finding and killing the man before the man killed his family. For the first time ever, Phan wished he'd never come to America.

12

6:56 p.m. on Saturday, October 9, 2004
Williamsburg, Virginia

STEVE PARKED HIS CAR AND HURRIED into the lobby of the Colonial Inne. He'd never met the people he was having dinner with, so he didn't know who to look for or what to expect. The invitation came from Giorgio Stassi, who called him at home earlier in the day. He identified himself as the executive assistant to Michela Baresi, the founder and president of La Fontana Cosmetics of Milan. Stassi said Ms. Baresi wanted to talk to him about Arul Ashirvadam. He assured Steve this evening was her only availability because she would be leaving Williamsburg early Sunday morning. He said she was staying at the Colonial Inne and would like to meet Steve for dinner in the hotel dining room at seven o'clock. Thinking he might learn something about Arul Ashirvadam that would help him administer his client's estate, Steve agreed to meet Ms. Baresi for dinner without knowing anything else about her.

The dining room's hostess waited at a podium just inside the entrance. An array of tables for four filled the room, lit dimly from chandeliers hanging near the center of each table grouping. Candles flickered on every table, while bow tie-clad waiters and waitresses darted around the tables taking orders or delivering delectables, giving the room an elegant, if not colonial, atmosphere.

"May I help you?" the young woman at the podium asked.

"Yes," Steve replied. "My name is Steve Stilwell and I'm supposed to meet someone for dinner. Her name is Michela Baresi. I believe the reservations are in her name."

The young woman checked her seating display. "Is it possible the reservations are in the name of Giorgio Stassi?" The woman winced with her question, communicating she wanted the answer to be yes.

"Yes, that's right. I believe Mr. Stassi is the woman's assistant."

The young woman smiled. "Excellent. Please, follow me." She led Steve toward the back of the dining room to an area off to the side of the nearest chandelier. The shadowy arrangement of tables gave the area a detached feeling, as though it were an island of its own away from those dining in the remainder of the restaurant. A young man in a dark suit sat at one of the tables. The other three were empty. The woman led Steve to the table where the young man waited. He stood up as they approached.

"Here is your table, Mr. Stilwell," the hostess announced, guiding him to a chair next to the young man. "Your server will be with you as soon as Ms. Baresi arrives."

"Thank you very much," Steve replied.

The young man at the table greeted Steve with an enthusiastic handshake and a thick Italian accent. "Hello, Mr. Stilwell. My name is Giorgio Stassi. I'm so pleased to meet you." The handshake continued throughout the introduction. "Please, do sit down. I will now go to Ms. Baresi and let her know you have arrived. I will return with her, shortly. Please, excuse me." He bowed in Steve's direction and departed.

The entire episode caught Steve off guard. When he saw the young man at the table, he presumed the hostess would take him to one of the other tables, not the one already occupied. He also couldn't help but notice how incredibly good looking the young man was. The slight shine to his designer blue silk suit coordinated nicely with his olive skin, neatly manicured mustache, and slicked back hair curling just above his shoulders. He had the air of a model about him, which made sense given Ms. Baresi's profession, although he typically associated cosmetics with female models, not males.

The other thing that caught Steve's attention was Ms. Baresi's delayed arrival until he was in place and seated. This was not unusual in a military or diplomatic setting. Junior people always had to be in their places before senior commanders or diplomats arrived. What was unusual was having Ms. Baresi's caste system imposed on him at dinner. Had she simply arrived after him, he would not have thought twice about it. But positioning Giorgio at the table to be sure he was in place before she arrived stuck in his egalitarian craw.

As he was pondering his situation, a waitress approached the table. "Good evening, Mr. Stilwell. My name is Kristina and I'll be your server this evening. I understand your guest will be joining you shortly."

Steve nodded and forced the semblance of a smile.

"Would you like to order a bottle of wine before she arrives? I hear she enjoys an Italian Barolo. We have a very nice one available this evening."

Steve sat speechless. Michela Baresi wasn't his guest, and he couldn't believe she or, more likely, Giorgio, had the gall to provide the waitress with her wine preference so it would be waiting for her when she arrived. He was beginning to dislike her on multiple levels. Her name even sounded like Michelle, a deceased high-profile estate client's unpleasant daughter he loathed working with. He wanted to get up and leave, but he knew that wasn't an option. For that matter, neither was saying "no" to the bottle of wine. After all, it was only for one meeting.

"That will be fine," he answered, looking up at the waitress. "I suppose it's expensive?"

The waitress smiled. "It's not so bad," she reassured him. "I'll have to check, but I think it's around one hundred and twenty-five dollars a bottle."

As the waitress announced the price, Steve felt a hand on his shoulder. He twisted his head around and saw Giorgio, with an elegant-looking woman in a royal blue off-the-shoulder cocktail dress standing to his right. The irony struck him immediately—she even looked like Michelle Siegel, so he braced himself for arrogance. Giorgio started the introduction while Steve was still twisting around in their direction.

"Mr. Stilwell, I am pleased to introduce you to Ms. Michela Baresi." Steve rose to greet her.

"I'm pleased to meet you Ms. Baresi," he said, offering to shake her hand. She accepted his offer.

"The pleasure is all mine," Ms. Baresi began, causing Steve to conclude at least one similarity with Michelle was already gone in that she was being gracious. "Shall we sit down?"

"Of course," Steve replied, continuing to stand while Ms. Baresi made her way around the table to sit across from him. Giorgio followed closely behind, pulling out her chair and making sure she was comfortably seated.

"I hope you don't mind if Giorgio joins us for dinner. I rely on him for everything and I want him to keep notes of our meeting. And, please, so that we get off to a good start, call me Michela. I find formalities can get in the way of good business being done. Do you agree, Mr. Stilwell?"

"I couldn't agree more," Steve responded. As he reached back and started to sit down, he added, "So please, call me Steve." Giorgio also sat down and scooted his chair up to the table. He took his folded napkin from the plate and placed it on his lap. Steve followed suit and got his napkin in place just as the waitress returned with the wine.

"Welcome to the Colonial Inne, Ms. Baresi," she began. "I hope you are enjoying your stay. Is this your first time in Williamsburg?"

"It is, thank you. I must say, I love it so far."

"Well, Mr. Stilwell has selected a wine for you this evening. It is a very nice Barolo." She poured Steve a small amount before serving the rest of the table. He swirled it in the glass to release the aroma, and then inhaled the fragrance before taking a taste. Although by no means a connoisseur, he had to admit the wine had a lovely flavor.

"This is very nice," he said, nodding to give the waitress his assent to serving the wine to the other guests. "As my guests are from Italy, though, I certainly defer to their judgment." He thought it best to admit his relative incompetence, rather than allow Michela and Giorgio to reach that conclusion on their own.

"I'm sure it will be just fine," Michela reassured him.

With the wine settled and poured, the waitress went through the featured dinner for the evening, a crab-stuffed filet mignon. Then, speaking directly to Steve, she added, "Would you like some time to look at the menu, Mr. Stilwell?"

"I'm sure our guests will need some additional time, thank you," he answered.

Giorgio spoke for the first time since sitting down. "Actually, Mr. Stilwell, Ms. Baresi has some very specific dietary requirements and we have already arranged for our meals. But please, feel free to take whatever time you require."

Steve looked at Michela as Giorgio spoke. She smiled and shrugged her shoulders. "What can I say, Steve? I think you would say in America, I am a picky eater." Steve laughed. He had to admit, his preconceptions about Michela were completely wrong. She was quite charming and so far, easy to talk to. She was also very beautiful, with perfect skin and a disarming smile accenting long black hair flowing across her shoulders. Although he felt quite good about his appearance when he left for dinner in his blue blazer, yellow and green striped tie, and khaki slacks, he wished now he'd worn a suit. In business meetings, he always found it better to be overdressed rather than underdressed. Tonight, he missed the mark.

"Well, the crab-stuffed filet mignon sounds wonderful to me," Steve announced. "I'd like to go with that."

"An excellent choice," the waitress confirmed. "Please, be sure to let me know if there is anything you need tonight." She bowed and departed for the kitchen.

"Let us begin with a toast," Michela offered, raising her wine glass. "To new friends and success." After Steve and Giorgio followed, Michela set her wine glass on the table. "I suppose you are wondering why I asked to meet with you tonight."

Steve took a sip of wine while Michela spoke and set his glass on the table, too. "When Giorgio called me this afternoon, he said it had something to do with Arul Ashirvadam's estate. Is that right?"

"In a manner of speaking, that is correct."

Steve picked up his glass and held it at the ready. "You'll have to elaborate as I'm not sure what you mean." He completed the motion with his glass, taking a slow, imperceptible sip.

"Can I speak frankly with you, Steve? I know we have just met, but I find it is always best in business to be honest with each another. That way, we know what each other wants and we can come to, how do you say, arrangements, that work for both of us. Don't you think that is a good approach?"

Steve's warning bells rang. Whenever a businessperson began a sentence by stating he or she wanted to speak frankly, Steve's experience told him it meant just the opposite. In fact, more often than not, what the speaker really meant was the other side in the negotiation should be honest, even if the speaker did not show all of his or her cards. Plus, the word "arrangement" nearly never had a good connotation. It almost always meant something under the table. His guard was up.

"Of course," Steve agreed. "Honesty is always the best policy, even for a lawyer."

Michela laughed and when she did, Giorgio did too. "Good," she said. "Then we are going to get along well. So, let me begin by admitting I am a wealthy woman, and I am not ashamed of it."

"Why would you be?" Steve thought her opening an odd way to begin the conversation.

"Sometimes men do not accept women with money. They see an attractive woman and immediately assume she got her wealth from her husband. They don't think she is capable of earning it herself. Do you know what I mean, Steve?"

Steve wasn't sure if Michela was trying to indict him, but he wasn't going to let her. "I'm sure some men, and maybe even some women think that, but I certainly don't jump to those conclusions."

"I'm sure that is the case, Steve, but like I said, I want to speak frankly with you. So, let me tell you what I know about you. You are a well-respected attorney in this town and you have had some very big cases. Am I right?"

"I hope that is the case, thank you." Steve wasn't sure where the conversation was going or what it had to do with Arul Ashirvadam, but he decided to play along just in case Michela took a productive turn. Besides, with his guard still up, he was sure he could avoid getting backed into a corner. "I can assure you," Michela continued, "it is true. That is why Arul wanted you to be his attorney."

"How do you know that?"

"As I said before, Steve, I am a wealthy woman, and Arul was a wealthy man. So maybe we attended some of the same functions in London and Rome, and maybe we met each other. Then we found out we had some things in common."

Steve was pretty sure that meant an affair, but he wasn't positive. If true, it undercut his client's dying declaration to take care of his family—the same family for which he proclaimed his devotion in the cover letter to his will. Since Steve represented Arul Ashirvadam's estate and owed no allegiance to Michela, and because she had emphasized the need to be frank, he decided to put her to the test.

"I take it that means you had an affair with Arul Ashirvadam?"

"Some things are better left unsaid," interjected Giorgio, bringing his napkin to his lips to wipe away a nonexistent drop of wine.

"Maybe so," Steve replied. "But I was just following Michela's instructions about speaking frankly." As he finished speaking, the waitress and an assistant brought their food and set it before them. The aroma from the beef called to Steve as soon as it arrived. He suddenly realized he was hungry and although the conversation was growing interesting, he had to eat something. He broke eye contact with Michela and Giorgio to cut his filet mignon.

"Spoken like a true lawyer," declared Michela. "And I shall honor your request, but I will expect the same in return." She paused to take a sip of her wine. "I don't want to call what Arul and I did an affair, although I am sure he loved me. From my perspective, we had sex on a few occasions, but we never made love. You understand the difference, don't you?"

"I'm not really sure I do, but I don't think I need to either," Steve replied, hoping to close the door on the awkward turn he had invited.

"A woman would understand. Our relationship was physical, not emotional. Maybe that is clearer, no?" Michela began to eat, seemingly at ease with the topic. Steve, on the other hand, couldn't wait for the subject to change. The level of sexual detail for a supposed business meeting made him uncomfortable.

After a piece of beef melted in his mouth and had him craving more, Steve set his fork on his plate to see if he could get the conversation back on topic. "What does this all have to do with my representation of Arul Ashirvadam?"

"You are so American, Steve. In Europe, we like to savor the conversation, letting it go where it may. Eventually, we will get to where we need to be, but it is a process and it takes time. You Americans are different. You want to get right to the point."

Steve cut another piece of beef. "That's the way we are, I guess. But we do get a lot of business done."

"Maybe so, but maybe you miss much more. Anyway, I will answer your question, but you must promise not to laugh." Michela paused.

When Steve realized she was waiting for his acknowledgement, he smiled and threw out a quick "I promise," before taking another bite.

Michela wasn't satisfied. "I am serious, Steve. I am about to tell you something deeply personal. I want you to promise you will be respectful." The stern look on her face reinforced this was not just idle table talk.

"I'm sorry. I didn't mean to come across as rude. Of course, I'll take you seriously."

Michela smiled and rested her elbows on the table. "I forgive you, of course." She clasped her hands and leaned forward to lessen the distance between them. "Perhaps I shall approach it this way. When we first started talking, I told you what I knew about you. Why don't you tell me what you know about me?"

Steve slid forward on his chair so he was closer to the table but didn't lean on it as Michela had done. "Now you're going to embarrass me. I must admit, I didn't know who you were until Giorgio called this afternoon. He told me you are the president of La Fontana Cosmetics, but I don't know much more than that. I did a quick search on the Internet and saw you were a model before you started La Fontana, and I see that La Fontana has grown to be one of the most successful cosmetic brands in the world. I'm afraid that's all I know."

"Then you are very trusting when a woman asks you to have dinner, am I right?" Michela smiled again.

"Maybe when her executive assistant calls and extends the invitation, then yes." Normally beautiful women intimidated Steve, but Michela's charm put him at ease. Her Italian accent helped, as did the fact that he had no interest in her. By now he felt like he was parrying with a long-lost high school friend, rather than a new business acquaintance he needed to be careful with.

"Let me tell you a little more so you will be able to understand. I have a degree in chemistry, but in those days, it was difficult for a woman in Italy to work in such a field, so I gave modeling a try. That worked out very well, so I decided to capitalize on my brand and start my own line of cosmetics. You can see the connection to chemistry, no?"

"I can. That's pretty impressive, Michela. Did you start from scratch, or did you buy an existing company?"

"I started it myself, with just an idea. I have always been fascinated by making women feel young, because when a woman feels young, she feels good about herself. Do you know the Fountain of Youth, Steve?"

"I do. The legend says if you drink from the fountain's water, you will remain young forever."

"Now you know why my company is La Fontana. It means 'the fountain' in English. Do you like that?"

"I really do, especially now that I know the story behind it. That's not embarrassing at all, Michela. Why did you think I would laugh?"

"Well, there's something I haven't told you yet. When my company was new, we did an advertising campaign linked to the Fountain of Youth. It was successful, of course. But I also became fascinated by the legends surrounding the fountain. I found Ponce de Leon's quest for the fountain in the New World very romantic. I shared this with Arul one night about a year ago when I visited his flat in London and he became very excited. He showed me a medieval letter he kept hidden that gave an indication where the fountain might be found."

Steve had stayed with Michela until her claim about the letter. He couldn't let it go unchallenged, but he needed to do so gently, especially given his promise to take her seriously. "I've got to say, Michela, you know that can't be true. The Fountain of Youth is just a myth."

"That is the difference between you and me, Steve. The lawyer in you says the fountain doesn't exist, while the entrepreneur in me says it's enough if people are intrigued by the thought of it." Still leaning forward, Michela took another sip of wine, as if she needed its energy to propel her through the rest of her explanation. "Don't you see the marketing potential of the letter? Whether the fountain exists really doesn't matter."

"Very nice, very nice indeed," Steve conceded. "Now I understand why you are a rich woman, Michela. You take advantage of opportunities others can't see."

"Precisely," Michela declared as if it were an established fact. "So, I asked Arul to let my company use the letter. To my astonishment, he refused. He said he wanted to keep it a secret to give him time to locate the place where the letter said the fountain could be found. He made me promise not to tell anyone."

"He couldn't have been serious, could he? I mean, Ashirvadam was an educated man. He had to know the fountain doesn't really exist."

Michela huffed. "You cannot stop being a lawyer, even for a minute, can you? Don't you see, the value is in the quest. If Arul could rekindle the legend, there might be money to be made. Anyway, I thought if I gave him some time and made him the right offer, eventually he would let me use the letter. To be honest, though, I eventually forgot about it."

Steve sat back in his chair. It was an interesting story, but it had no relevance to his representation of Ashirvadam's estate. He was ready for the conversation to move on. Aside from meeting Michela, the dinner thus far had been a waste of time. "Well, since the letter's in Ashirvadam's flat in London, I won't have any dealings with it. Perhaps you should contact the executor of his estate in the U.K."

"That's not the end of the story, Steve. But please excuse me for a moment."

She turned her attention to Giorgio, who was slowly working through his meal while the discussion progressed. He had yet to take any notes, making Steve wonder whether he was really an executive assistant or served some other purpose.

"Giorgio, if you would, please take care of the fare for the dinner now. Mr. Stilwell and I will meet you shortly."

With no indication that Michela's abrupt invitation to leave caused him any consternation, Giorgio set his utensils on his plate, took a final sip of wine, and dabbed his lips clean with his napkin. "Of course, Ms. Baresi." Standing up and backing away from the table, he bowed in Steve's direction. "Mr. Stilwell, it was a pleasure dining with you this evening."

"The pleasure was all mine, Giorgio. But please, you must let me pay."

"Don't be foolish, Steve," chastised Michela. "You were my guest tonight. Next time, perhaps I will be your guest." She smiled, and for a moment, Steve thought she actually seemed to be sincere about the possibility. Her smile faded as Giorgio wandered off in search of their server.

"Giorgio is a good man," she began, "but I thought we should finish our conversation with just the two of us."

"Now you've got me intrigued," Steve admitted. More accurately, he wondered what was going on. What could Michela possibly say that her executive assistant couldn't hear? Executive assistants sat in on everything— that's what made them executive assistants.

"Good," Michela replied. "Then you will listen carefully to what I have to say." She picked up her nearly empty glass of wine and drained the remainder with one final sip. "Okay, I am ready." She took a deep breath, leaned forward, and began to talk more quietly than before, making her difficult to understand. Her accent compounded the problem. Steve slid around to Giorgio's chair so he could hear her better, and they both eased closer to one another to facilitate the more private conversation.

"About a month ago," Michela continued, "Arul called me and said he thought he'd discovered the key to finding the Fountain of Youth. As if that wasn't enough, he said he wanted to share it with me. I would need to invest, of course, but he said he would take the initial step of getting the key. He swore that God himself had revealed it to him."

Steve didn't know how to respond. Michela seemed serious, but how could she be? At the same time, he wasn't ready to shut her down, as there had to be more to the story. He needed to draw it out of her, but he couldn't help being a little tongue-in-cheek. "So exactly what did God reveal to him?"

"You promised you wouldn't laugh, Steve. If you don't want to hear the rest of the story, you don't have to. But I do need your help anyway."

"I'm sorry, Michela, but you have to admit, the whole thing sounds pretty incredible—the Fountain of Youth and a revelation from God." Steve tried to lessen the impact of his skepticism by finishing his wine, just as Michela had done. He set his empty glass down and waited for Michela's response.

"I will be blunt. He has been collecting ancient tablets for years and has people watching for them. When something interesting becomes available, he acquires it."

Now Steve understood the relevance of Michela's story—she had to be talking about the tablet he picked up from Ashirvadam's post office box. Ashirvadam's final words flooded his ears, "I've sold my soul, Mr. Stilwell!" Ashirvadam's anguished cry had to be connected to his perceived revelation from God. He needed to know more.

"So how does he acquire them, legitimately or on the black market?"

"Who am I to say? Anyway, those details Arul never discussed. But I know he planned to acquire this tablet from someone in America. He told me it contains a map that will take us to the location of the fountain—he was certain of it."

"I guess he will never know, will he?"

"Don't be so crass, Steve. Besides, he may be dead, but I am very much alive, and I consider it my responsibility to pursue his dream."

Steve couldn't let Michela's last statement go unchallenged. "Remember when we started this conversation, you said we had to be honest."

"Yes, of course," Michela assured him. "There is no other way."

"Then I shall be honest with you. I think you don't really care about Ashirvadam's dream, but like you said earlier, there is money to be made from the quest. It seems like an ancient map showing the location of the fountain would be good business for La Fontana."

"Now you understand why we are having dinner, no? I want that tablet, Steve, and I know you either have it or you will find it as you handle Arul's estate. I am willing to pay the estate handsomely for it, but it must be a private sale, of course. The tablet cannot be made public until I am ready to do so."

"Ah, I see, I see." Steve knew there was an underlying business purpose to the dinner, but he never would have guessed it had anything to do with the tablet. Some of the puzzle pieces were coming together.

"Arul wanted to share the tablet with me—he would want me to have it. It is more than business, Steve. You must understand."

"And you must understand that I represent Ashirvadam's estate, which means I can only do what the law allows."

"Does that mean you have the tablet?"

"It's too early to tell what we have—we have just started to represent the estate. But now we'll be on the watch for it, and if we find it, we'll handle it just like we would any other valuable asset."

Michela gripped the arms on her chair and pushed it away from the table. As she stood, Steve rose, too. He stepped toward her and pushed her chair in. Michela drew close and reached out to hold his arm.

"You are not a good liar, Steve. Your eyes give you away. During dinner, they communicated you were here out of a sense of obligation. But when we spoke about the tablet, they lit up as you discovered the value of the object you have but did not understand." She drew even closer and he tried to pull away, but she held his arm to keep him in place. "Do what you have to do, but the price will go down over time, especially if others become aware of what you have. They may be less willing to pay for it."

Steve backed away. He wasn't sure if he'd just been threatened or warned, but either way, it made him feel uncomfortable. He didn't want Michela to know he'd been fazed, but he feared his eyes might give him away again. The best strategy seemed to be to change the subject and disengage.

"That sounds like a good note to end the evening on," Steve responded. "I'm sure Giorgio is wondering what happened to us." He held out his arm to direct Michela toward the foyer. She smiled politely and took the lead, walking to where Giorgio was waiting.

"Remember what I have said, Steve. You can always reach me through Giorgio. You can even visit me in Milan. Perhaps if you see what we do at La Fontana, you will feel more comfortable with my offer." Michela extended her hand, not as a handshake, but as a parting touch. Steve reached out to be polite and the two briefly held hands. "Goodnight Steve, I enjoyed the evening." She released his hand, not all at once, allowing her touch to trail off like the scent of a flower, and then left the dining room with Giorgio following close behind.

Steve wasn't sure what to make of Michela or which side of the law she was on. His initial impression was she was a businessperson through and through, but the possibility of her being connected with the illegal acquisition of stolen antiquities bothered him, to say the least.

As he turned to leave, his eye caught something familiar in a secluded corner of the dining room. There, at a table for two lit only by candlelight, sat Sarah with a man he didn't recognize. He could see a bottle of wine on the table and Sarah smiling and laughing, the way she used to do with him before they separated. He froze, unable to take his eyes off of her and the man she was with. As if she could sense his gaze, she turned her head toward him and made eye contact, then returned her attention to the man she was with, once again smiling and laughing.

Suddenly, the clay tablet didn't matter.

13

3:28 a.m. on Sunday, October 10, 2004
Turin, Italy

THE TURIN NIGHT WAS QUIET, JUST like every night in the old section, although the many lights along the streets hid the actual hour. The fall temperatures had already taken their downward turn, so the cool Alpine air crept through the streets unchecked, especially now that there was no warm Italian sun to hold it back.

The woman with golden-brown hair should have already switched to fall fashion. She looked out of place not only because she was on the street alone at three thirty on a Sunday morning, but also because she was dressed in a short skirt and heels with a light sleeveless top more fitting for July or August. Such a mistake could be forgiven elsewhere, but not in fashion-conscious Turin—women would notice. Men would notice too because she had a look they liked. She sauntered past the massive twin towers of the Palatine Gate, a huge red brick wall built by the Romans in the first century BC as a fortified entrance to the city. She stopped a few meters from the Commissariato Dora-Vanchiglia Police Station. The lobby area glowed with office lights advertising its twenty-four-hour police presence. She checked her watch; it was precisely 3:30 a.m. She brushed her hair off her shoulders, glanced toward the sky above the grassy area behind the Palatine Gate, then pushed the door to the police station open and strode to the counter.

"I need some help," she announced. A policeman hovering over a desk hurried over as soon as she made her presence known. He braced his hands on the counter and ogled her before answering.

"What kind of help do you need?" he asked far more politely than the woman's original demand merited.

"I've locked my keys in my car and I need you to let me in." There wasn't even the hint of a request in her voice. Like her summer fashion, her demeanor did not go unnoticed and sparked a response in kind.

"We don't do that," he said, backing a step away from the counter.

"Of course you do," she replied, her tone edging up one notch on the rudeness scale. "If you need something from someone's car, I know you can get into it."

"You're right about that," he admitted. "But you see, we don't need something from your car. You'll have to call a locksmith in the morning. Or, you can always break your window, can't you?" He grinned at the suggestion.

"You cannot talk to me like that," she insisted, raising her voice yet another level. "I want to see your supervisor right away. I cannot tolerate such insolence from a public servant."

The policeman looked at her with contempt, but dutifully turned toward the office behind the lobby to get the attention of the sergeant. He didn't have to summon his boss, though, because the woman's unruly behavior already had him heading for the counter to see what alcohol-induced fury his officer was dealing with.

"What is the problem here?" the sergeant asked, glancing at the woman on the other side of the counter but directing his question to the officer.

"This woman," the officer began, snapping his head in her direction, "locked her keys in her car. Now she's telling us we need to get them for her. I told her she would need to call a locksmith and she demanded to see you."

"I see," the sergeant said as if pondering the woman's request. "I'm afraid he's right. We can't do such things. There are only two of us here and if something happens, we would not be able to respond. We can help you call a taxi and you can come back in the morning to get your car. If you tell us your license number, I assure you we will not issue you a ticket."

The woman leaned over the counter, using her every tool to change their minds. "Surely there must be someone else who can help guard the desk," she said in her bedroom voice. "Then perhaps you could walk me to my car and unlock it for me. I would, of course, show my appreciation." She looked at the sergeant and moistened her lips.

The sergeant eyed the woman, then glanced down at the ring on his finger. "I'm very sorry. But like I said, we are the only two here and we cannot leave the station unless it is an emergency. Would you like us to call you a taxi?" He finished with a look of satisfaction for having been strong.

"I cannot believe I am being treated this way," the woman shouted, reverting to her original demeanor. "I want both of your names." She slammed her purse on the counter and reached inside, rooting around before withdrawing a handkerchief. Both policemen looked at her purse to see what would come out next. She reached inside and grabbed an inhaler, but instead of using it on herself, she turned it toward the policemen. Before they could react, she shot a toxic chemical agent in both of their faces while covering her own face with the handkerchief. Both officers started to choke and gag, struggling to suck in air. They fell to the floor writhing in pain.

The woman darted out the door and checked her watch. It was 3:42 a.m.—right on schedule. Moments later, she heard the whir of a chopper overhead and felt a blast of air heading from the southernmost green adjacent to the Palatine Gate. The chopper touched down and six commandos dressed in black jumped to the ground, all with automatic weapons strapped over their shoulders and most with packs on their backs. One headed straight for the police station and tossed the woman a weapon as he reached the door. The woman and two others ran to pre-assigned positions forming a defensive perimeter blocking the streets in front of the six-hundred-year-old Duomo di San Giovanni Battisti, also known as the Cathedral of Saint John the Baptist.

The other commandos raced for the front doors of the cathedral as a second helicopter touched down in the northernmost green adjacent to the Palatine Gate. Six more armed figures spewed from the aircraft. Three sprinted to positions around the north side of the cathedral, while the remaining three joined the force waiting at the cathedral's entrance. The first commando to reach the door pulled off his rucksack and removed plastic explosive charges. He positioned them around the main entrance's seventeenth century carved wooden doors. All the attackers scurried away as the charge detonated in a flaming flash, blowing the doors from their frame and launching them into the sanctuary.

Guided by flashlights, the team darted through the gaping hole and ran down the cathedral's left aisle, leaving the attacker who'd just spent his explosives to guard the door. They didn't stop to admire the priceless paintings of saints and Biblical icons watching over the precious contents of the cathedral. Nor did they peer through the majestic arches to their right serving as the boundary to the pews where worshipers would gather in a matter of hours for Sunday Mass. Instead, they sprinted to the end of the aisle to the left transept, where their fortified target awaited their arrival.

They stopped in front of a gold altar enclosed behind two floor-to-ceiling bulletproof glass windows bounded to the left and right by ornately decorated square marble columns. A red vestment draped over the middle of the altar hung down in front, with a scraggle of tangled thorns resting on top. No one talked or needed to; they had rehearsed the mission too many times for that.

They tossed the hassocks worshippers used to kneel in prayer before the altar out of the way, then sized up the glass panes separating them from the altar. Everything appeared exactly as it did on the mockup they used to perfect the mission's execution and timing.

One of the commandos took off his rucksack and pulled out cords of plastic explosives. He attached them to the perimeter of the window on the left. The attackers sought cover on the outside of the marble columns, but one tripped on a discarded hassock and fell. The handler detonated the explosives anyway and the resulting blast shook the floor and walls of the venerable cathedral and filled the transept with smoke and dust. Blood oozed from the fallen man's nose and ears as he lay unconscious on the floor.

Not waiting for the air to clear, the four remaining team members ignored their injured comrade and rushed back around to find the twisted metal window frame dangling from the ceiling, while the window itself lay in a shattered flexible glassy sea in front of the altar. The team stomped through the debris and rushed into the now penetrated chamber. A call over a radio the team leader had strapped to his belt added a Russian voice to the effort for the first time since they'd entered the cathedral.

"Siren approaching. Expect engagement soon."

The team leader didn't respond. It was enough to know the police were inbound, which they expected and planned for. That was why the other commandos guarded the streets leading to the cathedral. The key was getting out fast, and they were still on schedule. Another commando took off her rucksack and pulled out still more lines of plastic explosives, while the others swept everything off the altar holding the silver casket inside. After blowing open the altar, the female cut the rucksack from their disabled comrade and stuffed another line of explosives into the seam around the lid of the silver casket until the entire perimeter was stuffed full of the compound. Again, the commandos took shelter behind the marble columns and detonated the charge.

Vaboom! The casket's silver cover blew off and slammed to the floor, the crash reverberating throughout the chapel. As the air cleared, the team could now hear the distinct sounds of sirens and sporadic gunfire.

"Three minutes to departure," the Russian voice announced over the radio.

The team looked inside the casket. Down at the bottom, below the final bulletproof glass barrier, lay the most sacred relic in the Catholic Church, the holy Shroud of Turin. The cloud of dust hovering inside made it impossible to see the image of the crucified man, believed by many to be Jesus Christ, seared into the ancient linen, but that didn't matter.

"Set the final charge," the team leader barked in Russian. The last man removed his rucksack and attached two handles to the top of the glass case by twisting them down until suction cups on the bottom locked each one in place. He strung the final strand of plastic explosives around the central portion of the glass case, took shelter, and detonated the charge. A fireball flared upward, illuminating the interior of the Chapel of the Shroud with a fiery glow. As soon as it dissipated, the commandos returned and reached down to the badly damaged enclosure and tugged on the two handles. The fragment resisted at first, but with two men bent over and pulling with all their might, the heavy glass hatch created by the explosion lifted off and exposed the relic to the destructive air.

"What is your status?" the Russian voice shouted over the radio. "We are pulling the plug in two minutes. We cannot be taken alive."

"Get the cloth," shouted the team leader. The order need not have been given as the female team member had already begun to do so. She lit up the hole blasted through the Shroud's glass case with her flashlight and found the cloth intact without any visible burn or damage from the explosive charge. She pulled a large opaque green plastic bag from her rucksack and handed it to another team member, who opened it while she reached inside the case to remove the fragile linen even the most conservative estimates pegged at over seven hundred years old. She tugged on the center section and carefully pulled it through the opening, then loosely folded it in half-meter rolls as she extracted the full 4.5-meter linen from the case. When the Shroud was completely free, she doubled the bundle over one last time and set it inside the plastic bag, which she grabbed from her comrade.

"Let's go," she shouted.

"Target secured," the lead man yelled into the radio. "Extracting now." The other team members started running down the same side aisle they used on the way in, but the man with the radio stopped to assess the injured commando who was now conscious but unable to get to his feet. The injured man appeared disoriented and in shock but knew enough to reach up to his leader for help. "We cannot be taken alive, Alexi. You know the score." The man with the radio unslung his machine gun from his shoulder and fired a short burst into his team member. The man's body contorted as it absorbed the bullets and then slumped on the floor, waiting only for enough blood to drain before he died.

The shooter didn't re-sling his weapon, but instead gripped it by the barrel and sprinted for the door. By the time he reached the outside, he could hear sirens blaring and sporadic gunfire over the din from the two helicopters preparing to take off. The commandos who had entered the cathedral with him were already running back to the bird in the southernmost green. He sprinted to catch up but veered to the left to retrieve the team member guarding the police station and the woman who initiated the operation with her ruse. Bursts of anonymous gunfire continued to erupt, echoing down the offshoots from Via XX Settembre, the main road cutting through the middle of the action. Commandos shouted to each other and police lieutenants screamed out orders until both were drowned out by the sound of the first helicopter lifting off with its priceless cargo onboard.

The first chopper taking off signaled retreat to the remainder of the commandos securing the perimeter for the raid. They abandoned their positions and ran for the remaining helicopter on the northernmost field by the Palatine Gate. All converged on the helicopter and jumped onboard, trying to avoid the bullets they knew were flying around them but could not see. Then a burst of gunfire came from a building corner and a commando went down short of the aircraft, while several bullets struck the skin of the helicopter itself. The pilot immediately took his craft aloft, climbing into the night sky and shifting to forward motion as fast as the aerodynamics allowed. Soon it was zipping out of the city and heading to the northeast, flying low to avoid detection by radar.

The second helo's destination was a secluded farm outside of Navarro, a town a little more than half the distance between Turin and Milan. The plan was to land before daylight, disgorge the riders, and sequester the helicopter, together with all of the equipment from the raid, in a large ramshackle barn that already secretly housed a similar helicopter. The commandos and crew would then flee the area individually on pre-staged motorcycles waiting for them at the farm. The goal was to get to Switzerland or France and then disperse around the globe until the next high bidder required the team's services. To reduce the chances of being identified and hunted down, a charge would be detonated remotely to destroy the barn and everything in it as soon as all of the team members were safely across the Swiss and French borders. Then they could spend the hefty deposits in their offshore accounts with impunity.

The helicopter with the Shroud had a different escape plan. Instead of continuing to the northeast, the night vision equipped pilot raced the aircraft south at over 130 knots using black market military grade terrain following radar, allowing it to fly at treetop level to avoid detection. About an hour after the raid and still under the cover of darkness, the helicopter crossed over the Italian Riviera coastline between Genoa, Italy, and Nice, France, into international waters in the Ligurian Sea. As the helicopter neared the end of its fuel supply, the pilot vectored toward a large self-loading container ship plying the calm waters in a southwesterly direction. The ship had only a partial load of containers, which not coincidentally were loaded amidships to allow a helicopter to land and take off, although doing so would take a skillful pilot.

Incentivized by the nearly empty showing on his aircraft's fuel gauge, the pilot approached the vessel and hovered next to it, matching its speed and watching for any regular rolls or dips he might have to compensate for. Satisfied landing conditions were good, he slid the helicopter over the containers and gently brought the bird down onto the makeshift helipad.

"Get out now," he directed his passengers as he started to shut down the controls. Given that no one was tying the aircraft down and it was sitting on a bunch of shipping containers, they were in a precarious position. Everyone disembarked quickly and headed to a man waving from the exit point—a rope ladder secured to the top container and extending to the ship's main deck three containers below. All had their weapons and the female commando clutched the plastic bag containing the Shroud, which whipped and spun from the combined force of a slight sea breeze and the rotor wash from the helicopter.

The pilot was the last to leave, making sure all systems were completely shut down. Now it was time for the ship's cranes and crew to take over, attaching a line to the helicopter and dropping it over the side. It would be a difficult operation at night at sea, but the entire operation had been that way from the start. With the Shroud now in hand, they could not risk an aerial search or satellite spotting the helicopter on the ship. The vessel needed to appear as a container ship en route to its next destination, which indeed it was. The only difference was this ship had just helped complete the most spectacular heist of a religious relic since two merchants from Venice smuggled the bones of St. Mark out of Alexandria Egypt in a barrel of pork in 828 A.D. This time, though, the entire world would be on alert to help get the Shroud of Turin back.

14

9:07 a.m. on Monday, October 11, 2004
London, England

Dr. Jerome Gutmelder strolled into his office, hung up his brown suede jacket on a coat tree behind his door, and wandered over to an antique oak desk so big that it swallowed him up when he sat behind it. A slight man in his early seventies with thinning white hair and a matching beard, he'd developed a routine over his many years toiling at the British Museum in the slow-moving world of Babylonian artifacts. Monday mornings were catch-up days, spent going through emails and tying off ends left loose at the close of the previous week. This was also when he liked to do his professional reading because he could count on at least a couple of hours of quiet while everyone else in his department commenced their own workweek routines.

After clearing his desk of a few stray papers and pens left over from Friday, Gutmelder logged onto his computer and went straight to his email. He deleted or filed the first few messages dealing with news clips and upcoming meetings, but then came to one from someone he didn't recognize. The sender introduced himself as Ivan Lindor, a professor of archaeology at the College of William & Mary in the United States. Lindor admitted never having met Gutmelder, but was quite familiar with him by reputation. Then came the startling revelation—Lindor had seen what appeared to be an authentic clay tablet bearing a striking resemblance to a tablet found in 1899 in Sippar, Iraq, depicting the Babylonian map of the world. So similar, in fact, he presumed it could be a contemporaneous copy.

Lindor asserted the map on the new tablet was extraordinary because it depicted details to the south and southeast of Babylon missing from the pieced-together fragments forming the Sippar tablet. As if that wasn't exciting enough, the new discovery also had several inches of legible cuneiform—the writing used by the people in ancient Babylon—on the back. Lindor said that while he had no way to decipher the content or assess whether it offered anything new, given the notoriety of the Sippar map, he was certain this tablet would prove to be at least as significant, if not more.

Gutmelder could hardly control his exuberance and by now was speed-reading through the email. Lindor went on to note that while a law firm handling an estate currently possessed the tablet, he had not only observed it, but had also handled it and was quite sure it was authentic. A lawyer from the firm brought the tablet to Lindor because she needed to know more about it. In particular, she wanted to make sure it wasn't stolen. She wouldn't let him retain the tablet given its questionable title, but did give him 35mm photographs of the front and back, which Lindor attached to his email. He hoped Gutmelder would be able to assist him. In the event he could not, he was prepared to send the pictures to other experts in the United States.

Gutmelder scrolled a little further down the page past Lindor's signature to two JPEG files and clicked on the first one. It opened into a large, full-color image of the map.

"Oh, my goodness," he exclaimed. He couldn't wait to disrupt his colleagues from their Monday morning routines to show them his discovery. They were all intimately familiar with the Sippar map, not only because it was famous, but also because it was on public display at the British Museum. It depicted the ancient city of Babylon, the Euphrates River flowing nearby, two concentric rings enclosing a body of salt water, and triangular rays jutting from the rings depicting islands in the water. The map was incomplete, though, because everything outside the rings to the south and southeast was missing, having been lost forever to the passage of time. Now, as if time had reconstituted the desert's dust into a window to the past, the new tablet showed three triangular rays extending to the south and southeast, clearly labeled with cuneiform tags. Gutmelder couldn't wait to translate the tags to see what the rays represented.

Not wanting to leave the map but knowing he would clear his schedule for the rest of the day to study it, he opened the second JPEG file. The image displayed cuneiform script covering the back of the tablet in two long paragraphs. He wasn't sure whether it was the same as the hard-to-decipher text on the back of the Sippar map, which had nine shorter paragraphs, but it was certainly more legible. Although the different appearance could be attributable to something as simple as different scribes doing the work, the only way to find out for sure was to translate the new tablet and compare. He needed to get his team working on it right away.

Gutmelder banged out an email to his department informing them about an important new discovery and scheduling a meeting in his office for ten o'clock. To arouse their curiosity, he didn't disclose what the discovery was. He figured once his colleagues read the email, they wouldn't wait until ten o'clock for the meeting and would flock to his office right away. That was fine with him because he couldn't wait to share it with them anyway.

After hitting send, he began a short email response to Dr. Lindor. He thanked him for sending the photographs and told him he would have his team consider the material right away. He also assured him if the tablet turned out to be authentic and not stolen, the British Museum might be interested in acquiring it. For that reason, he asked Dr. Lindor to caution the lawyer he had spoken to not to dispose of the artifact without consulting with him first.

Gutmelder proofed his email to Lindor before hitting send. The tone had to be just right, expressing professional excitement without having the effect of inflating the price should the Museum decide to pursue the acquisition, as he suspected it would. Satisfied with his work, he launched the email just in time for the first person to come knocking at his door.

"Dr. Gutmelder?" the young man asked.

"Yes," Gutmelder replied. It wasn't a colleague coming to hear about the discovery, but one of the office staff who handled the administrative side of the department's business. Disappointed only because he wouldn't get to share his news, he invited the man in.

"Thank you, sir. You've received an overnight package from the United States."

"That's very nice, thank you. Who's it from?"

"I hope you don't mind, sir, but I did look on the way here. It's from the Federal Bureau of Investigation Art Crime Team."

"Ah, the FBI, very interesting. Let's have a look." Gutmelder took the cardboard envelope from the young man. "Thank you, again, but that should be all I require."

"Very well, sir," the young man replied. He turned and left the office.

Gutmelder inspected the yellow and red envelope from the outside before opening it. It was from the FBI's Art Crime Team, all right. He'd worked with them before helping to identify artifacts stolen from Iraq, so this was not the first time he'd received a package from them in the mail. What was unusual was that they sent it to him by overnight delivery, meaning they needed something in a hurry. Although that meant an infusion of always welcome cash into the department's coffers, it also meant he might not be able to get to the Babylon map project right away, depending upon what the FBI request entailed.

He pulled the cardboard tab on the side of the envelope and it opened along the perforated edge of the flap. He reached in and pulled out a small stack of documents, topped by a cover letter and followed, he surmised, by the standard contract the FBI used for such matters. Always an orderly man, he began by reading the cover letter, which was addressed to him personally, rather than to the Department of Conservation and Scientific Research more generally.

Dear Dr. Gutmelder,

Given your previous collaboration on the recovery and identification of certain artifacts stolen from Iraq, the Federal Bureau of Investigation Art Crime Team again requests your assistance. Unlike previous investigations, this case involves a homicide and an artifact we believe may be the motive for the killing. We do not yet have the artifact in custody, but we hope that by learning more about it, in terms of who might be interested in acquiring such an artifact and what it says, we may be able to locate the item and the person or persons responsible for the homicide. What we do know is that the artifact was recently discovered in the ruins of the ancient city of Babylon and smuggled from Iraq by a member of the U.S. military returning from his assignment there.

Enclosed you will find our standard personal services contract (the same contract we used before) for your review and signature. We are authorized to offer you $3,250 (U.S.) in payment for your services, provided you can complete the project within one week of the date of receipt of this letter. Please notify me immediately by email at the address listed below my signature block if you will accept this project. We can also arrange a conference call if you have any questions.

The only pictures we have of the artifact are attached to the personal services contract as an addendum. They are the best resolution we have.

Thank you for considering our request and we look forward to hearing from you.

Sincerely,

//Sheinelle Fields//

Special Agent

As much as he hated to do so, Gutmelder committed to prioritizing the case in front of the map of Babylon discovery. He flipped through the service contract, noting the contract price typed in on the first page and the many paragraphs of legalese he had no time for or interest in, until he finally made it to the addendum containing the color photos of the artifact. He could not believe what he saw.

"Bloody hell," he exclaimed, using two words not normally part of his academic vocabulary. There, as plain as day—color pictures of the front and back of the same map of Babylon he had just received from Dr. Lindor. "How can this be?" He couldn't fathom how the two cases might connect. Lindor said the artifact belonged to an estate represented by the lawyer who showed him the tablet. That had to mean that the deceased was the homicide victim. He looked again at the addresses on the communications he'd received. The FBI letter originated in Kansas City, while Professor Lindor worked at the College of William & Mary in Williamsburg, Virginia. Obviously, they did not know about each other, but that was about to change.

Special Agent Fields had offered him over three thousand dollars to decipher a cuneiform tablet in a week so she could try to locate it, and he was about to tell her where she could find the tablet for free. Now he had two meetings to look forward to, the one with his colleagues at ten and one with the FBI as soon as they were open for business in Kansas City. He could hardly wait for either one.

15

8:35 a.m. on Monday, October 11, 2004
Williamsburg, Virginia

STEVE SAT IMMOBILE AT HIS DESK on Monday morning with the door closed. He didn't feel like talking, especially to Marjorie. In fact, he rushed into the office early so he wouldn't have to walk past her at her desk. If he'd come at the normal time, she'd be sitting there waiting for him. The first thing she'd do was smile and ask about his weekend. He'd have to tell her about his dinner with Michela and Giorgio, which she knew nothing about since he made the arrangements with Giorgio on Saturday afternoon. Not that there was anything wrong with the dinner. It turned out to be surprisingly pleasant. But relaying that part of the story would cause what took place afterwards to cut deeper. Even now, he could picture Sarah's head turning his way in slow motion until her eyes locked on his. Then they shot him a silent but unmistakable message—it was over.

It wasn't so much that Sarah had been out with another man. After all, Steve had just finished eating dinner with another woman, albeit in a business setting and with a chaperone. Although he found Michela attractive, he had no feelings for her. It was also entirely possible Sarah had no feelings for the man she was with. That wasn't the point. Sarah's eyes said she was ready— no, she needed—to move on. Her turning back to her conversation with her dinner guest represented her turning away from Steve, and he knew it.

Although he didn't want to admit it, he'd known since the moment Sarah left him this day was coming. She'd always been an independent woman—she had to be as a Navy wife. She'd practically raised their two sons by herself while he deployed or worked long hours at the Pentagon. That meant the separation would be anything but temporary because it would remind her life without him was possible. His real fear, though, was she would learn it was preferable given her dim view of the prospects for changing his workaholic ways.

That was what happened. Sure, they paid lip service to getting back together, and had even gone out to dinner and looked happy with one another at college graduations and other family events with their two sons. But it was never the same, and it never could be. With each passing day they saw less of each other and grew further apart. The only saving grace was they were still technically married, and he clung to that thread. Now it looked like Sarah was ready to sever that thread, leaving him no choice but to admit he'd failed as a husband. The most horrible part of all, it was almost harder for him to admit failure than it was for him to accept he'd lost the love of his life.

Steve looked at his watch; it was coming up on nine o'clock. Two hours in the office and he had nothing to show for it. He needed to get a grip on himself. "Navy officers don't mope around," he told himself. "They get things done." The words, even if not spoken aloud, were enough at least to allow him to move. He shuffled some papers on his desk, trying to figure out what his next task should be, but he was lost somewhere between client and spouse. He needed to break free from one so he could focus on the other, and as reality set in, he knew that meant determining what had to be done in the Arul Ashirvadam case. He couldn't let his personal failures stand in the way of his professional obligations. At that moment, he knew Sarah's eyes were right.

A soft knocking at the door startled him. "Come in," he said just loud enough to be heard on the other side of his closed door. He tried to brace himself to deal with Marjorie's cheerfulness, or Casey's compassion once she sensed something was amiss, which she inevitably would. He mused Casey would have made a great shrink had she not gone into the law. Right now, her thoughtfulness and probing insight weren't what he needed or wanted.

"Good morning, Steve," Casey said, her voice as subdued as her knocks on his door. "May I come in?"

Steve sat upright and plastered a pleasant look on his face. He took the initiative to direct the conversation away from himself in case his happy face wasn't convincing. "Of course, Casey. Come on in. How was your weekend?"

"Productive. How about yours?" Casey walked in and sat down in one of the chairs in front of his desk. She sat back all the way, crossed her legs at her ankles with her prosthetic right leg on top, and rested a legal pad on her lap. The bullet points Steve could see on her legal pad indicated she had a number of things to talk about, so this would not be a one-and-done discussion. As long as the topics were business, he could get through it.

"Interesting would be the best way to describe it," he answered, intending to open the door to the discussion about Michela and Giorgio, but not Sarah. Casey needed to know all about his impromptu dinner meeting.

"How so?"

"You first," Steve countered. "I want to hear about productive first. Interesting is a lower priority."

"Okay then, I'll start. On Friday, I met with an archaeologist at William & Mary, Professor Ivan Lindor. It looks like we might have a valuable artifact on our hands."

Steve perked up, raising his eyebrows. "Did he say what it's worth?"

"No, but he did recognize it, at least sort of. He said it looked like a very famous Babylonian tablet that has a map of the world carved on it."

Steve nearly jumped out of his chair. "Our tablet is a map?"

"Well, yeah," Cased responded, apparently surprised by his enthusiasm. "I actually found it on the web this weekend. The professor's spot on. It matches perfectly. It's at the British Museum in London. I printed off a copy. See for yourself." Casey pulled a piece of paper with a picture of the British Museum's tablet printed on one side, together with a description of what the map depicts.

"This is incredible," Steve replied, his eyes darting between map and explanation. "This dovetails exactly with a discussion I had on Saturday night. You're not going to believe it."

"Believe what?"

"Well, Saturday afternoon, I got a call from the executive assistant for Michela Baresi. She's the CEO of La Fontana Cosmetics in Milan. She's also apparently the occasional lover of our late client."

"Did you say lover?" Now it was Casey's turn to raise her eyebrows.

"Like I said, you're not going to believe this. Ashirvadam wasn't quite the family man he led me to believe." Steve snapped his fingers. "It just hit me. That also explains the connection to the trustee in Milan, doesn't it?" He shook his head. "I can't believe I didn't recognize that before now."

"Anyway," he continued, "what she told me ties in exactly with what you just said. Michela said about a month before Ashirvadam died, he told her he'd found the key to locating the Fountain of Youth and wanted her to have it. He was certain about it." Steve paused then quickly added, "No, it was stronger than that. He said he'd had a revelation from God."

"Wait a minute," Casey interjected. "This is getting crazy. You don't believe that, do you?" Casey's face vacillated between grin and smirk, apparently unable to discern which side her senior partner would come down on.

"Of course not," Steve retorted, "but it doesn't matter what I believe. It's what Ashirvadam and Michela believed, and I'm pretty sure Ashirvadam believed he'd found the key to the real deal."

"What about Michela? Does she believe it? I mean, she must be a pretty sophisticated woman given her position."

"I can't tell, but I know she's sees money in the discovery. Not coincidentally, La Fontana means "the fountain" in Italian, so if she has the supposed key to the Fountain of Youth, it could be a marketing gold mine for her cosmetics line. That's why she arranged to have dinner with me. She wants me to give her the tablet as soon as we find it."

Casey grinned. "Ahhh, so she doesn't know we have it yet, then, does she?"

"Not yet, because we don't know if it's stolen."

Casey leaned forward and tapped her pen on her legal pad as if to make a point. "I might be able to shed a little light on that, or at least how we might be able to find out. Professor Lindor told me to contact the FBI's Art Crime Team. He said they'd be able to trace the tablet if it's been reported stolen."

"Did you tell him we'd take care of that, or is he going to?" Steve wasn't happy with either option at this point, thinking the step premature, but he didn't want Casey to feel bad in the event she'd committed either way.

"Neither," Casey responded. "I thanked him for the information, but said we weren't ready to go that route yet. I just gave him the pictures I took of the front and back of the tablet, and he's going to email them to some of his colleagues to see if they can tell us anything. After he hears back, we can decide if we need to go to the FBI."

"Perfect," Steve responded, relieved they didn't have to walk back a decision to go to the FBI. "If we do get any indication it's stolen, we'll notify the FBI right away."

"I agree," Casey concluded. "Does the same go for your detective friend in London? Will you let him know, as well?"

"Who, Cavendish?"

Casey nodded.

"That's a good question," Steve answered, rubbing his chin. "Off the top of my head, I think just notifying the FBI will be sufficient. If we get to that point, we'll need to tell the FBI about Cavendish. It'll all come out eventually anyway, and it may be better to be proactive so no one thinks we're trying to hide anything."

"That reminds me," Casey added, squirming a little in her chair. "Professor Lindor took the tablet out of the box, so he might have damaged any fingerprints on it and now his prints are on it, too. It happened so fast, I couldn't stop him."

"I don't think that'll be a problem," Steve reassured her. "They'll just take Lindor's prints to eliminate him from the list of those who've handled it recently."

"That's what I figured," Casey admitted, sounding relieved. "I still feel bad about it. By the way, knowing what the tablet might be worth, I'm a little concerned with keeping it safe. I thought I'd give it to Marjorie so she could put it in our safe deposit box at the bank. Are you okay with that?"

"That sounds like a great idea. Go ahead and make it happen." Feeling like they'd covered everything they needed to on the tablet, Steve dug his heels into the rug and used the leverage to tuck his chair up under his desk as far as it would go. He rested his elbows on the blotter and clasped his hands.

"Okay, what else do you have?" he asked. His abrupt change of subjects must have caught Casey off guard because she fidgeted in her chair before sitting up straight and puckering her lips as she consulted her notes. She checked the first item off her list, scanned the remaining items, and returned her attention to Steve.

"Okay," she said. "I'm guessing you haven't had the chance to speak with Ashirvadam's wife yet."

"Not yet," Steve conceded. "I've only gotten so far as finding out they're eight and a half hours ahead of us. Marjorie gave me her number, but I haven't made the call yet. I'll take care of that today."

"Why don't you let me take care of that? I'm thinking the last thing you need to be doing is talking to a grieving widow right now about where to bury her husband. In fact, if you take care of the interactions with the trustee in Milan and the court in Vienna, I can take care of the wife in India and the details with the churches. How does that sound?"

"I can't argue with that," Steve said. He wasn't sure why Casey thought dealing with Ashirvadam's widow was the last thing he needed now, but since she was right, he didn't bother to ask. Besides, their conversation had connected some dots in the Ashirvadam case and distracted him from Sarah, so he was feeling more upbeat than when he secluded himself in his office earlier in the morning. Even his voice had more spunk to it.

"What else is on that list for me?" He smiled to let Casey know she'd lifted his spirits.

Casey didn't look at her legal pad this time. She lay the pen down and held it in place with one hand, while she used the other to scoot herself forward on the chair. A serious look spread across her face—one he hadn't seen since she'd last had one of her increasingly rare bouts with depression. She looked ready to cry.

"What's wrong, Casey, are you alright?"

"I'm afraid I've got some bad news, Steve."

"You're not leaving, are you? Tell me you're not leaving." Casey's departure would be devastating. She'd just said she was going to assume a major role in resolving Ashirvadam's estate, so he hoped it wasn't so. But she'd proved herself a formidable litigator and built a stellar reputation with the Williamsburg bar so quickly that perhaps a bigger firm had taken notice and was wooing her away. He braced himself.

"Of course not." Casey smiled a small smile, like something was holding it back from getting as big as it should be. "I'm afraid you're stuck with me. Besides, you just made me your partner. I'm not going anywhere."

"Pfffew," he answered, exaggerating his demonstration of relief. "Then it can't be too serious."

"I got a call this morning from Janice Moore at Kennedy & Crocker—"

"—Yeah, I know them. They're pretty good, but they don't do trusts and estates. What do they want? Are we being sued for malpractice?"

"Janice gave me a heads-up, Steve." Casey covered her mouth, as if she were trying to decide if she had to say more. Her eyes teared-up and reddened. She kept herself from crying by taking a deep breath and went on. "It's Sarah, Steve. She's filing for divorce. I'm so sorry."

All expression vanished from his face and he froze, not sure whether he couldn't move or just didn't want to. Casey's announcement validated his earlier feelings of failure, dragging him back to the rut he was in when he sat alone in his office before she arrived. Now, he felt the added pressure to show resilience and the ability to compartmentalize his personal and professional lives. That meant brushing aside the news and moving on, but it was as if someone had pushed the pause button and he couldn't do anything until someone hit play.

"Are you okay?" Casey set her legal pad on the table next to her and, grasping the armrests of her chair, pushed herself to her feet. "Would you like a glass of water or a cup of coffee? I can get you anything you need."

Steve tightened his stomach and forced air across his vocal cords to form words. They were quiet and tentative, just loud enough for Casey to hear. "No thanks, Casey. I'm fine." He had more to say, although he wasn't sure what it was, so he said nothing. For the first time in his life, the silence wasn't awkward because it better expressed the way he felt—empty and alone. He summoned every last bit of concentration until his brain fired off enough neurons to allow him to cross his hands on his lap. He looked up at the zillions of holes in the ceiling tiles, unable to focus on any of them. "I guess I knew this was coming."

Casey sat down in her chair again and spoke softly to him. "When it's something you don't want to happen, knowing it's coming doesn't make it any easier."

"You can say that again," Steve added, trying to back away from the brink yet revealing a degree of emotional honesty he rarely shared with anyone.

"Why don't you go get a cup of coffee on DoG Street?" Casey suggested, referring to the shops in the colonial section of Williamsburg on the Duke of

Gloucester Street, just a block away. "Marjorie and I will take care of things here until you get back. The fresh air will do you some good."

Steve convinced his hands to grab the edge of his desk and push his chair backwards. "I think I will grab a cup of coffee, but our kitchen is good enough." He worked up half a smile and tried to sound resolute. "Then I've got a couple of calls I need to make on the Ashirvadam case. Getting those things done should be good therapy."

"Steve, don't fool yourself into thinking you need to be able to handle all that's happening on your own. Take it from someone who learned the hard way. Sometimes you need help to guide you through these things."

"Thanks Casey, I'll be fine," he reassured her. "Just tell me one thing—does Marjorie know?"

"I told her before I came in—I hope you're not angry. I thought it was something she needed to know."

"You're right, of course," he acknowledged. "I've got to admit, though, it's going to be difficult to talk to her with this in the background."

"Then don't leave it in the background. Get it out on the table right away so it's not something either of you have to dance around. Once you talk about it, you'll be able to move on."

Steve knew Casey was right, again. She'd lived through situations far worse than this and come out on top. Now it was his turn to deal with a little hardship, which, by the way, was largely of his own making. He mustered his courage and climbed out of his chair.

"Okay Casey, why don't you lead the way out. We'll get this over with so things can get back to normal." Steve knew down deep, though, he would never be over Sarah and things would never get back to normal. Sarah's eyes on Saturday had already told him what this morning's events now confirmed to be true. His life was forever changed.

16

12:34 p.m. on Monday, October 11, 2004
Williamsburg, Virginia

CASEY'D JUST COME OFF AN AMAZING weekend—amazing because it involved a Sunday afternoon spent with a handsome coach she met volunteering at a high school cross-country meet the day before. When she came to work, she couldn't wait to share her day with Marjorie, who would lap up every detail, smile for her, and cheer her on. That wasn't how her Monday unfolded. Instead, as soon as she arrived, Marjorie told her she could tell something was wrong with Steve. He'd been in his office with the door closed all morning and hadn't come out to say hello. Marjorie wanted to check on him, but this was so uncharacteristic of his normal behavior she figured he needed to be alone, so she let him be.

Then came the phone call from Janice Moore at Kennedy & Crocker, and Casey had to relay the news that rocked Steve's world. She helped him talk with Marjorie, who reminded him she'd been through a divorce, too. Marjorie promised there would be light at the end of the tunnel, but it might hurt getting there. Steve ended the matter by veering the conversation back to the Ashirvadam estate, making it clear he needed to work things out on his own.

Now she sat in her office on a Monday afternoon, preparing to call a grieving widow in India about burying her husband at a church she might object to and dictating to her how his estate would be handled. As Mondays went, this one had not been too good.

"Casey," Marjorie announced over the intercom. "The phone's ringing on the call to Mrs. Ashirvadam. You should pick up so you can say hello when she answers."

"Thanks, Marjorie," Casey replied as she picked up the phone on the outgoing line to India. The phone was still ringing.

"Vaṇakkam," a male voice with a distinctly Indian accent said on the other end of the line. Casey hoped he said hello and that he spoke English. Otherwise, this would be a very short and unproductive call.

"Hello, my name is Casey Pantel. I'm calling from the United States. Do you speak English?"

"Yes, of course," the man replied. Although his English was flawless, his accent made him difficult to understand, especially on the phone.

"I'm so glad," Casey responded. "I'm an American attorney representing the U.S. estate of Mrs. Ashirvadam's late husband, Arul. Let me begin by saying I am so sorry for her loss."

"Thank you for your expression of sympathy, Miss Pantel," the man said with British-like formality. "I'm sure you can appreciate this is a difficult time for the family."

"I can only imagine." Although the man appeared to understand Casey and it was she who was having difficulty, she found herself enunciating every word as if her listener were just learning English. "May I ask who I am speaking with?"

"My name is Abijith and I manage Mrs. Ashirvadam's affairs. How may I help you, Miss Pantel?"

"Thank you, Abijith." Casey jotted down his name, spelling it phonetically, so she wouldn't forget it. "As I mentioned, the firm I work with is representing the U.S. portion of Arul Ashirvadam's estate. I was hoping I could speak with Mrs. Ashirvadam about the estate and the burial arrangements for her late husband."

"You work with Mr. Stilwell, then, do you?" Abijith's answer surprised Casey.

"Why yes, how did you know?"

"As I said, Miss Pantel. I manage Mrs. Ashirvadam's affairs, so it is my job to know these things."

"Then you also understand my role and the things I need to speak with Mrs. Ashirvadam about."

"I understand Mr. Stilwell's role as the executor of Mr. Ashirvadam's American estate. I'm not sure I understand your role."

This wasn't exactly the conversation Casey expected. She'd hoped for a quick call with the widow. Instead, she found herself sparring with the woman's business manager. She wanted to be polite, but she also wanted to get her issues taken care of and he wasn't making it easy. She tried to explain.

"I'm Steve Stilwell's partner, Abijith, so I'm assisting him with Arul

Ashirvadam's estate. I thought I might be most helpful reaching out to Mrs. Ashirvadam, so that is what I am doing. Is she available by chance?"

"Well, Miss Pantel, I hope you realize it is after ten o'clock in Chennai. Mrs. Ashirvadam has gone to bed for the evening."

"I am so sorry for calling this late," apologized Casey. "I should have realized what time it is there. Perhaps we can schedule a time for me to call tomorrow."

"That's very kind of you, Miss Pantel, however I have advised Mrs. Ashirvadam not to discuss the estate over the telephone. As I'm sure you are aware, Mr. and Mrs. Ashirvadam are quite wealthy, so there is no telling who might try to take advantage of Mrs. Ashirvadam over the telephone. I'm afraid if you would like to speak with Mrs. Ashirvadam, you'll have to come to Chennai to do so."

Casey had no preplanned response ready for Abijith's intransigence. Although she'd mentally prepared herself for a range of possible issues, traveling to India before she could even speak to Mrs. Ashirvadam was not one of them. Like any good litigator, she quickly developed a viable option to put Abijith on the defensive.

"Of course, I understand your position, Abijith. However, as I'm sure you can appreciate, the cost and time involved with such a trip would be significant, to say the least. Perhaps we can arrange an acceptable alternative. For example, do you have a local attorney who represents Mrs. Ashirvadam that I might work through? That would allow you to verify my identity and legitimacy. In fact, I should be able to work everything through local counsel, although I have to admit, I would very much like to speak with Mrs. Ashirvadam. I want to tell her personally that we are committed to doing everything we can to expedite the handling of her husband's estate in the most professional manner possible."

"That is a very attractive option, Miss Pantel. I'm afraid, though, it is not one we will be able to accept. Mrs. Ashirvadam and I are quite resolute in our position. If you would like to speak with Mrs. Ashirvadam, you will have to come to Chennai. We have no intention of retaining local counsel for that purpose. Shall we say good-day, then?"

"No, not just yet, Abijith." Casey was ready to call his bluff, knowing Steve would support her. "I'd be willing to make the trip as long as I can be guaranteed a meeting with Mrs. Ashirvadam. I'm sure you can appreciate that I don't want to travel halfway around the world unless Mrs. Ashirvadam will see me. You already know Steve Stilwell is the executor of Arul Ashirvadam's U.S. estate, and since I am his partner, I'm sure you can see the importance of such a meeting. Plus, there are some burial details I really need to discuss with Mrs. Ashirvadam."

Now there was silence on Abijith's end of the line, making Casey think her willingness to come to India had caught him by surprise. As with Casey's pause, Abijith reentered the dialogue before the silence indicated weakness. "Well then, Miss Pantel, it is clear your desire to speak with Mrs. Ashirvadam is sincere."

"I can assure you it is, Abijith. I will not waste her time." Casey held out hope Abijith was caving on his in-person requirement.

"Mrs. Ashirvadam will be traveling with her children beginning on Saturday. She will not be reachable once she leaves. If you come to Chennai before that time, I will schedule a meeting for you with Mrs. Ashirvadam."

Although Casey was happy to be offered the chance for a meeting, the schedule seemed impossible. She had to negotiate better terms.

"That's very kind of you, Abijith, but it will be almost impossible to get there that quickly. It's at least a two-day trip, plus I'd need to get a visa, and it's already Monday. What if we scheduled an initial meeting by phone provided I commit to a follow-on meeting in Chennai? You have my word I will meet with Mrs. Ashirvadam in person."

"That is a wonderful idea, Miss Pantel, and under normal circumstances I would be happy to accept your offer. But with the death of Mr. Ashirvadam, these are not normal circumstances. I assume since it is impossible for you to arrive here before Mrs. Ashirvadam departs on Saturday, you will contact me in November to arrange an appointment?"

"No, that won't be necessary," Casey responded, determined not to let Abijith off the hook. "Let's schedule a meeting for this Thursday at one o'clock at Mrs. Ashirvadam's residence. If you guarantee I can meet with Mrs. Ashirvadam on Thursday afternoon, I will make it work."

"I will do the best I can Miss Pantel. As soon as you arrive, please call and let me know where you are staying. Then I will confirm the meeting with Mrs. Ashirvadam. For now, we can tentatively set it for Thursday at one o'clock, but you will likely need to be flexible. Mrs. Ashirvadam has two children, one of whom is ill, and she is very devoted to them. She will not hesitate to change her schedule if it is necessary for her children. I am sure you can understand that, can't you Miss Pantel?"

"Of course," Casey responded. "In fact, since this meeting will help us manage the estate in the most efficient manner, it will benefit her children as they are beneficiaries. I'm sure Mrs. Ashirvadam will appreciate that."

"Indeed," Abijith replied. "I look forward to your call once you arrive in Chennai, Miss Pantel. Now I must retire for the evening. Good day."

"Yes, I'm sorry for calling so late, Abijith. I will call you as soon as I arrive. Thank you so much for working with me. Goodbye."

Casey hung up the phone and threw herself against the back of her chair, which squeaked in protest as it rocked to its limit. She braced herself with her hands on the chair arms and thought about what just transpired. She'd committed to flying to India on notice so short she wasn't sure it was possible. She'd arrive in a city she knew nothing about and didn't even have a guarantee she'd get to speak with Mrs. Ashirvadam once she arrived. Yet the more roadblocks Abijith piled in front of her, the more she felt compelled to take the gamble. She sensed Abijith was hiding something. What could it be and why? And, was Abijith really acting on Mrs. Ashirvadam's instructions, or was he trying to prevent the meeting for his own purposes? The only way to tell was to get to Chennai in time for the tentative meeting with Mrs. Ashirvadam on Thursday.

17

~~~

2:17 a.m. on Tuesday, October 12, 2004
Williamsburg, Virginia

PHAN KNELT IN FRONT OF THE toilet he'd just scrubbed and retched violently. His stomach constricted in ever tightening knots, even after its contents had long since been expelled. He gasped for air after the last convulsion, trying to regain enough strength to stand up and do what he needed to do. The deep breath worked, with the inflow of oxygen sufficient to countermand his stomach's desire to purge. He pressed his hands against the stall walls on either side of the toilet and pushed himself upward, sucking in air like an Olympic sprinter finishing a race.

With his stomach still contracting, Phan reached down next to the toilet to retrieve the brush and rag he'd dropped when he started to heave. He scrubbed the inside of the bowl again, removing any signs of vomit, and then used the rag to make sure the toilet shined. Even the moral dilemma he faced could not keep him from making sure every inch of the Stilwell & Pantel Law Offices looked showroom fresh. He backed out of the stall and ran a mop over the floor around the toilet one last time, and then did the same to the men's room floor before he washed his hands, turned out the light, and exited.

Back in the lobby, Phan checked his watch. It was nearly two thirty on Tuesday morning. He'd agonized about this moment all weekend, unsure of what to do. He thought the decision would be made for him because not only was he unsure of what he was looking for, but he also had no idea where to find whatever it was. Even more than that, he reasoned if the brick was valuable enough for someone to steal, he was sure Steve and Casey would keep it secure, so he had no chance of locating it. Surely the man would understand—the guy who cleaned the offices couldn't know where such things were kept. Phan hoped once he explained reality and promised he would never tell anyone, the man would leave him and his family alone.

To keep all of his options open, he arrived at the office earlier than usual to look for the brick. He'd combed through Steve and Casey's offices, even looked in their desk drawers, and found nothing. He'd searched through Marjorie's reception desk and credenza and came up empty as well. That left him no alternative but to tell the man he couldn't find the brick and had no way to get it. Terrified about the potential impact on his family yet relieved he wouldn't have to betray his friend, he set about cleaning the office, all the time rehearsing what he would say when the man called. Then things changed.

As Phan vacuumed the Oriental rug around Marjorie's desk, he scooted her chair out to reach the area underneath. When he pushed the upright's handle forward, the unit hit something he couldn't see. Without switching off the vacuum, he looked and saw a shoebox-sized box shoved against the inside of the front panel of the desk, invisible to anyone unless they crouched down to peer into the shadowy corner. Thinking it might be an empty box Marjorie had accidentally kicked under her desk and then forgotten, he turned off the vacuum and opened it. He gasped when he saw the brick, at once grasping that he'd found what the man wanted and that his conundrum had returned. He set the box on Marjorie's credenza and glared at it.

At first, he resolved to take his original approach, lying to the man about not being able to find the brick. When that was the only option, he'd been able to rationalize that the man would have to understand and would leave him be. Now that he had the brick, what if he was wrong? What if the man did something to his family and he could have prevented it by simply turning the brick over to him? He tried to ignore the decision by leaving the box on Marjorie's credenza and continuing with his cleaning, but the issue so vexed him he eventually found himself heaving in the toilet. Now it was almost two thirty and he didn't know what he was going to do.

When two thirty arrived, he stood paralyzed in front of Marjorie's desk. He prayed the man wouldn't call and he'd never hear or see the man again. Then the phone on Marjorie's desk rang, cutting through the office like an air raid siren warning Phan to take shelter. As he reached out to answer, he noticed the caller's number displayed on Marjorie's phone. He ripped off a yellow sticky from a pad on Marjorie's desk and jotted down the number as fast as he could, still answering the phone just after it completed the fourth ring. The caller spoke first.

"Good, my man, good. I was beginning to think you wasn't gonna answer.

That would've been no good for your family, you know what I'm saying?"

This was the point of no return and Phan knew it. Lying about the brick was the obvious course, but the last time he'd lied in a life-or-death situation it went very badly. If Steve found out, he would understand—he had to. After all, his wife's and daughter's lives were at stake. Besides, maybe another option would materialize once he delivered the brick. The only way to find out was to promise to give the man what he wanted and see what happened. Perhaps he could make it turn out right after all.

"Please leave me and my family alone," Phan implored. "I only clean Mr. Steve's building. I not the right person to help you."

"That's where you're wrong, my man. You are the right person, and you better get me that brick tonight. You know what I'm saying?" The man's voice sounded deadly serious. "You got the brick or not?"

Phan's words came out without him realizing he was actually saying them. It was as if he were listening to someone else speak with his voice. "Yeah, I got brick. What you want me to do with it?"

"See, man, I knew you were the right person. Now listen here. You take that brick and go right out the front door of your building. There's a parking lot across the street with a white fence in front of it. Walk across that parking lot to the end where the trees are. Set the box on the ground just inside those trees and keep walking down the street away from your building. You got that?"

"Yeah, I got it." Phan could picture exactly what the man described because he parked his car in that lot every night. In fact, his car was there now, not at the end where the man wanted him to leave the brick, but at the other end, just beyond the lot's picket fence nearest his building.

"Okay, you got two minutes to drop that brick off, you understand? And don't try nothin' because I'm watching you close. You mess with me, my man, and your family's mine. Now hang up and get going."

With only two minutes to get the brick out the door and across the street, Phan didn't have time to think. He grabbed the box from Marjorie's credenza and shot out of the office door, jogging through the hall until he came to the building's front door. Before he went outside, he scanned the courtyard to be sure he wouldn't be ambushed. Seeing nothing, he jogged through the courtyard and across North Henry Street. He couldn't get over the picket fence carrying the box, so he headed left to Prince George Street, rounded the fence, and started walking briskly toward the trees at the back of the parking lot.

Three or four cars other than Phan's dotted the lot. As he neared the half-way point, a car he'd already passed started its engine but left its lights off. The sound of the engine turning over so close to where he had just been startled him, so he stopped to see what was behind him. As he turned to look over his shoulder, a car charged out of its parking spot and headed right for him. Phan started to dodge out of the way, but at the last second the car veered away, stopping next to him as the driver's side window rolled down.

"Gimme the box," the man demanded. Then he smiled at Phan and laughed. "You thought you was dead, didn't you?"

Something about the man's attitude made Phan snap. His heart was already beating so fast he could feel it leaping inside his chest, and his psyche couldn't accept the humiliation of the man laughing at his fear. Just like when he was doing full-contact martial arts in the Vietnamese Army, his right fist acted independently of the rest of his body, thrusting through the open window and into the driver's left eye. The man screamed as Phan withdrew his arm and thrust it in again and again in rapid succession, pulverizing the man's face like a jackhammer on concrete. The man finally escaped Phan's reach by leaning over the console between the driver and passenger seats, recovering enough to reach for the floor. Phan saw him making the move, so he tried to pull the door open, but it was locked. Now Phan could see the man pulling a pistol from under the seat. Calculating he would lose if he tried to subdue the man by going through the car window, he ran away to the end of the parking lot and out onto Prince George Street, still with the box tucked under his arm.

The man floored the vehicle after him, ripping through the parking lot. Phan knew the man couldn't follow him if he got off the road, so he climbed over the split rail fence around the field opposite the parking lot and started to run. The man's vehicle screeched to a halt and the driver's door flew open, with the man bringing the pistol up to the firing position and taking aim. A single crack followed and Phan crumpled to the ground. The man then followed Phan's path over the split rail fence until he came upon Phan, bleeding out of his back and gasping for air with every breath.

The man picked up the box next to Phan. "You one dumb son of a bitch, that's all I got to say." He opened it to confirm it had what he came for. He set the box back down into the tall grass and tucked the pistol under his belt at the small of his back. Then he grabbed Phan's arms and pulled them above his head.

Lapsing in and out of consciousness, Phan felt himself being dragged into the underbrush beneath a clump of trees. He was breathing very heavily and could not feel anything anymore. He thought about his wife and his beautiful little girl and how lucky they were to be in America. Then his eyes closed.

18

1:03 p.m. on Tuesday, October 12, 2004
Williamsburg, Virginia

TUESDAY WAS ALREADY BETTER THAN MONDAY. Now that Casey and
Marjorie knew as much as Steve did about Sarah's intention to pursue
a divorce, he didn't feel like he had to hide behind closed doors. Getting
everything out in the open freed him to think about other things, like
Ashirvadam's estate and his other clients. In fact, he'd worked on his other
clients all morning so he could focus on Ashirvadam's estate all afternoon.
Given the size of the estate, he took particular care because a mistake could
bring significant cost. Yet he couldn't get his mind off the Babylonian tablet;
where it might have come from and what it might be worth. He hoped
Professor Lindor would contact the office soon with whatever information he
was able to uncover.

"Mr. Stilwell," Marjorie called over the intercom. "Can you come to the
lobby, please? There are some people here who need to see you. They want you
to come to the reception desk."

"Of course," Steve replied, the end of his index finger turning red from
pressing too hard on his phone's intercom button. "I'll be right there. Do
you know who they are?" Steve assumed it was an old college buddy visiting
Williamsburg and dropping by to pay a surprise visit, as happened from time
to time.

"Mmmhhmm," Marjorie replied. She offered nothing more, adding
credence to his college buddy theory.

Steve put on his suit coat before heading for the lobby. As he approached the door, he could see a man and a woman, both in business attire, standing by the reception desk. He didn't recognize either one, so he approached the woman, who was standing closest to Marjorie's desk. He reached out to shake her hand as he welcomed them.

"Hello, I'm Steve Stilwell. Is there something I can help you with?"

The woman shook his hand. "Hello Mr. Stilwell. I'm Special Agent Sheinelle Fields with the FBI's Art Crime Team, and this is Special Agent Neil Crosby." Fields stopped shaking hands when she introduced Crosby, who reached forward to take over where his boss left off. His handshake was short and polite, not as friendly as Fields'.

As soon as the words "Art Crime Team" left Fields' mouth, Steve knew she had somehow connected him to the clay tablet. He didn't want to volunteer information on the off chance she didn't know as much as he thought she might, but if she asked the right questions, he'd cooperate fully and tell them what they needed to know. He would be as gracious as possible.

"Why don't you come into my office and we can talk. Would you like some tea or coffee before we get started?"

"That's very kind of you Mr. Stilwell, but we're actually not here to talk. Although I'd like to keep that option open, our purpose this afternoon is to execute a search warrant for an artifact stolen from Iraq. Neil, please show the warrant to Mr. Stilwell."

Steve tried not to look surprised and he hoped he was doing a better job than Marjorie. Her wide-eyed look telegraphed she was flabbergasted the FBI was about to search their office. Crosby retrieved the search warrant from his jacket pocket and unfolded it as he handed it to Steve. As if on cue, both agents produced their FBI badges to prove their identity and authority.

"We can make this very simple, Mr. Stilwell," Fields continued, withdrawing her badge and tucking it away as she spoke. "We're looking for the Babylonian tablet your partner, Casey Pantel, showed to an archaeology professor at the College of William & Mary last Friday. Give us that and a statement of how you acquired it, and Neil and I will let you get back to work. Or, we can do it the hard way and look through every space and container in your office big enough to hold the tablet until we find it. The choice is yours."

"I understand completely," Steve replied, realizing he needed to play things straight. "We do have a tablet, although I can assure you, Special Agent Fields, we didn't know it was stolen. In fact, that was one of the reasons we took it to Professor Lindor. We were trying to make sure it wasn't stolen. If he'd gotten back to us and said it was, we would have contacted you right away. As far as I know, though, we haven't heard anything from him yet."

"I don't doubt that at all," Special Agent Fields explained. "And I'm glad you'll be cooperating. It's much easier on all of us."

Steve nodded and turned toward Marjorie, who was sitting with her chair rolled back from the desk so she could peer underneath. She had a perplexed look on her face that made his hands sweat before he even knew what she was concerned about.

"Marjorie, can you run to the bank to get the tablet out of our safe deposit box? I'm sure Special Agent Fields or her partner will want to go with you."

"Can I talk to you for a minute, Mr. Stilwell?" Marjorie's expression conveyed urgency.

Steve couldn't imagine what was bothering her. Retrieving the tablet seemed like such a simple request.

"Sure. Special Agent Fields, will you excuse us for a second?"

"I'm okay with you conferring," Special Agent Fields responded, "as long as you to stay in the lobby. I'm sure you understand."

"Of course," Steve answered. "Marjorie, how about we step over toward the waiting area."

Marjorie was already halfway around her desk by the time Steve finished speaking. As soon as they reached the chairs in the lobby, Marjorie moved up close to Steve and started wringing her hands, which she never did. She spoke quietly, but her voice carried and was filled with alarm.

"We've got a problem," she proclaimed.

"What is it?"

"The tablet's gone."

"I'm not sure I understand," Steve replied, unable to fathom how the tablet could be missing. "Casey told me yesterday she was going to ask you to put it in the safe deposit box."

"She did, and she gave it to me right after we all talked yesterday morning. I was going to the bank right after lunch."

Steve could see where this was heading, but he had no idea how it would end. Regardless, it spelled trouble with the FBI agents just a few feet away. They would search the entire office if he couldn't produce the tablet. He glanced over and saw them talking to one another. Fields had her back to him; Crosby was looking his way and talking quietly. Steve assumed Crosby was relaying to Fields what was going on between him and Marjorie, so he brushed back his suit coat and slipped his hands into his pockets to portray calm, hoping whatever Marjorie revealed was easy to fix.

"I'm guessing you didn't take it to the bank or we wouldn't be having this conversation," Steve offered.

"No, I actually did," Marjorie responded, "The bank was closed. Yesterday was Columbus Day."

"Oh, that's right. I completely forgot," Steve admitted. "What did you do?"

"I brought it back and hid it under my desk all the way in back where no one would see it. I thought for sure it would be safe there until I could take it to the bank this afternoon with our deposit."

"Phwew," Steve whiffed. "I was afraid you were going to say it was broken or something. If it was under your desk when you left last night, it has to still be there. Let's go back and take a good look. You probably just kicked it out of sight and didn't realize it."

Marjorie looked unconvinced. "I hope you're right Mr. Stilwell, but I sure didn't see it."

The two walked back behind Marjorie's desk with Steve in the lead. He grabbed Marjorie's chair and rolled it out of the way so he could look underneath.

"Well?" inquired Special Agent Fields.

"I'm sorry," Steve apologized. Since the truth was actually the easiest option to explain, he decided to just describe what happened. "After Casey Pantel learned from professor Lindor late last Friday that the tablet might be valuable, we were going to lock it in our safe deposit box yesterday. Unfortunately, the bank was closed for Columbus Day. So, we hid it under Marjorie's desk and it must have gotten pushed back out of sight. I just need to get down on the floor and find it."

"Great," replied Special Agent Fields, eyeing Crosby. "Thanks for making this easy."

"You bet," Steve answered. He braced himself with his right hand on Marjorie's desk and lowered himself to his knees, then bent down to see under the desk. Nothing—no box, no tablet, no nothing. There was still an area underneath the drawers on the right side where something could get lost. It didn't look anywhere big enough for the box with the tablet in it. Still, he got down on all fours and looked under the drawers—again, nothing. If the tablet had been there, it was gone now.

Steve struggled to his feet and brushed the dust from his knees, then wiped his hands together a couple times to get any latent dust off them, too. All the time, he was thinking about how to break the news to Special Agent Fields.

"You're not going to believe this," he announced. "The tablet's missing."

"Neil, why don't you double check for Mr. Stilwell, just in case?" Fields suggested.

"Of course," Crosby responded. "Mr. Stilwell, can I ask you and Marjorie to step around the desk so I can get back there?"

"You bet," Steve replied, knowing Crosby wouldn't find anything. Crosby lowered himself to the floor in much the same manner Steve had, emerging from underneath the desk a few seconds later.

"There's nothing there," Crosby confirmed.

"What could have happened to it, Mr. Stilwell?" Fields asked. "Does anyone else have access to your office after hours?"

"Maybe Casey came by and got it before she left for India," Marjorie suggested. "She had to leave for Washington, DC, early this morning to get her visa, so she could have come in before we opened this morning. Maybe she decided to take it with her for some reason."

"Did Casey know you weren't able to put the tablet in the safe deposit box?" Steve asked. He thought if Casey had known, she would have told him as soon as she found out. She also would have come up with an alternative to leaving the tablet on the floor underneath Marjorie's desk. She was too concerned with the tablet's safety.

"Come to think of it, no," Marjorie replied. "She'd already left the office yesterday so she could get everything together for her trip. I guess it couldn't have been her."

"What about Phan?" Steve offered.

"Who's Phan?" Special Agent Fields asked.

"Phan's the man that cleans our offices at night," Steve replied. "Marjorie, is there any chance he could have found the box when he was vacuuming under your desk and thought it was trash? Maybe he threw it out not knowing what it was."

"I suppose it's possible," Marjorie conjectured, "but I really doubt it. Since it wasn't near my trashcan, Phan would've looked inside the box and seen the tablet. He never would have thrown it away without asking." Marjorie paused and then finished her assessment. "It had to be someone else."

"Well," Steve concluded, "if it wasn't you and it wasn't me and Casey didn't know it was there, I think we have to consider Phan. I don't see any other options."

"I can give Phan a call at home and ask him," suggested Marjorie.

"Any objection to that, Special Agent Fields?" Steve asked.

"None, as long as we can listen to the call. I'm sure you can understand we have to be careful once we've announced the search."

"Of course," Steve responded. "Marjorie, go ahead and give Phan a call and use the speakerphone so Special Agent Fields can hear what Phan has to say."

Marjorie nodded and flipped the phone around on her desk so she could dial it from where she was standing. The phone rang only once before Phan's wife answered.

"Hello, Phan?" the young Vietnamese woman asked. She sounded distraught.

"No, hello Linh. It's Marjorie from Mr. Stilwell's office. Can I speak with Phan?"

"Phan not home." The young woman started to cry. "I very worried. Phan not come home this morning and he not call. I afraid something happen to him and I not know who to call." Steve could hear the woman sobbing.

"Don't worry, Linh," Steve reassured her, although he, too, was alarmed. He'd known Phan for four years and no one was more reliable. Phan would have called his wife if he wasn't going right home after work because nothing was more important to him than Linh and their daughter. Something had to be wrong, or at least out of the ordinary. This wasn't the time, though, to share his gut instinct. Besides, he had a search warrant to deal with, and with the tablet and Phan both missing, he knew Special Agent Fields might jump to mistaken conclusions. He had to seize control of the situation, starting with talking Phan's wife away from the ledge. "We'll find him and we'll have him call you right away. He probably just fell asleep somewhere after working a long night."

"Thank you, Steve. You call me right away?"

"I promise," Steve pledged. "Just stay by the phone and I'm sure I'll be calling you shortly."

"Okay," Linh answered. "I wait for call." She was no longer sobbing, but Steve could hear her trying to catch her breath in between sniffles.

"Thanks, Linh. I'll talk to you shortly," Steve repeated. "Goodbye." He hung up the speaker phone, hoping he could fulfill his promise. First, though, he had to deal with Fields and Crosby. They could very easily take the hardline approach and turn his office upside down looking for the tablet. He had to convince them that was not the right course of action. The right course meant finding Phan without implicating him in the loss of the tablet. He had a narrow strait to navigate.

"Let me see if I've got this right," Special Agent Fields began. "The tablet is missing and so is the only person who had access to it last night. It sounds to me like we've found our suspect."

"I wouldn't go there yet, especially labeling Phan a suspect," Steve cautioned. "I can't in my wildest dreams imagine Phan stealing the tablet. Even if he found it, he would have had no idea what it was or that it might be valuable. After all, Marjorie had it in a box underneath her desk, which wouldn't be where you would expect to find a priceless artifact."

Marjorie started to cry for the first time in the six years she'd been working with him. "I'm so sorry, Mr. Stilwell. I never thought anything like this would happen if I kept it there just for the night. I should have locked it up in the file room. It's all my fault."

"Marjorie, don't you worry at all—I promise it's not your fault. I'm the one who should have realized the tablet was valuable when we first saw it last Friday and come up with a security plan. You had no way of knowing. This one's completely on me." Hoping he'd at least stemmed Marjorie's tide for now, he returned his attention to Special Agent Fields. "And, back to Phan, I would trust him with anything. He saved my life in Vietnam—that's why he works with us. There's simply no way he stole the tablet."

"Well, if there's no other explanation for what might have happened, it sounds like we've got to search your office." Fields pressed her conclusion. "I mean, we know Marjorie had it yesterday and you've told us there is no way anyone took it. So, it has to be in the office then, doesn't it?"

"Wait a minute, ya'll," Marjorie commanded, the tears no longer flowing but her cheeks still moist despite her attempts to dab them dry. "I'll bet I know what happened. What if Phan found the tablet and recognized it as something valuable, so he put it someplace to keep it safe? That would explain why we can't find it."

"You're a genius, Marjorie!" Steve replied, hoping to reinforce her recovery. "That's got to be it, and that's just the kind of thing I can see Phan doing. All we need to do is find Phan."

"I appreciate that, Mr. Stilwell. I really do. But Special Agent Crosby and I have a search warrant to exercise, and unless Phan would have taken the tablet out of the office to keep it safe, what you're telling me is it must be here someplace. So how about we get started with our search and we'll see if you're right about Phan."

Fields had him and he knew it. There was no way Phan would have taken the tablet out of the office, so it either had to still be here, or there was another explanation. He reverted to his Navy days of advising warfighters needing split second legal advice and came up with one more option.

"Special Agent Fields, I really do appreciate your patience and willingness to work with us, but I need you to give me just two more hours."

"Why should I do that? You said yourself the tablet must be here." Although Fields sounded skeptical, the fact that she asked the question gave him hope she might be receptive to his request. He just had to convince her his way forward would get her what she came for.

"Because there is at least one more possibility, and it's even more realistic than Phan moving the tablet to a safe place. If my partner, Casey, realized after she went home yesterday that it was a bank holiday, she might have come back to the office last night to get the tablet and take it home to keep it safe. After all, she was the one who took it to the professor, so she knew how valuable it was. She was also the one who expressed concern about keeping it in the office. She would have known to look around Marjorie's desk for it."

"Alright, I'm listening," Fields replied, conveying to Steve he was nearing the goal line but hadn't scored yet.

"Give us a couple of hours so Marjorie can see if she can track down Casey and ask her if she took the tablet. While Marjorie's doing that, I'll see if I can locate Phan and we'll find out what he knows. If either of those options work, you'll get the tablet, and we'll avoid all the evidentiary issues associated with searching material protected by the attorney-client privilege. Those issues will tie us both up in court, so we'd both lose." To avoid ending on a negative note, he added, "Two hours, Special Agent Fields. That's all I'm asking for. If I can't tell you where the tablet is in two hours, you can search the office. All you will have lost is a little time."

Fields looked at Crosby. "You okay with giving him two hours?"

"It's your call," Crosby responded. "I'm good either way."

Fields looked back at Steve, crossed her arms and slid her left foot out in front of her, so her posture reflected the finality of what she was about to say. "Okay, Mr. Stilwell, you've got two hours under the following conditions. First, you close your office for the rest of the day and Special Agent Crosby stays with Marjorie so we keep control of the search scene. Second, I go anywhere you go. While I'm willing to work with you because I feel like you're telling the truth, I can't stick my neck out any farther than that."

"That's more than reasonable," Steve responded. "I promise you won't regret it." He turned to Marjorie and switched on his command mode. "Okay, Marjorie, we've got two hours. See if you can track down Casey and find out what she knows. While you're starting that, I'll head out to the parking lot to see if Phan's car's still there."

"You got it Mr. Stilwell," Marjorie responded, already starting to work her way back behind her desk. "I'll also reschedule your afternoon appointments and put a sign on the door letting people know the office is closed."

"Sounds like a plan, Marjorie." Steve turned toward Crosby, who he'd not paid much attention to until now. "Special Agent Crosby, if you need a cup of coffee, there's a fresh pot ready to go in the kitchen." Steve pointed down the hall to show Crosby where it was. "Otherwise, make yourself at home." Steve turned back toward Fields. "Okay, Special Agent Fields, how about we go across the street to see if a car's still there."

Fields looked over toward Crosby. "Are you all set?"

"I'm good," Crosby declared.

"Okay, Mr. Stilwell." Fields looked at her watch. "It's 1:22. I'll give you until 3:30. If we don't have the tablet in hand by then, Special Agent Crosby and I will do what we came here to do."

"Fair enough," Steve replied. "Let's go check on Phan's car." Steve headed for the door and Fields followed close behind. When he opened it, he saw two Williamsburg policemen he didn't recognize coming down the hall. His immediate thoughts were someone must have hit his car in the parking lot and this was going to cut into his two-hour FBI grace period. He could already hear the clock ticking away.

"Hello, officers," he said, stepping forward to greet them. "May I help you?"

"Are you by chance Steve Stilwell?" the lead officer asked.

"I am."

"Do you know a Mr. Cường?"

"I do, very well. We call him Phan. Phan's his first name. Why, is something the matter?" Steve's heart raced. He knew the two officers weren't there to give him good news.

"I'm afraid he's been shot."

"Oh, my dear God," Steve exclaimed, not believing what he was hearing. "Why in the world would someone shoot Phan? Please, tell me he's okay."

"Someone just found him in the field across the street and we're taking him to the hospital now. He's alive, but you better get to the hospital right away. He's hurt pretty bad."

"I'm on my way," Steve announced. "Has anyone told his wife?"

"No, but we've got a squad car heading to his apartment now."

"No—you've got to let me call her first. I promised I would as soon as I found out where he was. She's Vietnamese, you know, and she doesn't speak English very well. She'll panic if she hears this from a stranger. Let me call her and tell her a squad car's on the way to take her to the hospital."

"You better hurry up," the officer said. "The car will be there any minute."

"Okay, Steve said, reversing direction and hustling back into the lobby so Marjorie could place the call.

"Oh, there's one more thing you need to know," the officer stated, following Steve and Fields into the lobby.

"What's that?" Steve said, still rushing toward Marjorie's desk and the phone.

"Mr. Cường was conscious when we found him. He told us to tell his wife and daughter he loved them. Then he said one more thing."

"What was that?" Steve asked, this time stopping and turning around to face the officer because he sensed what the officer was about to say was important.

"He told us to find you and tell you he was sorry."

"Sorry for what?"

"We don't know," the officer said. "Those were the last words out of his mouth. Then he passed out and he's not regained consciousness. We're hoping you would know."

Deep down, Steve knew why Phan apologized. It could only be one thing. The question, though, was why?

19

3:44 p.m. on Tuesday, October 12, 2004
Williamsburg, Virginia

STEVE STUMBLED TOWARD HIS DESK FEELING like something inside him needed to rip its way out. He'd gone to the hospital right after learning of the shooting only to find Phan already in surgery with a bullet lodged in his lung. Linh arrived sometime after he did because she had to find someone to take care of her five-year-old daughter before she could come to the hospital. He tried to console her, knowing it was an impossible task. Her family was halfway around the globe in Vietnam, with only Phan to rely on in America. Now with Phan barely clinging to life, she had nowhere to turn and no one to trust. Casey would have known just what to do, but she was out of the picture on her way to India. Worse yet, Steve had to leave Linh alone at the hospital so he could deal with Special Agents Fields and Crosby still waiting to search his office.

Fields and Crosby proved more than gracious. They obviously believed Marjorie's story about the tablet because they conducted little more than a cursory search. In fact, they left Steve's and Casey's offices untouched, searching only the common areas and avoiding a potential battle involving attorney-client privileged material. They left their business cards with Marjorie and said they would check in with the Williamsburg Police to interview Phan if and when he was capable of talking. They also asked that Casey call them as soon as she reached her destination in India. Then they departed, leaving Steve and Marjorie to cope with the attempted murder of their friend.

Steve collapsed in one of the chairs facing his desk, unable to make it all the way to his own seat. He buried his face in his hands, overwhelmed by grief and guilt. Phan trusted him, yet he'd subjected Phan to extraordinary risk since the day they met. He felt like he'd failed Phan again by exposing him to danger, although he wasn't sure how it came about. Phan had somehow become involved with the tablet—that was the only plausible reason for Phan to apologize. He'd taken it from under Marjorie's desk and it had gotten him shot. Why? There was no way Phan knew what the tablet was. Hell, Steve himself didn't know, other than it was ancient and valuable.

Perhaps Phan needed money but was afraid or too proud to ask for it. That had to be it, which meant Steve hadn't paid enough attention to Phan's needs as a new immigrant coming to America. As with Sarah, he'd so entrenched himself in his work, and most recently in the Arul Ashirvadam case, that he'd sacrificed the people he loved. Now two people had potentially vanished from his life forever, yet he felt so emotionally detached he couldn't even cry. He slid his hands around to the back of his head and with his elbows out, bent forward at his waist and stretched his back. He added a deep breath to help pull himself together.

"Mr. Stilwell," a quiet Tidewater Virginia voice said from the direction of the door. "Are you okay?"

Steve sat up slowly and twisted around just enough to make eye contact with Marjorie, then turned his head away so he was speaking to a phantom listener sitting at his desk. "Not really, Marjorie," he admitted, not even trying to be strong. "Between Phan being shot and Sarah filing for divorce, I feel like life's got me on the ropes. You know what I mean?"

"I do, Mr. Stilwell, I really do." Marjorie slipped into the other chair in front of his desk. "When I went through my divorce, it felt like the walls were closing in on me. Even though I wanted to get out of the relationship, I was so embarrassed once it happened. I couldn't talk about it at all. I even felt physically sick for months. I eventually moved on, Mr. Stilwell. You will too. Things will get back to normal again, just like they did for me. It just takes time."

Steve nodded. "I'm sure you're right, Marjorie." He paused to take in what he'd just agreed to, then decided he wasn't ready for a probing conversation. Like the crew of a damaged aircraft, he needed to eject. "I guess I better head back to the hospital now. Linh is all alone and I don't want her by herself if the news isn't good. I shouldn't have left her in the first place."

"You had no choice, Mr. Stilwell. The FBI was waiting for you."

"Marjorie, you just summed up my whole problem. Whenever I choose work instead of someone I care about, I always say I have no choice. I think I have a choice and just make the wrong one."

"Don't be so hard on yourself. From what I've seen, you always do the best you can."

Although he knew Marjorie was just saying that to cheer him up, her words actually did revive him because part of him agreed with her assertion. At times he felt like he really did have no choice, or at least no good one, and today seemed like one of those times.

"Thanks, Marjorie. Now, I better get going to the hospital."

"I need to tell you one thing before you go," noted Marjorie.

"What's that?" Steve asked, hoping it wasn't more bad news.

Marjorie hesitated, and then crossed her arms across her chest. Now it was her turn for a deep breath, which she followed with an exaggerated exhale. "Okay, I don't know how to say this, so I'll just come out and say it. I think Phan took the tablet last night."

"I think so too, Marjorie." Steve put his hands on the arms of the chair as if he were preparing to stand up. "In fact, I'm sure of it."

"You are?"

"Uh huh." Steve pushed upward with his arms and stood up, sounding more confident now that he had a mission to accomplish. "No one else had access to the office last night. And, why else would Phan apologize?"

"That's what I thought, too. And, there's one other thing, Mr. Stilwell. I didn't even think about it until you asked me to get the tablet and I couldn't find it."

"What's that?"

Marjorie produced a yellow sticky note she'd sequestered in her hand. She stood up as she handed it to him, acting like he might recognize it.

"What's this?"

"It's a telephone number somebody wrote on a pad of yellow sticky notes sitting on my desk," answered Marjorie. "I didn't write it and it wasn't there when I left my office last night. I just assumed you left it on my desk by accident and I forgot to ask you about it this morning. When we couldn't find the box, I realized someone had been at my desk and written down the number. It had to be Phan, but I didn't want to say anything when the FBI was here because I didn't know for sure and I didn't want to get him in trouble."

Steve took the note. "You did the right thing, Marjorie. No sense speculating in front of the FBI." He looked at the number and brought the note closer to his eyes even though he could clearly read it at the original distance. "Wait a minute. I think this is the same number we found in the box with the tablet. Are you sure you didn't write it down yesterday?"

"I'm positive, Mr. Stilwell. That's not my handwriting."

Steve hustled to his desk and pulled his planner from his briefcase. He flipped to the notes he'd taken when he inspected Arul Ashirvadam's safe deposit box and poked his finger on something he'd written to emphasize his discovery. "I knew it," he declared.

"What? Did you write the number?"

"No," he said emphatically. "Remember how the number in the tablet's box matched one of the two numbers I found in Arul Ashirvadam's safe deposit box?"

"Is this the same number?"

"It sure is. Why in the world would Phan write down the number of somebody associated with Arul Ashirvadam?"

"Do you think he saw it in your planner and tried to call it?"

"I can't imagine that," Steve countered. "He had to have come across the number some other way."

"What if somebody with that number called when Phan was here last night and he wrote it down?"

"That's much more likely, although I don't get why someone would call here in the middle of the night. Common sense would tell them the office was closed."

"Unless they were calling Phan and they knew he'd be here."

"It still doesn't make sense, Marjorie. I don't see any way Phan can be connected with Ashirvadam's estate or the tablet. I just can't figure out what the angle might be."

"Why don't you just ask him when he's able to talk again?"

"That's exactly what I'll do." A slight smile emerged on Marjorie's face, which was just the reaction he'd hoped for. Marjorie brought a lot of insight to the daily workings of the office, so it was always nice to acknowledge her contribution, especially on a big case like this. He knew she appreciated it.

"You know what, though?" he continued. "What if the information is time sensitive and Phan can't talk for several days, or even weeks? I think I need to do something now."

"Please don't call that number, Mr. Stilwell. If it belongs to whoever shot Phan, he might come after you, too."

"Yeah, and I suppose I might mess up things for the FBI."

"Just give it to the FBI, Mr. Stilwell. I'll bet they can trace it and find out who it belongs to."

Marjorie was right, of course, except he wasn't ready to turn it over to the FBI and leave Phan at their mercy. They might try to deport him, or worse yet, prosecute him if he was somehow involved in the theft of the tablet. Although Special Agent Fields had given him no indication she would do such a thing, the case was still in its early stages and lots of things could change. Besides, Marjorie said something that gave him an idea. It was extremely risky—actually beyond extremely risky. What if he could get the tablet back and give it to the FBI in order to get Phan off the hook? Phan had risked his life for him before. Maybe now was the time to return the favor. Otherwise, he might end up looking back on this moment as another situation where he convinced himself he had no choice, when in reality, he'd just made the wrong one.

"I think I've got another plan, Marjorie, but I need a few minutes alone before I head back to the hospital."

"Sometimes I don't know why I even bother." Marjorie put her hands on her hips, looking disgusted. "You're calling that number, aren't you?"

"Actually, no, at least not yet. I do need to make a call, though, and do a little research."

"Alright," Marjorie began as she started for the door. "I'll be at my desk if you need anything." She looked back just as she was getting ready to close the door on her way out. "Don't say I didn't try to warn you, Mr. Stilwell. I've got a bad feeling about whatever you're about to do." Marjorie frowned, then closed the door behind her.

Steve grabbed his planner and reopened it to the page containing the two phone numbers he'd found in Ashirvadam's safe deposit box. He pulled out a notepad and wrote the date and time at the top, then copied the Italian phone number he was about to call. He looked at his watch—it was just after four o'clock. The chances of anyone answering at this hour in Italy were next to none, unless by chance it was a personal phone. After he dialed, the second-long beep repeating after a longer period of silence told him he'd at least dialed the number correctly. A male voice answered.

"Pronto."

"Yes, hello," Steve replied. Although he fully expected if someone answered they would do so in Italian, he still fumbled with how to respond. "Uhmm, I'm calling from the United States. May I ask who I'm speaking with?"

"It is late here and I do not know you. Do not call me again." The man hung up, but not soon enough. Steve had only spoken with one man from Italy recently and there was no mistaking it, this was the same man. The Italian phone number in Arul Ashirvadam's safe deposit box belonged to Giorgio Stassi, Michela Baresi's executive assistant.

Steve began to assess the implications. Why would Arul Ashirvadam keep Giorgio Stassi's telephone number in his safe deposit box? After all, Ashirvadam was having an affair with Michela Baresi. Surely, he had her number memorized. Besides, a sexual liaison didn't seem like the kind of thing Michela would rely on her executive assistant to arrange. The phone number had to represent a business connection, and an under-the-table one at that. Otherwise, any above-board transaction would be fully visible to La Fontana stockholders. No, this was meant to keep something under wraps, and that something had to be the tablet.

Although Steve felt comfortable with that conclusion, he knew it didn't add up. Michela wanted the tablet to promote La Fontana, which would be hard to do if she obtained it using ways that would not stand up to shareholder and public scrutiny. Either she was lying about why she wanted it or perhaps Giorgio was double-crossing her. Steve intended to confront them to find out, because if either of them directed or recruited Phan to steal the tablet and then had Phan shot, he would make them pay. First, he had to get the tablet back, or at least make them think he had the tablet, because without it, he had no leverage. They would likely not even see him if they already had what they wanted. That realization settled it—he would make the next call.

Steve picked up his briefcase and hustled to the door, grabbing his suit coat and wrestling to put it on as he rushed into the lobby. He hurried past Marjorie's desk without stopping.

"Sorry Marjorie, I've got to go. I'll see you tomorrow."

"Mr. Stilwell, did you call—"

Steve didn't hear her. He was already out the door and heading for his car. He had a rendezvous with a telephone booth at the Williamsburg Amtrak station.

20

4:22 p.m. on Tuesday, October 12, 2004
Williamsburg, Virginia

Steve pulled out his wallet and sorted through the cards, pictures and notes jammed into one of the two leather slots with openings at the fold line. He found a crumpled piece of paper he'd hastily torn from a notepad, the penciled number on one side smeared with age. He wasn't sure why he'd kept the number, or why he'd even written it down. He'd come into work one Saturday to catch up on some reading and there it was when he listened to his voicemail. As each word flowed from his phone's speaker, he felt the swirling sensation of anger and relief vying for control. Three times he listened to it, and three times he sat transfixed by what he heard. He never told anyone else he received it, nor was he allowed to. The message was intended solely for his ears.

The first time the message played, out of habit he grabbed a pencil and wrote down the number the caller gave—not the caller's name. He couldn't bring himself to do that, and no way could he call back. Just listening shot shivers down his spine. The right thing to do was to delete the message, shred the note, and forget the call ever happened. He'd made it most of the way, pushing the delete button and erasing the voicemail forever. He'd even crumpled the paper into a tiny ball and tossed it into the wastebasket under his desk. Something made him sift through the trash and retrieve it. Against his better judgment, he smoothed out the note's wrinkles, folded the paper in three overlapping sections, and tucked it into his wallet. He'd not looked at it for over two years—until now. He had no idea whether the number was even valid anymore, although he was about to find out. It was the only way to get the tablet back, leverage his bargaining position with Michela, and make the situation right for Phan.

Steve dug into his pocket and retrieved the prepaid phone card he normally kept in his car's glove compartment for emergencies. The card wasn't registered to anyone so his call would be anonymous, which was just what he wanted. Before dialing, he looked around to see if anyone might be able to overhear him. A few people milled around the platform, but as it was a warm, sunny day, no one loitered in the shady area behind the terminal where he stood or was paying attention to what he was doing. Satisfied, he picked up the receiver and dialed the number on the card, then entered the PIN. Finally, when the recorded operator's voice told him it was okay, he entered the number from the note. He re-folded the paper and stuck it back in his wallet while the phone rang, which in and of itself was a good sign. After five long rings, he prepared to hang up, but was startled when someone answered.

"Hello?"

Steve immediately recognized the voice as the one in the message on his answering machine. It sounded tired, as if just awakened.

"Wendy, it's Steve Stilwell." He wanted to say more but couldn't find the words. Everything seemed awkward. He didn't even feel like he could be friendly. This was the woman who'd set him up when he was trying to help a friend jailed in Vietnam on bogus drug charges. She pretended to be on his side, offering to help, insinuating her methods involved seduction and bribery. He'd turned her down, of course, including her flirtatious advances. That didn't stop her from surreptitiously photographing their interactions, always capturing her advances but never his rebuffs. When she showed the pictures to his wife in a last-ditch effort to blackmail him, his marriage disintegrated. She then had the nerve to ask him for help when the people she fronted turned against her, and he did. None of that mattered now—he had to get over it. She was the only one who could help him and he was running out of time.

"Steve Stilwell—well I'll be. To what do I owe this pleasure?" Any hint of exhaustion evaporated and reemerged as sarcasm.

"Listen, Wendy, I'm sorry I didn't call you back. I just couldn't. I guess I was still reeling from what you did to me. I've got to admit, though, I was ecstatic to hear you were okay. I figured that's what you were calling to tell me anyway. Was I right?"

"That sounds about right. Maybe there was a little more to it than that. I think I might have been feeling sorry for myself and was calling to get you to cheer me up, but I guess I got by on my own."

"I don't seem to recall you ever having any trouble with that, Wendy."

Steve caught himself smiling. He was glad Wendy couldn't see him.

"So, now that you're a big-shot lawyer, you can't call me Gallagher anymore? I think we went through that once—my friends call me Gallagher."

Steve laughed, "Come on, Wendy, you've got to have a new name by now. I'm sure you don't use Gallagher anymore, or even Wendy for that matter."

"Like I said before, Steve, my friends call me Gallagher. But I'm sure you didn't call just to talk about my name. What can I do for you?"

"What makes you think I want something?"

"When a man waits two years to call me back after I leave him a message, it means he wants something. So, let's have it, what do you need?"

Steve put his hand over the receiver and looked around again to make sure no one had moved in close enough to overhear what he was saying. Satisfied he was still alone, he continued. "I'm sure you must still have certain connections in the Company."

"You know I gave that up a long time ago, Steve. My Company days are long gone."

"Don't B.S. me, Gallagher. I need a simple piece of information and I need it fast."

"Much better, Steve. You're learning. When you want something, at least pretend we're friends. Now, tell me, why in the world would a high-powered lawyer like you be using back channel ways to get information? Something interesting must be going on. You want to let me in on the details?"

As Gallagher spoke, memories roared back into his brain. All of his discussions with Gallagher followed the same pattern—attack, flirt, parry. She was witty, unpredictable and challenging, and he enjoyed talking to her. He didn't have time for that now, though. He had a mission to accomplish and needed her help. He had to convince her, and that meant giving in to her just enough.

"Okay, but this has got to be quick. I'm working another big case—"

"—Of course you are," Gallagher interrupted sarcastically.

"Let me finish. I've got this case and it involves a piece of art. It was in our office and someone convinced Phan—you remember Phan, don't you?" Steve didn't wait for Gallagher to answer. "Someone got Phan to take it from our office and then shot him in the back. I need to find who did it."

"I'm really sorry to hear that, Steve. Is he going to be okay?"

"I'm not sure. It's touch and go right now."

"How can I help?

"Can you write a number down?"

"Let me get something to write with."

Steve heard Gallagher set down the receiver and what sounded like a drawer opening and closing.

"Okay."

Steve read the number from the piece of paper, then repeated it. "You got it?"

"I do. Now what do you want me to do with it?"

"I need to know exactly where the person with that phone number is by midnight tonight."

"Wait a minute, Steve. Something's not adding up. You're not telling me everything. Why don't you just call the police?" When Steve didn't answer, Gallagher continued. "You haven't crossed over to the dark side, have you?"

"Let's just say it's complicated." Steve thought for a minute about how much he should say. It was complicated, all right, and the less Gallagher knew the better. He decided to play his trump card up front. "We can go into that later. For now, I just need you to get me the information. You owe me, Gallagher, and you know it. I saved your life. You get me this and I'll call us even."

Gallagher didn't flinch. "Steve Stilwell, I'm impressed. Going right for the jugular. It looks like I must have rubbed off on you after all. You didn't use to be like that, you know. But, since it is good to hear your voice and you did call me Gallagher, I'll see what I can do."

Steve felt a swell of relief break across every inch of his being. "I really appreciate that, Gallagher. I really do." He thought for a second about the practical side of what he just arranged. "How will you get me the information?"

"Give me your cell phone number and I'll call you tonight if I get it."

"That works," he replied. He gave her his cell phone number, as well as the number to his house as a backup.

"Speaking of works, Steve, you do know how this works, don't you?"

"I'm not sure. What do you mean?" Gallagher had him worried.

"Information like this isn't free. There's always a price."

"I've already paid in spades," he protested. "Like I said, I saved your life. And let's not forget, you did cost me my marriage." He could feel his temperature rising. She struck a chord by insinuating he'd owe her for the information. He'd more than paid in advance for a simple phone geo-location.

Gallagher huffed loud enough for him to hear. "Do we have to go there again? That was so yesterday. Besides, the Company won't see it that way. They'll see it as them doing you a favor, and they'll expect one in return. They may not ask now, or this month, or even this year, but you can bet they'll ask, and you'll have to pay. You won't have a choice, and sometimes the price can be high. Are you sure you want to do that, Steve?"

Gallaher's question jarred him. He knew he'd be putting himself in danger if he went after Phan's assailant. What he hadn't thought about was the unknown. How could he possibly agree to such an open-ended deal with the CIA? What if they wanted him to throw a case, or do something that might get someone hurt? He could never pay those prices. Asserting that now, though, meant not getting the information he needed. He had to take his chances with the deal if he wanted to find whoever shot Phan and possibly get the tablet back.

"I take it your silence means you've changed your mind?" Gallagher asked.

"No, I haven't," Steve replied resolutely. "I'm in. I expect a call shortly after midnight."

"Well, okay then," Gallagher responded, sounding surprised. "I'm not sure what happened to the Steve Stilwell I met in Vietnam, but I like the one I'm talking to now. I'll see what I can do. Do me a favor, though?"

"What's that?"

"Don't embarrass me and not answer the phone when it rings." Steve imagined Gallagher smiling at him as she spoke, knowing she was reading his mind.

"Just make sure the phone rings," he countered.

"It's been nice talking to you again, Steve. When this is all over, you'll have to buy me a glass of wine and tell me what this is all about."

"Thanks Gallagher. I've actually enjoyed talking to you, too, and I really appreciate your help. Now I better get going. I'll talk to you later."

"Goodbye, Steve."

Steve hung up the payphone, noticing for the first time a train moving slowly toward the station from the west. He had to admit, despite all Gallagher had done, there was something magnetic about her. She was edgy and seductive, like the forbidden fruit. But she was already in the rearview mirror, and what lay ahead was a phone call at midnight. That didn't give him much time to prepare, so he started to head to his car. As he did, he thought again about the conversation he'd had a little while ago with Marjorie. This time, he wasn't blaming the fates leaving him no choice about ignoring the needs of a loved one. He did have a choice—he just hoped he was making the right one.

21

———— ∽ ————

2:52 a.m. on Wednesday, October 13, 2004
Outside of Lorton, Virginia

STEVE FELT LIKE A DETECTIVE IN a B movie pulling into the parking lot of the dilapidated motel along the northbound side of Route 1 in Northern Virginia. The neon sign at the roadway was mostly burned out, symbolic of the establishment's guests, but a flashing vacancy sign let anyone traveling this outdated stretch of highway know they had a place to stay if they dared. From the looks of the parking lot, few took the offer, with just two eighteen-wheelers and four or five cars scattered around. Steve stopped near the lobby and walked to the door, only to find it locked. A short distance to his left, an open window with bars across and a plume of cigarette smoke hovering nearby told him the motel was still open for business even at three on a Wednesday morning. He looked over his shoulder as he walked to the window, making sure he didn't become the target of some local ruffian waiting for someone like him to walk by.

"May I help you, honey?" a smoke-ravaged female voice asked through the open window. When Steve heard her, he hustled the last few steps until he stood in front of her nighttime perch.

"I hope so," he replied, leaning over so he could talk closer to the open part of the window. So much smoke engulfed him, he was sure this exposure alone would plant the seeds of lung cancer. The woman was deeply tanned and skinny, her sun-damaged flesh barely clinging to her bones. She wore a sleeveless top that made her arms look even more emaciated, and her wrinkled face and bleached-blond hair puffed high on her head made her look every bit of seventy. She eyed him up and down.

"I hope so too, honey." The woman smiled—not a joking type of smile. She took off her glasses and crushed the end of her cigarette in an ashtray graveyard where seven or eight lipstick-stained filters sat waiting for more to join. "How can I help you?"

"I'm supposed to meet someone here," he began, hoping Phan's attacker was still at the address Gallagher provided when she called back just after midnight.

"Of course, you are," she sneered. "And I suppose you want to know if she's checked in, don't you?"

Steve shook his head. "No, it's not like that at all. I'm meeting a man."

"What a waste," she said, again eyeing him up and down.

Steve shook his head more emphatically. "No, you don't understand. This is business."

"Look honey, you don't have to explain." The woman paused to tap another cigarette out of the pack, lock it between her lips, and inhale a drag as the end glowed fluorescent red. "There's eight guests here tonight. Just give me the name and I'll call him to let him know you're here."

Steve reached into his front pants pocket and pulled out his wallet. He held it off to the side so the woman couldn't see and pulled out a fifty-dollar bill. He stuck his wallet back into his pocket, set the cash on the counter, and slid it toward her. One of her sundried hands reached forward and picked up the bill. She curled it into a tube in the palm of her hand and waited to see what he had to say.

"Okay, let me level with you," he began. "I don't know the guy's name, so I'm gonna need your help identifying him. Do you have any men who checked in by themselves today? You can rule out truck drivers."

"If this is drugs, I got nothing to do with it." Now it was her turn to shake her head no. "Just ain't no way I can help you, honey." She didn't dismiss him though, so he knew he was still in play. A little more incentive needed to change hands. He pulled out his wallet again and put another fifty on the counter.

"Hit me again," the woman said, tapping her finger on the bill. She'd obviously gambled before and knew when she had a winning hand. Steve pushed another fifty onto the counter.

"Okay," he said. "I need some information. How many men checked in by themselves today and when?"

"Four," she replied. "One this afternoon and three this evening. I seen at least two of 'em taking women to their rooms, but I seen nothin' from the other two."

"Tell me about the guy who checked in this afternoon," Steve instructed, zeroing in on him because Phan had likely been shot the night before and the hotel was a little over two hours away. The man must have done something in the interim before checking in. He hoped it didn't involve parting with the missing tablet.

"He's a black guy I never seen before," she replied. "Said he'd been up all night and needed some sleep."

"That sounds like him," Steve concluded, lightly slapping his palm on the counter. "You remember anything else?"

"Come to think of it, his eyes looked puffy, like he got hit or something. I asked him about it, but he said he was okay."

"That's him," Steve declared, reasoning Phan must have scuffled with the man before he got shot. "What room's he in?"

The woman tapped on the counter. "Hit me again," she smiled, fully exploiting her advantage. Steve dropped another fifty on the counter.

"He's in room 101, all the way at the end," she said, pointing in the general direction. "Anything bad goes down and I call the cops. You got it, honey?"

Steve ignored the question. "Is that his car parked in front of the room?"

"That's it," she confirmed. "He said he wanted the corner room. Didn't say why and I didn't ask."

"Does the room have a back door?"

"Nope, just the front. One way in and one way out."

Steve put another fifty on the counter. "What's the chance I can talk you into giving me a key?"

"Zero," she said, pushing the money back toward him. "I got no part of whatever goes down with the guests. You wanna get into the room? Go knock on the door. Like I said, honey, if anything bad goes down, I'm calling the cops."

"Got it," Steve said, smiling. "I owe you one." The woman nodded and took another drag from her cigarette, giving him one last look.

"What a waste," she said, shaking her head. She drew back inside the night office and sat down in front of the television.

Steve trotted back to his car and drove with the lights off to where the man was parked just outside of room 101. He butted his car up tight behind the man's car, backing up on an angle so it looked like Steve's right rear bumper hit the man's trunk. Steve's plan was to lure the man out of his room by claiming he'd accidentally backed into his vehicle. The tactic also had the advantage of hemming the man's car in. There was no way the man could maneuver out of there to make a quick exit. He would have to plow through Steve's vehicle first.

With his car in the blocking position, Steve shut off the ignition and reached over to the passenger seat to grab a can of pepper spray and a handful of extra-long zip ties. He planned to subdue the man with the pepper spray when he came to the door, zip tie his hands and feet, and tell the motel clerk on the way out to have the police come and arrest him. Just in case the pepper spray wasn't enough, he pulled one of his sons' aluminum baseball bats from the backseat floor. He intended to prop it up next to the door so he could get to it if he needed to; otherwise, it would play no part in his plan. He also left the driver's door ajar in case he had to make a quick exit.

As he walked from his car with the pepper spray in one hand and the baseball bat in the other, fear and reality set in. He was about to use a can of pepper spray to try to incapacitate the man who'd shot Phan. If things didn't go right, he could be killed. That wasn't the crazy part. He was a lawyer and respected member of the Williamsburg bar. Of all people, he shouldn't be taking the law into his own hands. And, what if he had to swing the baseball bat and he seriously injured or killed the man? It would be hard to argue self-defense since he'd tracked the man down. He might also taint the case against Phan's assailant and then Phan would have no justice. The right thing to do was to call Special Agent Fields and tell her where the man was. She'd have the local police there in minutes. Sure, he'd lose the tablet forever and any leverage he might have over Michela—his life and Phan's case were more important. He felt a sense of relief pour over him, his conscience having saved him in the nick of time.

Steve walked back to his car, threw the baseball bat onto the rear seat floor, and hopped in. He tossed the pepper spray and zip ties onto the passenger seat, started the car, and grabbed his cell phone from the console in front of the stick shift. Fortunately, he'd stored Detective Fields' number after she came by to search his office, so he was able call her directly rather than having to go through 911. The phone began to ring.

SSSlllaaapppp! A man's palm slammed against the driver side window. Terrified and not sure what happened, Steve dropped his phone and gasped. He looked outside just in time to see the man pulling his car door open.

"Man, what the hell you doing backing into my car like that?"

Steve didn't try to answer. He shoved his foot on the clutch and got ready to escape. Then he saw a gym bag and the box he'd picked up at the Vienna post office sitting on the trunk of the man's vehicle. The man had brought the tablet to him.

Steve knew the right thing to do was drive away, but with a stick shift and the man holding his door open, his exit would be anything but swift. Then actions started flowing faster than thoughts as his survival instinct took over. In a coordinated motion, his foot let up on the clutch and he looked away from the man to the passenger seat. The man was yelling louder now, but Steve couldn't discern individual words. He grabbed the pepper spray, flipped around, and pushed the button until his finger hurt, spewing the noxious chemical irritant directly into the unsuspecting man's eyes. The man screamed and pulled back from Steve's car, rubbing his eyes and trying to grab his shirt to wipe them dry.

Steve pushed his door wide open and jumped out of his car. The box with the tablet was on the opposite side of the man's trunk, which meant he'd have to run around the front of his car to get it and then retrace his steps. By that time, he was afraid the man might clear his eyes enough to get a shot off, so he held the pepper spray under the man's face and gave him another blast of the caustic chemical from point blank range. The man screamed and flailed his arms to stop the attack, hitting Steve's wrist with such force that he dropped the can and it rolled under his car.

With his only means of subduing the man gone, Steve bolted around the front of his car. By the time he reached the box, he could see the man wiping his eyes with his t-shirt sleeves and spewing a profanity-laced diatribe that included a promise to kill Steve as soon as he could see. Steve grabbed the box and flew back around the car at light speed, hoping he wasn't jarring the three thousand-year-old artifact to the point of disintegration.

By the time he jumped into his seat and slammed the door, the man was standing upright, rubbing his eyes with his shirttail. Steve turned the key and jammed the clutch to the floor, shifted into first, and poured on the gas. His car leapt forward but mercifully didn't stall. He'd gained enough speed to shift to second just as he was getting ready to jet onto Route 1 when his back window exploded—the man was shooting at him! Steve ripped the stick shift through third and fourth gears as fast as he could, trying to get out of pistol range. By the time he passed a dry cleaner about two hundred yards down the road, he figured he was safe.

Although his heart was still racing and he was drenched in sweat, he could feel himself transitioning back from instinct to rational thought. With this new clarity taking hold, he realized he needed to check the box to confirm it contained the tablet. He glanced into the rearview mirror to make sure he could safely open the box. "No!" he exclaimed as he saw a car speeding out of the motel parking lot about a half-mile behind him. He couldn't believe it—the man was coming after him!

Normally he would have no trouble losing someone that far behind on a busy road like Route 1, but at 3:30 a.m., the highway was deserted. He scanned the road ahead to see his options and then looked in his mirror again and saw the car speeding toward him at twice his speed. He shoved the accelerator to the floor and looked for a way to lose his pursuer. He clipped past a forty-five mile-per-hour speed limit sign doing sixty and climbing, yet the car behind him was still closing.

He cursed his stupidity for having entertained the idea of confronting the man. Why hadn't he just called the police? He knew why, of course, but didn't have time to psychoanalyze his emotional shortcomings. Five hundred feet ahead, the traffic light turned yellow. He crushed the accelerator again and his car blew through the intersection with the light turning red and a fresh produce truck approaching from his right. The truck now had the green light and the right of way, although he didn't think that would matter to the man chasing him. He heard screeching brakes and dueling horns, but no crash.

With unidentified headlights again gaining on him from behind, he sped down Route 1 until he could turn left onto Lorton Road. He had to stop in the turning lane to let two oncoming cars pass, then he wedged between the second and third cars and sped down Lorton Road heading west until he came to an apartment complex he could turn into. Hoping he'd finally lost the man but not completely sure, he wove through the complex's lot until he found an open spot. He backed in so his shot-out window wouldn't be visible to someone driving by, grabbed the box from the passenger seat, and jogged across the lot to the woods.

This time he wouldn't be caught in his car like he had been at the motel. In fact, he had no intention of being caught at all, especially having lucked into the leverage he needed. The next steps were the International Investment Bank, a quick call to Marjorie, and a flight to Milan to confront Michela. Then he remembered he'd left his phone in the car and had actually dialed Special Agent Fields before the ordeal with the man began. He wondered what she'd heard and whether she still was listening. Perhaps she was even geo-locating his phone.

He lifted the lid and tilted the box until the golden glare from a nearby streetlight confirmed he had the tablet. He couldn't turn it over yet. That meant returning to his car, hanging up the phone, and changing locations. His conscience spoke to him in a familiar voice, one he'd heard at the train station the day before. "You're drifting to the dark side," it said. "Turn back before it's too late." He grinned at the thought of Gallagher chastising him, but then the smile disappeared. The warning hit too close to home.

22

⸺ ⁂ ⸺

12:49 p.m. on Thursday, October 14, 2004
Chennai, India

W ITH OCTOBER'S MONSOONAL RAINS GUSHING DOWN, Casey's cab
pulled under the awning at the security gate at Rani Ashirvadam's
mansion in the upper class Nungambakkam district of Chennai. She felt
more than exhausted—she felt condemned. She'd left Williamsburg on
Tuesday morning and driven to the Indian Embassy in Washington, DC, to
get an expedited visa for her trip. Then she'd boarded a flight at Dulles Airport
early Tuesday evening, making it to the gate by the skin of her teeth. She spent
the next twenty hours jammed into the middle rows of packed airplanes,
hiking between flights to change planes, and trying to catch a modicum of
sleep en route before arriving in Chennai at midnight on Wednesday.

Although getting off the plane felt like liberation day, it was merely the
first step. Yet to come were standing in line to go through immigration,
picking up her baggage, and hailing a taxi to take her to her hotel. By the time
she checked in, it was two a.m. on Thursday, but because of the eight-and-a-
half-hour time difference from Williamsburg, she couldn't sleep. Now, as she
prepared for the most important and challenging interview of her trusts and
estates career, she hoped she could summon her "A" game, at least until she
finished her visit. There would always be time for sleep later.

The South Indian cab driver with jet-black hair looked over his shoulder
after talking to the security guard. "I am sorry," the driver began. "The guard
said he cannot let cabs inside gate. He said maybe you come back when rain

stop."

Casey looked outside and it was raining hard, not a windy or driven rain, but a steady downpour. She knew Abijith was behind the order. He'd made it clear when she called him from her hotel to confirm the meeting that Mrs. Ashirvadam's schedule was tight. She knew if she left now, he'd say she'd missed her one o'clock appointment and Mrs. Ashirvadam was no longer available. She wouldn't let that happen with any client, and she especially did not intend to give Abijith the satisfaction of winning. Besides, after having her lower leg severed in a helicopter crash, getting wet in a monsoonal shower didn't seem that bad.

"Do you have an umbrella I can borrow?" Casey asked, pulling her wallet from her purse to pay the driver.

"I'm sorry, no. Maybe guard does. He must walk here every day."

"That's a wonderful idea," Casey responded. "Would you ask him?"

"Yes, of course." The driver did as requested and received a curt reply. "He said no."

"I don't believe him, do you?" Casey asked. The driver shook his head indicating he cast his lot with Casey.

"Please tell him I will give him ten U.S. dollars if he will let me use his umbrella. I promise I will bring it back."

The driver nodded and relayed the message to the security guard. This time the guard's response was not so curt.

"He said he has umbrella, but if his boss sees you give it back to him, he will get fired. If you pay him twenty U.S. dollars, he give you umbrella."

"Tell him he has a deal," Casey said, smiling with the satisfaction of having taken the first step to get around Abijith. She passed a twenty-dollar bill to the driver to give to the security guard, who in turn handed his black umbrella into the car. "Now, how much do I owe you?" she asked the driver.

The driver pointed at his meter. "Four-hundred eighty rupees."

"I haven't had the chance to change any of my dollars into rupees yet, so if I give you twenty U.S. dollars, will that cover the fair?"

"Yes, of course," the driver assured her. "I give you change in rupees."

"That's okay," Casey replied. "You helped me get the umbrella, so the rest is for you." She gave the driver a parting smile, then looked out the window one last time to mentally prepare for jumping into what she knew had to be a cool, drenching rain. She staged the umbrella next to the door, zipped her purse and briefcase closed, and pushed the door open. With a deep breath akin to that of a paratrooper jumping from a plane, she propelled herself outside and deployed her new umbrella. Partly sheltered from the rain, she reached back into the cab and grabbed her briefcase and purse, said goodbye to the driver, and shoved the car door closed with her prosthetic foot, the only part of her lower extremities that didn't already feel wet. She then set her sights on the long walk to the mansion's garden and front door, which she could see was already propped open with someone standing there to watch her approach.

Intent not to appear flustered, Casey made way her to the house at her usual pace. By the time she reached the garden made lush by the nonstop tropical rain, she could see an older man with gray hair she assumed was Abijith in a business suit waiting for her at the front door. She could tell by his scowl she'd won the first round simply by showing up on time and undeterred, albeit soaked from her thighs down. To complete her victory and avoid giving him even the slightest satisfaction, she refused to mention she was wet and uncomfortable.

"Miss Pantel, I presume?" Abijith asked as if it were possible she might be someone else.

"I'm pleased to meet you, Abijith," Casey said with a fleeting smile as she arrived on the columned porch. Out of the rain, she turned away and shook her umbrella before completing her introduction. She set the umbrella to the side of the door and reached out to shake Abijith's hand. She wanted him to feel the water running down her arm so he'd realize her very presence was an act of defiance.

"I'm pleased to meet you, as well," Abijith replied. Casey knew he was lying. His voice hadn't the slightest degree of warmth or sympathy for her miserable condition, nor did he offer her a towel to dry off. "As we discussed on the phone, Mrs. Ashirvadam's schedule is very tight today. I'm afraid she will only be able to speak with you for a few minutes. Please follow me to the sitting room where she will be joining you shortly. Oh, yes," he added condescendingly, "it is our custom to remove our shoes before entering the house. You may leave them on the mat by the door." Abijith started to turn to the left, away from a curved marble staircase at the end of the wide foyer, toward the sitting room.

"Abijith," Casey called out. "I'm afraid it can be very difficult for me to put my shoe back on, especially once it's wet."

"I don't understand," Abijith replied, turning back toward her. He showed little patience for her implied request for an exception to house rules.

"It's nice to know it's not that noticeable, Abijith, but you see, my right leg is prosthetic. She pulled up her pant leg to reveal a portion of the titanium shaft, then looked at Abijith and grinned. Abijith looked too socially horrified to smile back. With no way to reconcile custom and reality, he took the only option Casey left him.

"Yes, of course, Miss Casey—excuse me—Miss Pantel. We can make an exception for you under the circumstances." With his decision made, he continued where he left off, turning and escorting Casey to the sitting room.

"If you will wait here, Miss Pantel, I will tell Mrs. Ashirvadam you are here."

Casey nodded as Abijith's instructions didn't merit a response, especially since they did not include any invitation to sit down. She didn't know if it was because she was wet or because she was expected to remain standing until she could be introduced to her host. The wait did give her the chance to look around. The room was exquisitely furnished, which made Casey feel bad about walking on the hardwood floors and hand-woven rugs with her wet shoes. After all, it was Abijith she didn't care for, not Ashirvadam's widow.

She noticed a large oil painting of what she presumed was the family hanging on the wall opposite the foyer entrance to the room. Ashirvadam's wife immediately drew Casey's eyes. Standing behind her two sons in a shimmering gold sari with a hand on each of their shoulders, she perfectly balanced elegance and beauty with her role as her sons' mother and protector. Arul Ashirvadam, who looked to be much older than his wife, stood next to her with one arm around her and the other at his side, separated from his children. He wore a slight smile, as did the boys, but his wife looked like she posed with a purpose—one hidden from anyone who did not take the time to look and seek to understand.

"Hello, Miss Pantel. I'm so delighted to meet you."

Casey turned and saw a woman even more striking than her image in the painting coming across the room to meet her. Her ivory sari with an alternating blue and gold floral pattern accentuated her bronzed skin and pulled-back black hair, giving her a regal appearance. Abijith stayed in the background, but Casey could feel his watchful eye. She approached her host to greet her.

"Hello Mrs. Ashirvadam. Thank you for seeing me on such short notice and please accept my condolences for the loss of your husband. I know this must be a very difficult time." The two women shook hands, then Mrs. Ashirvadam stepped back and looked at Casey up and down. Casey felt self-conscious with her shoes on, now fearing she had committed a serious cultural faux-paux.

"Look at you, you are soaking wet." She turned to Abijith. "Why did we not escort Ms. Pantel from the front gate?" She turned back toward Casey without giving him the opportunity to explain. "I am so sorry Miss Pantel. I know you cannot be comfortable in those wet clothes and that is no way for us to talk." Before Casey could say anything, she turned again to Abijith. "Please, arrange for some tea and coffee while I take Miss Pantel to get some dry clothes."

"Of course," Abijith answered, exiting from the room to fulfill his charge.

Mrs. Ashirvadam held out her arm, showing the direction to the door leading from the room. "Please come with me, Miss Pantel." Casey started to head in that direction, with Mrs. Ashirvadam taking the lead when Casey reached her side.

"You're very kind, and I apologize for wearing my wet shoes in your house. Please forgive me as I don't want to appear rude."

"There is no need to apologize. Mr. Abijith mentioned you could not easily remove your shoe because of your foot. You need not worry about that anymore." She led Casey up the winding red marble staircase and continued as they climbed the last few stairs to the second floor. "I noticed we look to be about the same size. I am sure we can find a nice sari you will look very beautiful in, if you don't mind dressing like a woman from Chennai."

"I would like that very much, but I don't want to impose on you."

"It is no imposition at all. In fact, it is the least we can do after making you walk through the rain." Mrs. Ashirvadam escorted Casey into a huge master bedroom with an area for morning tea in front of large windows overlooking a tree-filled backyard. A young female attendant greeted them at the door and followed them into the room, which was meticulously arranged around a king-sized bed angled so its occupants could enjoy the view through the window.

"What colors do you like to wear?" Mrs. Ashirvadam asked.

"Whatever colors you think would look best will be fine for me. You are so beautifully dressed, I trust your fashion sense much more than I trust my own."

Mrs. Ashirvadam gave some instructions to her attendant in their native Tamil language and the young woman disappeared into a mammoth walk-in closet to find just the right garments. She returned moments later with a beige, ivory and muted orange cotton sari with a matching geometric patterned blouse. "That is exactly the one," Mrs. Ashirvadam remarked. "It's one of my favorites and it will look so pretty on you."

"You don't have to let me wear one of your favorite saris. Why don't you pick one you don't like so much?"

"Don't be silly. Of course you should wear this one. And, since you are sharing my clothes, now you must call me Rani." She smiled at Casey, making an offer of genuine friendship.

Casey returned the smile. "Only if you call me Casey."

"Then we have a deal, Casey, don't we?" Rani held out her hand so they could cement their new friendship with a handshake. "Since you probably have not worn too many saris before, if you step into the closet, my attendant will show you how to wear it. She will also take your wet clothes and dry them for you."

When Casey emerged from the closet, she was a different woman. Having shed the staid clothes of the Virginia bar, she now looked and felt more feminine. "This feels so comfortable and it's so pretty, I won't want to take it off," Casey commented.

"You won't have to. It's my gift to you for coming all the way to Chennai to talk to me."

"Rani, this is very kind of you, but you don't have to do that. I can give it back as soon as my clothes are dry."

"Nonsense." Rani emphasized her dismissal of the idea by shooing it away with a backhanded wave. "Of course you shall keep it. And, now that you are comfortable, we should get down to business. Why don't you join me by the window and we can talk. Mr. Abijith will not dare join us here and we can have an honest conversation." She turned to her assistant. "Please tell Mr. Abijith that I will be meeting with Miss Pantel in my room and to have the coffee and tea brought up. If he is angry, tell him too bad." She smiled at the attendant, "don't really tell him that." The attendant grinned and rhythmically wobbled her head in a unique Indian mannerism indicating she understood her instructions and left the room.

"So why is it that you thought it so important to talk to me in person, Casey?"

"That's an excellent place to start," Casey began. "As I'm sure you're aware, your husband asked my senior partner, Steve Stilwell, to be the executor of the portion of your husband's estate located in the United States. Mr. Stilwell is a very skilled attorney and well respected, and he was actually with your husband at the restaurant when he died. There are other executors for the portions of his estate in England and India, so Mr. Stilwell is responsible for identifying all of your husband's assets in the United States, paying off his liabilities, and then, according to your husband's will, putting all of the remaining assets into a trust for you and your children."

"I see," Rani replied, pulling her sari a little higher on her shoulder. "That is as my husband and I agreed. I assume, though, there must be more to it or you would not have come all of this way."

A woman from the kitchen staff entered the room with coffee, tea and biscuits. She set them down on the table between the two women and stood by waiting for further instructions.

"The coffee and tea are safe," Rani reassured Casey. "We make them with bottled water so they will not cause problems for your stomach. We know Americans visiting India are told not to drink the water, but you need not worry here."

"I would love some coffee," Casey responded, stretching the word love to emphasize her request. "I'm afraid the jet lag is starting to take its toll."

"You have made a wise choice, Casey. Indian coffee is very strong and tasty, and it will definitely keep you awake. In fact, I will join you and have a cup myself." The staff member looked to Rani who nodded slightly, giving her the clearance to pour the coffee.

"Thank you, this is very good," Rani informed the staff member. Taking that as her cue to leave, she bowed and departed. "You were just about to tell me the reason you felt obligated to come all the way to India to speak with me."

Casey finished taking a tiny sip of hot coffee that nearly burned her lips, then set the cup and saucer on the table. "Okay," she began tentatively, expecting this part of the conversation to be difficult. "Your husband sent our office a letter with some instructions. He first directed that his body be buried at St. Thomas Syro-Malabar Catholic Church in, and I'm sorry if I'm not pronouncing it correctly, Palayur. The letter says he discussed this with you and you might object."

"He is right about that, I'm afraid. How can his children visit his gravesite if it is in Palayur? We are in Chennai on the east coast. Palayur is in Kerala province on the west coast. For me, I do not care, but for my children, it is important he be buried here." Rani crossed her arms and straightened her back, setting down a non-negotiable marker. "I've already instructed the authorities in London to have his body returned to Chennai as soon as possible."

"Do you have any idea why he would want to be buried in Palayur?" Casey asked.

"Of course," Rani declared, her tone terse now that the conversation had shifted from pleasantries to her deceased husband. "He loved everything about St. Thomas the Apostle, having grown up attending San Thome Basilica here in Chennai. Both our families attended that church—that is how we met. I don't know if you are aware, but St. Thomas came to India and started the Christian church here. The first church he established is in Palayur on the west coast. He left there after about ten years and came to Chennai, where he was martyred. In fact, the Portuguese built the San Thome Basilica over his tomb. For all of us who go to Mass at the Basilica, St. Thomas is revered."

"That's really fascinating," Casey commented. "I wasn't aware."

"There's more, Casey. For Arul, St. Thomas was something even more special. He had a dream when he was a teenager St. Thomas would be his protector. Because of that dream, he believed St. Thomas watched over him and helped make him successful. For all of his life, he has prayed to St. Thomas for protection and in return, he has always been very generous with the church. He said when he died, he wanted to be buried at Palayur, where St. Thomas brought the faith to India. He felt like it was the ultimate act he could do to thank St. Thomas for his protection."

"Okay, that makes sense," Casey acknowledged, "and it may also answer the next question I was going to ask."

"I take it there is more in the letter?"

"There is," Casey responded, glancing around the room to see where she'd left her purse and briefcase. "While I can remember the name of the church in Palayur, I can't remember the name of the other church in Italy. Excuse me for a second as I've got some notes in my briefcase." Casey retrieved her briefcase and purse from just outside the closet and pulled out a spiral notebook and pen. She flipped to the first page where she'd written down the details from Arul Ashirvadam's letter for quick reference. Before she had a chance to announce the name of the church, Rani cut in.

"If the other church is in Italy, it's because of that woman."

"That doesn't sound good," Casey remarked, leaving room for Rani to fill in the details. It was too late to pull her foot off the landmine without causing an explosion, so she decided to by sympathetic and let Rani vent. Although it might be unpleasant if Rani saw her as her husband's agent, which in a way she was, an angry Rani might provide more useful information than a friendly but guarded Rani.

"I cannot even say her name. She owns a cosmetics company in Milan."

"Oh, no. I can see where this is going."

"I hate to say this, but she is a whore, Casey. There is no other name to call her but whore. If she lived in my country, my family would kill her."

"I'm so sorry, Rani. I didn't mean to open these wounds. I'm so sorry."

Rani stood up and gazed out the window. "It is not you, Casey. You are just doing your job. I blame that woman and Arul. They only thought of themselves. They didn't care who they hurt. Arul had two children who needed a father at home, not one who slept with other women around the world." Rani wiped tears away from under both eyes, but her voice remained strong. "I know guilt for these sins had to be part of the reason he killed himself. He knew I could never forgive him, and he could not have a divorce. He let his lust lock him in a cage. He took the only way out he could find." Rani turned back around, her eyes red and tear-filled. "I'm sorry, Casey, for acting this way. So much has happened and I'm having now to deal with my youngest son's sickness alone. I am so angry at Arul for all he has done. I don't even feel sadness with his death. I am just so angry about everything."

Rani's moist eyes turned to sobs, leaving Casey wondering what she should do. In America, she would hug the woman to console her, but she didn't know what was culturally appropriate in India. Thinking it better to err on the side of compassion, she rose out of her chair and embraced her. Rani broke down and cried in her arms, and Casey felt tears running down her own cheeks. She didn't move until Rani slowly released the embrace and took a step back. She managed to force a partial smile.

"I'm sure this was not what you intended, was it?" Rani asked, again wiping tears from her eyes.

"I'm not sure what I expected," Casey replied, sniffling. "But I knew this would be hard for you."

"Even with my anger toward Arul, it is harder than I thought it would be. Why don't we sit down and finish so we do not have to think about these things anymore."

"That sounds like a good plan," Casey replied, borrowing a phrase she'd picked up during her four years working with Steve.

"You were about to tell me about a church in Italy, I believe." The corners of Rani's lips edged up into an expression falling short of a grin, but signaling a willingness to move forward.

"Yes, that's right," Casey answered while consulting her notes. "It's the Cathedral of San Giovanni Battisti in Turin, Italy. The letter instructed us to give any money we found in your husband's safe deposit box to that cathedral. Do you have any idea why he might have wanted to do that?"

"You would have to ask that woman," Rani replied in a voice devoid of emotion. "I have no idea about the things he did in Italy. They are between Arul and her."

"Well, we found 100,000 euros in the box, which we cannot give to the church as your husband desired. Because his letter isn't part of his will, it has no legal affect. That means the money will go into the trust to be spent as the trustee directs. If you want to give effect to your husband's request, you'll have to ask the trustee to do so."

"And who is the trustee?"

"I'm afraid it's Bertrolli & Associates in Milan. It's a—"

"—Of course it is. Why wouldn't it be?" Rani pointed her finger at Casey, "God forgive me, but I do not want even a single rupee going to a church in Italy. I don't want the money, either. You can donate it to San Thome Basilica or give it to the poor in Chennai. I don't care. As long as I have a say in matters, nothing will go to anything in Italy. Now, is there any good news in the letter?"

"There actually is, Rani. When your husband ended the letter, he stated very clearly that you and your two children were very precious to him. He wanted everyone to know he loved his family."

"Those are just words from a deceitful man. I don't believe them, and neither should you."

Casey decided further questions would only undercut her newfound relationship with Rani and it would be best to end the conversation. She had what she'd come for, anyway, and she might need Rani's cooperation down the road.

"Well, that's all I've got to tell you about," Casey concluded. "Because you and your sons are the beneficiaries of the trust we are transferring your husband's U.S. holdings into, we will keep you informed of the progress with the estate. It's quite complex, though, so it will take time."

"I do not worry about such things, Casey. I must admit, Arul was a very skilled businessman, so I am well taken care of. He also gave me two wonderful boys. I love them with all of my heart, and as you can imagine, they are having a very difficult time. Especially the youngest one, who is battling leukemia and is not responding to treatment. I cannot lose him too, Casey. I will not let that happen. You understand, don't you?"

"I do, Rani. I do. You are a strong woman, which is just what your son needs. Would you mind letting me know every now and then how he is doing? I'll be thinking of you and your boys."

"Thank you, Casey. I will do that. Now, we should go back downstairs to find Mr. Abijith. I am sure he is seething mad now." Rani chuckled. "He is a cranky man, Casey, but he has always looked out for me like a daughter even though he was Arul's business manager. I do not know what I would do without him."

"Let's go see how mad he is then." Casey grinned. Although she didn't share Rani's enthusiasm for Abijith, Rani's praise made her think she had judged him too soon. After all, he was only doing his job. Perhaps once Rani had the chance to tell him about their conversation, he might become an ally in resolving the estate.

"Would you like to change into your clothes before you go? I don't want you to feel uncomfortable wearing a sari if you are not used to it."

"No, I have to admit, I love the way this feels. For at least a little while longer, I can shed those boring American lawyer clothes." Casey knew, though, as soon as she walked out the door and headed to her hotel, she'd revert to her legal role. That meant contacting Steve and letting him know what she'd found out, in particular with respect to Rani's veto of Arul Ashirvadam's burial instructions. She also wasn't sure where to go next or what angle of the case Steve might be working on. It was time to synch up their efforts.

23

12:53 p.m. on Thursday, October 14, 2004
Milan, Italy

STEVE HAD NO IDEA HOW BAD he looked. If he had, he wouldn't have been standing in the posh lobby of La Fontana Cosmetics demanding a meeting with Michela Baresi. Although he'd changed his clothes and shaved at Dulles Airport before boarding his multi-legged flight to Milan, it was now Thursday afternoon and he'd not showered for two days. The hair on the back of his head was all matted down from a fight with an unruly airline seat, and a lone gray eyebrow hair broke ranks from the others, protruding like a crossing gate long enough to keep waiting cars off railroad tracks. His khaki pants looked like he'd slept in them, which in fact he had, as did his button-down shirt. Only his blue sport coat and polished penny loafers looked fresh, but even they were out of place in this old world high fashion environment. Had his name not been Steve Stilwell, he would have been shown the door.

"Ms. Baresi's assistant is coming to get you," the receptionist promised. She looked like a La Fontana cover model, her makeup perfect in every respect. Her smile disarmed some of his anger.

"Ciao, Mr. Stilwell," he heard a familiar voice announce from somewhere behind him. He turned to see Giorgio Stassi reaching out to shake his hand. "It's good to see you again." Giorgio's face displayed little emotion, leading Steve to believe maybe it wasn't as good as Giorgio wanted him to believe.

"Thank you for seeing me," Steve responded, wrapping up his handshake and withdrawing his hands to his pants pockets. "I hope Ms. Baresi will understand, I've been on a plane all night, but it's imperative I see her."

Giorgio frowned and sucked in air through the corners of his mouth. "I'm afraid that won't be possible, Mr. Stilwell. Ms. Baresi has a full schedule this afternoon. I am sure you can appreciate as La Fontana's president, her schedule is booked weeks in advance." Giorgio shrugged his shoulders. "I'm afraid there is nothing I can do."

"Tell her I have what she is looking for," Steve directed, "and if she wants to hear about it, she needs to make room on her schedule this afternoon. Otherwise, she can read about it in the newspaper."

"Very well," Giorgio responded, conveying no indication what Steve said was significant. "May I tell her what it is?"

"She'll know," Steve answered, remembering Michela excused Giorgio before bringing up the tablet at their Williamsburg dinner. He began to casually look around the lobby for a place to sit, signaling his impatience with the conversation. Phan getting shot and twenty-four hours of international travel had seriously eroded his usual cheery disposition. Giorgio picked up the signal, nodded, and left via the way he arrived. Steve took a seat in one of the chairs he'd spotted and ran through exactly what he intended to say to Michela as soon as he saw her, which he had no doubt he would. She would not pass on what could be her final opportunity to obtain the tablet. Barely ten minutes went by before Giorgio reappeared. Steve stood up; he hated the power dynamic of talking up to Giorgio.

"Mr. Stilwell, I have good news. Ms. Baresi was able to shift her schedule and she can see you now. Please follow me."

"Thank you, Giorgio." This time it was Steve's turn to convey little emotion, making the gesture more perfunctory than genuine. He couldn't place it, but there was something about Giorgio that didn't sit well with him. His designer clothes and handsome looks had something to do with it as both made Steve feel unsophisticated, which indeed he was compared to Giorgio. It was more than that, though, and it emanated from Michela's dismissing Giorgio from the dinner table. Something told him Michela didn't fully trust Giorgio, her own executive assistant, and that perception tainted his impression of the man. It would be a difficult hurdle for Giorgio to overcome.

After a short ride to the third floor, the elevator doors opened to an expansive area of uncovered light hardwood floor. A receptionist even more striking than the one in the main lobby sat toward the back of the room, with La Fontana Cosmetics in raised cherry-red script on a glossy white wall directly behind her. She was talking on the phone when they arrived. Before they reached her desk, Michela emerged from an office to the receptionist's right.

"Steve," Michela said, the smile on her face evincing the first genuine welcome of the afternoon. "I am so glad to see you." She walked over and shook his hand, making the gesture even friendlier by adding her other hand and embracing his hand between hers.

"Thank you for adjusting your schedule to see me," Steve answered politely, withdrawing his hand from the greeting. "Giorgio said you are very busy today." His response was formal, not warm. After all, this was not a social visit. He suspected Michela was at least partially responsible for Phan's shooting. Not because she ordered it—he couldn't see that, but because her thug was the one who stole the tablet so she could sell more cosmetics. Just thinking about it roiled him.

"Why don't you come into my office, Steve? Giorgio says we have some things to talk about." Giorgio had stepped back from the conversation, but nodded when Michela mentioned his name. "You will excuse us, Giorgio, won't you?" she asked.

"Of course, Ms. Baresi." He nodded again and turned toward Steve. "Before I go, would you like some coffee, Mr. Stilwell? It may help you recover from your long flight."

"No thank you, I'm fine."

"Please, join me in my office," Michela repeated, this time retreating with an inviting smile and tilting her head in the direction he needed to follow. Once they were both inside her office, she closed the door and led him to a sitting area in front of her desk. She sat in one of the chairs and directed him to the couch. "You look like you need the sofa more than I do, Steve. You look very tired."

"I must admit, I am. It was a very long trip. So, why don't we get down to business while I'm still awake enough to talk."

"Very well," agreed Michela, sounding much more businesslike. "I understand from Giorgio you now have the tablet we discussed in Williamsburg." Michela sat all the way back in her chair and crossed her legs.

"I do, but I suspect you know that already, don't you?"

Michela looked surprised. "Why would I know that? You just told me."

"When we met over dinner, you said we must be frank with one another. Now it's my turn to be brutally honest."

Michela looked confused. "Of course. What is it you have to say?"

"We both know how much you want that tablet, Michela. You even told me Arul Ashirvadam had people out looking for it. I can only imagine now that he is dead, his people are your people."

Michela's face grew stern. "There is a difference between being honest and careless, Steve. I am afraid you are being careless. Arul was the collector, not me."

Steve didn't back down. "You said yourself you are an entrepreneur, and

La Fontana stood to profit if you could get the tablet."

"Legitimately, Steve. Legitimately. What good would it do me to have a stolen tablet? I could not use such a thing. It would be a liability."

Steve chuckled. "Come on, Michela. You don't expect me to believe that, do you? You had to know the tablet was smuggled from Iraq when you offered to buy it from Ashirvadam's estate if we found it." Steve looked directly into Michela's eyes. "And you knew very well we would find it, didn't you?"

"Let me ask you a question first, Steve. Why haven't you turned the tablet over to the police yet? As you say, you have to know that the tablet was smuggled out of Iraq." Michela stood and walked behind her desk, leaving Steve at the sofa. She turned before she sat down, looking deep into his eyes. "Is it because, at least for a while, you held out hope the tablet was not stolen? Or, are you holding it for some other reason? You need to ask yourself these questions, Steve Stilwell, before you accuse others of doing something wrong."

Michela adjusted the jacket to her suit and took a seat at her desk. It was Steve's turn to talk and she was waiting for his reply, but her probing questions hit hard. She was right. He hadn't initially called the police. What she didn't know was before he boarded the plane at Dulles, he'd called Marjorie and told her to inform Special Agent Fields the tablet was safe. He'd also instructed her to tell Special Agent Fields he'd hand it over to her as soon as he returned. He didn't have the tablet with him; he never would have cleared customs with it. Knowing that, he'd stopped by Security International Bank in Vienna, Virginia, on his way to Dulles Airport and locked the tablet in Ashirvadam's safe deposit box. He'd intentionally kept that information from Michela because he wanted to see how she'd react. So far, it was not as expected. He decided to put everything on the table.

"On Tuesday morning, someone stole the tablet from my office and shot a very close friend of mine."

Michela covered her mouth and gasped. Her reaction was spontaneous, not staged. For the first time, Steve doubted his own accusation. He had to remind himself Michela could still be behind the plot to get the tablet. Besides, if she wasn't, who was?

"Was your friend killed?"

"No, thank God. I called after I arrived in Milan to check on his condition and it looks like he'll recover. He was very lucky." Steve braced his hands on his knees and pushed his back into the sofa, releasing Phan-related tension for the first time. He fought to stem his emotions. He hoped Michela didn't notice.

"The man who shot him left him outside to die," he continued, "but someone found him and called an ambulance. He was barely alive. He came to America from Vietnam and has a wife and daughter he loves very much. I think he stayed alive for them."

"It sounds like a miracle," Michela commented softly.

"I think so, too," Steve added, his anger dissipating with Michela's compassion.

Michela stood up and walked back to the sitting area. Instead of taking one of the chairs, she sat down next to Steve and put her hand on his arm. "I am very sorry to hear about your friend, Steve. I can tell he means very much to you and I promise I had nothing to do with it. As much as I would love to have the tablet, I would not steal or kill for it." Her lips relaxed into something just shy of a smile, then she stood up and returned to her original seat across from him. "I would, however, pay a great deal of money for the tablet if I could buy it legitimately."

Steve still wasn't convinced, although he also wasn't as sure as he had been when he stood in the lobby demanding to see her. He felt jet lag kicking in, clouding whatever remaining concentration he had. He feared, though, if he broke off the conversation, he might not get another chance to talk with Michela. He had one more person he had to ask about.

"Thank you, Michela," he began. "I really appreciate your honesty and compassion. I hope you won't mind, though, if I ask a few more questions before I go."

"Of course," Michela responded. She looked at her watch. "I have a few more minutes before my next appointment. What is it you want to know?"

"I can't help but notice every time we talk about the tablet, you excuse Giorgio. Does he know about it?"

"Giorgio knows everything. Sometimes I think too much." Michela smiled. "A woman needs to have some secrets, wouldn't you agree?"

"I would, except I don't get it. If he knows everything, why do you ask him to leave when we talk about the tablet?"

"Shall I be frank again?"

"That's what you promised to do."

Michela hesitated, then proceeded even more slowly than usual, giving Steve the impression she was choosing her words carefully. She began with a faint grin. "Giorgio is very smart and very talented. He is also a beautiful young man, so I enjoy having him around." The smile disappeared. "He also knows who I have seen and when I have seen them, and perhaps that can be sensitive information. Do you understand?" Steve didn't respond, not knowing if he was supposed to and also not completely comprehending what she meant.

"You are so naïve, Steve. Maybe some of the men I have seen discretely were married, like Arul. Now do you understand?"

Steve half-nodded, indicating he was only partially there. "That explains why you keep Giorgio around, not why you excuse him when you talk about the tablet."

"Because I do not—." Two quick knocks on the door followed by Giorgio stepping inside her office interrupted Michela. Giorgio said something to her in Italian.

"Sì, sì, sì," she responded. "Steve, I must apologize. My next appointment is here. I'm afraid I cannot speak with you any longer." She turned her attention back to Giorgio. "Please, tell them I will be with them shortly."

"Very well," Giorgio responded. He slipped out of the office leaving the door open.

"Because I do not completely trust him with all things," Michela whispered. She returned to her full voice. "You must tell me where you are staying, so perhaps we can meet for dinner, or at least maybe a glass of wine afterwards."

Giorgio poked his head back in the office. Michela reacted before he had the chance to say anything. "Just one more minute, Giorgio." Giorgio nodded and disappeared again.

Steve hesitated to tell Michela where he was staying, yet for some reason he felt like it was the right thing to do. He knew as soon as his head cleared, he'd have more questions to ask her, especially about Giorgio. He might even want to tell her he'd found Giorgio's number in Arul Ashirvadam's safe deposit box. He decided to leave the channel open, plus, he enjoyed talking to Michela. She was self-assured and engaging. Even if he didn't learn anything more about Giorgio or the case, dinner or a glass of wine with Michela would be pleasant. He didn't notice Giorgio standing at the door when he spoke.

"I'm staying at the La Macrón," he responded. In fact, I'm heading there now to take a nap. It's been a long couple of days." He stepped toward Michela and shook her hand again. "Thank you again for seeing me, Michela. I really appreciate it."

"It was my pleasure, Steve." Again, she turned her attention to Giorgio. "Giorgio, please have one of our couriers take Mr. Stilwell to the La Macrón Hotel. Goodbye, Steve."

Steve headed out of the office, following Giorgio, who detoured once in the lobby to escort the next group of visitors into Michela's office. He returned moments later.

"Please be seated, Mr. Stilwell. I will have someone here shortly who can help you get to your hotel."

Steve sat in a waiting area to the left of the receptionist, who was still busy answering calls. Now he was really intrigued. Why didn't Michela trust Giorgio with conversations about the tablet, despite trusting him with the identities of her indiscretions? Something wasn't adding up. He hoped Michela would follow through with her offer to meet him for a glass of wine. Perhaps in the more informal setting, with a bottle of her favorite Barolo uncorked, she could be more forthcoming. For now, though, his most important mission was to get to La Macrón, check in with Marjorie about Phan and Casey, and get some sleep.

24

3:07 p.m. on Thursday, October 14, 2004
Chennai, India

CASEY FELT HER NAILS INVOLUNTARILY DIGGING into the seats of the vehicle Abijith tasked to take her back to her hotel. Although she'd flown Army helicopters into hotspots in northern Iraq and piloted countless missions where danger lurked everywhere, she could hardly bear to watch the driver weaving in and out of oncoming traffic to pass a horde of motorcycles and three-wheeled yellow auto-rickshaws moving too slowly for his liking. Other motorcycles crisscrossed all around them, some with a husband driving, two children tucked in behind him, and his wife riding sidesaddle in a sari teeming with primary colors. When Casey's driver missed a turn he needed to take across a divided road, then turned around and drove headfirst into three lanes of oncoming traffic to go back and take it, she almost got out of the car to walk the rest of the way. Since pedestrians on the side of the road looked even more exposed to danger, she decided to dig deeper into the leather and tough it out until they finally arrived at her hotel.

"Thanks for the ride," Casey said to the driver as she handed him a fresh new ten-dollar bill. "I'm sorry, but I haven't had the chance to get any rupees yet, so I hope American dollars are okay."

The driver smiled. "Oh, yes. Thank you very much." He jumped out of the car and opened her door for her.

"Goodbye," Casey said as she pulled her briefcase and purse from the car and headed for the boutique hotel's lobby. She waved and smiled at the young woman at the front desk who'd checked her in when she first arrived.

"Miss Casey," the young woman called out. "You look very nice in an Indian sari."

"Thanks," Casey replied, too tired to stop to talk or explain how she came to wear it. She could feel the jet lag gripping her with the relief she needed in the form of a nap just a few short stairs away. She trudged up to her first-floor room, unlocked the door, and flung herself on the bed in the cool breeze from the ceiling fan whirling over her head. She knew she should take off her new sari and crawl under the covers, but she couldn't muster the energy. Maybe after a couple of hours, but for now sleep was her first order of business.

Just as she was drifting off, she heard four hard knocks on her door. Not wanting the housekeeping staff to walk in on her laying on the bed, she dragged herself up and stumbled to the door. "I'm coming," she announced so they did not attempt to enter on their own.

With no peephole to see who was there, she stood with her hand on the doorknob until she could tell it was safe to open the door.

"Who's there?"

"It's Abijith, Miss Pantel. I need to speak with you."

Casey hesitated. She didn't like the idea of a man she barely knew coming to her hotel room. She was also surprised the hotel staff gave him her room number, but she chalked everything up to cultural differences. Given her very positive meeting with Rani, she decided to take the chance and open the door. When she did, she saw Abijith with another man she hadn't seen before standing behind him. Given that he had the same kind of white shirt on that her driver wore, she assumed he was Abijith's driver.

"Hello, Abijith. What can I do for you?"

"May we come in? There's something we need to talk about." Abijith had a serious look on his face, so whatever it was, Casey figured it wasn't good. Regardless, she didn't want them in her room—that was not a good precedent to set.

"Why don't we go down to the lobby, Abijith, and talk there. I don't feel comfortable conducting business in my room."

"I'm afraid you do not have a choice, Miss Pantel." Abijith thrust his right foot and right hand out to block any attempt by Casey to close the door. Then he flicked his head in the direction of the room, signaling to the man behind him it was time to enter.

"What the hell do you think you're doing?" Casey said forcefully as the man tried to push past her to get into the room. She reached out to shove him back, but he was much bigger and stronger and pushed her backwards, throwing her to the floor. Her survival instinct kicked in and she started to jump back up to get into a defensive position, but the man pushed her again even harder, this time whipping her head back and causing it to strike the corner of a half-wall jutting out at the end of the foyer. While all this was going on, Abijith entered the room and closed the door behind him.

"Stay where you are and listen to me," Abijith demanded.

"You better get your asses out of here now or I start screaming," Casey countered, making it clear they had not come close to subduing her.

"Let me remind you, Miss Pantel, you are in India. Do you think anyone will hear a foreign woman screaming? I can tell you, they will not."

"What is it you want?" she snarled.

"It is not what I want, Miss Pantel, it is what I demand. I must have respect. Did you think you were being clever by meeting with Mrs. Ashirvadam alone in her room, cutting me out of the discussion?"

Casey remained defiant. "That was your fault, Abijith, and you know it. You could have allowed my cab to come to the house."

"Don't be so impressed with yourself. Cabs are a security risk and you are not that important. I hate to tell you, but you were not worth the risk."

"You know as well as I do that Mrs. Ashirvadam invited me to her room. I would never have suggested that on my own."

"You should know our customs when you visit our country. Mrs. Ashirvadam was only being polite. She did not really want you to come to her room. You should have refused and held the meeting as planned. Now, I shall make sure you never meet her again."

"You do what you need to do, Abijith. I'm not going to try and argue with you." Casey could feel herself cooling down. She needn't be combative anymore. That reaction's purpose had run its course. Now it was time to de-escalate and get Abijith and his goon out of the room without suffering further injury.

"I'm glad you see it that way, because there is one more thing I must do." He barked some orders in Tamil and the man in the white shirt started looking around the room.

Recognizing something more was about to happen, Casey tried again to back the situation down. "Look, you've made your point. There's no need to draw this out. I have no intention of trying to see Mrs. Ashirvadam on this trip again."

The man in the white shirt stepped away from Casey and walked to her suitcase on the luggage rack. When he started to unzip it, Casey tried to stand up, but felt dizzy from hitting her head on the wall. She still managed to get up, but when the man started to come toward her, she took a few steps to the bed and sat down. She put her hand behind her head to feel if there was a bump, and there was. Her hair also felt sticky. When she brought her hand back around and looked at it, her fingers were covered with blood.

The man with the white shirt stopped a few feet from Casey but didn't touch her. He looked toward Abijith, who again gave him more directions in Tamil. With Casey watching, he returned to her suitcase, finished unzipping it, and dumped its contents onto the floor.

Casey reached for the phone on the nightstand, but the man in the white shirt saw her and grabbed the receiver from her hand. He shoved her back on the bed and ripped the wire out of the back of the phone.

"Don't be foolish," Abijith told her. "You are just prolonging what must be done." The man in the white shirt looked at Abijith, who nodded at him. He scanned the room until he saw where Casey had set down her briefcase and purse before she plopped on the bed to take her nap. He poured the contents of both onto the floor, then trod with his leather sandals on everything that would break. When he saw Casey's passport, he picked it up and gave it to Abijith.

"I want you to remember this day. All I can say is I hope your discussion with Mrs. Ashirvadam was worth it." He opened the passport and ripped the pages from the cover, then tore the pages again and again until they fell from his hands like snowflakes. He cast the remnants and the passport cover to the floor.

"Goodbye, Miss Pantel. Next time you should be more careful about opening your door in a foreign country. Do not attempt to call the police. I think you will find the hotel staff never saw anyone come to your room. You see, they must live here after you leave."

Abijith flicked his head in the direction of the door, signaling to the man in the white shirt it was time to go. When the man reached the door, he held it open for Abijith, who left without saying more. The man turned for one last look at his handiwork and chuckled. Then he pulled the door closed behind him, leaving Casey to deal with the aftermath.

Casey picked herself up off the bed and slowly stood up, making sure she wasn't too dizzy to walk. Confident she could make it, she navigated to the door and secured it with the deadbolt. Although it was too late to matter, hearing the lock engage gave her at least a minor measure of comfort. Her main concern now was making sure she didn't need to go to the hospital to get stitches. She took a few tentative steps to the bathroom and tried to use the adjustable makeup mirror attached to the wall to inspect the cut, but it was a little to the left of center on the back of her head and she couldn't get the mirror in the right place to check it out. Her only option was to call the front desk, and then there would be questions for which she would need answers.

As she walked out of the bathroom to make the call, she remembered the man in the white shirt ripped the wire out of the back of the phone. She looked at it to see if it would still work, but the wires were completely torn away from the connector. Now she'd have to go to the front desk to ask for help, yet she wasn't thrilled with the thought of leaving her room so soon after her attackers departed. Even more concerning, though, was having a possible open head-wound in a tropical environment, so she grabbed her key from the nightstand and made her way out the door. Two short flights of stairs and a quick jaunt further and she stood at the front desk where the young woman who complemented her sari sorted through paperwork.

"Hello Miss Casey," the young woman said, smiling. "May I help you."

"You can," Casey said, trying to appear as cheerful as possible. "I fell in my room and hit the back of my head. I can tell it's bleeding, but I can't tell how badly it's cut. Could you take a look and tell me if I might need stitches?"

The woman looked more closely at Casey and noticed the blood on her hand. "Oh my, Miss Casey," she said, jumping out of her chair. "Please sit down and I will call the hotel doctor."

Casey took the woman's suggestion as the back of her head throbbed. "That may not be necessary if it's not too bad. It might just be a small scratch."

"Let me take a look." The woman walked behind Casey and pulled apart her hair to reveal Casey's scalp. Casey felt her hair tug on the cut and it made her wince. "Ooh, Miss Casey, we need to call the doctor. He will come right to your room so you won't have to go to the hospital unless he says it's necessary."

"That sounds like a good idea," Casey admitted. She put her elbows on her knees and rested her chin in her cupped hands. She just wanted to lay down for a nap and wake up to find this had all been a bad dream. "I tell you what," she said, lifting her head just enough so she could do more than mumble through her fingers. "Would you mind helping me back to my room? If I walk alone, I'm afraid I might fall again."

"Of course, Miss Casey. Let me call the doctor first and get someone to come to the front desk for me, and I will take you to your room so you can lay down." The young woman opened the desk drawer next to Casey and pulled out a thin three-ring binder. She flipped through a few of the well-worn pages until she found the number for the hotel doctor and then rang him up. She spoke in Tamil, but Casey sensed the urgency in her voice, which was both comforting and alarming. After the doctor, the young woman made one more call and a young man arrived to work the front desk while she escorted Casey to her room.

"Do you feel well enough to go, Miss Casey? If not, you can wait here for the doctor."

"I can make it," Casey replied, not knowing if it was true. She held the young woman's arm and they retraced Casey's steps to her room, where the young woman took Casey's key and unlocked the door.

"Oh, Miss Casey, what has happened to your room? Your belongings are all over the floor." Casey didn't respond, instead walking slowly under her own power toward the bed. Without the adrenaline of the confrontation, her head pounded with every pulse of blood through her veins. The young woman persisted.

"The two men who came to your room did this, didn't they Miss Casey?" Casey still didn't answer, she just sat on the bed.

"Can you get me a towel to put under my head until the doctor comes?" I don't want to get any blood on the bed."

"Of course." The young woman scurried to the bathroom and returned with an unused bath towel, which she folded in half and then covered the pillow at the head of the bed. "You can lay down now, Miss Casey. I will stay with you until the doctor comes."

"Thank you so much," Casey replied, drawing her feet up on the bed and resting her pounding head on the pillow. Lying down finally brought a measure of relief.

"The two men who came to your room did this—there is no other way for this to happen. I am so sorry for letting them come to your room. They said they were business associates and needed to tell you something important. This is my fault."

Casey managed to string together a few more groggy words as sleep became irresistible. "It was not your fault at all and—and I appreciate you helping me."

"I will call the police, Miss Casey. We must tell them what happened."

The woman's suggestion momentarily brought light back to Casey's eyes. She tried to sit up but couldn't. "No, you mustn't do that." She gripped the woman's wrist and held it tightly. "Promise me you won't do that."

"I promise, Miss Casey. I promise."

Casey felt her hand slip free. She didn't have the strength to pull it back to the bed. She just wanted to sleep.

25

8:26 p.m. on Thursday, October 14, 2004
Milan, Italy

STEVE PAID THE DRIVER AND GOT out of the cab in front of Michela's flat in Milan's Moscova district. It looked unassuming at first—a single section of a street-long row of four-story apartments. The entrance was inside an archway located just off the sidewalk on the right side of the street. A passerby would never suspect that one of Italy's richest women lived inside.

Steve tried to pretend this was just a follow-on business meeting, but he was actually looking forward to seeing Michela. He'd missed her call because he'd fallen asleep after instructing the front desk he was not to be disturbed. When he woke up two hours later and rang the front desk to remove the restriction, they told he had a message from Michela Baresi inviting him to join her for dinner at eight thirty. She left instructions to meet her at her flat, where they could walk to a restaurant and continue their conversation of earlier in the day over a glass of wine.

He felt guilty, of course. Sarah had only filed for divorce on Monday and he was already thinking about another woman. He wasn't trying to think about her; it was just happening. Michela was brilliant, self-assured, and beautiful by any man's standards, so he rationalized feeling an attraction toward her was only natural. Yet this felt like more than a passing fancy. He wanted to talk to her and learn more about her. He realized she was out of his league in terms of age, sophistication, and wealth; even that didn't stem his enthusiasm. After all, she had asked him to join her, albeit under the pretense of a business discussion. Although it would never get beyond that—it couldn't because he represented Arul Ashirvadam's estate—he still felt nervous about ringing the doorbell and saying the right thing. It had been too many years since he'd had to think about such things.

He entered the archway and checked his watch; it was eight thirty sharp. He pushed a button to the right of the door, not sure whether it was a doorbell or a something that activated an intercom. Either way, it worked, as Michela cracked the door open a few moments later.

"Hello, Steve." She smiled and opened the door the rest of the way so he could see the expansive room behind her. Instead, his eyes were on her. She looked incredible, with her hair up and wearing a loose fitting olive drab top and jeans. He hoped he wouldn't say something stupid. She continued with her welcome before he had the chance to find out. "I'm so glad you got my message. This time I summoned you on short notice. I think that makes us even, does it not?"

"I'm glad you did, Michela. I'd fallen asleep and if you hadn't called, I would have skipped dinner. You saved my evening."

"Good then," she said. "Look how I am being a bad host. Please come in. There is someone here you need to meet."

"I'd love to," he replied, hoping he wasn't sounding too eager. He was also getting hungry, so he hoped the introduction wouldn't run long. He hadn't had anything to eat since the flight from Dulles to Rome, and he needed to get something in his stomach.

Michela led him into her flat, through the foyer and the formal living room, and around the corner to a bar. A man in a gray suit stood with his back to them, holding what Steve surmised in these surroundings had to be a gin and tonic. He thought it odd the man didn't turn around. Michela's heels on the tile floor left no doubt of their approach. Steve assumed the man must be of such a stature that he wouldn't turn before everyone else was in place, much like Michela waited for him to be seated in Williamsburg before joining him at the table. Michela did nothing to end the suspense, making no announcement or introduction.

"May I get you something to drink, Steve?"

"Yes, that would be nice," he replied, so focused on the salt and pepper hair of Michela's other guest that his words stumbled out as if not connected. "I'll—I'll have whatever he's drinking." He couldn't understand why Michela was acting as if the other man wasn't there.

"A very good choice," the man said with a voice Steve had heard before but couldn't place because it lacked context. The man started to turn, slowly revealing his facial features.

"I'm sorry, I don't believe we've met," Steve began.

"Such a short memory," the man continued, his English accent finally triggering Steve's recognition. Steve couldn't understand how this could be. He looked at Michela, but she paid him no attention as she mixed his gin and tonic.

"Detective Cavendish?"

"You do remember," Cavendish declared. "Indeed."

"Why are you here?" Steve uttered.

Cavendish took another sip of his drink. "Perhaps you should ask your host, Mr. Stilwell."

Steve again looked at Michela, who was now handing him his drink. "Here you go, Steve. Now I will join you with a glass of wine. The drinks will make everything better, don't you think?"

"I don't know what to think, Michela. Why is Detective Cavendish here?"

"It is very simple, no? When you told Giorgio you had the tablet, I called Detective Cavendish while you waited in the lobby. He thought it would be a good idea to talk to you in person, so I asked you to dinner and he flew here to meet with you. Now that we are together, we can talk about something we all find very interesting—"

"—the tablet," Steve asserted.

"Very perceptive, Mr. Stilwell," Cavendish began. "I must say, I would not have picked you as someone who trafficked in stolen artifacts. You seemed too naïve for that. Very good on you, though; I am not often wrong about people."

"Wait a minute," Steve barked. "Who said anything about trafficking in stolen artifacts? I've done nothing of the sort."

"Of course you haven't," Cavendish remarked snidely. "Let's look at things from my perspective, shall we? I am certain I mentioned to you on the night Arul Ashirvadam died that he was suspected of dealing in stolen artifacts. Yet when you recover one, you don't inform me. Instead, you liaise with Ms. Baresi to arrange a possible illicit sale. That doesn't sound very innocent now, does it, Mr. Stilwell?"

"Is that what you think?" Steve felt his face turning red with anger. "That couldn't be further from the truth. I came here because someone shot and nearly killed one of my closest friends, and I thought Michela had something to do with it."

"So, you dangled the tablet in front of her as an enticement?"

"I had no choice," Steve asserted, citing his favorite excuse. "Besides, the FBI knows I've got the tablet. I had my office report it to the Special Agent working the case. We told the FBI I'd deliver it to them as soon as I return to the States."

Michela looked downcast as a frown spread across her face. "You came here to lie to me, Steve?" She slid onto a barstool and sipped her wine, waiting for him to answer.

"No," Steve began, looking for the words to explain his motives without further indicting himself. Twenty minutes ago, he was excited to talk to Michela and now he was on the verge of alienating her forever. "I came here to find out the truth about what is going on." He opted to keep the final arrow in his quiver, that Michela had lied to him about the purpose of this evening's meeting, in case he needed it later.

Cavendish walked around the bar and refilled his glass with gin and ice, leaving the tonic aside. He took a sip without wincing and set the glass on the bar next to Michela. "Something you said intrigued me, Mr. Stilwell. You said you notified the FBI. I assume you didn't do it out of the goodness of your heart."

"I have no obligation to notify you, Detective Cavendish, if that's what you're getting at." Steve went out of his way to sound indignant. "If you must know, I came across the tablet during the course of representing my client. When I had sufficient reason to believe the tablet was stolen, I notified the FBI. It's that simple."

Steve stepped forward and thumped his glass on the bar, putting an exclamation point on his explanation. He also had no intention of touching his drink again. If his previous interaction with Cavendish at Scotland Yard had taught him anything, it was that Cavendish was a savvy interrogator. Steve needed his full wits about him to avoid being backed into a corner, even though he had nothing to hide.

"Spoken like a true lawyer," Cavendish remarked, "except I think you must be leaving something out."

"Why do you say that?" Steve asked.

"Because you are very calculating, Mr. Stilwell. You don't do anything without thinking it through and considering all of the ramifications." Cavendish backed away from the bar, leaving his drink on the counter. "Even this conversation is deliberate, isn't it? You've not said a single word you haven't carefully selected, have you?"

"I suppose the same goes for you, Detective Cavendish, doesn't it?"

"Touché," Michela remarked, following her jab with a slow sip of wine. She looked Steve in the eyes for the first time, confusing him as to whose side she was on, if indeed she was taking sides.

"I won't argue with that," countered Cavendish. "I also won't be distracted. Let's be honest with one another. You told the FBI you had the tablet because you had to, not because you wanted to. Otherwise, you would have held onto the information to exploit it, just like you tried to do with Ms. Baresi. I'm right on that, aren't I?"

"Look, Detective, you obviously didn't fly here from London at Ms.

Baresi's whim. You don't even have law enforcement jurisdiction in Italy, so there's nothing you can do unless you call the Italian police, which you have obviously chosen not to do. So, what is it you want from me?"

"It's quite simple, Mr. Stilwell. I want you to leave Italy immediately. You're poking your nose where it doesn't belong."

"Now you're the one who's leaving something out, Detective. Why in the world would you want me to leave?"

"This is a law enforcement matter, Mr. Stilwell. I'm sure you're quite aware of that."

"Of course, it's a law enforcement matter. That's not good enough. Someone stole the tablet from my office and left my friend for dead in a field. I will do everything in my power to find out who did it and make sure they're held accountable."

"I'm afraid that's not your job, now is it, Mr. Stilwell?"

"Then give me something, detective. Give me something that lets me know you're closing in on whoever is responsible. Surely you can do that."

Cavendish retrieved his gin, then drained it in one long swig, leaving only the ice behind. He returned the glass to the bar and walked closer to Steve, close enough that he could talk quietly and still be heard. "Very well, Mr. Stilwell, but I want your commitment to leave Italy tomorrow. If you won't, you will leave me no choice but to notify the Carabinieri."

"I'll leave tomorrow," Steve promised, since he'd planned on doing so anyway. He slid backwards to increase the space between him and Cavendish. He hated people invading his space. Michela remained seated at the bar, continuing to sip her wine, as if the entire conversation was irrelevant. Steve wondered how she'd become Cavendish's middleman.

"Very well, then." Cavendish rubbed his chin like Steve's dad used to do when they played chess and he was plotting his next moves. "You will recall when we first met, I indicated there were things I was not prepared to talk about."

"Actually, I do," Steve responded. "I got the sense I was being summarily dismissed."

Cavendish snickered. "You were, in fact. What I said was true, of course. The black market for these antiquities has become quite sophisticated, particularly in London."

"Are you telling me Al Qaida's involved?"

"That's what we suspected at first. It turns out there's no evidence of Al Qaida in this case. There's someone or something else behind it, and that's what we are trying to track down."

"Then why does it matter if I'm here? I can't be interfering in anything."

Cavendish looked Steve in the eye and said nothing.

"Wait a minute," Steve said, pointing his index finger upward to emphasize his epiphany. He looked at Michela. "It's Giorgio, isn't it? That's why you're involved, and that's why you always send Giorgio away when you want to discuss the tablet."

"This is between you and Detective Cavendish," Michela responded.

"That's got to be it," Steve reiterated. "That also explains why I found Giorgio's cell phone number in Arul Ashirvadam's safe deposit box. He was working directly with Giorgio, wasn't he?"

Michela looked surprised. "How can that be? Arul would not go behind my back to talk to Giorgio. You must be mistaken."

"I'm afraid it's no mistake, Michela. I called the number before I left Virginia and Giorgio answered."

"What did you say to him?" Cavendish asked.

"I don't recall exactly, other than I was calling from the United States and I asked him who he was. He told me not to call again and hung up. I recognized him, but I don't think he recognized me."

"Now I'm concerned," Cavendish remarked. "If he recognized you, he's going to wonder how you got his number, and if he didn't recognize you, he might become suspicious."

"I don't know if I can keep doing this," Michela announced. "I am very close to Giorgio. If I know too much, he will see it in me."

Steve wanted to ask if they were lovers; he assumed they were. Perhaps this was more than sex to her this time, unlike Arul Ashirvadam had been. Michela's relationships seemed complex and intertwined, yet somehow devoid of emotional substance.

"You must continue to work with us, Michela, you know that," Cavendish declared. "You're in too deep to back out now."

"How did you become involved?" Steve asked.

"We will need to save that discussion for another day, won't we, Mr. Stilwell," Cavendish remarked. "I do have one question, though. I believe I heard you say you informed the FBI agent working the case that you have the tablet. What case were you referring to?"

"To be honest, I'm not sure," Steve admitted. "All I know is two FBI agents from the Art Crime Team had a search warrant for the tablet. I would have given it to them, except someone stole it from my office and shot the man who cleans our building at night. I promised to contact the agents if I found it, which I've now done."

"Interesting," Cavendish responded. "And how did you recover the tablet?"

Steve grinned. "I guess we'll need to discuss that another day, Detective Cavendish, won't we?"

Cavendish flashed the trace of a smile, then quickly regained his stoic composure. "I'll reach out to the FBI today," he began, "and I hope you will continue to cooperate once I connect with them."

Steve nodded. "As long as I can do so ethically, you have my word. In fact, I've brought something with me that you might find interesting."

"I thought you didn't have the tablet with you," interjected Michela.

"I don't. But I do have the next best thing—35mm photographs. Perhaps it would further the case if we knew what the tablet said. I'm told it's an ancient map of Babylon and that it's extremely valuable."

"Like the Sippar tablet?" Cavendish asked.

"Precisely," Steve responded, surprised Cavendish knew what it was. "How did you know?"

"I marveled at the Sippar tablet in the British Museum as a lad with my father. I used to imagine what might have been on the parts of the map that were missing."

"Well, now you'll know. The tablet I've got is intact."

"That does sound intriguing, doesn't it?" Cavendish's face softened, and for the first time, Steve thought he saw the semblance of a genuine smile. Cavendish rubbed his chin again as if debating what he was about to say. "I tell you what, Mr. Stilwell. If you can get to London tomorrow morning, I will set up a meeting for you with Dr. Jerome Gutmelder at the British Museum. He's an expert in ancient Babylonian tablets and will be more than willing to help. I'll recommend he translate the tablet as soon as possible, recognizing, of course, that anything he says will become part of our investigation."

"You've got a deal," Steve announced. "I'll make the arrangements as soon as I get back to my hotel. How can I get in touch with you to let you know when I'll arrive in London?"

Cavendish reached into his suit coat and pulled out his wallet. "Here's my card. You can ring me on my mobile anytime. I'll set up the meeting with Gutmelder as soon as I know your schedule."

"What about me?" Michela asked. "What am I supposed to do?"

"Nothing has changed for you, Michela," Cavendish replied tersely. "We need you to continue being our eyes and ears. Something is happening and we need to figure out in advance what it is."

Michela acknowledged what Cavendish said but didn't look happy. Steve again wondered why she was working with Cavendish. Was she just being a good citizen, or did he have something on her? From his perspective, it really didn't matter. At least it appeared like she wasn't behind Phan's shooting because she was working with Cavendish, although maybe Giorgio was. With Cavendish actively on Giorgio's trail and the opportunity to have the tablet translated hanging in front of him, this looked like a good time to say goodbye to Italy and leave the case up to law enforcement. He'd done all he could.

"I'm afraid I must be leaving now," Cavendish announced. "I've got some meetings in Rome tomorrow morning, so if you will excuse me, I will show myself out."

"Of course, I will show you out," Michela insisted. "I cannot allow a guest leave on his own." She followed Cavendish, who was already making his way to the foyer.

"I should be going now too, Michela," Steve added, falling in line behind her. "I've got some airline reservations to book."

Michela looked over her shoulder and gave him a look he didn't understand. When Cavendish reached the door, she opened it for him and he stepped outside into the entranceway, blocking Steve's departure.

"Goodnight, Ms. Baresi. I appreciate you hosting this meeting." He didn't wait for Steve or ask him if he needed a ride. He simply turned and left, leaving Michela and Steve standing in the doorway. Steve broke the silence first.

"Since we've made it a point of speaking frankly with one another, I'm not sure if I should thank you or be angry with you for hosting this meeting tonight. It was not the friendly dinner discussion I expected."

"I could say the same thing about you, Steve. You led me to believe the tablet might be available, but you knew it was not. So, how am I to feel? Maybe you have used me, no?" Michela leaned up against the doorframe, making it impossible for him to slip by without coming dangerously close to her. He could tell she wanted more than a cursory conversation.

"Okay," he admitted. "Maybe I shouldn't have done that, but I thought you were involved in hurting my friend."

"Is that what you think of me, Steve? I thought we had a nice dinner together in Williamsburg and I liked you. You must think I am a very bad person to be capable of such things."

"That's not it at all."

"Then what was it? Why did you think I would hurt your friend?"

"I didn't think you intended to hurt anyone. I did think you might have paid someone to get the tablet, and my friend got in the way. If that was true, I wanted justice for my friend."

Michela looked perplexed. "I am not sure what I should think about that, Steve. I am willing to forgive you, though, because you were concerned for your friend. Maybe we can make a fresh start, no?"

Steve smiled. There was something genuine and soothing about Michela that wiped away his misgivings. Even the sound of her voice, with her pleasant Italian accent, made him feel more at ease. He decided to take her up on her offer and depart on good terms.

"Okay," he answered, "let's make a fresh start. Deal?" He offered to shake hands.

Michela broke into a broad smile and began to shake hands with him. "Deal."

"Well, now that we are on good terms, I should be going."

"We haven't eaten dinner yet. My favorite restaurant is right around the corner. Why don't you join me for dinner like we planned?"

"I'd like that very much, Michela, if we don't make it too late. When I get back to my hotel tonight, I'll have to make my reservations to fly to London in the morning."

"I can help with that too," she said. "After dinner, we will come back to my flat and I will help you make your reservations before you go back to your hotel. What do you think of that, Steve Stilwell?"

It was an offer he couldn't refuse, so he didn't. Michela closed the door behind them and they went out to dinner on a breezy moonlit evening in Milan.

26

3:02 a.m. on Friday, October 15, 2004
Milan, Italy

Mᴵᴄʜᴇʟᴀ sᴛɪʀʀᴇᴅ ʙᴇɴᴇᴀᴛʜ ʜᴇʀ ʙᴇᴅᴄᴏᴠᴇʀs ᴛʀʏɪɴɢ not to wake up. Once she did, she'd start thinking about all she had to do at La Fontana and she'd never go back to sleep. She pulled the sheets over her exposed shoulder to fend off the cold and tried to drift back to the dream she was having before she woke up.

Her room was pitch black; she needed it that way to sleep. Now that she was partially awake, the red digital numbers on her clock beamed 3:03 a.m. so brightly that she could see the image of the block numbers on the inside of her eyelids after she closed her eyes. To make matters worse, every time she shifted her weight, the crackle of the feathers in her pillow sounded like thunderous applause at her favorite play.

She tried snuggling under the covers knowing there was no way she'd be able to go back to sleep. She was already thinking about her morning appointments. Her only chance was to start reading the magazine she kept on her nightstand and hopefully drift off to sleep over the course of the next hour or so.

She turned on the lamp and light exploded across the room. She reached over and pulled the magazine onto her lap, resigned to the fact that she would be reading salacious articles until it was time to get up and go into the office. Then the doorbell rang.

No one ever came to her door at three o'clock in the morning. Her mind raced about who it could be. She ruled out Steve. He'd been gone for hours. Could it be the police coming to give her bad news about a loved one, or a drunk male friend stopping by on his way home hoping to rekindle some forgotten night of passion? Her first instinct was to ignore it, then it rang again, longer and more determined.

She sat up and picked up the phone on her nightstand. She would dial the police and they would come quickly. They knew who she was and where she lived. They would also be able to tell her if they were the ones at the door. If not, they could dispense with whoever was out there and she could try to go back to sleep. She pressed the phone against her ear and started to dial.

"Oddio," she declared. "How can it not work?" She pushed the hook switch repeatedly to see if she could bring the phone back to life. Nothing worked. She threw the phone on her bed in frustration, then the doorbell rang a third, fourth and fifth time in quick succession. She felt anger boiling up, replacing her initial fear. She hopped out of bed and went to her closet, pulled on the jeans she'd worn earlier in the evening and threw on a La Fontana sweatshirt. She would go downstairs and look through the peephole to see who was there, then retrieve her recharging mobile phone in the kitchen and call the police. Then the doorbell rang again, and again, and again, and again. It did not stop.

"Shut up!" she shouted. She threw open her bedroom door and burst into the hallway, debating whether to give the person at the door a piece of her mind or settle for calling the police. A black-gloved hand grabbed her by the throat and she gurgled a terror-filled scream. A second black-gloved hand grabbed the back of her head while the first hand slid over her mouth. She reached for the man and tried to bite, but a powerful twist of her head snapped her neck with a sickening crunch. She was unconscious by the time she hit the floor.

The black-gloved assailant couldn't wait. He picked her up and carried her to the stairs, then held her as if she were standing at the top. He gave her a violent shove and she tumbled downward until she came to a stop two-thirds of the way down. There, death mercifully took her. The doorbell stopped ringing.

27

⟿

12:02 p.m. on Friday, October 15, 2004
London, England

"Thank you for making time for me on a Friday afternoon," Steve declared, taking a seat in front of the large oak fortress of a desk separating him and Dr. Gutmelder. The desk lamp's cream-colored shade tilted toward Gutmelder, casting long shadows around his nose and eye sockets. The only other light shone behind them, illuminating material strewn about a drafting table at the rear of the office.

"It's my pleasure," Gutmelder replied with a genuineness only significant self-interest could explain. "Detective Cavendish mentioned you have a clay tablet you'd like to talk about."

"That's right," Steve confirmed. "He said you might be able to tell me a little about it."

"If it's what I think it is, I will be able to tell you quite a lot about it." Gutmelder put his elbows on his desk and leaned forward over them. "Did I hear correctly that you think the tablet is a map of ancient Babylon?"

"That's exactly what it is," Steve answered. "It's very similar to one you already have at the museum."

"You are familiar with the Sippar tablet?" Gutmelder rocked even further forward over his arms.

"I've seen it, but to say I'm familiar with it would be a stretch. The other attorney in my office showed me a picture. The tablet I have is the same, except it's in much better shape. You can actually see the entire map."

Gutmelder's excitement boiled over and he slammed his hands on his desk. "I knew it," he exclaimed. "You're an attorney in Williamsburg, aren't you?"

"Why, yes I am," Steve answered, startled and confused by Gutmelder's response. "Why do you ask?"

"Because an archaeology professor at the College of William & Mary said a lawyer brought the tablet to his office. He sent me pictures, so I've seen what you have. It is remarkable, Mr. Stilwell."

"That was my sense, too," Steve replied, picking up on Gutmelder's enthusiasm. "Especially since people have been willing to kill for it."

"Yes, that's very sad," commented Gutmelder, the excitement draining from his expression. "Very sad, indeed. The FBI told me the American soldier who smuggled it out of Iraq was killed by someone trying to steal it from him, and he killed one of his assailants." Gutmelder crossed his arms over his chest. "You need to be very careful with this tablet, Mr. Stilwell. You will be a target as long as you have it, so you should consider giving it to someone who can safeguard it. When people find out what it says, you will not be able to protect the tablet or yourself."

Gutmelder's response surprised Steve. He'd intended his allusion to the man who shot Phan to spur questions by Gutmelder, who could not have known what happened to Phan. Instead, Gutmelder revealed two deaths Steve was not familiar with. Now he knew why Special Agent Fields wanted the tablet. It wasn't just that it had been smuggled out of Iraq. It was because the smuggler had paid for his indiscretion with his life. Steve surmised Fields had contacted Gutmelder about the tablet and asked for his expert assistance. Gutmelder then connected the dots between Fields' case and the professor at William & Mary.

"I appreciate your concern, Dr. Gutmelder, and I can assure you the tablet's in a safe place where no one can get to it except me."

"That's precisely my point, Mr. Stilwell. This puts you in grave danger. Two people have already died, and I'm afraid more will die until the tablet is adequately secured. Now, if you don't mind me asking, how did you come to possess the tablet? Do you represent the estate of the soldier?"

"No, not at all. I didn't even realize a soldier had been killed until you just mentioned it."

Gutmelder backpedaled. "Perhaps I spoke out of turn. I hope you won't spread what I said in case it is something I should not have disclosed." Gutmelder looked worried.

"I'll keep it between us," Steve assured him, holding back that he'd already tied all of the threads together.

Gutmelder breathed a sigh of relief. "Thank you, Mr. Stilwell. Then let me ask again. If you don't represent the soldier, who do you represent and why are you working with Detective Cavendish?"

"I represent the U.S. estate of Arul Ashirvadam. He's a wealthy businessman who—"

"—committed suicide in a London restaurant a few weeks ago."

"Exactly. Are you familiar with the case?"

"Everyone in London is. In fact, I'm also working with Detective Cavendish on it. That explains why he sent you to me. Ashirvadam had the tablet, didn't he?"

The question made Steve squirm. He needed to be forthcoming so Gutmelder would tell him what he needed to know. At the same time, he needed to protect his client's interests. He took the middle ground and hoped it would be good enough.

"Let's just say it's part of Ashirvadam's estate, how about that?"

"Of course, I understand," Gutmelder replied, picking up on Steve's professional caution. "We both need to be careful, don't we? Now, what can I help you with?"

"I need to know what the tablet says, Dr. Gutmelder. Two men have been murdered, another committed suicide, and one of my dearest friends was shot over this thing. I need to know why. If I leave you pictures, will you translate it for me? I'll pay you out of Ashirvadam's estate."

"That won't be necessary."

"Please, Dr. Gutmelder, I need to know what the tablet says."

"I meant it won't be necessary for you to leave any pictures. I already have them and I know what the tablet says. I'm just not sure I can share it with you."

"I don't understand," Steve countered. "What could possibly be on the tablet that you can't share?"

Dr. Gutmelder pushed his chair back and stood up as if he were preparing to lecture a class of freshman archaeology students. "This tablet is a key, Mr. Stilwell. It's a key that's been lost for over three thousand years. It unlocks a door some people may not be prepared to go through."

"I appreciate it's a significant find, Dr. Gutmelder, but you're going to have to give me more than that. What does the tablet unlock?"

Gutmelder took a step back and stood behind his chair, gripping the back like a lectern. "I've not told anyone about my findings yet, Mr. Stilwell, and I'm not sure I should tell you. After all, you are representing the man who acquired what he had to know was an ancient artifact smuggled out of Iraq."

Steve stood up and nonchalantly put his hands in his pockets. "Isn't it possible Ashirvadam thought he was acquiring it legitimately?"

"Don't fool yourself, Mr. Stilwell. He was a sophisticated antiquities collector. He knew exactly what he was acquiring, which is why the transaction took place in the shadows. I'm afraid your client was a criminal, and to some extent responsible for the killings. There is no way around it."

Steve wished he hadn't asked the question because it appeared to make Gutmelder more resolute about not disclosing the translation. Yet Steve sensed Gutmelder really wanted to tell someone about what he'd discovered, but for some reason hadn't done so. If he could find the right approach, he was sure Gutmelder would talk.

"I hope that's not the case, Dr. Gutmelder. Since I do still have the tablet, it seems the only way I'll be able to adequately safeguard it is if I know what it says. That means if you aren't able to tell me, I'll have to find someone who will, and they might not appreciate the need to be discreet. Wouldn't it be better for you to tell me so you can control the publicity?"

Gutmelder stroked his beard two or three times before responding. "Alright, Mr. Stilwell. I'll tell you what it says; however, you must first agree to abide by my terms."

"Of course," Steve replied, gambling the terms were something he could agree to.

"First," Gutmelder began, "You must not to go to the press with what I am about to tell you without consulting with me first. I am the one who translated the tablet, so I deserve a say in how the discovery is made public."

"I have no problem with that," Steve answered, hoping the remaining conditions were that easy.

"Second, I am certain either the FBI or Scotland Yard will try to take possession of the tablet since, as I think we can all agree, it was stolen from Iraq. When that happens, you must make sure they understand this is a priceless artifact and that they safeguard it accordingly. This tablet cannot be relegated to an evidence locker in some low-security warehouse, Mr. Stilwell. Do you understand?"

"I'll do what I can, Dr. Gutmelder, although I can't control what the police do. You know that, of course."

"I do indeed, but you can influence them, and that's what I expect you to do."

"I will," Steve promised. "Is there anything else?"

"Yes," Gutmelder replied as he started to walk around his desk and approach Steve. "This is most important. There is no doubt the tablet will have to be returned to Iraq. To do so now would be a travesty. Iraq is in no condition to receive a treasure like this. So, when the discussions take place about returning the tablet, I want you to advocate for the British Museum serving as a repository until it can be safely repatriated."

By now, Gutmelder was standing in front of Steve, looking anxious and prepared to stand his ground. As Steve thought about what just transpired, he couldn't help but grin.

"Is something funny, Mr. Stilwell?"

"You'd thought about those three points and had them ready for me before I even arrived, didn't you?"

A small smile wormed its way onto Gutmelder's lips. "I'm not a very good actor, am I?"

"Good enough to get what you want," Steve replied. "I'll do the best I can. The last one, in particular, will be tough. Our governments will make the decisions about where the tablet lands, and I suspect what it says will have a bearing on who ultimately gets it. That said, I'll make sure the British Museum is in the mix. Deal?" He reached out to shake Gutmelder's hand.

"Deal," Gutmelder responded, vigorously shaking Steve's hand. "Now, follow me to my workbench and I'll show you what you've got." Gutmelder led Steve to the drafting table at the back of his office. He stood at the foot of the table and adjusted the neck of the desk's lamp so the light shined brightest on the picture of the front of the tablet. Steve stood next to him so he could see whatever Gutmelder pointed to without having to look from an odd angle.

"As you indicated," Gutmelder began, "your tablet's map is the same as the one on the Sippar tablet, so we already know how to read it. Babylon is this horizontal bar in the center, divided by a vertical bar, which is the Euphrates River." Gutmelder used a pen to point to each location as he described it. "These two outer circles represent a sea, and the rays jutting from the circles are specific islands, but because the Sippar tablet was missing everything outside of the sea rings to the south, we didn't know what was there."

"And now you do," interjected Steve.

"Precisely," Gutmelder replied. "There is one island of particular interest—Dilmun." Gutmelder pointed the pen at the ray extending south/southeast of Babylon.

"What's Dilmun?"

"Dilmun is the Sumerian version of paradise. You probably studied about Sumer in primary school, at least we do here in the U.K. The Sumerians were the first civilization to leave a written record, and their writings describe the island of Dilmun as a garden paradise where no one grows old or dies."

"Like the Garden of Eden," suggested Steve.

"Precisely," Gutmelder replied again. "In fact, some historians believe Dilmun is the Garden of Eden. They've just never been able to prove the connection."

"And I suppose you are going to tell me this tablet does?"

"You tell me," challenged Gutmelder. "Just looking at the map, Dilmun is very likely the island of Bahrain in the Persian Gulf. I'm not sure it could be anything else."

"That's fascinating," Steve began, trying not to sound underwhelmed. "I've got to admit, though, I don't see how associating the island of Bahrain with Dilmun is so revolutionary."

"You're right, of course. It's not. In fact, several scholars have associated Dilmun with Bahrain before. What is revolutionary is what's on the back of the tablet." Gutmelder slid the picture of the back directly under the light. "This is what is revolutionary." He circled an area of the tablet with the non-writing end of a pen.

"It looks like a bunch of chicken scratches to me," mused Steve.

"Far from it, Mr. Stilwell. This is very well-preserved cuneiform writing, which is the writing developed by the Sumerians. I've spent my life studying and translating tablets like this, and I've never seen anything like it."

"What does it say?" Steve asked, growing impatient with the build-up.

Gutmelder retrieved his notepad from the stack of material littering the desk and started to explain. "The first part of the text talks about Dilmun as a paradise where no one grows old because people there eat from the Tree of Life. It even references the story of a Sumerian hero, Gilgamesh, who is on a quest to find the tree, which thrives in the center of Dilmun."

"Okay, so the Tree of Life is in Dilmun," Steve commented. "I'm still not seeing how this gets beyond an interesting story."

"It's what the end of the description says that's important. It explains that God, and the reference is singular which in itself is significant, said people could no longer eat from the tree because they had proved themselves unworthy. God then put a guard in front of the tree with a flaming sword and instructed the guard to turn all away until his face reappears in the garden."

"Okay, I think I'm starting to see how this is coming together," Steve replied. "Ashirvadam was seized with finding the Fountain of Youth. About a month before he died, he told his lover, Michela Baresi, he'd found an ancient Babylonian tablet that would lead them to the Fountain of Youth. If you equate the Tree of Life with the Fountain of Youth because they both keep people young forever, I guess you get to the same place. Either way, though, I don't see how this discovery puts anyone in danger. It's an interesting story but not earth shattering."

"Unless you're a biblical scholar, Mr. Stilwell. This story of God barring access to the Tree of Life predates the Bible's account in Genesis by a thousand years, yet the story is precisely the same."

"Ahhh," Steve said, the light finally coming on. "People will think this undercuts the Bible's story of the Garden of Eden, won't they?"

Gutmelder turned and looked toward Steve. "Some will, Mr. Stilwell, and they'll want to discredit or destroy it as heretical. Others will see it as consistent with the Biblical account and say it supports what Genesis says. Still others will look at it as an historical treasure that ties together thousands of years of history. You can be sure of one thing—no one will be neutral. The tablet has immense historical and religious significance and it will bring out people's passions."

"I guess the right thing for me to do is to turn it over to the FBI, isn't it?" Steve asked, not mentioning he'd already committed to doing so.

"If I were you, that's exactly what I would do."

"I still don't get what Ashirvadam thought he could do with it. He dangled it in front of Michela Baresi to use with her cosmetics firm, yet he had to know it would be of limited use if it was stolen. Maybe he thought he could hang onto it long enough for the trail to get lost."

"Or maybe he just wanted to admire it," Gutmelder suggested. "Detective Cavendish also found an extraordinarily rare copy of the Prester John letter on private display in Ashirvadam's flat after he died. No one knew the copy existed, let alone that he had it."

"What's the Prester John letter?"

"A very good question. It's a medieval letter long thought to be a hoax from a legendary Christian king known as Prester John. He wrote it to the Roman Emperor in Constantinople in the twelfth century when the Crusaders were having a rough go of it in Jerusalem. Prester John offered the Emperor and the Crusaders his assistance. There are only about one hundred authentic medieval copies of the letter known to exist, and Ashirvadam's appears to be one of them." Gutmelder paused for a second, pulling his beard until it came to a point at the bottom and then let go. "Hhmm. Now that I think about it, it ties in quite well with the tablet, doesn't it?"

"I'm not following you."

"Yes, of course. Without reading the letter, it would be impossible, wouldn't it? Let's just say the letter describes Prester John's kingdom as being in the vicinity of Paradise. I wonder if that wasn't what Ashirvadam was really looking for—the Garden of Eden."

"Well, he didn't find it, did he? In fact, just the opposite—whatever he found caused him to kill himself."

"The entire episode is tragic, Mr. Stilwell, and, I'm afraid it is just the start.

"We'll never know now, will we?"

Dr. Gutmelder paused for a second, again pulling his beard until it came to a point at the bottom and then letting go. "Interesting, isn't it, Mr. Stilwell?"

"What's that?"

"How Arul Ashirvadam's death and the FBI's case in America intersect."

"I guess everything had to come together at some point since we're all working around the same clay tablet. I'm just not sure we've identified all the players yet. Ashirvadam's dead, yet someone tried to steal the tablet from me and kill the person who cleans my office at night. Like you said, I don't think this is over."

"And now you know why, Mr. Stilwell."

Knocking at the open door presaged the entry of a familiar face.

"Detective Cavendish," Gutmelder began. "I wasn't expecting you this afternoon. I've got some information about the tablet I need to discuss with you. Why don't we let Mr. Stilwell depart first. He was just leaving."

"I'm sure he was," Cavendish declared. "But I'm afraid I'll have to ask him to come with me. You and I will have to schedule a time to talk later."

"Of course, Detective," Gutmelder replied. "I must say, though, that the information is important, so we should talk as soon as possible."

Steve looked at his watch. "I'm sorry, Detective Cavendish. I really need to see about making arrangements to return to the United States this evening. Dr. Gutmelder was very helpful and I've got some follow-on work to do, beginning with turning the tablet over to the FBI."

"That's all well and good, Mr. Stilwell, isn't it? I'm afraid it will have to wait. You see, there's been an accident."

"An accident? What kind of accident?" Steve couldn't see how an accident could have anything to do with him.

"It's Michela Baresi."

"I hope it's not serious," Steve replied, fearing it was since Detective Cavendish had returned to London to tell him the news.

"I'm afraid she's dead, Mr. Stilwell. Either she fell down the stairs at her flat late last night or someone made it look that way."

The news sucked all the air out of Steve's lungs; he couldn't breathe or talk. He just stared at Detective Cavendish and waited for him to say it was a tasteless joke.

"The Carabinieri want to talk to you and I suggest you cooperate."

"I don't understand. Why would they want to talk to me?"

"Because they have you on a security camera leaving Ms. Baresi's flat late last night."

Steve was stunned he was a potential suspect. "I didn't do anything, if that's what you're implying. We went out to dinner after you left and then we went back to her flat so she could help me book my flight to London. I promise you, she was perfectly fine when I left."

"That's what you need to tell the Carabinieri then, isn't it?"

"I guess so," Steve admitted. "When do they want to talk to me?"

"They've asked to talk to you this afternoon."

"We better get going then. I want to get this cleared up as quickly as possible." Steve shifted what remained of his attention to Dr. Gutmelder. "Thank you for your help today, doctor. I'll let you know as soon as I turn the tablet over to the FBI."

Gutmelder nodded. "Good luck, Mr. Stilwell."

"I will contact you later this afternoon, Jerome," Cavendish added. He motioned for Steve to head to the door and they departed Gutmelder's office in silence.

Steve felt emotionally numb. Last night he actually thought he'd met a woman who could help him get through losing Sarah, and now she was gone forever. Worse yet, as with Phan's shooting, he felt responsible for Michela's death because she'd asked him to spend the night and he refused, saying he wasn't ready. Had that been the only reason, he might have been able to deal with it. But down deep he knew the real reason was his concern for the ethical implications of a relationship with his dead client's part-time lover. Even though refusing her invitation was the right thing to do, he'd let his business persona once again hurt someone he cared about or was at least starting to care about.

With Phan in the hospital and Michela dead, Arul Ashirvadam's pursuit of the Tree of Life seemed less and less important. In fact, he couldn't wait to jettison responsibility for the tablet by handing it over to Special Agent Fields. Perhaps once that happened, the killing would stop. More importantly, he could leave figuring out what was going on and who was behind it to Cavendish and Special Agent Fields. He just had to convince the Italian Carabinieri he had nothing to do with Michela's death.

28

2:35 p.m. on Friday, October 15, 2004
London, England

IT WAS A CONFERENCE ROOM, NOT an interrogation room. Steve didn't care. As far as he was concerned, this was an interrogation. He could see out the open door to the office area, where Cavendish conferred with a man he assumed was an Italian detective. Cavendish had been much friendlier during this visit to Scotland Yard compared to their first meeting after Ashirvadam's suicide. He sensed Cavendish knew he had nothing to do with Michela's death, especially since Cavendish had seen how he and Michela interacted earlier in the evening. The interview was just one of those things that had to happen when an unexplained death like Michela's occurred, and he intended to bend over backwards to cooperate. He needed to clear his name as soon as possible so he could try to get Michela off his mind and plug back into his practice in Williamsburg.

He looked at the floor underneath the conference table as a wave of emotion swept over him. He could feel his soul reaching out for the routine life he'd longed for when he retired from the Navy. Michela's death made that vision foggy and unrecognizable. He heard a voice calling him—it was too distant to understand. He'd shrugged off Casey's advice to talk to someone about the body shots life had thrown him recently. He wasn't shrugging now.

"Mr. Stilwell, are you alright?"

Steve looked up and saw Cavendish and the Italian detective standing opposite him at the table. "I'm sorry Detective Cavendish. It might be the jet lag finally catching up with me."

"Yes, of course," agreed Cavendish. "I was about to introduce you to Detective Bruno Alfano from the Italian Carabinieri. If you need another moment to collect yourself or would like a cup of coffee or tea first, we can give you a few more minutes."

"Thank you, that won't be necessary." Steve offered his hand across the table. "I'm pleased to meet you, Detective Alfano." Alfano was a short, mustached man with closely cropped hair. Steve had to lean over the table to seal the introduction.

"Thank you for your cooperation, Mr. Stilwell. Why don't we sit down so we can talk?" Alfano gestured for Steve to take his seat, bowed slightly, and sat down across from him. "I have invited Detective Sergeant Cavendish to join our discussion. I hope you do not mind." Alfano spoke slowly in short, clear sentences, enunciating every word as if he were translating from Italian before he spoke.

"I will be taking notes, Mr. Stilwell," Alfano continued, pulling a small spiral notebook and pen from his suitcoat's interior pocket. "You are welcome to do the same, of course. Do you need anything before we begin?"

"No, I'm fine, and I do want you to know I had nothing to do with Michela's death. As Detective Cavendish can corroborate, I met her at her flat last night to go out for a glass of wine and dinner. After we returned, she helped me book an early morning flight to London and then I left. That had to be a little after midnight because I got back to my hotel just after twelve thirty. Michela was fine when I left."

"I appreciate what you are saying, Mr. Stilwell, and to be honest, we are quite sure you were not involved in Ms. Baresi's death. If I may have your confidence, we know someone else entered her flat about two hours after you left. We believe that individual murdered Ms. Baresi. We also know you were with her until after midnight, so there is a chance you may have information that will help us identify the killer."

Steve gripped the edge of the table and pushed out until his elbows straightened, then exhaled to release the anger overflowing inside him. "I am just so—so pissed that someone killed her, detective. How could someone do this?" Neither detective said anything, creating the silence Steve so hated in a discussion. "She gave no indication of anything—anything. If I had sensed any danger at all, I would have stayed with her. I should have stayed with her." Steve held his head in his hands, closed his eyes, and fought back his emotions. Navy officers don't get emotional, he repeated to himself over and over. When he pulled his head back up for another deep breath, he noticed both detectives staring at him, making him feel even more self-conscious about his emotional display. He forced himself to calm down and tell them what he could.

"I'm sorry, detectives. Like I said, I think the jet lag is catching up with me." He chiseled out a grin and Alfano reciprocated.

"I appreciate this is difficult for you, Mr. Stilwell. As you know, we must try to reassemble all of the pieces of the puzzle so we can determine what happened. I need to ask you, did Ms. Baresi receive any telephone calls or talk to anyone while you were with her?"

"No, not that I recall, but I wasn't with her one hundred percent of the time. While we ate dinner, she left to use the restroom and one time at her flat, she left to get wine. I suppose she could have spoken with someone during those times. I'm sure you can check her phone records."

"What about the wine, Mr. Stilwell? How much did she have to drink?"

"She wasn't drunk, if that's what you're getting at." Steve thought for a moment, mentally adding up what they drank over the course of the evening. "We split a bottle of wine at dinner, and then had another glass each when we returned to her flat. It was spread out over three or four hours, so it wasn't too much at all. Michela seemed fine when I left."

"Yes, I see," Alfano remarked. "Was she angry when you left? I mean, you said you should have stayed with her, but you did not. Did she ask you to stay with her? I only want to know to understand her state of mind when you left."

"If you must know, she did ask me to stay," Steve admitted. "When I told her I couldn't while the case was going on, she understood."

"And that case would be?"

"Oh, I'm sorry. I'm representing the U.S. estate of Arul Ashirvadam, and I'm afraid seeing Michela might have been perceived as a conflict of interest. You understand, don't you?"

"Yes, of course, Mr. Stilwell. I suppose it was a very honorable decision."

Steve wasn't sure what Detective Alfano's last comment meant. It certainly wasn't the validation of his decision he was hoping for. As angry as he was with Michela's death, he couldn't let Alfano's comment go unchallenged.

"I'm not sure I understand what you mean, detective."

"I mean Michela Baresi was a beautiful woman. Most men would not hesitate to sleep with her. Unless, of course, you already had sex with her before you departed."

Steve could feel his face growing red hot with anger. First, he did not understand why the question was relevant. Second, he did not appreciate Alfano's insinuation that he had misled them to sound honorable. He had to maintain his composure to get through the interview, but he also needed to put down a marker about what he considered acceptable.

"I guess I'm not like most men," he replied sarcastically, "and I don't see the relevance of your statement. Just to make it clear, Michela and I went out to dinner and she helped me with my airline reservations. That was it."

"Very well, Mr. Stilwell," Alfano replied, closing his notebook and sticking his pen back in his suit pocket. "I think that is all I will need for now. I do hope you will be willing to testify when we find the person responsible for Ms. Baresi's murder."

"I would be happy to," Steve said, calming down now that the interview was drawing to a close. Before he could say anything further, his phone rang. He assumed it was Marjorie checking in, which caller ID confirmed, so he asked for a moment to answer and tell her he would call her back. Alfano nodded and Steve took the call still sitting at the table.

"Hello, Marjorie. Can I call you back in a couple of minutes? I'm finishing up an interview."

"Mr. Stilwell, I'm so glad you answered." Marjorie sounded anxious, so Steve let her continue. "Detective Fields is here with another search warrant. She says she can't wait any longer for the tablet, so she needs to know where the safe deposit box is or she'll have to take your files and go through them at her office. She doesn't want to do that and says it would be much easier if you simply told her where the tablet is."

Steve couldn't deal with this crisis sitting at a conference table with two detectives listening to his every word. Not that anything he would say would give rise to any suspicions. He just needed some space to think his way through this.

"Hold on for a second Marjorie. Let me wrap up the interview here." He left the phone's microphone open so Marjorie would be able to hear what was going on.

"Detective Alfano," he began, "there's a crisis at my office I need to help with. Are we finished here?"

"We are," Alfano responded. "Thank you for your cooperation and I am sure we will speak again."

"I'll wait for you outside," Cavendish added.

"Thank you, detective. This should only take a minute."

Cavendish and Alfano departed the room, standing just outside with the door open. Rather than push his luck by closing the door, Steve turned his back to the detectives and began to speak as quietly as he could, using his free hand to muffle his conversation.

"Okay, Marjorie, I can talk now. Let me get this straight. Special Agent Fields has a new warrant to get information about the safe deposit box where the tablet is?"

"Yep," Marjorie said with her usual gift of bluntness. "She and that other detective she came with before say they'll search your office if they don't get safe deposit box information now. They say they can't wait until you get back."

"Mmmhhh," Steve murmured. "Let me think about that for a second." With both him and Casey out of the office, it made delaying the search much more difficult. He fully intended to turn over the tablet as soon as he returned, but he wanted to get it out of the safe deposit box, not have the FBI do it. If they proceeded to go after the tablet themselves, there was the matter of the hundred thousand euros in cash in the box, as well as the post office box rental agreement and the paper with the telephone numbers on it. He wasn't sure what Special Agent Fields would do with those items, although he presumed she would confiscate them. His main concern was ethical—would he be failing to zealously represent his client if he gave Special Agent Fields the box information without a fight? Given that fighting might result in lots of client files being taken from his office, he decided his best option was to give Fields the information she wanted.

"You still there, Mr. Stilwell?" Marjorie asked.

"Sorry, Marjorie, I was just thinking through the options. Here's what you need to do. Go ahead and turn the name and address of the bank over to Special Agent Fields and give her the box number. Ask her, though, to wait for me to come back so I can open the box and give her the tablet. Tell her I've got the key with me and I'll meet her at the bank as soon as I return. I'm trying to fly back to Washington, DC, tonight, so I could be there as early as tomorrow. How does that sound?"

"I'll give it a try, Mr. Stilwell, but she seems pretty determined."

"Just do the best you can. I'll call you back after I'm done with this interview so you can tell me what she said."

"Got it Mr. Stilwell."

"Oh, and can you also see if you can find me a flight back? I'd need to leave out of London Heathrow no earlier than nine p.m. Don't buy it yet because I need to make sure I can get to the airport in time, but I'd like to at least know what my options are. You can tell me what you find when I call you back."

"No problem, Mr. Stilwell. I better get back to Special Agent Fields. She's starting to look impatient."

"Okay, I'll talk to you later, Marjorie. Goodbye."

Steve tucked his phone into his jacket and went to the door to tell Cavendish and Alfano he was ready to go. He hoped they wouldn't ask him to stay in the U.K. He really needed to get back to Williamsburg and sort things out. The case was whooshing by in a swirl and he was losing his grip. He had to put down an anchor and chart out his next steps before the events charted his next steps for him. He also needed to touch base with Casey. He hadn't spoken with her all week and had lost the bubble on her side of the case. Casey needed to hear what he'd found out, too, so they could coordinate their efforts. It would take some magic from Marjorie to patch through a conference call on three different continents, but if anyone could pull it off, Marjorie could. Then perhaps he could come to terms with all that had transpired over the last two weeks. Just thinking of it made him feel tired, very tired.

29

6:23 p.m. on Friday, October 15, 2004
London

"I CAN HOLD AS LONG AS YOU need me to," Steve said, sitting at a pay phone near his Friday night flight's boarding gate at Heathrow Airport. Marjorie had just enough time when they first connected to tell him Casey had been in the hospital with a head injury. She didn't say more because she said she wanted to leave the details to Casey. Now that they were having trouble reconnecting, he was really worried. Anything serious enough to warrant a hospital visit in a foreign country couldn't be good.

"Mr. Stilwell, are you still there?" asked Marjorie from her desk in Williamsburg.

"I am," Steve replied.

"Casey, can you hear Mr. Stilwell and me?"

"Yes," Casey replied from her hotel room in Chennai.

"Hallelujah," Marjorie declared. "Go ahead, Mr. Stilwell. We're all on the line."

"Thanks, Marjorie. I need to ask right off, Casey, are you okay?"

"I'm fine, Steve. I promise it's nothing for you to worry about. I hit the back of my head on the corner of a wall and it split the skin, so I needed a few stitches."

"Oh, my goodness, Casey," interrupted Marjorie. "That doesn't sound like nothing to me."

"Me either," chimed in Steve. "How in the world did you hit the back of your head? Did you fall?"

"That's the troubling part," Casey admitted. "I was pushed and when I fell back, I hit my head."

"Oh, my goodness," Marjorie repeated. "I was afraid when you said you were going to India, but I held my tongue."

"Who pushed you Casey?" Steve asked. He needed details so he could assess if Casey was still in danger. He also wanted to hold someone accountable.

"It's a bit of a long story, so let me give you the abbreviated version in case we get cut off. I spoke with Ashirvadam's widow. Her name is Rani, and I thought we hit it off."

"I'm not surprised," Steve commented. "You hit it off with everyone. That's why we sent you to Chennai in the first place."

"Not quite everyone. There's one person in particular who hates me—Ashirvadam's business manager. He's extremely protective of Rani and he thought I crossed him, so he showed up at my hotel room with a thug to intimidate me." Casey relayed the details of what happened.

Steve fumed and his voice intensified. "This wasn't your fault Casey—Abijith had no right to come to your room to bully you. The bottom line is he hurt you and he needs to be held accountable. Did you call the police?"

"I'm sorry, Steve. I know I should have, but I couldn't. Abijith made it clear if anyone at the hotel supported my story, they'd never work in Chennai again. He's a powerful man here. No one in Chennai is going to cross him, especially for a foreign woman. We just need to let this one pass."

"I'll be honest, Casey. I don't know if I can do that right now."

"Let it go, Steve," Casey replied, using a conciliatory tone. "We just need to administer Ashirvadam's estate. Abijith is a sideshow. Let's not given him the satisfaction of thinking his actions had any impact on our representation."

Steve shifted the receiver to his other ear. Casey was right, of course. That didn't make backing down any easier. "I guess we don't have a choice, do we?"

"I'm afraid not," confirmed Casey.

"Does that mean you're finished in Chennai?" Steve asked.

"It does and I've got some bad news. Rani nixed everything her husband proposed in his letter. She won't let him be buried in Palayur because, although her relationship with him seems to have been on the rocks, she wants their two boys to be able to visit his gravesite. That means burying him in Chennai. She also knew about his affair with Michela Baresi and she detests the woman. In fact, she called her a whore and refused to donate money to any church in Italy because she felt the donation had to be motivated by her husband's relationship with Michela."

"She doesn't have to worry about Michela anymore," Steve lamented. "She was murdered shortly after I left her flat in Milan."

"Oh, my goodness," Marjorie declared.

"Whoever did it made it look like she fell down the stairs in the middle of the night." Then Steve surprised himself by delving below the surface and touching on the way he really felt about Michela. "In the short time we'd known each other, I'd come to admire her. Now I just feel sad she's gone."

"I'm so sorry, Mr. Stilwell," consoled Marjorie. "I knew this was going to be another one of those crazy cases. It's not worth half a million dollars. Phan almost died, somebody beat up Casey, and the FBI is coming to the office with search warrants. You need to withdraw from this case, Mr. Stilwell, before it's too late."

Steve heard himself saying "I'm afraid that's not an option," knowing full well it was an option. He just wasn't ready to consider it yet. His mental calculus told him the danger stateside would be over as soon as Special Agent Fields took custody of the tablet, and he presumed Casey would be safe since she wouldn't see Ashirvadam's widow again. That left only him and, frankly, he didn't care about himself right now. Still, he knew he had to say more to dispel Marjorie's fears. Her loyalty warranted a more thoughtful response.

"I don't think the judge would let me off the hook even if I felt it was the right thing to do. We're in this too deep, Marjorie, and it might harm the interests of our client. We've just got to do the best we can. Besides, as soon as the FBI takes possession of the tablet, I think we'll be completely off of the bad guy's radar."

"Who is this bad guy?" asked Casey.

"That's a good question," Steve answered. "I'd say it was Arul Ashirvadam at one time, but he's dead and somebody's still trying to get the tablet. At least now I think I know why."

Marjorie flew back with a "Why?" before Steve's lips finished forming his final word.

"I know this may be a little hard to get your head around, but it's because the tablet pinpoints the location of the Garden of Eden in cuneiform writing predating the biblical account in Genesis."

"I don't get it. What does that mean?" asked Casey.

"It means the Sumerians wrote about the Garden of Eden a thousand years before Moses did, and they knew where it was."

"That news will rock the religious world when it becomes public," Casey declared.

"Precisely," Steve acknowledged. "I don't think we can even begin to comprehend how controversial the tablet will be. Whoever wants the tablet must understand that."

"Forget what it means," Marjorie interjected. "Where's the Garden of Eden?"

"It's in a place the Sumerians called Dilmun, on the island of Bahrain in the Persian Gulf."

Marjorie continued with her practical line of questions. "Well, now that we know where it is, can we go there to see it?"

"I don't think so," Steve responded. "Both Genesis and the tablet indicate God closed the Garden and put an angel there to guard the way to the Tree of Life. I think that means there's no way for people to see it."

"The whole thing sounds like some ancient myth to me," Casey commented, "and I'm glad it will be the FBI's problem shortly."

"Speaking of problems, Mr. Stilwell, I've got some bad news I need to tell you about."

"What's that, Marjorie?" Steve could hardly believe what more bad news there could be and felt himself cringing in anticipation of whatever Marjorie had to relay.

"I took a phone call from a retired Navy commander, Jack Matzen. He said he was a good friend of yours."

"Oh, no. Don't tell me there's something wrong with Jack. He's way too young."

"It's not Jack, Mr. Stilwell. Admiral Frank Bancroft passed away unexpectedly from a heart attack on Wednesday. Jack Matzen wanted you to know the funeral is at the Naval Academy Chapel tomorrow at one o'clock."

"Ahhh, I'm so sorry to hear that. He was a great leader."

"Who was he, Steve?" asked Casey.

"He was the admiral commanding the USS Saratoga battle group I deployed with to the Mediterranean. He taught me what it meant to be a lawyer in the fleet. I'm going to need to get to that funeral."

"That's what I figured," answered Marjorie. "Since you are getting in late tonight, I've already made you reservations at the Hyatt right outside of Dulles. You can drive to Annapolis tomorrow morning. Do you have the clothes you need?"

"I don't, but I can stop at a department store on the way to Annapolis in the morning. What about Special Agent Fields? Do I need to meet her at the bank tomorrow?"

"No, she said that wouldn't be necessary. She's going to the bank first thing in the morning to execute the search warrant. She said you could call her on Monday if you have any questions."

Steve could see people boarding his flight to Washington. The waiting area was emptying and he could ill afford to miss his plane. He needed to wrap up the call.

"It looks like my flight is boarding now, so I've got to go."

"Is there anything else I need to do in India?" Casey asked. "I can't travel right away because the doctor thought I might have a mild concussion. I'm free if you need me to do anything."

"I'd say just relax and get better," Steve responded.

"Amen to that," added Marjorie.

"Okay, I'll look at booking a flight out of here as soon as I can," responded Casey. "I've also got to get my passport replaced. My guess is I'll be back in the office on Thursday or Friday."

"Take the rest of the week off, Casey," Steve suggested. "Then we can regroup and figure out where we are. I've got to run—they just announced the final call and I heard them mention my name. Safe travels to everyone and enjoy the weekend."

Steve hung up and hurried to board his flight. At least it was a direct flight and he might be able to sleep. He couldn't believe Admiral Bancroft was gone. He was the one who referred his first big case to him and really kick-started his civilian law practice. Showing up at the admiral's funeral was the least he could do. It also added to the long line of sorrows he'd felt within the last couple of weeks. Maybe what he needed was a good, long vacation somewhere far away from the practice of law. Casey was good enough now to manage things for a couple of weeks while he got himself back together. The thought of it gave him something to look forward to. He just had to get through the next twenty-four hours.

30

12:50 p.m. on Saturday, October 16, 2004
U.S. Naval Academy, Annapolis, Maryland

Although he'd walked into the U.S. Naval Academy main chapel many times before, Steve had to admit it looked amazing today with the sun's rays pouring through the giant rotunda's windows. The natural light accented the blue of the center aisle carpet and the side balconies' rails against the cream and beige stone walls and arched ceilings of the one-hundred-year-old architectural gem. Straight ahead above the altar, a stained glass portrait of Jesus walking on water looked out over those waiting for Admiral Frank Bancroft's Saturday afternoon funeral Mass, while the Navy and Marine Corps flags flanked the chamber and reminded attendees where they were. There could be no better place for a naval officer's farewell, save Arlington National Cemetery, which would be Admiral Bancroft's final port of call once his family and the cemetery settled on his burial date.

Steve walked down the center aisle in the off-the-rack suit and tie he'd hastily purchased at a mall en route to the funeral. The new clothes hid the bone-deep fatigue he felt after his whirlwind trip to Italy and the U.K. Only the wrinkled shirt he'd put on right out of the package reflected his true condition. He hoped it wasn't too noticeable. About halfway to the altar, he saw a familiar face turn around to look at him.

"Jack Matzen," he said, taking care not to be too enthusiastic greeting an old friend at such a solemn occasion. "It's great to see you." Jack stood and the two shook hands, then Jack slid towards the middle of the pew to make room.

"I really appreciate you giving my office a call to let me know about the admiral's passing. I would have missed this if you hadn't called."

"I knew you'd want to know," Jack responded. "He was a good man."

"Are you still teaching at the Naval Academy? Navigation, wasn't it?"

"I am," Jack replied. "You've got a good memory."

"I can't think of a better way for a retired ship driver like you to finish out a Navy career. How's the family?"

"Everyone's doing great. How about you and Sarah? You should be empty nesters by now."

Steve glanced away to ponder how to respond and saw a Navy chaplain in his Roman Catholic vestments making his way to the altar as the organ switched from background music to the entrance hymn. "We better continue this after the Mass," he instructed, ducking Jack's question. Jack nodded and they both turned their attention to the priest. Neither opted to join in the hymn.

Steve had so many things clogging his mind that the Mass and whatever the priest was saying were barely audible above the caffeine induced ringing in his ears. The funeral made him think of Ashirvadam and all the work he and Casey had to do to probate the estate. It also seared Michela's death deeper into his psyche. The guilt of not staying with her and possibly fending off her attacker dueled with the guilt he felt for being attracted to her in the first place. When the priest started lacing his eulogy with history—a subject Steve could never get enough of—his ears tuned in.

"You see, my friends," the priest continued, "there is no better place to gather and recognize the life of an officer in the United States Navy than the Naval Academy Chapel, for here lie the remains of one of our greatest naval heroes, John Paul Jones. His crypt in the basement to the chapel is a fitting monument to all who have served in the Navy. I encourage you to visit before you leave today because it symbolizes the first half of Admiral Bancroft's journey as a brave and dedicated sailor in the service of our nation.

"While you're in the basement, take a moment to study the beautiful stained glass windows in St. Andrew's Chapel. In particular, look at the window depicting St. Brendan. He was an Irish monk who sailed the seas during the sixth century in search of Paradise and God's Promised Land. His story was widely known during the Middle Ages and represents Admiral Bancroft's current journey—his eternal reward in the Promised Land."

Steve's brain fixated on St. Brendan. The monk wasn't the only one looking for the Promised Land—Ashirvadam was too. So was Michela for that matter, although she couched her search as looking for the Fountain of Youth. But like St. Brendan, they believed the fountain could be found in a physical place they could visit and possibly cheat death out of its otherwise inevitable sting. Unlike St. Brendan, Ashirvadam had a clay map to navigate by, but there had to be more to it than just knowing where the Garden was. Historians and explorers had already combed every square inch of the Middle East in search of Eden and couldn't find it. Unless it lay on the sandy floor of the Persian Gulf or had so morphed as to be unrecognizable to the modern eye, it would have been discovered if it really existed. Maybe the Garden of Eden was an allegory and not a real place after all, and maybe the tablet was an interesting ancient document but worthless as a key.

Realizing he had again drifted away from the sermon and had no idea what the priest was saying, he looked up toward the pulpit to make one last attempt to tune in. This time the altar distracted him—it was so beautiful he couldn't help but admire its every detail. In particular, the stunning blue stained glass image of Jesus walking on water drew his attention. Of course, the water theme made it a fitting image for the seagoing services' chapel. Yet he couldn't take his eyes off the vibrant blues of the water and purples of the sky, culminating in the figure of Jesus in the middle. He stared at it to take it all in. Then it hit him like a blinding flash of the obvious—the tablet wasn't the key, and if he hadn't come to the funeral, he never would have realized it.

Steve couldn't sit through the rest of the funeral. It was all he could do to keep from shouting out his new theory to all the gathered mourners. He knew he had to test it first to see if it was viable. And, either by divine providence or an amazing coincidence, Jack Matzen was just the man to do it for him. The best thing to do, of course, would be to wait until after the Mass and then ask Jack for his help. Steve's impulse to solve the case drove him to the second-best option. He hoped Jack wouldn't be too angry and leaned toward him to get his attention.

"Jack," Steve whispered as he got as close to Jack as he dared come. "I know this is a bad time, but would you mind stepping to the rear of the chapel with me for a minute? I've just thought of something really important I need to run past you. I'm afraid it can't wait." Steve's face twisted into an awkward look, his eyebrows and one corner of his mouth raising slightly, conveying his uncertainty about how Jack would respond.

Jack shrugged and nodded, wearing a similarly awkward expression. Without saying anything, he turned and quietly followed Steve from the pew. They walked toward the back of the chapel as inconspicuously as they could. Steve still saw every head in the rows they passed turning in their direction and registering disapproval. The treatment reinforced his inclination never to sit in the front half of any venue. As the two retired Navy officers reached the back of the chapel, the priest concluded his sermon. Jack pushed the door open and they stepped outside.

"What's up?" Jack asked.

"I'm so sorry for asking you to leave the funeral, Jack, but I've been involved in a pretty serious case over the last few weeks. It involves an ancient clay tablet a sailor smuggled out of Iraq."

Jack smiled. "You've got to love the ingenuity of the American sailor, even if it is a little misplaced sometimes."

"Yeah, but this time somebody killed the sailor and stole the tablet from him."

"Geez, you weren't kidding when you said it was serious."

"I know, and I can't stop thinking about it. Anyway, something the priest just said may have helped me figure out what's going on. If I'm right, more bad things will happen soon."

"What do you need me for?" Jack put his hands in his pockets and eased one foot forward. Steve could tell he was listening but not yet committing.

"I need you to tell me how long it would take for a ship to get from point A to point B."

"I can certainly do that. I'm going to need to know what kind of ship and where points A and B are."

"Do you have any charts of the Med and Persian Gulf in your office?"

"You bet. My office is in Luce Hall. It's a five-minute walk from here. You up for it?"

"Sure. Why don't you go back to the funeral first and I'll wait for you here. I'm too antsy to sit through to the end."

"Look, Steve. I know you well enough to know you wouldn't have pulled me from the funeral if it weren't important. I'll tell you what. You fill me in on the details on the walk over and we'll get this done right away."

"Roger that," Steve declared, recalling the adrenaline surge he experienced working with the ship drivers and pilots on Admiral Bancroft's carrier battle group staff. He rationalized working with Jack to test his theory paid a more honest tribute to Admiral Bancroft than daydreaming at his funeral. He realized Jack might not share the same exuberance once he briefed him on his theory of the case.

"Here's the deal," Steve began as they started their trek toward Luce Hall. "I have a super-wealthy client who committed suicide while I was talking with him at a restaurant in London. He pulled out a gun and shot himself in the head right there at our table."

"My God," Jack declared. "You really weren't kidding when you said this was a serious case. What on earth caused him to kill himself?"

"I'm not completely sure, but I know it had something to do with that clay tablet the Seabee smuggled out of Iraq last year. As I said, someone stole it and killed him in the process, but not before he took out one of his assailants. Whoever stole it mailed it to my now dead client, and the FBI is getting ready to take it from me if they haven't already."

"Damn, man. You JAGs always did have the best stories," Jack responded, referring to Steve's former life as a Navy lawyer. "I see things haven't changed. Tell me again, though. What does the tablet have to do with me?"

"We haven't even gotten to the crazy part yet. It turns out the tablet is a three-thousand-year-old map pinpointing the location of the Garden of Eden to the island of Bahrain."

"That doesn't surprise me," Jack said matter-of-factly.

Steve stopped in his tracks. "What do you mean that doesn't surprise you?"

"That was always the story when I was in Bahrain."

"I didn't know you were assigned in Bahrain. What did you do there?"

"DESRON FIFTY," Jack responded, referring to Destroyer Squadron Fifty, headquartered in Manama, Bahrain, along with the U.S. Navy's Fifth Fleet in the Persian Gulf. "One of the things we all used to do was drive out to the Tree of Life, which legend said was from the Garden of Eden."

"You're messing with me, right?"

"No, I swear to God," Jack replied. "It's actually pretty amazing. You have to drive about an hour from the base out into the middle of the Bahraini desert. It's sand and rocks as far as you can see. Then, out of nowhere, there's this big, beautiful green tree growing in the sand. There's no water around and it never rains, yet this tree is always lush and seems to thrive in the desert. Because nothing else is able to survive out there, people say it's the Tree of Life from the Garden of Eden."

"We'll I'll be," replied Steve. "I can't believe I've never heard of it before."

"I hadn't either, until I worked in Bahrain. For some reason, it doesn't get a lot of attention."

"All I can say is I think that's about to change," asserted Steve.

"We're here," Jack said, pointing as they approached the front door of Luce Hall. "Let's head on up and we can pull out the charts you need." Jack held the door for Steve as they went into the building and wound their way to Jack's office. Jack unlocked the door and they went inside. It was meticulous, just like Jack's desk when Steve worked with him in the Navy. Framed photographs of all the ships Jack served on adorned the walls.

"Pull up a chair and I'll grab a couple of charts of the Med and Persian Gulf."

"Sounds good," Steve replied, standing behind a chair at the table in front of Jack's desk. He didn't bother to sit down, knowing that as soon as Jack brought over the charts, they'd both be poring over them.

Jack went to a tall box in the back corner of his office and rooted through the rolled-up charts standing on end, all with handwritten labels along their top outside edges. He pulled out two in quick succession and joined Steve at the table.

"What do you want to see first, Med or Persian Gulf?" Jack asked.

"Let's start with the Med," Steve instructed. Jack set the Persian Gulf chart on the arms of one of the empty chairs and unrolled the chart of the Mediterranean Sea on the table. He used a stapler and a tape dispenser to pin down the top edges so it wouldn't roll up while they were looking at it.

"What are you looking for?"

"A port at the top of Italy's boot on the west coast," Steve replied.

Jack swept his left hand across the chart to flatten it out and help focus his attention on Northern Italy. He bent over to get a closer look and then put his finger down next to a large city in northwest Italy. "What about Genoa?"

Steve joined Jack in bending down to look at the city's location more closely. "That's perfect," he responded. "Let's make Genoa the starting point."

"Check," confirmed Jack. "I assume the next point is the destination?"

"That's right—Bahrain."

Jack retrieved the other chart and unrolled it over the Med, using the same stapler and tape dispenser to pin down the corners. He repeated the sweeping motion with his hand and put his finger on the island of Bahrain in the Persian Gulf, just off the coast of Saudi Arabia. "There you go—Bahrain."

"Perfect," Steve declared. "Now, what I really need is to know how long it would take a merchant ship to travel between those two ports."

"What kind of merchant ship?" Jack asked. "It makes a big difference. Most container ships can go through the Suez Canal, while big oil tankers have to go around the Cape of Good Hope off the southern tip of Africa. If a ship has to do that, it adds about two weeks to the trip."

"Let's assume it's your run-of-the-mill container ship doing whatever the average speed is."

"Alright, that's easy," Jack remarked. "We don't even need the charts for that—I can look it up online." Jack left the table and scooted around his desk, taking a seat at his computer. He logged in, found the website he was looking for, and put in Genoa as the starting point, Bahrain as the ending point, and a speed of eighteen knots. "Looks like it's just over 4,500 miles, which would take ten days and twelve hours at eighteen knots, but you still have to account for the trip through the Suez Canal."

"How much will that add on?" Steve asked.

"I'd figure a day-and-a-half to two days, just to be safe. It's possible the ship could get lucky and there'd be a transit slot available right away, but more likely it will have to wait until the next day to catch a convoy going through. Then it will take another twelve to sixteen hours to complete the transit. If you add two days to the trip, you should be pretty close."

"Okay, so that means it's about twelve-and-a-half days from Genoa to Bahrain, including the Suez transit?"

"That sounds about right to me," confirmed Jack. "What else do you need?"

"I think that should do it, but let me think for a minute." Steve started rubbing his chin and tucked his free hand under his armpit, giving him the appearance of one of Jack's academic colleagues pondering the origin of the universe. He didn't want to waste his opportunity with Jack. Once he left, it might not be so easy to get his questions answered. "Can we look at the Med chart again?"

"Sure." Jack switched around the charts so the Mediterranean Sea sat on top. Steve again bent down and stared at it, knowing he needed more information but unable to think of any more questions.

"You know," Jack continued, "if you tell me what you're looking for, I might be able to help."

"All right, that's a deal," Steve announced. "I just came up with a new theory for a case I've been working on. It's still pretty rough, but I'm willing to talk about it if you are. You've just got to promise me one thing."

"What's that," Jack asked, putting his hands in his pockets.

"If this is too half-baked, you've got to be honest with me and tell me. I don't want to look like a complete fool when I go to the authorities."

"That sounds ominous already. You know me, though. I'll tell it like it is."

"Okay, then," Steve began. "Why don't we take a seat and I'll lay it out for you." Both men pulled out adjacent chairs so they would have a good view of the charts stretched across the table. Steve took a deep breath and then started rolling out his theory as best he could, even though he was still mulling over how all the seemingly extraneous details might tie together.

"So," he continued, "do you remember about a week ago when an armed group flew into Turin, Italy, and stole the Shroud of Turin?"

"Hell yeah, it was all over the news. Pretty damn bold, I might add. I can't believe they got away with it."

"Me either, but now I'm thinking it might be linked to my case somehow."

"You've got to be kidding me." Jack paused like that was all he wanted to say, then his eyes lit up with a new insight. "Wait a minute. When did your client die?"

"Good point," Steve conceded. "My client died on September 30 and the heist was only a week ago."

"So how can they be related?"

"I know there are other people involved—I just don't know who. In fact, they've been trying to get the tablet from me ever since I picked it up from my client's post office box. Somebody even shot and almost killed the guy who cleans my office at night because they thought he could steal the tablet from me. There've got to be heavy hitters involved to pull off that kind of stuff."

"You aren't kidding," Jack responded. "As I recall, there were two helicopters and a bunch of armed mercenaries involved in the raid. I figured there had to be terrorists or some rogue country behind it. It was a major deal."

"That's what I thought, too," Steve said. "Maybe this won't be plausible—let's see. How far is it from Turin to the Med?"

"I don't know, but we can find out." Jack grabbed the dividers he kept on the table and opened them so one end rested on Turin and the other on Genoa. Then he compared the distance to the chart's latitude scale. "Looks like about a hundred miles."

"So that's easy helicopter range, isn't it?"

Jack pulled away from the chart and leaned back in his chair. "Okay, I see where you're going. There's nothing easy about this. It'd take some real pros to pull this off. They'd have to fly in the dark and under the radar all the way from Turin to the coast somewhere around here." Jack tapped his finger on the chart between Genoa and Nice, France. "Then they'd have to cross into international waters and rendezvous with a merchant ship equipped with a helo pad. I'm sure the authorities thought of that on a theft this big. Any ship with a landing pad or a helo on board would have been looked at right away."

"I'm with you, Jack. But what if the ship didn't have a landing pad. Couldn't a helo land on containers if they were configured properly?"

"Yeah, it could be done, but again, it would take some real pros—ex-special forces types. You're getting into a pretty elite group. And what about the helo? It'd stick out like a sore thumb if they tried to tie it down to the containers, and the authorities would have found it for sure had it refueled and gone back to shore."

"So maybe we should be looking for a self-loading container ship with a crane. Once the helo delivers the Shroud, the crane ditches the helo over the side. Then it's easy to hide the Shroud even if the authorities board and search the vessel."

"Hot damn," Jack said, slapping the chart-topped table with the palm of his hand. "I've got to admit, it's do-able. It'd take balls, but it's do-able." Jack started to push away from the table as if satisfied with the resolution, then stopped short. "Wait a minute, Houston. We got a problem. I thought the authorities found the remnants of two helos in a burned-out barn about a hundred kilometers northeast of Turin? Didn't the Italians determine those where the helos the thieves used?"

Steve thought for a moment. "That's what the news said, but what if one or both of those helos were decoys? What if instead only one of the helos used in the raid flew to the barn and the thieves staged another helo there in advance so the authorities would think they'd found both birds. Then they'd stop looking elsewhere, at least long enough for the culprits to get away with the Shroud."

"You think whoever it is has the kind of money that they can just torch two helos and not worry about it?"

"Yeah, I do. Two helicopters would be budget dust for my client alone, and based on what you're saying, I'm thinking someone much bigger is involved. After all, we're talking about the Shroud of Turin here."

"I guess it's pretty obvious now that I think about it."

"What do you mean?" Steve asked, surprised that Jack now seemed to be arguing his side.

"These guys are going to ask the Catholic Church for a billion-dollar ransom, and if the Pope says no, they'll threaten to destroy the Shroud. The Church will have to cough up the money because they can't let anything happen to it. If they won't pay, everyone will say the Church knew the Shroud wasn't the real deal. And, if the Pope believes it is the real deal, the Church'll pay anything to get it back." Jack grinned. "I've got to hand it to them, Steve. It's evil, but it's brilliant. Bloody brilliant."

Steve snapped his fingers and left his hand suspended with his index finger pointing in mid-air at Jack's invisible revelation. "Of course, why didn't I think of that before? That's got to be it, Jack. You're spot on." Steve put his hands behind his head and rocked on the back two legs of his chair as he ran through the ramifications of Jack's theory.

"Okay, counselor," Jack interjected. "I recognize that look. All you asshole JAGs get that same damn look whenever you're about to tell us ship drivers why we're wrong." Jack chuckled and half-smiled as if he'd been waiting for years to make his observation.

Steve was too focused on analyzing his case to react to Jack's jibe, instead treating it as a helpful critique to better flesh out his theory. "No, I really think you're spot on, Jack, but there are a couple of things that come to mind now that you mention it." Steve stopped rocking and planted his elbows on the table with his hands clasped. "First, I don't think they'll ever really destroy the Shroud. It's their insurance policy. As long as they have it and can threaten to destroy it, no one will dare touch them. They might damage it to show they mean business, but I don't think they'll ever destroy it entirely. If they do, they know they'll be as good as dead."

"I'll buy that," Jack commented. "Kinda makes their plan even more brilliant in a way, doesn't it? Now that they have the Shroud, they're untouchable." Jack started shaking his head in disbelief. "I still can't believe they got away with it. So—what's the other point?"

"It's the reason my client got involved in the first place—the tablet. He must have wanted the Shroud because he thought it was the key to the Garden of Eden."

"You're going to have to give me more than that, Steve. You completely lost me."

"Of course," Steve agreed. "When my client came across the tablet on the black market, he must have had someone translate it for him from photos. On the front is a map that shows the Garden of Eden in Bahrain. Like you said, that's not particularly astounding news in and of itself. But on the back, there's a passage almost identical to the Bible's account of God closing the Garden of Eden."

"I still don't get it," Jack admitted. "Why's that such a big deal?"

"Because there's a phrase on the tablet that's not in the Genesis account. It says God put an angel with a sword in the Garden to block the entrance and guard the Tree of Life until the face of God reappears."

"Sorry, Steve, but I'm not a damn biblical scholar. What's the phrase on the tablet that's not in Genesis?"

"Until the face of God reappears."

"Holy shit," Jack exclaimed. "Sorry about that language when we're talking religion here, but are you thinking what I think you're thinking?"

"I'm afraid I am. The Shroud of Turin is on its way to Bahrain as we speak. When it gets there, someone's going to see if the face on the Shroud unlocks the Garden and the secrets of the Tree of Life."

"Yeah, and if it doesn't work, they've still got a billion-dollar ransom coming." Jack shook his head again. "Like I said, it's evil and brilliant at the same time. Except, if finding the key to the Tree of Life was such a big thing to your client, why did he kill himself after setting everything in motion?"

"I haven't figured that out yet," admitted Steve. "I didn't even see the connection to the Shroud until the chaplain started talking about St. Brendan's voyage to the Promised Land. That's when it hit me that the Shroud must be on a ship heading for Bahrain."

"What are you going to do now?" Jack asked.

"That's a good question. I need to think through this a little more and then tell the FBI and Scotland Yard what I've come up with."

"Man, Scotland Yard's involved in this, too?

"Yeah, they've been involved since my client shot himself in London."

"Like I said, you JAGs always did have great stories." Jack slid the stapler and the tape dispenser off the charts and they started rolling up out of their own inertia. "You need these? I've got extras."

"Yeah, why don't you let me take them just in case. I'll get them back to you when this thing's over."

"Why don't we head back over to the funeral and pay our respects to Mrs. Bancroft," Jack suggested. "I'm sure it must be over by now."

"I'm sorry about that, Jack. I should have waited until after the funeral. I suppose this could have waited, but you've been a huge help. You've taken this from a raw theory to a plausible plan. I can't thank you enough."

"Don't worry about it, Steve. You know Admiral Bancroft wouldn't have wanted it any other way. I would stash those charts in your car before we see Mrs. Bancroft. No sense advertising we left early."

"Sounds like a plan," Steve replied as he gathered up the charts and walked out of the office with Jack locking the door behind them. Now was the tough part—convincing law enforcement his theory was plausible and needed to be taken seriously. Jack's ransom addition made perfect sense as far as the Shroud of Turin was concerned. The harder sell would be connecting the Shroud to Arul Ashirvadam. It all seemed so fantastic. His client was a smart, sophisticated entrepreneur, as was Michela Baresi. They had to know the authorities would eventually tie them to the theft of the Shroud and bring down their empires. Michela must have realized it first and started to cooperate with law enforcement to salvage La Fontana. Had only Ashirvadam been involved, he could have forgiven Michela's sin. But whoever Ashirvadam partnered with—which Steve now realized was what Ashirvadam meant when he said he sold his soul—couldn't tolerate the defection. And, with Ashirvadam and Michela both out of the picture, Steve couldn't comprehend why the conspirators would risk taking the Shroud to Bahrain. Something didn't add up. He had a three-hour drive to think about it and figure out what it was, as long as he could keep from falling asleep and killing himself in a ditch. He felt like he was running on empty.

31

7:47 a.m. on Monday, October 18, 2004
Williamsburg, Virginia

STEVE PULLED HIS CAR INTO HIS parking space behind his office and left the key in the ignition. He needed a moment to get his head together before going into the office. He had so much to do, he felt a tightness in his chest. Wasting all day Sunday didn't help. He woke up early on Sunday afternoon from a jet lag induced coma, even more exhausted than before he fell asleep the night before. He tried to reach Detective Fields, but she didn't answer or return his calls and it was too late to call Casey in India and Detective Cavendish in London. He ended up moping around all day eating junk food and running uninteresting Internet searches. He finally called it quits around eleven, but with his internal clock still confused as to what time it was, he couldn't sleep. The last time he remembered seeing the clock, it was just after two on Monday morning and he had to get up at six thirty to be in the office by eight.

Now, with his head no more together than before his pause, he took his keys and opened the door not quite wide enough to intrude on the empty parking space next to him. As he slid his foot out onto the pavement, a gray sedan with a male driver and a female passenger zoomed into the spot next to him, barely missing his open door. The sedan lurched forward as its brakes dug into the discs and stopped the vehicle with the front bumper hanging over the top of the concrete barrier at the end of the space. Steve pulled his leg back in the car and closed the door, irked but not wanting to get in the way of whatever hurry the people next to him were in.

No sooner had his door closed than the doors to the sedan opened and Special Agent Fields hopped out. The driver got out too; all Steve could see was a man in a suit he assumed was Special Agent Crosby. As he looked up at Fields, she knocked on his window.

"Good morning, Mr. Stilwell. Can we talk for a minute?"

Steve opened his door slowly to avoid contact with the sedan and climbed outside. Fields stepped back, but the restricted space between the cars gave Steve little room to maneuver. Assuming Fields' Hollywood entrance didn't portend anything positive, he took a guarded approach.

"You cut that a little close, didn't you?" Steve asked, directing his question to Crosby.

"Shit happens," Crosby replied half under his breath yet loud enough for Steve to hear.

"Yeah, well maybe it shouldn't happen so close next time. And by the way, you're not getting this conversation off to a very good start." Feeling like he'd registered as much disapproval as he dared, he offered Fields an olive branch. "How about we head into my office and you can tell me what's going on."

"Thanks, but that won't be necessary," Fields replied in a friendly-enough tone to let Steve know she'd accepted his offering and was reciprocating with one of her own. "We heard you were back and wanted to touch base with you." Crosby leaned against the sedan's trunk while Fields did all the talking.

"There has to be more to it than just wanting to touch base," Steve countered. "You could've done that by telephone. Why don't you level with me and tell me what's really going on."

"Fair enough," agreed Fields. She reached out and grabbed the sedan's door handle as if she needed the support to convey her message. "You need to watch your back. This thing just got bigger—lots bigger."

"After what I just went through in Europe, I can't imagine it getting any bigger, but okay."

"Yeah, we talked to Detective Cavendish," Fields continued, "and we know about Michela Baresi. I'm afraid there's more."

"Well, it shouldn't involve me now that you've got the tablet. Whoever wants it must know that."

"That's just it," Fields remarked. "We don't have the tablet."

"What do you mean you don't have the tablet? Marjorie called me when you brought the search warrant to my office. She should have told you exactly where to find Ashirvadam's safe deposit box."

"She did, and the tablet's gone."

"That can't be. It was in Ashirvadam's safe deposit box—I put it there myself. No one should have been able to access it without a key."

"We know," acknowledged Fields. "We saw you on the bank's surveillance tape."

"Then what's the problem? Why don't you have the tablet?"

"Because last Friday, somebody got to the bank employee responsible for safe deposit boxes. He had a locksmith drill the lock along with two other boxes they were cleaning out. Now the tablet and the bank employee are missing. It doesn't look good."

Steve thought for a moment. "If they have the tablet, why should I have anything to worry about?"

"You're probably right," conceded Fields, "but we wanted to warn you just in case they want to cover their tracks. You and the guy who cleans your office know what their man on the street looks like, and thanks to that stunt you pulled at the motel, he might have an incentive to even the score."

"I've got to admit," Steve replied, "that was pretty stupid. I don't know what I was thinking."

"You weren't thinking," Crosby chimed in. "You're lucky you're still alive."

"Any idea who's behind this?" Steve asked.

"We've got our theories, but that's all they are," Fields admitted. "We initially thought it was your client. With all that's happened since he killed himself, though, there has to be someone else calling the shots."

"You think Ashirvadam was innocent?"

"I didn't say that," Fields replied. "I think he was in deep—maybe too deep—and that's why he killed himself. We'll get to the bottom of this. It just may take a while."

Steve knew he'd reached the point in the conversation where he could float his Bahrain theory. Fields had been a straight shooter since their first meeting and he liked the way she ran her case. He would have to get her to take a quantum leap, though, to connect the tablet, the Shroud of Turin, and the Tree of Life. He surmised Cavendish might be more plugged into the Shroud heist because it took place in Europe, making it more likely he'd be able to visualize a connection between the tablet and the Shroud. Still, cooperating with the FBI now might be better for him and his practice in the long run, so he decided to test the waters with Fields.

"I'm not sure you've got as much time as you think," Steve asserted.

"What makes you think that?" Fields asked.

"I've got a hunch the theft of the tablet and the Shroud of Turin heist are related."

"The Shroud of Turin heist?" Crosby asked skeptically.

"Yeah, from a cathedral in Turin, Italy. It happened a week ago yesterday. You familiar with it?"

Crosby pulled away from the trunk. "Of course, I'm familiar with it," he snapped. "It's my job to be familiar with art thefts. I just don't see where you're coming from. Can you prove it?" Fields stepped sideways to help bring Crosby into the discussion, but he made no move to come closer. He seemed satisfied to throw grenades from a distance.

"To be honest, I can't at all," Steve admitted. "It's just a hunch. But if I'm right, a ship with the Shroud of Turin will be in the vicinity of Bahrain as early as this Thursday. This might be your only opportunity to get the Shroud back before it goes underground."

Fields picked up where Crosby left off. "Why don't you tell us why you think the Shroud is on a ship heading for Bahrain."

"Are you sure you don't want to step into my office?

"I think we're good," responded Fields, sounding skeptical.

"Okay," Steve said, taking a more relaxed pose by resting his backside against his car and turning slightly sideways to see Fields and Crosby. "I guess the best place to start is with the tablet. Have you seen a translation yet?"

"Not yet," answered Fields.

"Then here are the basics. The front of the tablet contains a map indicating the Garden of Eden is on the island of Bahrain. The back contains text that says God closed the Garden and placed an angel there to guard the way to the Tree of Life."

Crosby crossed his arms, looking disinterested and impatient. "That's all very interesting," he interjected, "but what's it got to do with the Shroud?"

"I'm getting to that," Steve said. "When the passage talks about the angel, it says he'll guard the way to the Tree of Life until the face of God returns."

"Don't tell me," Crosby said, cracking a cynical smile. "Since the Shroud supposedly has the face of Jesus on it, you think taking the Shroud to Bahrain is going to magically reveal the Garden of Eden." Crosby huffed, emphasizing his contempt for the thought before lambasting it further. "Do you actually believe that, Stilwell? We'd get laughed out of the department if we took that rot back to headquarters. You're talking about an ancient myth scribbled on a hunk of clay. We're wasting our time, Sheinelle."

"Let the man finish," Fields chided. "Until somebody gives me a better theory, I'm all ears."

"Look, I understand this sounds a crazy, but it's not what I believe or what you believe that matters. It's what whoever has the tablet and the Shroud believe. And I'm thinking somebody believes that if they take the Shroud of Turin to the Tree of Life in Bahrain, something will happen."

"What Tree of Life is that, Mr. Stilwell?" asked Fields.

"Believe it or not, there's actually a tree called the Tree of Life in the Bahraini desert. I'd never heard of it either, so I looked it up on the web. Sure enough, in a place that otherwise looks God-forsaken, there's a big tree thriving in the desert."

"I can't believe I'm saying this," relayed Crosby, "but let's say I buy your theory that someone believes getting the Shroud to the tree gets them into the Garden of Eden. Why in the world would it happen on Thursday?"

"Because that's how long it takes a ship to travel from Genoa, Italy, to Bahrain, assuming it goes through the Suez Canal."

Crosby kept his cross examination going. "What makes you think the Shroud is on a ship? I don't recall any information indicating a ship was involved."

"I've got to admit, that's speculation on my part. I'm thinking that one of the helos involved in the heist could have landed on a ship in the Mediterranean without being detected. The ship would be free and clear to sail to Bahrain."

"I'm sorry," Fields began, "I'm afraid I've got to agree with Special Agent Crosby. As I recall, the Italian authorities announced they found the wreckage of the two helos involved in the theft. Aside from that, everything you're telling me is conjecture and hunch. You're not giving me any facts to hang my hat on."

Steve stood up and put his hands in his pockets. "What do you have to lose by alerting the Bahraini authorities? All they need to do is keep an eye on the Tree of Life and check out any unusual activity. You don't have to tell them why."

"I tell you what," Fields said. "As soon as we get back to Washington, we'll update Detective Cavendish at Scotland Yard. If he wants to pursue it, he can. Our interest is in the tablet, anyway. Nothing about the Shroud is under our jurisdiction."

"Unless, as I suspect, the people behind the tablet and the people behind the Shroud are the same," countered Steve. "Then it would be your concern."

"Alright," stated Fields. "We know your client was involved with the tablet, so why don't you start by telling us what you know."

"I've told you everything I can, Detective Fields, you know that. The whole reason you came here today was to warn me because you know very well someone in addition to my client is involved."

A look of satisfaction streamed across Crosby's face. "I guess we're at an impasse, then, aren't we Stilwell?"

"I'm afraid we are," conceded Steve. "But you will tell Detective Cavendish, won't you? Otherwise, I'll need to call him myself."

"We'll call him as soon as we get back to Washington," Fields replied. She smiled politely and stepped forward to shake Steve's hand. "I guess we better get going." Crosby didn't bother to say goodbye. He retraced his steps around the back of the sedan, jumped into the driver's seat, and started the car.

"We'll be in touch," Fields said as she began her own withdrawal by climbing into the passenger seat and closing the door. She never looked back at Steve, instead focusing on something in her lap. Steve stood by his car and watched her drive away. He wasn't sure he bought her explanation for coming to see him. She could have called him and warned him of any potential danger. As with everything, there had to be more to the story, although he was starting to care less and less about what it might be.

32

8:11 a.m. on Monday, October 18, 2004
Williamsburg, Virginia

STEVE STARED AT THE STEAM RISING from the fresh cup of coffee Marjorie set in front of him, hoping somehow it would discern his next move. Instead, it just drifted upward and disappeared, offering no insight or deeper meaning. He picked up the cup by the handle and brought it gingerly toward his lips, not wanting to burn himself on his first sip and ruin the rest of the brew. He blew ripples across the milky brown surface until he thought it was cool enough to drink. Just as he was ready to give it a go, Marjorie returned to his office.

"You seem a little down this morning, Mr. Stilwell. Is something wrong?"

"Can I be honest, Marjorie?"

"Of course, you can." Marjorie sat down in a chair in front of his desk and edged forward as far as she could go. Her eyes looked both worried and concerned, making Steve regret he'd opened the door to being vulnerable with someone he worked with. He decided to say just enough to sound convincing without going over an imaginary line he had yet to draw.

"I've got to admit, the—," a ringing telephone interrupted him mid-sentence.

"I'll run get it," Marjorie declared, propelling herself out of the chair.

"I've got it," Steve countered, recognizing he'd just been granted a reprieve, which already made him feel better. He motioned for Marjorie to keep her seat. "I'm sure this will only take a minute." He picked up the phone and switched to his best client service voice.

"Law offices of Stilwell and Pantel, this is Steve Stilwell speaking."

"Steve, hi, it's Casey. How are you?"

"Oh hi, Casey. It's great to hear from you. Let me put you on speaker. Marjorie's here with me." Steve pushed the speakerphone button, turned the volume up all the way, then hung up the receiver. "Can you hear me?"

"Loud and clear," Casey replied.

"Fantastic, we've got you the same. How are you feeling?"

"Muuuuuch better. In fact, the doctor said I can travel Wednesday, so I'll make my reservations as soon as I get my new passport. With a little luck, I'll be back in Williamsburg Wednesday night."

"That sure is good news," Steve replied. "Why don't you plan on taking off the rest of the week. So much has gone on with this case, we'll need to regroup next week and rethink our approach. Besides, I'm hoping the crazy stuff, as Marjorie likes to put it, is behind us."

"Well pardon the French, but it's about damn time," Marjorie said in the most exaggerated Tidewater twang she could muster. She looked down her nose and eyed Steve, conveying her Mayberry expression meant more than humor—she felt genuine relief.

"I second that," Casey added.

"I must say, though," Steve reflected. "I did learn an interesting fact at Admiral Bancroft's funeral on Saturday."

"I knew it was too good to be true," Marjorie interrupted. "You attorneys just can't let things go."

"I'm not sure there's anything we can do about it this time," Steve reassured her. "This one's out of our hands."

"I'll believe that when I see it," replied Marjorie, crossing her legs and resting her hands on the legal pad in her lap.

Steve grinned. "Point taken, Marjorie. I'll let you be the judge. You remember when somebody stole the Shroud of Turin last week?"

"Yeah," Marjorie responded.

"Well, I'm thinking whoever has our tablet is also behind that theft."

"Wait a minute," interrupted Casey. "Shouldn't the FBI have our tablet by now?"

"They should," Steve answered, "but they don't. I spoke with Special Agent Fields this morning and someone beat them to it." Steve relayed what Fields told him about the theft of the tablet from the bank and his theory about taking the Shroud of Turin to the Tree of Life to unlock Paradise.

Casey spoke tentatively. "Can I be honest with you, Steve?"

"Of course."

"I don't buy it—it's too far-fetched. Do you really think someone would go to all of the trouble to steal the Shroud just to see if it opened some mythological gate to the Garden of Eden? I'm having trouble taking this conversation seriously."

"If I had the Shroud, I'd try it," Marjorie admitted, unaffected by Casey's skepticism. "Just think if you got to see the real Garden of Eden, even if for a moment. Wouldn't that be worth it?"

"Actually, money's what I think it all comes down to," Steve replied, recalling his conversation with Jack Matzen at the Naval Academy. "The Catholic Church will have to pay whatever ransom the thieves ask for. If they don't, it would be like admitting they think the Shroud is a fake."

"Now that I can buy," Casey declared, "except for one thing."

"What's that?" Steve asked.

"Think about it. If the purpose of the theft is ransom, why take the Shroud to Bahrain and risk being caught with it? Isn't it much more likely they'd hide the Shroud until they get their ransom?"

Steve thought for a minute. Casey's point was valid—it was the biggest hole in his theory. But if she was smart and quick enough to spot the problem, she was also smart and quick enough to figure out the solution. He turned her question back around on her.

"You've got me on that one, Casey. What do you think, though? If it were you, why would you take the Shroud to Bahrain and risk everything?"

Marjorie couldn't restrain herself. She actually popped out of her chair and started to argue her case holding her notepad, just like she'd seen Steve and Casey do time after time when they were trying to convince each other of their latest legal theory. "Don't ya'll get it? There's millions of people out there who'd risk everything to see the real Garden of Eden. If you throw in the chance to touch the Tree of Life, forget about it. I'll bet there's someone who's paying a lot of money for that chance."

"Okay, Marjorie," conceded Casey. "I can see that, except the pool of people who are rich enough and religious enough to do all that has to be pretty small, especially now that both Ashirvadam and Michela are dead. Either way, I don't think we care. Like you said, Steve, it's out of our hands."

"I'm afraid so," Steve replied. "I told the FBI my concerns and now it's up to them. Let's regroup at nine next Monday and figure out where we need to go. Now we know for sure we're representing the estate of a person who was involved in some pretty serious criminal conduct, so we'll have to see how that affects our representation. Is everyone okay with that?"

"Works for me," Casey replied.

"Me too," chimed in Marjorie.

"Alright," Steve concluded. "Have a safe flight back, Casey. We'll see you on Monday. Please give me a call when you're back in Williamsburg so we'll know you're safe. Marjorie will hold down the fort until then."

"Bye, Steve. Bye, Marjorie," Casey responded, ending the call. Steve pushed the speaker phone button to make sure the call disconnected, then looked back over his desk toward Marjorie.

"Okay, Mr. Stilwell, what do you need me to do?"

"Hmmm. Let me think about that for a minute." Steve knew what he needed to do—look at his pending cases, catch up on the estates he'd let slide while he was in London and Milan, and come up with the outline of a new game plan for the Ashirvadam estate. He couldn't get there, though, because the conversation with Casey and Marjorie reverberated through his thoughts. Casey was right. If someone intended to hold the Shroud for ransom, they would be unlikely to risk sending it to Bahrain. But Marjorie was right too. There were likely millions of people, rich and poor, who would risk everything for a chance to walk in the Garden of Eden and eat from the Tree of Life, even if that chance came from a clay tablet buried in the Iraqi desert for 3,000 years. In fact, Ashirvadam proved Marjorie's point. He'd killed himself over the tablet. Then the connection hit him.

"I've got it, Marjorie."

"Got what?"

"I can prove the tablet and the Shroud thefts are related." He turned around to his credenza and rooted through the stack of open case files. When he got to Ashirvadam's file, the item he was looking for was right at the top clipped to the left side. "This is it. It was right in front of our noses all the time."

"What is it, Mr. Stilwell?"

"Do you remember the letter we received from Ashirvadam giving us instructions about how to handle his estate?"

"Sure, though I don't recall anything about either the tablet or the Shroud. What's it say?"

"It directs us to provide the euros from Ashirvadam's safe deposit box to the Cathedral of San Giovanni Battisti in Turin." Steve set the file down and began to bang out text in the Google search field on his computer. He hit enter and waited for the results to appear. When they did, he clicked on the first link. "That's it, Marjorie. The cathedral Ashirvadam wanted us to give the money to is the one that housed the Shroud of Turin. He must have felt guilty about the plot to steal it, so he directed us to give the church money to ease his conscience."

"I told you, Mr. Stilwell. Some people would risk everything to see the Garden and the Tree. I don't think what our client did had anything to do with money—it was his religious beliefs. He just got a little off track when he started committing crimes to get the keys to the Garden."

"I'm with you on that, Marjorie. Although there is one more thing that doesn't make sense."

"What's that?"

"If Ashirvadam wanted to see the Garden so badly, why did he kill himself? I mean, if he believed he was going to see the Garden and the Tree of Life, wouldn't he try to hang on until he actually saw them? Something doesn't add up."

"Maybe he did it for someone else."

"That's got to be it, Marjorie. The question is who?"

"I can't help you with that, Mr. Stilwell."

Steve locked onto the thought. The one person he could see Ashirvadam doing it for was Michela, and she was dead. Yet if his theory about Ashirvadam's motive for conspiring to steal the Shroud was correct, someone could be making their way to Bahrain right now to rendezvous with a ship bringing the relic to the island, if they weren't already on the ship themselves. Other than connecting his client to the plot, which he could not tell anyone about at this point, he had no proof it would happen. Still, he was convinced he was correct and that Thursday would be the day of reckoning.

The problem was, although he told Special Agent Fields about his suspicions and she promised to relay them to Detective Cavendish, they weren't in a position to take action. His theory was pure speculation, bordering on the ridiculous. It required wealthy, educated people to believe if they took the Shroud to some forlorn tree in the middle of the Bahraini desert, they'd somehow get a supernatural ticket to Paradise. No self-respecting FBI agent or Scotland Yard detective would react to that, which meant those responsible would escape justice. They'd almost killed Phan and murdered Michela, both attacks Steve felt somewhat responsible for. The least he could do was help find out who was behind them. That left him only one alternative.

Marjorie stood up to leave. "Is there anything else you need me to do, Mr. Stilwell? You've got the rest of the day open, so you've got time to catch up on things."

"You know, there is one more thing." He paused to make sure he wanted to go down this road, then remembered his mantra from his Navy JAG Corps days—be bold. This might be his last chance to make a difference in the case and he didn't want to let it get by. "I tell you what. Can you book me on a flight to Bahrain leaving out of Washington tomorrow? I need to check out one last thing."

Marjorie frowned and put her hands on her hips. "Like I said. You attorneys just can't let things go." She headed for the door, then turned back to retrieve the full cup of cold coffee still sitting on his desk blotter. "And I'll get you a fresh cup of coffee while I'm at it."

Steve smiled. "Thanks Marjorie. I don't know what I'd do without you."

Marjorie kept walking out the door and into the lobby. "Me either," she shouted without looking back. Then she disappeared around the corner on her way to the kitchen, while Steve set his sights on Bahrain.

33

3:13 p.m. on Wednesday, October 20, 2004
Manama, Bahrain

Hot didn't begin to describe the afternoon—inferno seemed more apropos. The temperature itself wasn't bad, about ninety-two degrees, normal for an October Wednesday afternoon in Bahrain and nothing Steve wasn't used to in Williamsburg. The difference was the sun. Steve sensed the gods holding a magnifying glass far above him in the cloudless skies of the Persian Gulf, trying to incinerate him like the ants he'd mercilessly fried as a kid. He walked down American Alley, weaving around the trash littering the sidewalk in front of the numerous fast food restaurants, trying to nab a few seconds of shade any time a building's shadow allowed. When he reached the end, he came to the entrance to Naval Support Activity Bahrain and showed his retired military identification card to the petty officer manning the gate.

"May I help you, sir?" the petty officer asked.

"Yes, I'm here to meet with Captain Phil Nash from the Fifth Fleet staff," Steve replied, referring to the major Navy command located within the installation.

"Yes, sir. Please come this way." The petty officer led Steve through a metal detector and into a waiting area where a short, stocky Navy captain in a desert camouflage uniform waited. The gold-embroidered wings above his left breast pocket announced him as a naval aviator. Steve approached him to introduce himself.

"Captain Nash, thanks so much for meeting with me today. I'm Steve

Stilwell." He stuck out his hand and the two men shook hands.

"Phil Nash, glad to meet you," Nash replied, sounding like he was fresh off the boat from New York City. "How about we take a walk to the NAVCENT headquarters building and chat along the way. You ever been here before?" Nash led the way out of the Pass and ID Office and onto the main street leading into the base complex. Steve couldn't help but look around. In contrast to the litter and dust-ravaged American Alley, the base looked pristine, with sand-colored buildings and palm trees dotting the landscape. The base streets were limited to pedestrians, but almost no one was outside, making the fortress feel empty.

"No, I never made it to the Persian Gulf, just the Med," Steve replied as they strolled along the street. "In fact, I just got in a few hours ago. I was able to catch a flight out of Dulles yesterday morning and got in around twelve. How about you? How long you been here?"

"Got here six months ago on one-year orders. Six months to go, but it doesn't seem like that. We're so slammed with Iraq and Afghanistan, time flies by. You know how it is, not enough hours in a day. So, what's this case you want to tell me about?"

"As I mentioned on the phone, I took on a very wealthy client back in Williamsburg, Virginia, and it looks like he got mixed up in the black market for ancient artifacts. The one that's causing all the problems is a clay tablet smuggled out of Iraq last year by a Seabee."

"That doesn't sound good," Nash replied as they rounded a corner by the base medical center. "What happened to the sailor—did he get court-martialed?"

"I'm afraid he's dead."

"Because of the tablet?"

"Yeah. He advertised it online and somebody killed him and took the tablet. He did manage to knock off one of his attackers in the process. A little while later, my client ended up with the tablet."

"No shit?"

"It gets even more convoluted than that, but at least that gives you an idea of what I'm dealing with."

"Okay, you got my attention, but what's all this got to do with me? Did the sailor know me or something?"

"No, nothing like that," Steve reassured him. He stopped in the shadow of the Security Barracks where it was more comfortable to talk. "Look, Phil, I know you're a busy man these days, so there's no need for us to go to your office. I'll just be straight with you."

"Okay. What do you need from me?"

"Here's the deal. I think a container ship is going to pull into Bahrain in the next forty-eight hours from Genoa, Italy. It's possible it could anchor offshore within helo or water taxi range. My guess is, though, it will pull up pierside. It's also possible the ship didn't leave from Genoa, but it had to be in the vicinity of Genoa immediately before it started its voyage on October tenth."

"Why October tenth?"

"Because that's the day someone stole the Shroud of Turin."

"Wait a minute," Phil said, taking a step back and crossing his arms over his chest. "Are you telling me this ship had something to do with that raid?"

"That's exactly what I'm saying."

"No shit?" he replied, echoing an earlier phrase. "Why are you telling me? I'm sure the Italian authorities must be all over this."

Steve put his hands in his pockets, hoping to convey confidence in his theory. "Let's just say I've told the FBI and they promised to tell Scotland Yard. To be honest, though, I'm not sure they're in a position to follow-up on it."

"I don't understand—why's that?"

"Because I've got no hard proof—it's just a hunch. That's where you come in. You should be able to tell me if there's a ship that meets the profile."

"Come on, man. You were a flippin' JAG. You know I can't give you that kind of information. We're done here." Phil uncrossed his arms like he was ready to start leading Steve back to the main gate.

"Wait a minute, Phil. I'm not asking for anything classified. If there's a ship that meets those parameters and the information is classified, just tell NCIS. They can run with it. I can even email you the name and contact information for the FBI agent handling the case. That said, if you can do it with unclassified sources, all I'm asking is that you give me a call. All I need is the name of the ship and when it will arrive. I'll take it from there."

Phil re-crossed his arms over his chest, indicating Steve had successfully backed him away from the ledge. "I guess once the ship's in port or at anchor, it's public knowledge," he rationalized out loud.

"Exactly," Steve confirmed. "I don't want to touch anything classified—just unclassified information."

"How do I know you're not just some crackpot with another conspiracy theory?"

Steve reached into his pocket and pulled out a small stack of business cards. "Here, this has my website on it. You can check it out and make your own judgment. You can also call the JAG front office at the Pentagon and ask them about me. They won't know anything about this case, but they'll know about me. Then you can reach your own conclusions."

"I'll have to think about it. I've got to make sure I'm not doing something illegal."

"Look, I wouldn't ask you to do something illegal because that would make me guilty too. If you find a ship that meets the criteria, ask your JAG before you get back to me. If he says it's wrong, you'll never have to talk to me again. But if he says it's okay, you just might be helping get the Shroud of Turin back from whoever stole it."

"Alright, I'll consider it, but no promises. And, if it turns out you're asking me to do something illegal, I'll turn your name over to NCIS."

"That works for me," Steve replied.

"If I do get the information, what are you planning to do with it? I mean, you can't go on the ship and do anything. This is Bahrain, for crying out loud. They'll lock your ass up, and since this is Ramadan, they won't have any patience for westerners who muck up their observance."

"It's Ramadan?" Steve asked.

"Yeah, we're right in the middle of it. I've hit a couple of Iftar suppers myself with officers from the Bahraini Navy."

"That explains something else, then doesn't it?"

"What's that?"

"Why they're pulling this off now. They might have thought security would be more lax during Ramadan."

"Security for what? For that matter, what do you expect to happen when the ship pulls in? You never told me."

"Well, here's where it gets a little crazy," Steve admitted.

"I've got news for you, Steve. Everything you've said so far sounds crazy. Hit me with it anyway."

"Okay, you asked for it. I think the Shroud of Turin is on that ship and somebody's going to take it to the Tree of Life to see what happens."

"What do you mean, see what happens? Why would anything happen?"

"Because that smuggled tablet we talked about said it will."

"You've got to be kidding me? Your wasting my time because you think somebody stole that Shroud just to take it to the Bahraini desert to see what might happen?"

"I'm afraid that's it," Steve conceded. "But it's not what you and I believe. It's what whoever has the Shroud believes, and that's what I think they're going to do."

Phil uncrossed his arms again and ran his hand down the back of his neck. "Okay, you made your pitch and I got it. Anything else you want me to know?"

"Like I said, just let me know if you see a ship that was in the vicinity of Genoa on October tenth arrive in the vicinity of Bahrain in the next couple of days. If you can't tell me, tell NCIS and give them my name. Just please don't ignore it. I'm not asking for anything else."

"Roger that," Phil responded. "How about we head back to the gate so we can both get on with our days." Phil motioned with his hand and the two men started retracing their steps to the main gate.

"Oh, there is one more thing," Steve said, the back of his shirt between his shoulders darkening with sweat from his renewed exposure to the intense Gulf sun. "I'm staying in the Jewel Hotel at the end of American Alley across from the grocery store. I'm in room 803. I don't know what the telephone number is, but I'm sure if you call the front desk, they can put you through."

"Got it," Phil replied, sounding abrupt and disinterested. "I know exactly where that is."

Steve knew he'd lost the fight when Phil made no attempt to write down the name of the place or the room number. At this point, he knew Phil just wanted to get him off base so he could get back to work. He'd probably even report Steve to the Naval Criminal Investigative Service, or NCIS, as someone to watch out for. Either way, it didn't matter. Now he had to figure out another way to learn if there were any ships arriving from Genoa. The only other option he could think of was to stake out the Tree of Life and wait, but if it was in the middle of the desert like Jack Matzen said, there wouldn't be any place to hide.

Phil's rebuff left him little choice. Come to think of it, he'd been so focused on identifying the ship, he hadn't thought about how he was going to get to the Tree of Life or what he would do once he got there if the bad guys showed up. He had at least the beginnings of a plan, though. Go back to his room, shower, catch a quick nap, and hit American Alley for dinner. If the seven-hour time difference didn't get to him first, he'd figure out his next moves before hitting the rack for the evening. He was confident the fates brought him to Bahrain for something. Now he needed the fates to tell him exactly what that was.

34

7:22 a.m. on Thursday, October 21, 2004
Manama, Bahrain

THE YOUNG WOMAN CHOSE A TABLE for two in the lounge where she had an expansive view of the elegant surroundings. She admired the muted lime-green shade of the chair's cushions, noting how the pastel flowed into the color of the tinted glass table top. Before she could sit down, a waiter wearing a uniform from a by-gone era helped her with her chair.

"Good morning, miss," the waiter replied with an accent the young woman had recently become familiar with. "I hope you are doing well." He smiled warmly, making her feel welcome.

"I am, thank you. How are you?"

"I am quite well, of course." He smiled again, wagging his head slightly from side to side, as if surprised he'd been asked the question. "Would you like some coffee or tea this morning?"

The woman looked up at him, tightening her lips as she tried to decide whether coffee or tea would be a better fit. Having slept well in a room she could easily become accustomed to, she opted for the more civilized option. "I'd prefer tea, thank you."

"Of course," the waiter responded. "Would you like milk and sugar?"

"No thank you. But I would like a croissant with a few slices of cheese and fresh fruit, if that's possible."

"Yes, of course. Is there anything else?"

"No, that will be splendid." She surprised herself with her response. She wasn't trying to be formal, but something about breakfast tea at the Crown

Palace Hotel made the Queen's English an imperative, even if it did have a distinctly American accent.

The waiter bowed and smiled before taking a step to the rear and retreating from the area. She grasped the chair's arms and lifted herself farther back onto the oblong cushions. They felt firm and comfortable, making it easy to lean back and take in all of her surroundings. She felt like she blended in well. She'd brought along cool linen pants and short heels for just this type of occasion, together with a conservative blue blouse she'd ironed after arriving yesterday at the hotel. The silk scarf tied under her chin and covering all but her bangs further transformed her appearance. She felt culturally connected with her surroundings.

She had a clear line of sight to the lobby from her table and could even see the check-in counter, although it was hard to discern individual faces. Still, she didn't want to be too obtrusive—she wanted to blend in and watch.

"Here is your breakfast, miss."

The waiter's reemergence startled her. She hadn't noticed him come up behind her and she flinched. The waiter ignored it if he noticed at all. He set the croissant, fruit and cheese down first, then poured her tea, leaving the pot for her to refill her cup as she desired.

"Thank you," she said, looking up at the waiter and smiling

"It is my pleasure, miss. May I bring you something else?"

"No, this is plenty for now."

"Very well then." The waiter repeated his much-rehearsed step to the rear and departed.

She started her breakfast with a sip of tea. The cup had already grown hot and she pulled away after only a few drops of the liquid trickled over her lips. She brought her napkin from her lap and dabbed the point of contact, hoping the cloth would absorb the heat activating the nerve endings on her bottom lip. A bite of fresh melon proved to be the solution, with the cool fruit neutralizing what remained of the heat.

She set down her fork and did a visual sweep of the room like the guard on a watchtower scanning the surroundings of a fire base in Northern Iraq. She was acting on a hunch so speculative she hadn't even told Steve. If it played out, she'd have something to tell him. If it didn't, she'd simply enjoy a few relaxing days at the Crown Palace, pampering herself before she returned to the office on Monday. After all, Bahrain was on the way back from Chennai to Williamsburg, sort of. Her calculus was simple. Where would an incredibly wealthy person stay during a short visit to Bahrain? Her Internet searches in Chennai unanimously pointed to the glamorous Crown Palace Hotel.

Casey tried another sip of tea and it was cool enough to drink. The warm liquid tasted refreshing and light, well-suited to a hot Bahraini Thursday, although she wasn't sure if she'd spend any time outside experiencing it firsthand. She looked at her watch—it was almost eight a.m. She'd only met Rani Ashirvadam once yet she was confident she would recognize her again. She assumed Rani would stand out in her sari, although she was surprised at how many Indian women she'd seen since arriving in Bahrain. Rani was striking and elegant, making her noticeable no matter what the surroundings. Plus, if Rani did show, Casey expected her to have one or both of her boys in tow.

Casey looked around the lobby and locked-on to each woman, one at a time. Seeing no one who looked like Rani, she began to question her assessment of the factors giving rise to her suspicions. First, Rani left India just two days after she met with her, which, by coincidence or not, would put her in Bahrain in time for the arrival of any ship carrying the Shroud. Second, and it bothered her that she even had these thoughts, Rani told her during their meeting that her youngest son had leukemia and was not responding to treatment. Casey remembered when Rani said that she seemed both desperate to save her son and determined not to lose him. Putting it all together, maybe Rani was desperate enough to bring her dying son to the Bahraini desert to see if the Shroud of Turin and the Tree of Life could save him.

The whole thing seemed so preposterous, she couldn't believe she was staking out the Crown Palace lobby as if it could happen. Even if, through some supernatural miracle, what the tablet said was true and the Shroud actually could open a vortex to Paradise lost, Casey couldn't fathom Rani devising a plan on her own to steal the Shroud. She seemed too genuine for that. Her only thought was that Rani's husband, Arul Ashirvadam, with his obsession for the Garden of Eden and eternal youth, had convinced Rani it was worth the gamble.

"Ohhh!" Casey let loose a muffled gasp as an open hand fell heavily on her shoulder from behind, the fingers squeezing tightly onto her collar bone. She tried to stand up, but the hand pushed back, trapping her in her seat. A second hand came down on her other shoulder, the force driving her deeper into the chair's cushion. She looked over her shoulder, seeing only the dark hands of a man standing behind her. "Let go or I'll scream, I swear to God," she declared.

The hands loosened their grip and one patted her on the shoulder, making her think it was someone she'd met long ago who was trying to surprise her with a boyish prank unsuitable to the circumstances. The man's response dispelled that possibility.

"So, Miss Pantel, it seems you did not learn much during your visit to Chennai. That is too bad." He took his hands off her shoulders and walked around to the seat opposite her, pulling back the chair. "May I?"

Casey remained defiant. "Does it matter, Abijith? You wouldn't respect my answer if I said no, would you?"

Abijith shrugged and sat down, motioning for the waiter to come to the table.

"Yes, sir?"

"A cup of black coffee, and bring it immediately. I do not have much time. Do you understand?"

"Yes, sir," the waiter replied. "Miss, may I bring you anything else?"

"I'm fine, thank you," Casey said politely, fuming over Abijith's tactics. She took satisfaction, though, in knowing that his presence meant she made the right choice to come to Bahrain.

"Very well," the waiter said, departing in his usual manner.

"You should not have followed us here," Abijith declared. "This is not the typical behavior of a trusts and estates lawyer, in your country or mine. What is your game?"

"I should ask you the same thing," Casey countered. "Intimidating people is not the job of a business manager in your country or mine."

"You are very naïve, Miss Pantel. Intimidation is very much a part of business in both of our countries."

The waiter returned with Abijith's coffee and poured it for him. Before the waiter could say anything, Abijith dismissed him with a wave of his hand. The waiter made a hasty departure.

"I see you are rude to others and not just me," Casey observed. "I suppose there's a degree of comfort in that."

Abijith's face tightened. He took a long sip of his coffee, then barked a question as soon as he returned the cup to its saucer.

"Why are you here?"

"I'm here for the same reason you are, Abijith. To visit the Tree of Life."

Abijith's eyes widened. "Who are you and what do you want?"

"You already know who I am. I'm an attorney assisting Steve Stilwell and we're handling Arul Ashirvadam's estate. I've told you that from the very first time we spoke."

"Don't bullshit me," Abijith said angrily, his voice growing louder. "If you were just an American attorney, you would not be here. Who are you working for—I demand to know."

"Who are you speaking to like that, Abijith?" a woman asked from behind Casey. Again, Casey could not see the speaker, although this time, she had an idea who it was. She stood up and turned around to look into the woman's eyes. The woman looked confused, like she recognized Casey but reasoned it couldn't be her because of the context. Casey greeted her warmly.

"Rani, it's me, Casey Pantel. I spoke to you at your home last week."

A big smile came over Rani's face. "Casey, it's so good to see you again!" The two women hugged like longtime friends. "Let me introduce you to my two boys, Nihal and Jivan." Rani turned and reached behind her, shepherding two young boys who'd been hiding in the folds of her burgundy and gold sari. One boy was completely bald and looked particularly shy.

Casey bent down on one knee, her prosthetic leg in front of her, and reached out to the boys to shake their hands. "Hello there," she said, not wanting to mispronounce their names. "My name is Casey. I'm from America. Where are you from?"

The younger boy retreated into Rani's sari and held tightly to his mother's legs. The older boy announced "India" in the voice of a confident ten-year-old. He took Casey's hand and shook it up and down several times. The younger boy followed suit, his hesitant hand slipping out from behind the protection of his mother's colorful fabric shield.

"That's really cool," Casey said, hoping the boys understood American slang. "I was just in India last week and I visited with your mom. I'm so glad I got to meet you today. I hope you have a fun time in Bahrain."

"We're going to see the Tree of Life," the older boy announced.

The boy's innocent revelation confirmed her hunch. "That sounds like lots of fun. That's why I'm here, too. I flew to Bahrain on my way back to America so I could visit the Tree of Life. I hear it's awesome." She smiled at the boys and then worked her way back to her feet.

"I cannot believe we happened across you this morning," Rani said. "Have you already visited the Tree of Life?"

"No, not yet. I was going to finish breakfast and then see if I could arrange a visit through the concierge. I'm sure it can't be too difficult."

A big smile came over Rani's face. "Oh, Casey, you must come with us. We just finished breakfast and we are preparing to go. Why don't you join us?"

Casey glanced at Abijith. He wore a neutral expression, although she knew he had to be seething. She could think of no better way to get back at him and knew she would be safe as long as she was with Rani. She wondered, though, where the Shroud was and what the implications might be if she were there when they unveiled it. Abijith might not allow her to escape. She decided to decline the offer. Before she could, Abijith jumped into the conversation.

"I think it is an excellent idea for you to join us, Ms. Pantel. You can ride with me in my car." Abijith smiled, like a poker player believing he had the winning hand, or at least being able to bluff others out of the game.

"That's very kind of you," Casey replied, "but I don't want to intrude on Rani's family time. You go ahead and I'll make my own arrangements. Perhaps we could meet later for lunch or dinner."

"Nonsense," Rani replied. "I shall not take no for an answer. It would be silly for you to go on your own when we are going to same place. And, as much as I'm sure you would like to ride with Abijith, we can make room in my car so we can talk along the way. I'm sure my boys would love to hear about America."

Casey felt boxed in. She wanted to turn down the invitation but feared Abijith would grow even more suspicious if she did. At least riding with Rani, she would be safe. If she saw the Shroud, she would contact the Bahraini police as soon as she returned to the hotel. In fact, she decided she would inform the front desk where she was going just in case something bad happened.

"Okay, you've convinced me," Casey responded, pretending to be enthused by the opportunity. She knelt down again, a little more labored than the first time. "Only if you two tell me about the fun things you are doing on your trip."

"Wonderful," Rani said. "Abijith, why don't you go see if the cars are here and the boys and I will follow with Casey as soon as she is done with her breakfast."

Abijith glared at Casey just long enough to register his displeasure. He took one final swig of coffee and left the mostly full cup on the table. He didn't offer to pay, but stood up and addressed Rani, ignoring Casey and the boys. "I will be waiting with the cars," he responded. After what Casey thought might be a slight bow, he departed and headed for the lobby exit.

"Please, finish your breakfast, Casey. I am happy to sit and chat while you do."

"That's kind of you, Rani, but I'm ready to go. I just want to stop by the front desk on my way out." She searched quickly for a reason to justify the stop. "I need to see if I've received any messages before we go."

"Oh, are you expecting a message? We can ask them to call my cell phone if it is important."

Casey had to think fast once again. She hadn't expected Rani to try to accommodate a call she knew wasn't coming. "Thanks, that won't be necessary. Steve Stilwell usually checks in with me when I'm on travel like this to make sure things are going okay. If he calls, it'll be easy to call him when we get back."

The waiter reappeared while the two women were still standing by the table. "Will there be anything else for you today?"

"No, thank you," Casey replied. "Can you add it to my room bill? It's room 702 and my name is Casey Pantel."

"Of course, Miss Pantel."

"Well then, shall we be going?" Casey asked.

"Do you need to change?" Rani inquired.

"No, I think I'm all set. As long as these low heels work in the sand, I should be fine." Casey pushed in her chair and the women and both boys, each holding one of their mother's hands, started walking to the waiting Toyota sedans via a short stop at the hotel front desk. Abijith held the rear door of the second sedan open for Rani and the two boys, while Casey got her own door and climbed into the front passenger seat. Once everyone was in place, Abijith closed the door and headed for the first sedan. When the first sedan set out, the second sedan followed.

"I'm so glad you are able to join us today, Casey."

Casey twisted in her seat and looked back over her shoulder. "Me too. Thank you so much for allowing me to tag along."

The boys started asking Rani how long it would take to get to the Tree of Life. She assured them it would not be long, then returned her attention to Casey.

"Why did you want to see the Tree of Life, Casey? It is not something many people have heard of or visit. I would imagine that is especially the case for Americans because it is so far away." Rani looked puzzled. "I must say, I am surprised not only to see you at our hotel, but also that you happen to be going to the same destination we are. Don't you find that odd?"

Rani's questions worried Casey. Did she suspect something? Or was she just being curious? Casey decided to take a light-hearted approach to address Rani's concerns. "I'd call it an amazing coincidence," she assured Rani. Then she made up a simple excuse that would be easy to remember in case it came up again with Abijith. "I actually learned about it at my church, so I thought it would be worth the quick stop in Bahrain to see it." Casey adjusted the scarf over her bangs. "I'd also never been to Bahrain, so that made the stop doubly interesting."

"I see." Rani sounded skeptical. "Yes, I must agree, it is quite a coincidence." She looked directly into Casey's eyes as if she were probing for the truth. "Did you bring a camera so you can take some good pictures to show your church?"

Casey smiled and met Rani's eyes with her own. She knew Rani had no interest in whether she had a camera. The question was Rani's way of saying I don't believe you—if you really wanted to tell your church about the Tree of Life, you would have brought a camera to take pictures so you could show them. It was too late to change stories now, she had to stick with where she was and try to change the subject even though she suspected her cover was blown.

"I never have been much of a photographer," Casey countered. "I just planned on snapping a few pictures with my phone. I'm sure I'll be able to get some postcards at the hotel's gift shop."

Rani nodded as the last vestiges of her smile disappeared. Her youngest son tugged on her arm and said his stomach hurt.

"I'm so sorry, Rani. I'm taking you away from your family time. Please, just pretend I'm not here and enjoy the time with your boys. We can talk some more when we get to the tree."

Rani didn't react to what Casey said. She'd already put her arm around her sick son and pulled him as close to her as his seatbelt allowed. He buried his head in her side, but said nothing more. Casey felt terrible for him, knowing he was fighting a losing battle with a potent disease, and doubly so because his sudden sickness had just rescued her from Rani's inquisition. She turned and faced out the front of the car to end their dialog and figure out what she would do if Rani started to question her again. This was not the friendly ride with Rani to the Tree of Life she expected when she set off from the Crown Palace Hotel.

35

8:04 a.m. on Thursday, October 21, 2004
Manama, Bahrain

STEVE PICKED UP THE TELEPHONE RINGING in his room at the Jewel Hotel. "Mr. Stilwell," said the Indian clerk at the front desk. "There is someone in the lobby who wants to see you."

"Did he say who it is?" Steve answered, taking a sip from the tepid instant coffee he'd managed to conjure up with the coffee maker in his room's kitchenette.

"I'm sorry, sir. He did not."

"Can you ask him for me?"

"He is talking on his phone, sir, so I cannot interrupt him. He told me to tell you it is very important."

"Okay, thank you." Steve hung up the phone. The visitor was lucky Steve was awake and dressed given he'd barely slept last night. With seven-hours of jet lag, it felt like one a.m. and he was dragging, hence the instant coffee. He grabbed his wallet and room key, and passport just in case, and headed out to the elevator after making sure his room was locked. Eight floors later, the elevator opened and he rushed out as if pushed by a tailwind to see who so desperately needed to meet with him. A man wearing khaki pants and a sport shirt stood at the other side of the lobby with his back to Steve and a phone stuck to his ear. The man said goodbye, shoved the phone in his pocket, and turned around as Steve approached.

"Phil, what are you doing here?" Steve asked. "I thought I'd never hear from you again." The two men shook hands.

"To tell you the truth, that was the plan. Your story was so crazy, I was pissed I'd taken the time to meet with you in the first place."

"What changed your mind?"

"I don't know what made me do it, but after we spoke yesterday, I asked my staff to let me know if there was a merchant ship that met your parameters." Nash put his hands in his pockets.

"And?"

"I'll be damned, Steve, but there's a Cypriot flagged self-loading container ship that arrived here last night. It left the Ligurian Sea west of Genoa on the tenth. Just for the heck of it, I asked if that was a common route. The staff said it rarely happens."

"I knew it," Steve exclaimed. "We need to tell the Bahraini authorities right away. There's no time to waste. Someone could be taking the Shroud off the vessel as we speak."

"The first thing I did was tell the NCIS agent on staff and he's running with it. He said he'd tell the Bahraini Police, but expects they'll want more information before they do anything. He said they'd never react just because a container ship arrived from Genoa. There's also nothing out on Interpol or anything else they can hang their hats on, so he's calling NCIS headquarters in D.C. to see if they can help."

"I was afraid of that," Steve lamented. "We're missing the window, Phil. If I'm right and that ship has the Shroud on it, somebody's going to take it out to the Tree of Life as soon as possible—before anyone figures out what's going on."

"So, what's your plan?"

"Get a driver and get out to the Tree as fast as I can."

"What in God's name are you going to do when you get there? Be real, Steve. You've got no car, no weapon, and no options. You better let this one go."

"Drive out there with me."

"What?"

"I said, drive out there with me."

"What the hell can I do? I've got no weapon either."

"Look, Phil, you wouldn't have left headquarters and come over here if you thought nothing could be done. You've got a car and I assume you know how to get there. Maybe we'll see something that'll give the Bahrainis the evidence they need. Then you can call NCIS and we'll get out of there right away. What do you say?"

Nash shook his head slowly from side to side and sucked air deep into his lungs. "I can't believe I'm even considering this."

"It's now or never, Phil. The window might already be closing and the ad of Turin could be lost forever."

"Alright, Stilwell, I'd hate to be the one responsible for that," Nash replied sarcastically. As they rushed for the door, he added, "If this keeps me from making Admiral, your ass is grass." He reached over and slapped Steve on the shoulder and smiled. So did Steve. This was the Navy brotherhood in action.

36

9:32 a.m. on Thursday, October 21, 2004
Manama, Bahrain

THE TWO LATE MODEL TOYOTA SEDANS rushed over the dirt road leaving a trail of dust floating high into the hot desert air behind them. The first sedan stopped about twenty-five yards from the Tree of Life and the passenger door popped open the instant the car's forward momentum ceased. Abijith got out and slammed the door behind him as the second car pulled alongside so he was in the perfect position to open Rani's door. Rani's older son came barreling out, having been cooped up too long, and ran for the tree. Her younger son was more cautious, clinging to Rani for both social and physical support. Casey opened her door last and after getting out, walked around the front of the car to where Rani and Abijith waited.

"Isn't it remarkable?" Rani asked. "Just look. We are in the middle of the desert with nothing but lifeless sand for miles in every direction, yet this tree grows broad and full and green."

"It's even more amazing in real life than the photos I've seen," Casey added. "It's like a lone tree painted on an otherwise empty desert canvas." She paused for a second to take it all in. "I love how its tangled lower branches scrape the sand while its green leaves stretch across the dusty blue sky. I can't imagine how it stays alive out here."

"It is a miracle, I believe," Rani replied. "We must walk up to it. I want my boys to touch and enjoy this gift from God."

"It is too hot," Rani's younger son complained, speaking English for the first time. "I don't want to go to the tree. I am too tired. Let me stay in the car with Mr. Abijith."

"You must go, Jivan. We have traveled very far to see this tree, especially for you. Come, and I will go with you." Rani held out her hand and he took it. She led him slowly toward the tree, with Casey walking on the other side of the boy.

"He tires so easily after his treatments," Rani explained. "It takes a few days for his energy to return." Up ahead, Nihal was already climbing on the tree's lower branches.

"Nihal, you must come out of the tree at once," Rani directed. "This is a very special tree and we must show it respect. God gave us this tree to admire, not to climb."

"How do you know that, Mama?" Nihal asked, stopping his upward momentum but not coming out of the tree.

"Come sit with your brother and me under its cool shade and I will tell you." Nihal grimaced as he jumped to the ground a few feet below. He continued his protest by dragging his feet as he slid toward Rani and Jivan, leaving a trail in the sand behind him.

Casey looked back toward Abijith. He was on the phone, too far away for her to hear what he was saying. Behind him in the distance, she could see a black SUV racing down the same dirt road they had traveled. A column of dust rose high above the vehicle into the sun-filled desert sky.

"It looks like someone else is coming to visit the tree," Casey informed Rani. Rani shrugged and continued to lead Jivan by the hand until they joined Nihal under the tree.

"Boys, look at how beautiful this tree is. It is so big and has so many green leaves, yet there is nothing else here—not even any water. Can you discover its secret?"

"What secret is that, Mama?" asked Nihal, his gloom at having to abandon his climb disappearing after learning the tree might involve a secret.

"The secret of how it lives when nothing else around it does," Rani responded.

Jivan's face lit up. "Is that why they call it the Tree of Life, Mama?"

"You are exactly right, Jivan. The Tree of Life must have great wisdom to survive here, so maybe there is something we can learn from the tree. Why don't you and Nihal explore around the tree and then we can talk on our drive back to the hotel about what you learned." Jivan looked back at his mother and smiled. Casey could tell Rani made him feel safe and loved.

Nihal didn't need any further incentive to explore, he leapt up and retraced his steps to the tree's lower branches. He yelled back to Rani without turning to face her. "Mama, what if the secret is in the top of the tree? If I don't climb it, we won't learn what it is." He paused to wait for his mother's response.

"I am sure the secret is available to everyone, Nihal, especially to those who show respect for the tree by not climbing it. Why else would there be fence around its trunk? Now go, and not another word about climbing the tree."

By now the black SUV was pulling up next to the two parked sedans. The door on the passenger side opened and a young man with slicked back hair and a moustache jumped out. He surveyed the area, including checking the route he had just traversed. He caught the eye of both women, and for the moment the Tree of Life was not the most important scenery in the desert. He strode across the sunbaked soil toward Rani and Casey without regard to the dusty mix of sand and dirt clinging to the finely polished leather of his Oxford shoes. He looked out of his element, but confident nonetheless. Neither woman approached him; they waited until he reached them to speak.

"Hello, Rani," he said in an accent Casey didn't recognize. His use of Rani's name surprised Casey. He and Rani seemed to be from different worlds; he in his designer clothes and she in her burgundy and gold sari. He held out his hand and she took it, then he kissed her cheeks. The kiss looked innocent, familiar but not romantic, yet there seemed to be more. She didn't let go of his hand when the kiss ended, the touch lingering in the silence between his greeting and her response.

"Hello Giorgio." Rani smiled coyly, like an infatuated schoolgirl trying hard not to reveal her obvious interest. "When did you arrive?"

"Last evening. And you?"

"Early yesterday afternoon."

"I see the boys are here and doing well. How is Jivan?"

Rani tried to smile, but sadness spread across her face. She turned to see where Jivan was, waving at him when his eyes met hers. She looked back to Giorgio and answered slowly, as if she hated being forced to articulate such painful words. "He is not responding to the treatment, Giorgio. He grows weaker every day."

"Perhaps today will be a good day for Jivan, no?" he replied.

"I pray it will be so." Rani's eyes welled with moisture but did not release a tear.

"Who is your friend?" Giorgio asked.

"Oh, yes of course. I am sorry to be so rude. This is Casey. She works with the lawyer representing Arul's estate. By coincidence, she was staying at our hotel and was planning to visit the Tree of Life today, so I asked her to join us."

Giorgio's eyes widened at Rani's disclosure. He greeted Casey warmly, nonetheless. "Hello, Miss Casey," he said, offering to shake her hand. "I am pleased to meet you."

"I am pleased to meet you, as well," Casey responded, shaking his hand firmly. "Where are you coming from, Giorgio?" She quickly ran through her conversations with Steve trying to recall if Giorgio's name had come up. Her instinct told her he had to be connected to Michela Baresi, but she didn't want to jump to conclusions.

"From Italy," he said, offering no more specificity. "And you?"

"From the United States," she replied, returning the favor. Another vehicle heading across the desert toward them distracted her. "This seems to be a busy place. Another car is coming."

Giorgio turned and watched the vehicle approach. As it got closer, a second vehicle could be distinguished following right behind. They sped toward the tree, unrestrained by speed limits or traffic. The telltale dust cloud trailed them like a wake in the ocean.

"Why don't you two spend some time with Nihal and Jivan in the shade under the tree," Giorgio instructed. "I will wait in the car."

Rani nodded and turned away to be with her boys, while Giorgio headed toward the cars. Before he made it, two dust-drenched late-model SUVs pulled up next to his car. This time, five men and women got out. Instead of immediately heading toward the tree, they fanned out around the cars as if staking out a perimeter. None expressed any obvious interest in the tree, causing Casey to suspect the main event was about to go down. Not wanting to raise any suspicion, she retreated under the tree with Rani and the boys. She kept her eyes on Giorgio.

Giorgio walked to the front of one of the SUVs, where one of its disembarked male passengers lit a cigarette. Giorgio started to lean up against the vehicle, but pulled back after his hand touched the hot metal surface. The two men spoke briefly, then walked around to the rear of the vehicle and opened the back. Giorgio emerged towing a large black wheeled suitcase. The man with the cigarette left the back of the SUV open and returned to his perch at the front of the vehicle. As Giorgio neared the tree, Abijith began heading in the tree's direction. Another dust cloud appeared on the horizon.

"Do you know what's going on, Rani?" Casey asked. "I'm a little concerned with all these people. It doesn't look like they've come to visit the tree."

Rani looked up from helping Jivan explore the tree's leaves. "I'm sure people visit the tree for many reasons, Casey. I would not worry." She looked out toward Giorgio, who was almost to the outer reaches of the tree's branches. "If you are worried, why don't you walk behind the tree and take the picture for your church. Now would be a good time I think, don't you?"

"That's a good idea," Casey replied, realizing if she stayed, she would likely see the Shroud of Turin and might be considered a witness the conspirators could not afford to let live. She started walking with her back to Rani and

Giorgio away from the tree, in a direction where she could still see the collection of cars and the group of people surrounding them. When she got about twenty yards from the tree, she turned and took out her cell-phone. She didn't take any pictures just yet, instead clutching her phone and waiting for the right opportunity to do so.

From her vantage point, she could see Giorgio opening the suitcase and removing a folded cloth she assumed was the Shroud. He called to Rani and they began to unfold it, holding it by the corners like a giant table cloth and spreading it on the ground under the tree's low-hanging limbs. As they did, another vehicle pulled into the area where the other cars were parked. Two men emerged and hustled around to the front of their car. Abijith, who was now under the shade of the tree but still removed from where Giorgio and Rani were spreading out the Shroud, pulled out his phone again and began to dial.

"He's making a call," a woman helping form the perimeter around the vehicles shouted. Giorgio and Rani stopped laying out the Shroud and turned to see who was shouting, but Abijith paid no mind. He put the phone up to his ear until two quick cracks echoed across the desert, then he crumpled to the ground.

"Oh my God," Rani screamed. "What have you done to Abijith?" She started to run to him, but Giorgio grabbed her hand and pulled her back.

"You can do nothing for him now," Giorgio shouted. "We must finish with the Shroud and leave before it is too late. Grab Jivan and bring him here." Rani scooped up Jivan, who stood paralyzed with fear staring at Abijith. The wounded man lay on his side in the hot Bahraini sun, moaning and trying to plug the holes in his abdomen.

"What happened to Mr. Abijith," the older boy asked, getting ready to head in Abijith's direction to investigate.

"Stay where you are, Nihal," Giorgio commanded. "Your mother needs you to be still."

When the shots rang out, the two men who'd started heading for the tree hit the deck. "Go call for help," one man yelled to the other before he regained his feet and started sprinting for the tree. Casey watched as he darted toward where Giorgio and Rani worked. She couldn't believe it.

"Steve," she yelled. He stopped just short of the tree when he heard her and looked in her direction. *Crack, crack.* The piercing sound echoed in every direction and for a moment, Casey could tell neither origin nor target. Then Steve collapsed.

"No, you bastards!" Casey shouted. She ran toward Steve.

"Oh my God," Rani cried again. "It was not supposed to happen like this. What is happening, Giorgio?"

Casey pulled up short of Steve when she heard a familiar but distant sound reverberating across the terrain. Everyone else heard it, too, but Casey knew precisely what it was. The perimeter group started to return to the vehicles, except for the man with the cigarette. He motioned to the member of his team who had fired the shots that took down Abijith and Steve and they marched toward the tree. Casey looked up and saw a spot in the sky getting bigger and bigger. Its silhouette confirmed what she already knew; a Blackhawk helicopter would arrive any minute. Convinced help was on the way, she ran to Steve, who lay gasping for air and bleeding out his chest and upper thigh.

"Hang in there, Steve," Casey yelled, putting pressure on his chest wound to stop the bleeding. Blood streamed between her fingers, so she pressed harder. She looked at his face and his eyes were big and round and full of fear. Blood oozed out of the corner of his mouth as he gazed up at her. His eyes made her flash back to the nightmares she had about the death of her copilot, when she could hear him yelling "do something Casey, do something" as their helicopter crashed to the ground. Steve's eyes silently yelled the same message, except this time, it wasn't just a bad dream.

By now, the man with the cigarette and his sniper had reached the cover of the tree. "We need to leave now," he commanded, his Russian accent adding to the chaotic mix of nationalities.

"We are not done here," Giorgio shouted.

"I don't give a shit," the Russian replied. "We are taking the Shroud."

"Wait," Rani screamed. She gathered the face of the Shroud in her arm and pulled Jivan close to her. "Jivan, you must listen to me. Hold on to this cloth and the tree very tightly, and do not let go until I say. Do understand?"

The boy nodded, sobbing and afraid.

"Read it now," Rani demanded. "Read it now!"

Giorgio pulled the clay tablet and an index card with the translation typed on it from his sport coat pocket, the sweat from his trembling hands staining the tablet's dry clay surface. He read from the card, "And God placed an angel with a flaming sword in the Garden of Eden to guard the way to the Tree of Life until the face of God reappears."

"Your face has returned, oh God," Rani cried, "I beg you to heal my son!" She dropped the Shroud and wrapped her arms around Jivan and cried in anguish.

"I'm taking it now," the Russian declared. "If you want to get out of here, you need to come now."

As the Russian grabbed the Shroud and stuffed it back in the suitcase, the Blackhawk helicopter landed about forty yards to the right of the row of parked cars. The leaves in the tree rustled from the gale force rotor wash, and dust blew in every direction.

"Wait here and take out the pilots," he directed the man with the rifle. "They won't expect you to be here. The moment you get a clear shot, take it. We will take care of the others. Then rejoin us at the cars." Impervious to the commotion and the whirling sandstorm precipitated by the Blackhawk's slowing rotors, the Russian grabbed the suitcase and started walking back to the SUVs.

"We must go, Rani," Giorgio shouted. "Bring the boys now."

"You go, Giorgio. I will stay here with the boys."

"Nonsense. You will spend the rest of your life in jail, separated from your boys. You must come with us. We will be safe as long as we stay with the Shroud."

Rani picked up Jivan and called out to her other boy. "Come quickly, Nihal, we must go. Follow your brother and me." Nihal ran to Rani and grabbed onto her sari as they trailed after the Russian carrying the suitcase.

By now, a group of about eight Bahraini policemen had jumped out of the helicopter and started to deploy. Before they'd gotten more than a few steps, the Russian commandos opened fire and three policemen fell. Three more made it to the safe side of one of the parked vehicles, but two tried to run back to the helicopter and were gunned down. The rotors on the helicopter, which had slowed to a near stop, started to rotate faster again, but then a crack rang out from under the tree and the pilot's helmet exploded, dropping him lifeless on the controls. When the copilot realized he, too, was exposed, he opened the door on the right side of the bird and vaulted to the ground. He pulled his sidearm from his holster and started running to where three of his fellow policemen were pinned down behind the vehicles. Still in the open and with shots raining all around him, he stopped, took aim, and emptied his magazine. This time, the Russian leader with the suitcase went down, hit multiple times by the fire from the brazen copilot. The copilot paid for his bravery, though, as the commando with the rifle took him out as he ran for the safety of the cars.

"Get the suitcase," the female commando yelled from behind the cover of one of the SUVs. The man with the rifle ran in that direction, but a hail of bullets from the three remaining policemen kept him from getting close.

Giorgio lost it when he saw his Russian guardian dead on the ground. "We are doomed," he cried out, and he dropped to his knees and started to cry.

"Get up, Giorgio," Rani yelled, and she yanked him by the shoulder to pull him to his feet. Instead, he wailed even louder, his words unintelligible if they were words at all. Unable to budge Giorgio, Rani used her body to shield her two boys and pushed them along in front of her. "Run back to the tree," she screamed. "Nihal, run fast and hide behind the tree." The boy flew forward and got behind the tree and the small wrought iron fence surrounding its trunk, then turned and called to his mother and brother.

"Mama, Jivan, run. Run!"

Rani kept pushing Jivan in front of her, always keeping between him and the danger. No bullets came her way, though, as the action had shifted to the commandos around the car and the three remaining policemen pinned down behind the vehicles. As one of the commandos used an automatic weapon to hold the policemen at bay, the others piled into the SUVs. In one of the vehicles, the rear window came down and a commando with an automatic weapon prepared to employ suppression fire to cover their escape.

"Break off the engagement," the female commando ordered in Russian. The remaining commando immediately stopped firing and retreated into one of the waiting SUVs, leaving the suitcase behind. As he did, the first SUV sped away, heading back along the same route it had come by. Once the final commando was in the second SUV, it sped off in a cloud of dust, with automatic rifle fire peppering the vehicle sheltering the last three Bahraini police. When the firing finally stopped, the policemen emerged from behind the car to take control.

"This man is dying," Casey cried out, trying to stem the flow of blood from Steve's wounds. Captain Nash ran over to her to help. "Get a tourniquet on his leg," she instructed, having long since shed the boundaries of rank. Nash pulled off his belt and forced it under Steve's leg, then pulled as tightly as he could to stop the bleeding. It worked, but he couldn't let go or the belt would loosen and the bleeding would start again. He called to the police officers.

"You need to get an ambulance now," he instructed.

"We have called," the policeman responded, "and cars are on the way. It will take some time for them to arrive, and then the hospital is more than thirty minutes away."

"He'll never last that long," Casey countered. "They need to send a helicopter."

"That will take time, too," the policeman responded, now standing over the trio on the ground. "We have badly wounded policemen, too. We can put them in the cars and drive them to the hospital. It is the only way."

Casey looked around. There was one other way. She'd not been able to bring herself to climb back behind the controls since the mishap over Iraq severed her right leg and killed her copilot. It wasn't her physical disability that held her back, but the deep-seated feelings of guilt for letting the mishap occur, even though there was nothing she could have done to prevent it. Now, she stood to cost another dear friend his life, this time not because of some mistake she might make piloting the bird, but because she wasn't willing to take the risk. She'd managed to deal with the guilt the first time. This time she knew if she didn't try, she'd never wash the blood from her hands. She knew what she had to do.

"Help me get him into the Blackhawk," she instructed Nash.

Nash, still pulling tightly on the tourniquet, looked up in amazement. "Don't tell me you can fly a Blackhawk?"

"I'm hoping it's like riding a bike," Casey responded. "You get Steve into the helo and keep pressure on his chest wound while I get the bird going. We good?"

"Roger that," Nash responded. He let loose on the tourniquet and hopped into position above Steve's head. He grabbed him under his shoulders and started dragging him to the helicopter. Casey yelled out to the other policemen.

"Get your wounded and that suitcase into the Blackhawk," she instructed. "I'll need one of you to come with me and show me where the hospital is. The other two stay here and guard the others until help arrives." She pointed to Giorgio and Rani and spoke loud enough for them to hear. "If either of them tries to escape, shoot them. Do you understand?"

"I understand," one of the policemen said. "I will come with you." He turned and barked orders in Arabic to the other two, grabbed the suitcase, and joined Casey running to the helicopter.

When Casey opened the helo door, a grotesque scene awaited her, with the pilot slumped over in his seat and the controls spattered with his brains and blood. Undeterred, she reached inside and unbuckled him, then yanked him until he fell out onto the desert. It wasn't the way she wanted to treat a man who had just given his life for her and others, but she had no choice. She couldn't let more people die.

Casey climbed into the seat and surveyed the controls. She didn't have time for a safety check—she had to trust the bird was still flightworthy after its brief stop in the desert. She hesitated, wondering whether she was doing the right thing. She hadn't flown for years and there were controls she didn't recognize. What if she crashed again and killed them all? Then again, what if she didn't crash and some of them lived because she got them to the hospital in time to save them? That was the answer and she knew it.

Because the batteries, generators, and auxiliary power unit were already engaged, she quickly fired up the engines. The turning blades whirled faster and faster, finally creating the lift she need to get the chopper airborne. "Here goes," she shouted. She pulled back on the stick, lifting the Blackhawk off the ground. She hovered momentarily at about fifteen feet, testing the controls to make sure she could navigate. When she was ready, she gave the policeman a thumbs up and he pointed in the direction she needed to fly. The Blackhawk tilted forward and began to move, gaining altitude and speed.

Casey zipped across the desert, fueled by adrenaline and a mix of emotions. The flight was exhilarating and she felt alive again, like she had when she flew in the Army. For now, the guilt was gone and the freedom of flight returned as the Bahraini desert zoomed by beneath her. Unable to communicate by radio, she trusted that whatever hospital the policeman was directing her to would be able to accommodate them. In just a matter of minutes, the policeman pointed to a landing pad near a large hospital complex.

"Land there," he yelled. "It is the Bahrain Defense Force Hospital."

Casey nodded and started her descent, circling the hospital to make sure there were no hidden obstacles inhibiting her approach. Seeing none, she brought the Blackhawk in and set it down lightly on the pad, as if her nine-year flying hiatus never occurred. She quickly shut down the engines to help with the wounded, but before she could release the blood-soaked straps from across her chest, the landing pad was awash with medical personnel evacuating the wounded.

Casey's next mission was to find Steve to make sure he was getting the care he needed. That's what she would have done with any member of her crew. Once she knew his status, she'd call the U.S. embassy and Marjorie back in the states to let them know what was going on. Then she could get cleaned up, come to grips with what had just happened, and figure out what she needed to do next. She prayed it wouldn't involve attending Steve's funeral.

37

12:12 p.m. on Monday, October 25, 2004
Manama, Bahrain

STEVE HATED VISITING PEOPLE IN HOSPITALS. The patients were sick or hurt and didn't want to be there. He was convinced he'd take home some debilitating disease floating outside the room of some unfortunate soul who should have been quarantined. Now, in his own room after nearly four days of being confined in intensive care, his visitor outlook changed. When a nurse announced two people were waiting to see him, he was thrilled. Casey came in first, beaming from ear to ear.

"Howdy stranger," she began. "You don't know how good it is to see you. I'd give you a big hug, but I'm afraid I'd hurt something." She walked up next to his bed, clasped her hands, and just kept smiling.

"It's so good to see you too, Casey," Steve said with a raspy voice so weak it surprised even him. "I guess I haven't been talking enough." He tried to laugh, but it came out as a muffled cough. He was embarrassed he couldn't cover his mouth. Now he felt even greater sympathy for the unfortunate souls he'd secretly wished were quarantined. "I guess my throat's a little sore, too."

"That's probably because you had a tube jammed down your throat for the last three days," quipped Casey. "I promise you won't need to talk much now. There's someone else here who's got lots of news to tell you."

Steve twisted his head to see beyond Casey to the door, but his chest hurt too much to move that far. It didn't matter, because on cue, Detective Cavendish walked into the room and stood right behind Casey, ceding the best real estate to her.

"Hello, Detective Cavendish," Steve said, his voice hoarse and cracking. He managed to lift his arm off the bed and force a small wave. "I must say, I'm surprised to see you here. You certainly didn't have to come."

"Oh, yes I did," Cavendish retorted. "You were quite instrumental in solving our case. You provided the critical piece of the puzzle we'd somehow overlooked." Steve sensed it pained Cavendish to admit the omission.

"You've got to listen to him, Steve. You won't believe how convoluted everything was."

"Why don't you both pull up a chair and stay for a while? I'm told my schedule's free this afternoon."

"The doctor only gave us a few minutes," Casey replied, sidestepping the invitation to find a chair. "How about we let Detective Cavendish tell you what he knows. You're going to feel a lot better when you hear it."

"Sounds like a plan," Steve said, swallowing hard but finding comfort in one of his favorite overused phrases. "Before we start, could one of you pour me a small glass of water? My throat is really dry."

"Of course," Casey replied, filling a plastic cup from the tray next to the bed and helping him take a few sips.

"Thank you so much," Steve said, his voice rejuvenated. "Okay, Detective Cavendish."

"Brilliant," Cavendish declared, using an overused phrase of his own. "I must say, I didn't want to burden you with this today, but Casey told me you would want to know how everything turned out. Since I'll be heading back to London this evening, this is the only opportunity we'll have. I hope you won't find my being here too inconvenient."

Steve shook his head. "Not at all. Casey was right—I'm a captive audience."

"Well then, I guess the best place to start is with our first meeting at Scotland Yard, isn't it? I'm sure you recall that meeting."

"It's etched in my mind," Steve whispered. "I don't think I could forget Arul Ashirvadam's suicide even if I tried."

"Indeed," Cavendish acknowledged. "Well, when we spoke, I mentioned the unfortunate situation in London regarding antiquities stolen from Iraq."

Steve nodded. "I remember, and as I further recall, you weren't willing to share any information with me. I left Scotland Yard quite frustrated."

"As well you should have. I assure you I can be more forthcoming today, especially since we've been able to fill in many of the details. For example, we now know this episode began back in September when Ashirvadam saw photographs of the smuggled clay tablet posted on online. Since he was an avid collector of cuneiform artifacts and would have been familiar with the Sippar tablet in the British Museum, he recognized the smuggled tablet's map and potential value. He forwarded the photographs to a German scholar he'd previously used to decipher other tablets in his collection. When the scholar told him what the smuggled tablet said, he had someone in America acquire it for him and paid the German scholar quite handsomely to keep the discovery secret."

"If he paid the German to keep quiet, how did you find out about the arrangement?" Steve asked.

"Let's just say our intelligence sources told us Ashirvadam had possibly gotten his hands on a priceless artifact smuggled out of Iraq. Although we had no other details, we approached him to let him know we were watching. We told him if he didn't cooperate and our intelligence turned out to be correct, he would lose everything. He said he didn't know what we were talking about, but we are convinced our visit fueled his paranoia. That's where the story gets interesting."

"It sure seemed interesting to me already," remarked Steve.

"Me too," added Casey.

"Well, perhaps interesting was a poor choice of words," admitted Cavendish. "Complicated might be more accurate."

"What do you mean?" Steve asked.

"Let me explain," Cavendish continued. "When the German scholar told Ashirvadam Bahrain was the place to look for Paradise, Ashirvadam mentioned it to Michela Baresi as a way to curry her favor. He told her what the tablet said without divulging how he acquired it. She recognized the marketing potential for her cosmetics company, of course, but she also realized the tablet had likely been smuggled out of Iraq. So, she contacted the Italian Carabinieri and agreed to work with them. The Carabinieri had no idea we were already watching Ashirvadam, so we didn't have access to Michela or her information."

"Then why did Michela call you instead of the Carabinieri when I saw her in Milan last week?" interjected Steve.

"Because when Ashirvadam's suicide hit the press, the Carabinieri reached out to Scotland Yard and I began to work directly with Michela. As I'm sure you can appreciate, we have a close working relationship with the Carabinieri on these types of cases."

"Okay, I can buy that," Steve admitted. "But one thing I still don't understand is why you were coming to the restaurant for Ashirvadam. Your sudden appearance seems to have pushed him over the edge."

"I must ask you to keep this conversation in confidence, Mr. Stilwell. I'm only telling you because you were so instrumental in solving the case."

"As long as it doesn't compromise my client's interests, you have my word."

"That's good enough," Cavendish declared. "I suppose it should come as no surprise that we have sources in the black market who, how shall we say, are more than willing to cooperate in return for their continued freedom." Cavendish grinned, apparently amused at his own understatement. Steve grinned too, recognizing this was an opportunity to stroke Cavendish's ego and maybe get him to divulge even more if he saw Steve as a kindred spirit.

"We started to hear rumblings that something big was in the works in the relics world and that it might involve the Russian mafia. We had no information about what it was or where it might take place. We simply noticed some known Russian mercenaries go off the grid all at the same time, so we wanted to visit your client and offer him a way to save himself in return for telling us what he knew. At that point, we had no idea he was the catalyst behind the rumblings, although he must have thought we did."

"I don't get it," Casey complained. "I see the tablet thing. But going from the tablet to stealing the Shroud of Turin—that's a quantum leap."

"A quantum leap, indeed," agreed Cavendish. "As we talk with Giorgio Stassi and Rani Ashirvadam, we hope to learn more. Based on what we know now, we think it all comes down to blood, guilt, and money."

"You need to explain a little more than that," Steve protested. "Whose blood are you talking about?"

"Ashirvadam's youngest son, Jivan, of course. Jivan had a rare form of leukemia and wasn't responding to treatment. Ashirvadam and his wife were desperate to save their son's life, and if that meant stealing the Shroud of Turin and using the text on the tablet to see if it opened the door to the Tree of Life, they were willing to take the chance. Although they were wealthy enough to finance the heist on their own, they needed connections to pull it off. That was where Giorgio Stassi came in. He overheard Ashirvadam's overtures to Michela and offered to make the connections with the Russians. He predicted the Catholic Church would pay an enormous ransom to get the Shroud back and he wanted a piece of it. Whilst it might mean living in exile in Russia, Ashirvadam and his wife found that acceptable as long as Jivan survived, and Giorgio thought his newfound wealth would offset any inconvenience."

"What about the guilt?" Casey asked.

"The guilt was Ashirvadam's," answered Cavendish. "His wife knew about his affairs, including his most recent one with Michela Baresi. She confronted him and told him he had neglected her and his sons when they needed him most. She told him she would expose him unless he made things right. The guilt he felt for letting down his family led him to concoct the Shroud of Turin scheme after he saw the translation of the back of the tablet."

"I take it the money part is the ransom you mentioned?" Steve asked.

"Precisely," Cavendish confirmed. "They had the Catholic Church and they knew it. The Church would pay anything to get the Shroud back, and

Ashirvadam told Giorgio that he and the Russians could keep it all after the Shroud's rendezvous at the Tree of Life. That's why when Giorgio told the Russians he suspected his boss was threatening their payoff by cooperating with the Carabinieri and Scotland Yard, they killed her."

"I hear all that," Steve submitted, "but it doesn't explain why you trusted my hunch enough to come to Bahrain."

"I'm sorry to say it wasn't just you, Mr. Stilwell. We did have one other source."

"Who's that?" Steve asked.

"Abijith."

"Abijith?" Casey asked angrily. "That can't be. He assaulted me in Chennai."

"Yes, and I am sorry about that," apologized Cavendish. "He wasn't trying to hurt you, of course. He was afraid you were going to interfere with the case, so he wanted to scare you off. He just took it too far."

"I'm glad that's the way you see it," Casey asserted, crossing her arms and sounding unconvinced. "I think he fully intended to bully me."

"It didn't work then, did it, Miss Pantel? It seems you were right in the thick of things. By the way, you do know, Mr. Stilwell, that Miss Pantel kept you alive and flew you to safety. You wouldn't be talking to us today if it weren't for her."

Steve tilted his head toward Casey. "That's what I've been told. I can't thank you enough, Casey. I owe you my life."

Casey smiled. "You would have done the same for me, Steve, and you know it. As you say in the office all the time, it's a team effort."

"What about the man who shot Phan?" Steve asked. "Did the FBI catch him?"

"Not yet," Cavendish responded. "I spoke with Special Agent Fields yesterday and they are closing in on him. She said it is just a matter of time."

"Speaking of time, it looks like my doctor is heading this way." The doctor entered the room, together with one of the nurses from the station just down the hall.

"Good afternoon, everyone," the Bahraini doctor said, walking to the opposite side of Steve's bed. "I think you have visited long enough for today. Mr. Stilwell is not going anywhere soon. There will be plenty of time for you to visit again. Now, I must ask you to let him rest."

"Did you hear that?" Casey asked. "The doctor just ordered you to get some rest."

"I second that," Cavendish declared, sporting a reserved British smile. "I've got to be going anyway to catch my flight to London, although I do want to mention one last thing. As I said earlier, your communication to the FBI about the Shroud possibly being on a ship helped us position ourselves to recover the relic. I can say this much. Although we knew from Abijith that Ashirvadam's wife and two boys would be coming to Bahrain on the way back to India after Jivan's cancer treatment in France, we had accepted the Italian Government's theory that the two helicopters involved in the Turin raid were found destroyed in a barn. As a result, we didn't consider the seaborn possibility until you explained your theory. In hindsight it seems obvious. At the time, we wanted to believe the Carabinieri, so we did. Had it not been for you, we would not have recovered the Shroud."

"Thanks for the kind words, Detective Cavendish. Like Casey said, it's a team effort." Steve grinned a tired grin. The conversation had sapped all of his energy. His eyes grew heavy and he wanted to nap. He didn't realize the nurse was administering a sedative through the IV flowing into his arm. Where just a few minutes ago there had been conversation with Casey and Cavendish, now there was sleep.

38

4:17 p.m. on Monday, October 25, 2004
Manama, Bahrain

STEVE FELT GROGGY, LIKE HE WAS in a semi-conscious state, unable to discern reality from dream. He sensed he was in a hospital bed, with the lights in the room neither on nor off. He looked around the room and saw no one, yet he felt the warmth of someone holding his hand. The logical side of his brain told him to pull his hand away to confirm his perception. The emotional side fought the impulse because the thought brought him comfort and made him feel at peace. Consciously or sub-consciously, he channeled his energy to squeeze his hand to let the phantom know he was aware of its presence. He felt the hand grip tighter. It had a distinctly feminine touch, soft and warm and pleasant.

He fought harder to open his eyes to see the source of the touch. The room started to get lighter, but his eyes felt dry and he struggled to open them. He was on the verge of punching through to full reality, if he could just overcome the last barrier and open his eyes. He sensed movement next to his bed. He could see his bed clearly—even his feet at the end creating rolls in the covers. For some reason, his mind continued to filter out the source of his comfort. He heard a female voice call out his name. The voice was strangely familiar yet unrecognizable. He had to find out who it was. He focused all of his mental energy, and with the neurological equivalent of a laser, commanded his eyes to open. A horizontal slit of light appeared, cutting through the dusk-like fuzziness, but so bright that it whited out everything in the room.

"Steve?"

The voice was clearer this time and his mind was zeroing in on the speaker, although he could not comprehend either those that remained as possible candidates or those that had been eliminated. He sent another order to his eyes and they opened further. More light, more dryness, more blindness to his surroundings

"Hi Steve," the woman said. She sounded friendly and happy, and he wanted to see her. His mind continued to dwindle down the candidates. He gave a final push and his eyes opened and he could see the room clearly now, although the lights were too bright. Yes, someone was holding his hand, and he turned his head to see who it was.

"It's so good to see you again, Steve," the woman said. She leaned over and gave him a kiss on his cheek. "Don't you know who I am?"

Steve forced a response. "I'm sorry, I'm still a little out of it," he whispered. "Do you think you could help me with a drink of water?"

"Sure," she replied. She poured water from a pitcher on a rolling cart near the bed into a plastic cup. He looked at her as she did. She was dressed conservatively in a fire-engine red blouse and gray pants, but her blond hair brushed over her shoulders gave her a model-like appearance.

"Here you go," she said, handing him the cup, which he brought to his lips and started to drink. He handed the cup back and looked into her hazel eyes.

"Gallagher!"

"It took you long enough." Gallagher smiled and feigned a look of disapproval. "As I recall, you weren't very good at making first impressions with a girl, were you?"

Steve couldn't hide his astonishment. "What in the world are you doing here?

"Are you disappointed?" she asked in typical Gallagher fashion.

"No, not at all. It's really good to see you. But I have to admit, it was the blond hair that threw me."

"Do you like it?" she asked, twisting around and tossing her hair off her shoulders as if auditioning for a shampoo commercial.

"I actually do," he admitted. "But tell me again, what in the world are you doing here?"

Gallagher reeled in her playfulness and reached out and took his hand. "Okay, I'll be serious for a moment, but only if you promise not to dwell on what I'm about to say."

"I promise," Steve said, wondering what he was getting himself into.

"Well," she began. "The last time we saw each other, I was the one in the hospital bed and you were the one standing next to me."

"I remember that all too well. You were in pretty bad shape."

"Yes, I was," Gallagher said, getting even more serious. "I thought there was a chance I might die."

"I'm afraid I thought you might too," agreed Steve.

"Do you remember what I asked you?"

"You asked me to hold your hand."

"And you did," Gallagher said, using her free hand to wipe a stray tear from under her eye. "When I heard through my contacts that you were in intensive care halfway around the world, I thought I'd return the favor. There you have it—that's why I'm here."

Steve was genuinely touched. This was the first time he'd seen this side of Gallagher. She'd always been the devil-may-care former CIA operative, with superior self-preservation instincts and an uncanny ability to advance her own agenda. This version of Gallagher actually valued relationships, although Steve wasn't completely convinced she didn't have some ulterior motive. In fact, remembering her feisty and playful personality, he almost would have been disappointed if there wasn't.

"Thank you, Wendy. I hope you know how much this means to me."

Gallagher smiled and squeezed his hand. "Knock off that Wendy, stuff, you hear? How many times do I have to tell you, my friends call me Gallagher." She let go of his hand and put her hands on her hips, pretending to be angry. "You are my friend, Steve Stilwell, aren't you?"

"I am," Steve answered. "I can truly say I am."

"Well good, then." She smiled and brushed her bangs away from her eyes. "I tell you what. How about as soon as you get back to Williamsburg, we go out to dinner? You pick the place and you buy, and I'll show up. Then we can catch up on what's been going on."

"Wait a minute. I want to make sure I heard right. Did you just ask me to take you out to dinner?"

"You don't have to if you don't want to, you know." Gallagher smiled. She had an irresistible energy about her that filled the room. It made Steve remember why he found her so intriguing, even after all she had done to him.

"You know I'd like that," Steve confirmed.

"I know." Gallagher laughed and gave him another kiss on the cheek. "You've still got my number?"

"I do," Steve replied. "Thanks again for coming by, Gallagher. And please tell your contacts thanks for sending you my way."

Gallagher turned and started toward the door, then stopped and looked back over her shoulder. "You can count on that, Steve Stilwell." She turned all the way around toward Steve and pointed her finger at him. "Don't forget to call me this time, Steve. You won't get another chance." She smiled and waved before turning and walking out the door.

Steve wasn't sure what just happened. Was Gallagher really just returning the favor, or was she interested in him? He hadn't given her any thought, although he had to admit, he enjoyed her company. She was spontaneous and full of life, and her dark side was nowhere to be found. He started to run through the list of restaurants in Williamsburg he might take her to. The thought of it reinvigorated him and made him want to recover as soon as possible so he could get back to Williamsburg and get on with his life. Then a nurse walked into the room and interrupted his pleasant thoughts about the road to recovery. She started checking his vital signs.

"You must be quite the ladies' man, Mr. Stilwell."

The comment took Steve aback. If there was one thing he was not, it was a ladies' man. He also thought it unusual coming from a female nurse in Bahrain's military hospital.

"I don't think so at all," he replied. "Why would you say that?"

The nurse spoke as she wrapped the blood pressure strap around his bicep. "Because while you were visiting with one pretty lady, another one came by to visit you. When she looked through the door and saw you already had a visitor, she asked me to tell you she stopped by. She apologized for not being able to stay and wanted me to tell you she is glad you are doing better. She wished you well."

Steve couldn't fathom who the visitor might be. He didn't know anyone in Bahrain or in the Middle East, for that matter. Plus, traveling in the Persian Gulf while the wars in Iraq and Afghanistan raged wasn't something most people he knew did. Except, of course, for Navy officers assigned to the Fifth Fleet Headquarters in Bahrain. He tried to think of who the senior Judge Advocate might be assigned to work for the Admiral. If it was a woman, she would be the most likely candidate for his visitor. Aside from that possibility, he was at a loss. Unable to come up with a name, he gave in and asked.

"Did she give her name?"

"She did," the nurse replied, pumping the blood pressure sleeve full of air. "She said her name was Sarah."

The name hit Steve like blunt trauma to the head, with pain shooting through every nerve in his body. "O, shit," he heard himself saying. Normally he would have apologized after using such language in a setting like this, but his world had just gone from an emotional high to an emotional low in the span of a single second. "Did she say where she is staying?"

"No, Mr. Stilwell, and you've got to sit still so I can take your blood pressure."

"You don't understand. I've got to go get her. That was my wife."

"Oh, I see," the nurse replied, stopping what she was doing. "I'm sorry Mr. Stilwell. I'm sure she's gone by now. It's been at least fifteen minutes since she left."

"Please, I beg you," Steve implored. "Can you call the main entrance and see if she's still there? I've got to see her before she goes. Please." The nurse did as he asked, but it was too late. The front desk saw Sarah get into a cab just a few minutes before.

Steve was beside himself. If Sarah came to express concern and wish him a speedy recovery, that was one thing. He doubted that was the case, because she could have done that by picking up the phone. Instead, she traveled seven thousand miles to see him in person. She had reached out, yet another encounter with Gallagher blocked her way. Now his dinner with Gallagher in Williamsburg loomed large, a dinner he was elated about just minutes before.

Steve buried his face in his hands. Things had become so complicated, he wasn't even sure he wanted to go back to Williamsburg. Perhaps once he finished handling the Ashirvadam estate, he could slip off the grid for a few months and think about what he wanted out of life. Casey and Marjorie could keep things afloat well enough. First, though, he needed to call Marjorie to see if she could work some magic and find out where Sarah was staying. Maybe it wasn't too late after all and he could convince Sarah to come back to the hospital to talk things through. If not, at least he could take comfort in knowing he tried. For once he didn't accept that there was nothing he could do. If the fates hoped to defeat him, they would have to play a stronger hand.

"Steve," a voice called from the door. "Can I come in?"

Steve pulled his hands away from his face, revealing the person at the door. He didn't speak, his mind telling him it might be the medicine and not a real person calling his name. A tear beaded up and rolled down his cheek.

"I thought you'd gone," he said to Sarah as she waited by the door.

"I thought so, too," Sarah replied, easing her way toward him. She stopped when she reached the side of his bed. She didn't reach out to him, instead clutching the handles of her purse with both hands.

"How are you, Steve?"

"I'm doing fine, Sarah. The doctors say I'll make a full recovery." Steve felt another tear forming, so he used his finger to wipe it away before it started following the track of its predecessor. "Why did you come back?"

"I don't know—I'm asking myself the same question." Sarah spoke without inflection or emotion, as if she were trying to hide her true feelings. "Was that the same woman you met in Vietnam on the Sapphire Pavilion case?

"It was," Steve said, not offering further explanation. He was afraid Sarah would interpret anything he said as an excuse, so he waited for her to draw it out of him on her terms.

"Have you been seeing her?"

"No, not at all. That's the first time I've seen her in years."

"Then how did she know you were here?"

"She's a former CIA operative. I called her to use her contacts to help get some information I needed for the case I'm working on. I thought the call was the end of it, but apparently her contacts told her I'd been shot, so she came to visit me. She was repaying a debt because I stood by her when she almost died after our car accident in Virginia."

"I want you to think long and hard about the next question, Steve." Sarah spoke with a newfound intensity indicating the small talk had ended. "I don't want the first answer that pops into your head. I want the real answer—the true answer—the one that comes from your heart."

"Of course, Sarah," Steve replied, as if that was what he always did. "What's the question?"

Sarah looked deep into his eyes. "Do you love her?"

Steve looked back at Sarah so his gaze would confirm the truth of what he was about to say. "I don't need to think about that, Sarah, because I think about it constantly. The only woman I love is you." He thought about stopping there, but it wasn't the whole story. He knew he might not get another chance, so he decided to tell her the whole truth. "I'll be completely honest with you. I was devastated when you filed for divorce and I was trying to look beyond you. I never could. I still love you and I always will."

Sarah's lips formed a small smile and she reached out and took his hand. "Now I know why I came back, Steve."

Steve smiled, too. "I'm so glad you did, Sarah."

"When I heard you'd been shot, I got on the first plane I could. I've got to confess something, too, Steve. I tried to look past you, too, and I couldn't. As much as I tried not to, I'm afraid I still love you. It just took you almost dying for me to realize it."

Steve squeezed Sarah's hand. "It was worth getting shot to hear those words." He smiled broadly. "Where do we go from here?"

"Why don't we give us one more try," Sarah suggested. "I'll instruct my lawyer to drop the divorce. Then it will be up to us see if we can put the pieces back together."

"I'd like that," Steve replied. "I'd like that very much."

Steve had so much to talk about with Sarah, he didn't know where to start. He wanted to hear about every aspect of her life, from how she'd been spending her days to what new TV shows she enjoyed. He also couldn't wait to tell her about the Ashirvadam case, just like he used to tell her about all of his cases before they separated. For now, though, it was enough to smile.

EPILOGUE

⁓

Three months later
Manama, Bahrain

THE PRISON GUARD AT BAHRAIN'S ISA Town Prison for women led Rani from her overcrowded cockroach-infested cell to a room where she could speak with her lawyer. Normally such accommodations were impossible, especially given that Rani was a foreigner, but her wealth made things possible even from behind bars. When she arrived in the room, the guard pointed for her to sit in an empty chair and shoved her in that direction. He hovered behind her, making sure he brushed up against her back so she would know he was close at hand. He always was with such a beautiful woman.

Rani was a far cry from the woman she had been just three months before. Gone were the fashionable saris; in their place the orange jumpsuit of a prisoner. Prison guards replaced the servants in her daily routine, and she lived in abhorrent conditions lacking in adequate sanitation, food and health. With thirteen other women jammed into her ten-bed cell, maintaining even a modicum of dignity proved impossible. News about her boys was rare and movement in her case even rarer. She didn't know yet if the Bahrainis intended to prosecute her for conspiracy in the deaths of the Bahraini policemen, or whether they would be content executing the Russians they'd captured trying to escape after the firefight in the desert. The Italian government also wanted to extradite her to stand trial for the theft of the Shroud. Given that an Italian prison would be a godsend after Isa Town, she told her lawyer not to oppose the request. If it happened, she would move her boys to Italy and pay someone to raise them until she could someday be released.

A door opened on the other side of the room and a black-haired portly man in his fifties entered wearing a Western business suit. It was her lawyer. He pulled out the chair opposite her and sat down. He was the best lawyer money could buy in Bahrain. She'd also hired an English litigation team to defend her just in case. Even though her Bahraini lawyer seemed like a nice man with nothing but her best interests at heart, she didn't trust that he was completely on her side because she was a woman and therefore expendable in his eyes.

"Good afternoon, Mrs. Ashirvadam," the lawyer said in English, which was one of the conditions of his hire. "I trust you are doing well today."

"Thank you for coming, Mr. Saif. While I appreciate your concern, it goes without saying I will never be doing well as long as I am here. Has there been any change in the status of my case?"

"I am afraid not. We are still waiting for a decision by the Public Prosecutor's Office. I have nothing I can tell you in that regard."

"I understand," Rani said mechanically. "Then why did you come? It's about Jivan, isn't it? Tell, me—tell me what it is," she demanded.

"You are right. It is about Jivan," he responded, starting to grin. "I have good news."

"Oh, dear God, please tell me what it is," she begged.

"Jivan went for his treatment four days ago. I am pleased to tell you he is responding for the first time. They had to call in several doctors to confirm, but it looks like the cancer is going into remission. The doctors said it is a miracle."

Rani buried her head in her hands and wept. She heard nothing her lawyer said after that point, nor did she need to. The key had just released her from the only prison that mattered.

THE END

Photo of David E. Grogan by Bob Bradlee

DAVID E. GROGAN WAS BORN IN Rome, New York, and was raised in Cleveland, Ohio. After graduating from the College of William & Mary in Virginia with a BBA. in Accounting, he began working for the accounting firm Arthur Andersen & Co., in Houston, Texas, as a Certified Public Accountant. He left Arthur Andersen in 1984 to attend the University of Virginia School of Law in Charlottesville, Virginia, graduating in 1987. He earned his Masters in International Law from The George Washington University Law School and is a licensed attorney in the Commonwealth of Virginia.

Grogan served on active duty in the United States Navy for over 26 years as a Navy Judge Advocate. He is now retired, but during the course of his Navy career, he prosecuted and defended court-martial cases, traveled to capitals around the world, lived abroad in Japan, Cuba and Bahrain, and deployed to the Mediterranean Sea and the Persian Gulf onboard the nuclear powered aircraft carrier *USS Enterprise*. His experiences abroad and during the course of his career influence every aspect of his writing. He has written two books in the Steve Stilwell Thriller series, *The Siegel Dispositions* and *Sapphire Pavilion*.

Grogan's current home is in Savoy, Illinois, where he lives with his wife of 36 years and their dog, Marley. He has three children.

You can follow Dave on Twitter (@davidegrogan) and Facebook (davidegrogan), and learn more about him at: www.davidegrogan.com.